JOHNNY QUARLES

"BRINGS A FR[...]
TO THE CLAS[...]
Elme[...]

"A RISING STA[...]
OF WESTERN [...]
Johnny Quarles demonstrates a rare knack
for plotting and characterization
designed to keep the pages turning."
Amarillo Sunday News-Globe

"ONE HELL OF A STORYTELLER . . .
Johnny Quarles is the genuine article . . .
He just keeps getting better and better."
Terry C. Johnston

"QUARLES PROVIDES AN EXHILARATING
PICTURE OF THE UNTAMED WEST."
Kliatt Book Guide

"IN THE TRADITION OF
LARRY McMURTRY . . .
Quarles's folks are far more colorful
and a whole lot more fun than
those found in the usual western."
Judith Henry Wall, author of *Handsome Women*

"JOHNNY QUARLES MASTERFULLY BRINGS
HIS COLORFUL CHARACTERS TO LIFE,
SPINNING A DARN GOOD TALE
IN THE PROCESS."
Youngstown, Ohio, Vindicator

Other Avon Books by
Johnny Quarles

FOOL'S GOLD
NO MAN'S LAND

SPIRIT TRAIL

JOHNNY QUARLES

AVON BOOKS ◆ NEW YORK

.

SPIRIT TRAIL is an original publication of Avon Books. This work has never before appeared in book form. This work is a novel. Any similarity to actual persons or events is purely coincidental.

AVON BOOKS
A division of
The Hearst Corporation
1350 Avenue of the Americas
New York, New York 10019

Copyright © 1995 by Johnny Quarles
Published by arrangement with the author
Library of Congress Catalog Card Number: 94-94470
ISBN: 0-380-77656-1

First Avon Books Printing: January 1995

AVON TRADEMARK REG. U.S. PAT. OFF. AND IN OTHER COUNTRIES, MARCA REGISTRADA, HECHO EN U.S.A.

Printed in the U.S.A.

RA 10 9 8 7 6 5 4 3 2 1

First, I want to thank God for any abilities I might have. A special thank you to Cindy Greven, my typist, and to Sarah Colgan's daddy, Tom, at Avon Books. And as always, thanks to Wendy, a good wife and partner who gives me more inspiration and comfort than I deserve.

People never cease to amaze me with their kindness and support. I don't understand anyone who doesn't feel that we all need each other. I use my book dedications to continually recognize those who made a difference in my life, be it a casual acquaintance or a deep friendship. I would like to recognize more of these fine people:

Gerald Fluman; Bing Erikson; Brad Boring; Bud Kain; Ken Bolenbaugh; Irv and Ruth Honigsberg; Dan Mugg; Pat Walker; Dan Dunn; Jo Ann McGuire; Steve Stubblefield; Gordon Steier; Jerry Long; Cindy Read; Mike and Suzanne Ware; Lynn Steier; Keith Lea; Jody Brumfield; Roy and Shirley Sanders; Wendell Crist; Donnie Dennis; David Root; Dr. Keith Wilson; John and Lois Clausing; Tharon Fox; Wayne Warrington; Dan Sims; Steve Bundy; Jack Light; Lonnie Atnip; Anna Maly; Ralph Mitten; Greg, Amy, Scotty, and Kyle Morgan; Ben Haines; Dr. Dan and Honey Washburn; Paul Giberson; Greg Thompson; Bill Venable; Richard Kliewer; Don and Paulette Winbolt; John and Marla Chadwick; Greg Purdum; Robert and Gayla Williamson; Cloyd (Blackie) and Martha Williams; Bob McKinnon; Darrell Herndon; Jeff Chapman; Catherine Cook; Richard and Judy DeVaughn; Jon Butler; Donna Ginter; Jim Maddox; Dawnette Bell; Larry and Mary Jane Mendenhall; Beverly Hill; Hiram Walker; Jim Kimbrell; Fabian Forte; Doug Netter; Leigh Ann Wikoff; Todd and Liz Robinson; Allen

Robinson; John Ireland; Nancy Nuss; Sandy Anderson; Leroy McKee; Raymond and Barbara Hendrie; Dick Noyes; Steve Harris; Jim Loucks; Gary Don and Vicki Johnson; Robert McKeag; Melvin Stephens; Jim and Terry Kelly; Bob Carpenter; Skip Moon; Tina Johnson Irvin; Junior and Frances Scott; Kent Shoemaker; Wayne Pierce; Gary Nugent; Wes Hurlbutt; Craig Simmons; Jerry Long; Robert Claborn; Jack Seltenreich; Merle Schultz; Bob Parks; Leland George; Danny Barnes; Dale Crabb; Alan Smith; Forrest Phillips; Brian Meyer; Joe and Jamie Smith; Steve and Gretchen Boyer; K. D. Zerby; Larry Allen; Tom Sedberry; Bo Gregory; Erie Layton; Buddy Rogers; Reggie and Gail Logan; John and Letha Lieb; Pam Billingsley; B. J. Ellison; Glen "Squeaky" Astley; Jim Baker; Jim Hannon; Betsy Thomas; Larry Everett; Jack Winkle; Bob and Pat Anderson; Jim Warnock; Lyle and Marian Suter; Dan Smith; Randy Walker; Donald Hughes; Joyce Roller; Bill Vickers; Mike Kapka; Henry Senters; Forrest Ridgeway; Daryl Thompson; Mary Kate Maco; Tony and Marlene Rodriquez; Tim Broomfield; Rodney Burtram; Jim Loucks; Jack Winkle; Anna Mary Ridgeway; Louis Ausbrook; Glenn Blazer; Darrell McDaniel; P. J. Kimberlin; Smith and Virginia Legg; Mike Murphy; Dr. Don Gooch; Bo Gibson; Jeff Hughes; Wayne Kelly; Rick Hilburn; Rick Daniels; Charlie Scott; Frank Terrell; Phillip and Diane Lewis; David Bortel; Willie Paradis; Mike Martin; Daryl Miller; Sharla Brehm; William Verduin; Sidney Brown; Eugene Poe; Robert Wentz; Thaddeus Badura; Clay P. Jones; Larry Harmon; John Jones; Floyd Jackson; Corinne Gooch; L. O. Huenergardt; Sue Gerleman; Tim Priest; Greg Jacoby; Monty Cole; Don Paddock; Sandra Campbell Regier; Gerald Radcliffe; Steve McKeever; Kenneth Logan; Jeff Huston; Judy Graber; Dr. Gary and Marcia Patzkowsky; Denise Dunnigan; Rhonda Fifer; Walter Correll; Jeff and Debbie Turnbow; Richard Mildren; Joe Antonini; Henry Lemmerman; Betty Riley Dennis; David McCreary; more of my Army buddies, Tipton, Doty, Jordan, Perez, Derfler, Rideout; and Parks;

Gene Burkett; Jerry Denney; Darrell Senters; Art Rodriguez; Patty Garrett; Carol Sue Hodson; Shirley Daughtry; Daymond Myers; and the greatest football player I ever saw, Dicky Shaw.

More writers I admire:

Melvin Duncan; Janet Dailey; Wanda Sue Parrott; the beautiful Kat Martin; the rugged Larry Jay Martin; Deana James; Richard S. Wheeler; Mary L. Hall; Charles W. "Chuck" Sasser; Dr. Wilson (Bill) Buvinger; Nancy Berland; Mark Duncan; Jean Hager; Marilyn Brewer; Gennell Dellin; Art Burton; Steve Wilson; Anne Rice; Sandra Johnston; Peggy Goodrich; Violet Freeze; J. Madison Davis; Louisa McCune; Debbie Chester; Nancy Williamson; Dusty Richards; Cheryl Anne Porter; Betty Martin; Eve K. Sandstrom; Michael Wallis; Sherron Miller; Dr. Frank Adelman; Kevin Anderson; Virginia Henley; Audrey Schubert; Clint "Happy Trails" Jones; Ralph Compton; Jim Yates; Mary Groman; Barbara Taylor; Micheal Schubert; and Allison McCune.

To a wonderful artist and friend of mine, Native American and proud Cheyenne, Jerome Bushyhead.

As you may have noticed, I like to travel in my books. While writing this particular effort, I kept thinking about my ten years as a conductor/brakeman/switchman/engineer trainee on the Frisco Railroad, which is now the Burlington-Northern. I have never worked with a finer group of individuals than the wild bunch that rode the rails with me. As I look back on those days, I remember their wit, sarcasm, belly-aching, laughter, hell-raising, and general outlook on life, and it makes me think that all politicians should be required to spend some time with these modern-day cowboys. I truly think they have a better grasp of what life is all about than anyone I've ever been associated with.

To my friends, the railroaders, I dedicate *Spirit Trail*.

1

Samson Roach sucked in his breath and held it. The pain that generated deep inside his head made him wince and wish he were somewhere else, or better yet, somebody else. At his side, his hand still cradled the whiskey jug. It was nearly empty. He'd drunk himself into a stupor, taking half the night to achieve his current state.

With some kind of effort, he opened his eyes into narrow slits. Then, with another deep breath, he managed to pull them open wider.

All around him, the world was as he'd last seen it, except for a glistening of white frost that covered everything. The brightness stretched as far as his aching eyes could venture to look. Samson looked down at his buckskin clothes. He, like the world, was covered with frost. Funny, he thought, how he hadn't noticed the cold while he slept. Now all of a sudden his body felt as stiff and cold as a dead man's.

Slowly, he pulled up on his elbows and dragged himself next to a tree, then leaned carefully against it. The whiskey made a sloshing noise, and he pulled out the cork to take a long gulp, hoping the burning liquid would generate some heat through his body. Absently, he wiped his mouth and tried to look out around him. The sun was just starting to show itself over the glittering landscape. The yellow rays pierced his eyeballs so badly, he moaned with pain and held his eyes shut for a while. His head was spinning, and he congratulated himself for the fool that he was.

"You! Samson Roach!"

The man's voice called out from nowhere, causing Samson to jerk. He dropped the jug and turned his head in the general direction of the voice. The movement sent new waves of pain and nausea through him. He let out a groan and grabbed his head, trying to pry his eyes open.

"Who the hell wants to know?" he said irritably.

The man stepped up closer, to where Samson could see. "Name's Joseph Mellner," he said. He motioned to a second man standing at his side. "And this here's Bill Wheeler. We're from Pennsylvania. The man at the tavern up the creek told us you can guide us up to Oregon."

Samson ignored them. Instead, he groped for the jug and took another drink, smacking his lips and savoring the small amount of relief he was starting to feel. Finally, he raised his gaze and studied the two men for a moment. It irritated him that they had made it their business to disrupt his morning.

"He done told you wrong, mister," he said.

The man named Joseph Mellner appeared not to have heard what Samson said—that, or he didn't care. "We're looking for a man who knows his way to Oregon," he repeated. "And we've been told you're just the man."

"Go away," Samson moaned, waving his jug at them. "I ain't goin' to Oregon. I ain't goin' nowhere."

Mellner still wasn't paying attention. He said, not unkindly, "Now, look here, Samson Roach. We heard what happened to your family. And that's a pity. A real shame. But life goes on."

Samson glared up at the men as best he could. "You don't know nothin' about nothin'," he said. He wiped his arm over his brow as a sorrowful look crossed his face.

The memory of his wife and child was a heavy weight that Samson carried in his heart. It had been this time last year, in April, that he had been in charge of leading thirty-five wagons toward Oregon. They'd been gone nearly two weeks when his nine-year-old son, Cordry, had drowned in a river.

The death had somehow pulled Samson and his wife, Nancy, apart. They had dealt with their grief separately. Samson had taken to drinking, giving little care to anything but forgetting about the emptiness inside him. Nancy had grown numb and wary of life. She had rarely spoken a word to anyone and kept mostly to herself.

It was during one of Samson's drunks when the five Indians had ridden into camp. They had appeared to be friendly, offering moccasins in exchange for bread and honey. The travelers obliged them; someone gave them liquor as well. Before long, the Indians were drunk, too. They had moved outside of the wagon circle and were lying about, laughing and talking in loud voices.

The wagon train was camped by a river. Nancy had wandered down to the water's edge and sat down. She was aimlessly pitching stones, content to be alone in her own thoughts.

Suddenly, one of the Indians happened upon her. She jumped to her feet and tried to run away, but the sight of the beautiful woman stirred the drunken Indian's desires. Savagely, he had raped her, then smashed her skull against a rock.

Some of the wagon train women had found her the next morning as they went to the creek to draw water. She was lying on the bank, her head crushed beyond recognition. The Indians were gone, and Samson lay outside his wagon on the bare ground, passed out and helpless as a pup.

Filled with grief and self-pity, Samson had left the traveling group. He no longer had the will to be a part of the living. Only the heavy shroud of liquor could chase away the ghosts of guilt and misery. He drank away all of his and Nancy's four-years' savings, spending his days and nights wherever he could find a place to lie. When the money ran out, he swapped the family belongings and horses, down to his guns and hunting knives.

Now, as he lay before the two men, Samson's guts were wrenched with misery as he thought back one more time. Slowly, he lifted the jug, when Mellner again spoke.

"I'm not leaving here without you, Roach. One way or another, you're going to see us to Oregon."

"Are you crazy?" Samson said. He tilted the jug toward his lips and drank. Then he said, "You best git now, both of you, elst I might have to persuade you some." He reached down to his hip for his hunting knife, but it was gone.

"If you're planning on cutting or shooting us, I'm afraid you're out of luck," Mellner commented. "We saw your knife and guns at the tavern. I'd say you're drinking that knife away right now. Least, that's what I've been told."

"Go to hell, and take your friend here with you," Samson said, sounding more bitter.

Mellner nodded at Wheeler. "Come on. We're going to take him back with us."

Bill Wheeler hesitated a moment, then stepped back. "We best leave him alone, Joseph. Can't you see the man doesn't want to go? Besides, he's not in any kind of shape to lead anybody anywhere." He stared down at Samson doubtfully.

Mellner shook his head. "That's where you're wrong, Bill. The fellow at the tavern says there's none better than Samson Roach." He pulled his hat down tighter over his brow and tried again. "Now, look here, Samson. We got families waiting. Why, there's pert near eighty wagons! People's lives, every cent they've got in the world! They're all tied up in dreams of going to Oregon. It's your duty as a fellow human being to lead us there." He pointed to his chest with emphasis. "You take me and the missus. We've got five children. Been saving for this trip ever since we first heard about it back in '40. I think you need to crawl up out of that hole you've dug yourself. Stand up like a man again. Get your respect back." He nodded shortly. "Yep, one way or the other, you're coming with us. Take his shoulders, Bill. I'll get his feet. We'll take him back and sober him up. Maybe then we can talk some sense into him."

Reluctantly, Bill Wheeler grabbed hold of Samson under the arms and tried to pull him away from the tree. Joseph Mellner took hold of his feet.

Even in his drunkenness, it incensed Samson that someone would take such liberties with him. Suddenly, he sprang on them like a mountain lion. He kicked Mellner in the chest, sending him flat on his back. Instantly, he had spun around and taken Bill Wheeler in a headlock. He drove his fist hard in Wheeler's face, then, cursing wildly, he began to throw punch after punch.

Gasping for breath, Joseph Mellner ran to his horse and retrieved his Kentucky rifle. Wild-eyed, he raced back, raised the rifle, and crashed the butt hard against the back of Samson's head.

Samson's right fist was raised, ready to strike again, when he felt the blow. Pain flowed to the front of his head like water running through dry sand. Then everything turned black. His body slumped forward and his face bounced against the icy earth. He was out cold.

"Like it or not, Samson Roach, you're going to Oregon," Joseph Mellner said, still trying to catch his breath.

2

The sight of Joseph Mellner and Bill Wheeler riding in with a man who was not only strange, but unconscious to boot drew the attention of several children. They crowded around, trying to get a better look-see.

"His head's bleedin'," one boy pointed out.

"Looks like he might be dead," another boy said. "Is he dead?" he asked Mellner.

Mellner frowned. "You young'uns go on, now," he said. His words were spoken in a loud and stern manner, but they had little effect on the curiosity of the children. They moved back for a moment, then slowly pressed forward again to stare at Samson.

The children were soon joined by adult onlookers. A big circle formed around the scene as the crowd grew. There were mumblings and comments running back and forth as folks speculated on what had happened.

Reuben Cook, who owned the tavern, pushed his way through the crowd. He bent over Samson and studied his bloody head.

"You fellers do this?" he asked Mellner and Wheeler.

Mellner nodded in affirmation. "It was the only way we could get him here. Why, he was slobbering drunk!" he said, as if that explained everything. Beside him, Wheeler nodded in agreement.

Reuben Cook stood erect and rubbed his chin, studying the situation. Finally, he looked seriously at Mellner. "Well, maybe he'll die. That's about your best bet," he said.

"Die? Are you out of your mind?" Mellner almost shouted, "He *can't* die! He's going to take us to Oregon." He gave a short laugh. "We surely didn't go to all this trouble to watch the man die! No sir!"

Reuben Cook removed his dirty hat and wiped his glistening forehead with his sleeve. Although the morning was cool and damp, he was sweating. He shook his head at Mellner. "He'll kill you," he said.

Mellner looked irritated. "Shush, man!" he said. "I'll not hear any of your cheap talk. Why, it was you yourself who said that Samson Roach is the best man alive to lead us to Oregon."

Again, Reuben shook his head. His face took on a deep reflective look once again. He said slowly, "I'm sorry for that. I'm even sorrier I told you where to find him."

Bill Wheeler absently reached up and touched his swollen face. His cheek had already turned purple. "I don't like this, Joseph," he said. "The man was drunk. And even then he was like a mad dog. I'd hate to see what he'd do sober!"

"Not you, too, Bill," Mellner said. He looked disgusted at Wheeler. "You're surely not going to let a couple of bruises mess up your thinking, are you?"

Wheeler, still holding his swollen face, took a look down at Samson, then at Reuben, then at Mellner. "It's not that, Joseph," he finally said. "It's just that Mister Cook, here, could be right. Why, we both saw how this man Samson fought us like a mad animal back there!"

A determined man and stubborn to the core, Joseph Mellner turned away from the others and stomped away, filled with disgust. Mellner carried only one purpose in life, and he carried it close to his heart. He was going to get his family to Oregon. Samson Roach was the only logical means to that end. Besides that, he figured he was doing Samson a favor as well. If there was anything Mellner detested, it was drunkenness. He hated it with a passion. His own father had been a drunk, and Mellner carried some painful memories of the fact. To see someone like Samson fall onto the same path, especially when Mellner needed him so, was more than he could stand.

It was several minutes before anyone in the crowd seemed to realize that some medical help was needed. Finally, a couple of women hurried up, shooed away the children and the curious, and tended to Samson's head. The Kentucky rifle of Joseph Mellner had raised up a respectable-sized bump on Samson's head. The skin was split open right down the middle.

All during the women's tending to his wounds, Samson lay there as limp and lifeless as a dead man. The women wanted to move him to a wagon, but Reuben Cook persuaded them to let Samson convalesce in a back room at the tavern. That way, he assured them, maybe they could talk the man out of killing somebody when he came around.

No sooner had they settled Samson on a rough table with a burlap sack for a pillow, than Reuben began to have second thoughts. All of a sudden, his stomach was churning. It had been a big mistake, he thought, shooting his mouth off about how this Samson Roach would lead them to Oregon. After all, he'd only been speculating when he made such claims. And look what had happened. Reuben swallowed hard and stared down at Samson's face. Such foolishness could get a man killed, he thought. Dizzy with the idea, he stumbled out back of the tavern and fetched a jog of buttermilk from the cold water in the spring. Instead of pouring a cupful, he put the jug to his lips and tipped it up high, taking in a huge gulp. Smacking his lips gratefully, he carried the jug with him into the tavern and plopped down in a chair. He drank some more, letting the buttermilk cool and soothe the burning in his stomach. *Why,* Reuben thought, *buttermilk must be just about the finest thing there is.* He liked to slush it around in his mouth, letting it slide over his tongue. Sometimes a little bit would seep out from between his lips and run down into his beard and turn dry. Not being a man who worried about such trifles as vanity, Reuben didn't much care. Neither did Gertie.

He'd given his wife her name after he traded a pack-horse, two gallons of whiskey, and a long coat for her from her Oglala father. It had been four years ago, when he'd been camped out on the Republican and had run into the Indians. Her Oglala name was Dark Water, but Reuben couldn't see himself calling his wife that. He'd had an aunt named Gertrude once, and he recalled thinking highly of her in his youth. So, all in all he considered the gesture a fine tribute, and Gertie didn't seem to mind.

Reuben was a man of little self-discipline, and he kept after that jug of buttermilk until his stomach had swollen to the point where he thought it might burst. Samson was going to come to any minute now, and Reuben knew he ought to check on him. Rubbing his belly, he summoned Gertie from her perch behind the bar.

"Go see if Samson has come around yet," he said.

Gertie's eyes widened, but Reuben motioned her to go. He knew he should go himself, being as how Samson had little feeling for Gertie. Oh, it wasn't anything personal against Gertie. It was just that Samson hadn't had anything good to say about Indians since his wife's death. Sober, they never even entered his conversation. But once he'd taken a few pulls off a jug of whiskey, he'd curse their very existence.

"Go," he said, irritated. Gertie wasn't moving fast enough to suit him.

A minute later, she returned. "He is moving," she said.

"He's moving," Reuben repeated with a sigh. Frowning, he took another drink of buttermilk, even though he was already stretched full. With an effort, he rolled out of the chair and shuffled off toward the back room, unable to stop the huge belch that sounded throughout the tavern.

Samson was sitting up, holding his head in his hands. Reuben quietly took a seat on a stool next to the table. Samson looked like a young boy, Reuben thought, sitting there cradling his head. In the year he'd known Samson, he'd never realized he was such a small man. Whereas Reuben stood nearly six feet, Samson was a quarter inch shy of five-seven and didn't weigh much more than 130. What there was of Samson was solid, though. He was lean, rock-hard, and athletic. But even that was not what made folks take notice of Samson Roach. The fact was, Samson was the toughest man Reuben had ever encountered. Never in his life, as a scout, or a trapper, or a tavern owner, had Reuben ever come across a man more vicious and determined in a scuffle. No, size was not the way to measure a man where Samson was concerned, especially not when he was riled.

Reuben wanted to offer some of his buttermilk to Samson. He didn't know for certain if buttermilk would help a body get over a hangover, but he was sure it could make a stomach feel better. This really wasn't a perfect offering-up time. Still, he hated to see a man suffer. Poor Samson, he thought. There he sat, drunker than a wet hoot owl and probably not even remembering what had happened. Yet.

Reuben couldn't begrudge him his being drunk. No, he couldn't begrudge any man for having his own demons in life. He liked to pull on a whiskey jug himself, and did so most every day. Not so much that he'd let himself get drunk, like Samson did. No, Reuben drank just enough to where he felt right about things. Only on such occasions as a cold or rainy night would he drink himself nearly blind.

Samson sat holding his head and Reuben sat watching him for several minutes. Finally, Samson slowly raised his head and squinted until he recognized the man beside him.

"Oooooh, my head! It's hurtin' bad. Give me a drink, will you, Reuben?" he moaned.

Reuben studied Samson, especially his eyes, then cautiously handed him the jug.

Samson grabbed up the jug and took a couple of deep breaths before he tilted it up and took a long drink. Suddenly, his eyes flew open wide and he started to gag. It reminded Reuben of a child who's been forced to take a bite of something unpleasant.

"What in hell? Buttermilk!" Samson spit. "You tryin' to poison me? I hate buttermilk!"

Reuben's eyes blinked wildly. His heart started to pound in fear. He hadn't even given a thought to what was in the jug when Samson had demanded a drink. He was sorry, but he was too scared to say so. Instead, he just sat there, staring, and waiting for Samson to jump off that table.

To his relief, Samson only groaned and laid his head back in his hands.

"What am I doin' here?" he asked. "My head. Did somebody bust up my head last night, huh, Reuben? It hurts awful!"

Samson rubbed his hand lightly over his forehead. Reuben winced when he saw the deep gash on the side of Samson's head. He'd forgotten how bad it looked. Again, he wished he could take back all he'd told Mellner and Wheeler. Then maybe he wouldn't be sitting here all worried with this drunk and unpredictable man. He couldn't help feeling responsible for the whole thing. He stared sadly at Samson's suffering.

"Well, hoss, you might as well know right now. A feller by the name of Mellner from Pennsylvania knocked you in the head."

The instant the words left his mouth, Reuben was leaning forward, his body tensed as he watched for Samson's move.

But Samson didn't even look up. "Why? Were we fightin'?" he asked.

Reuben shook his head. "I wish it were so, hoss, but the truth is, the man knocked you colder'n a glacier, then dragged you back here. Says you're gonna take him and his bunch to Oregon."

Reuben's own voice surprised him. He sounded calm. Outside, he'd given Samson the news in a matter-of-fact tone, when inside, he wasn't feeling matter-of-fact at all.

3

Somewhere in the deep recesses of his memory, Samson could recall a conversation about somebody going to Oregon. But hard as he tried to remember more, nothing would come out clear. There were small fragments that passed by, but nothing coherent enough to relate to anything else.

As the cobwebs started to clear from his vision, he looked at the man sitting next to him. It was the closest person to a friend he had. Reuben Cook.

"What are you saying, Reuben? You mean some immigrant done this to my head?" He paused to consider such a thing, his eyes narrowing. "He must of whipped me good. Well, go fetch the man. I wanta see what he can bring to the fight whilst I'm sober."

Samson tried to put emphasis to his words by standing up, but as soon as he rose from the bed, his head started swirling in big circles. All of a sudden, he felt the urge to vomit. He cupped a hand over his mouth and gasped.

Reuben took an involuntary step backward off his stool. He watched, wide-eyed, as Samson groped behind him for the bed, then slowly lay back down, just before he passed out again.

Some time later, Samson awoke. The first thing he noticed was the sound of heavy rain pounding on the roof above. He was alone. The single tiny window in the back room of the tavern let in just enough light to tell him that evening was approaching. He lay there a moment, testing the feelings that ran through his body. His head felt heavy, with a dull throb on one side. His stomach had a tenderness to it that usually meant he'd been drinking heavily.

But that was all he knew. Where he was and how he had gotten there was a total puzzlement. Slowly, he sat up and tried to shake off the disoriented feeling. He looked around at the small room, hoping to identify its contents. But nothing seemed familiar.

He reached up to rub his sore head, and was startled to feel a large bump there. Samson sat and stared out the little window. None of this made any sense. Not that this was the first time Samson had awakened like this, having to take a few minutes recollecting what had transpired the night before and where he had ended up.

He was still musing over his predicament, with no revelations in sight, when Reuben came back. Samson could barely recognize him in the semidarkness.

"Well, hoss! You gave me a scare, you did! I thought you was a goner, the way you passed out this mornin'! You hardly moved a muscle all day long." Reuben took his seat across from the bed and grinned with relief.

"What am I doin' here?"

Reuben got up, and this time he offered Samson a drink of whiskey before he proceeded to tell him the story all over again.

Samson was dumbfounded that some immigrant had come along and managed to render him so helpless, while he didn't remember a thing about it. That was a bitter pill to swallow. "He must've sneaked up on me," he said, giving Reuben a questioning look.

"Dunno, hoss," Reuben said. "All I can tell you for sure is he and another Pennsylvanian brought you in this morning with that big knot on your head." He paused, waiting for some reaction, but Samson only sat there. "Anyway," he went on, "that other feller, name of Wheeler, I think, was busted up some. So I'd say you got in some licks yourself. The way I figure, it was while you were fightin' the one that the other came and busted you from behind."

Normally, such an occasion would have made Samson angrier than a grizzly bear. Instead, he slipped into a reflective mood, pondering what had happened. Had he really fallen this far, he wondered. Reuben Cook and the little tavern room were forgotten as Samson sorted through his life. He couldn't keep his thoughts from traveling back to his wife, Nancy, and son, Cordry. After his son's death, he'd become drunk and helpless, even up to the day when Nancy was killed. Samson's stomach churned into a knot. What kind of man would allow such a thing to happen? He should have been there, he thought, right by her side. Then she'd still be with him. The painful thought tore through him. But even that ache wasn't as deep as the one he carried over Cordry. The day his son had drowned, something inside Samson had died, too. His own father had been a drinking, abusive man who had never loved or bonded with his son. Samson had grown up a suspicious and dubious person, trusting few and asking of no one. It was hard for him to show any emotion, even with his own wife, though he liked and admired her. Nancy had had a hard time dealing with the fact, but over time she had made her adjustments.

Then Cordry had come along. It was like a washing of sunshine in Samson's life. Everything changed, as Samson found someone who was a part of himself—the one person he could love with all his heart and know the love would be returned without question. He and the boy were inseparable. Samson took him hunting and taught him the ways of the woods. He taught him how to read signs, how to know a buck's track from that of a doe. How to pick the best swimming hole and swing from a tree.

Nancy had been somewhat jealous and a little hurt over being excluded from the special twosome. Cordry was getting all the love from Samson that she so desperately craved and deserved. But she loved her son, too, and she knew she had to learn to be content with the life she'd been dealt.

Samson had been aware of his wife's sufferings, even though she'd never voiced them. He could read a person the same as he could read an animal's tracks, and he never missed the wounded looks that so often crossed her face. He did love her, without question, in his own way, and he didn't want her to be unhappy. Still, he just didn't have it in him to take her in his arms and hold her tight. She was supposed to understand that, he told himself. She should realize that it just wasn't his way to show the kind of affection a woman wants. Why, she could surely see that he loved her just by the fact that he was present in their marriage and treated her so kindly.

Those were the thoughts that Samson had used to fight the guilt that gnawed at him. From the day Cordry had died, he had turned all his thoughts over to the power of the whiskey jug. He'd had every intention of drinking himself to death, and it was a miracle that he hadn't succeeded.

Now, a year later, here he sat in a small dark room with Reuben Cook offering up even more whiskey, feeling as hopeless as a man can feel. He'd been wrong to neglect Nancy and ignore the pain she felt after Cordry's death. He should have looked at his wife and considered the demons that haunted her soul. He should have been a man and stood by her side, been her comfort. He should have joined his strengths with hers and gone on with their life together. Samson knew that if he'd been a husband to Nancy, she'd be alive and with him today. Suddenly, Samson could see his own father in himself, and it made him feel sick.

The melancholy of his thoughts caused his eyes to water. He wanted to lie down and cry like a baby, and if he'd been alone, he would have. Instead, he sniffed and fought back the tears and wished Reuben Cook would go away. Suddenly, he felt angry at the man for not allowing him that small courtesy.

4

It was a pathetic state of affairs, but Samson had ceased caring. There was a gray comfort that came from pulling up inside himself and letting the world keep turning without him. It was nonproductive, but safe. At least no one could blame him if things didn't go right. The fact that he'd lost pride in himself and the esteem of others hurt him some, but not enough to make him want to stand up and make an accounting.

He was sitting there, waiting for Reuben Cook to get frustrated and leave him alone, when a door opened. Sudden light flashed across the room. Samson glanced quickly up and back down at his lap, cursing to himself at the new intrusion.

The man who stepped inside was vaguely familiar. He moved a few steps closer, stopped, and put his hands on his hips. Samson could feel him staring. The man stood there so long, Samson finally had to look up.

What he saw irritated him even more. The visitor was surely full of himself. With a cocksure attitude, his eyes raked over Samson with naked disgust.

"So Reuben, have you talked some sense into him?" the man asked.

Reuben Cook looked sheepishly at Samson, then back at the man. Meekly, he shrugged his shoulders.

At the sound of the man's voice, Samson's eyes narrowed. Momentarily, he forgot the pain in his head and the ache in his heart. He'd heard that voice before, and it didn't bring back any pleasant memories. Still, he couldn't place it. He rubbed his forehead. Reuben Cook was about the last fragment of a friend he had left, and this brazen fool was making Reuben uncomfortable, too. Besides that, he was having to think, and that made him even more angry.

"Whatever you're after, mister, just spit it out and leave us be," he said in a gruff voice. He knew he didn't want to deal with this man, but he also knew he couldn't stand to wait forever for him to make his business known. Indecisive people drove him crazier than anything.

"All right," the man said. "My name's Joseph Mellner. MELLNER. Don't you remember?" He shook his head at Samson's confused expression. "Of course you don't. You were too drunk to remember anything." He sat down on a barrel and took a deep breath. "I, along with several others in my party, would like to employ you to take us to Oregon. Cook, here, says you're the best man for the job."

Samson's hard eyes momentarily left Mellner's and fell upon Reuben Cook. "You've got a big mouth, Reuben. And a lyin' one at that."

"Wasn't just Mister Cook, here, who said it," Mellner said. "Folks know your name from here to Pennsylvania. Word has it you're a great hunter and tracker. Could find your way straight out of hell." He made a show of looking Samson over. " 'Course, if you want my opinion, I'm a mite disappointed in you. You certainly don't look like the caliber of man who would attract such high compliments."

Reuben Cook's eyes flitted nervously back and forth between the two like a rabbit that's been caught between a bobcat and a coyote. He didn't know which way to run or which side to take. The two men were staring at each other while the hostility hovered between them like a heavy cloth. Reuben cleared his throat and nodded his head at Mellner. "You best go on and leave Samson be," he said in a tentative voice. "This here ain't the time nor place to do any negotiating. He's still hurt 'n' all . . ." His voice trailed off.

"This is absurd!" Joseph Mellner snapped with indignation. His face turning red, he ignored Reuben Cook and his warning and directed his comments at Samson. "See here, man," he began, jumping up to pace angrily back and forth. "Despite what I think about you, we still need you to guide us to Oregon. We simply have no one else to ask."

Samson's headache reared up again, not only from the big goose egg on his head. His stomach was churning. He wished this stubborn wretch of a man would just get out from in front of him and go away. Surprisingly, he didn't feel any of the raging anger that usually came when someone tried to confront him. Instead, he felt unbelievably tired.

"Mister, I ain't takin' you or anyone else nowheres. Now, if you don't mind, I'd like to be left alone. Please."

But Mellner didn't move an inch. He had stopped his pacing, and was standing over Samson again, his face suddenly deep in thought. He rubbed his forehead with his hand, then scratched the side of his nose. Samson watched him carefully, studying his every move and trying to guess what he was going to say next. Samson noticed that look of self-pride that he despised in others.

But Mellner did look proud, especially when he spun around and faced Samson with a new look of hope. "Here's our offer," he said. "We've agreed to pay you a handsome sum of money. In addition, once we reach Oregon, we'll give you the first choice of any parcel of land. I'll buy back all the weaponry you traded in on liquor, in exchange for your services."

To his surprise, Samson still felt no anger at the man. Even though he had no intentions of accepting the offer, he still couldn't push away the secure feeling the words brought to him.

Just about everything he had owned now belonged to Reuben Cook. How he would love to start all over again in life, he thought. But it was all impossible. Samson swallowed hard. Somewhere out there, far away, lay the bodies of his wife and son. Nothing would bring them back. All the land and possessions in the world couldn't take away the awful hurt he felt inside.

Softly, he said, "Mister, whatever your name is, I'm

askin' you to leave me be. There's others that can take you to Oregon. Others better than me."

"I won't argue with that," Joseph Mellner said. "But they're not here, and you are."

Just then, Reuben Cook stepped in front of Mellner. "It's time to leave now," he said. His eyes were pleading.

Mellner glanced at Reuben Cook, then turned again to Samson. "Well, all right, but I'll be back. You can be assured of that."

Once he'd seen Joseph Mellner out the door, Reuben Cook gingerly sat back down. "I'm sorry, hoss," he said. "That woman of mine shouldn't have let him in here."

Samson shook his head. "It's okay," he said. He stared a moment at nothing in particular. His irritation was gone and the empty feeling was returning. "I guess the man's got a right to pursue his life. I just ain't the one to be leading him anywhere."

Reuben couldn't think of anything intelligent to say, so they sat there in silence for several minutes. Samson tried to turn himself back inside to his original feelings of self-pity, but couldn't. Something new had been stirred inside him. Finally, he spoke up, and in such a loud voice Reuben jumped up off his chair.

"What in hell's the allure?" he said. Without waiting for Reuben's startled reply, he went on. "Why, I had the same wanderlust myself, once. Oh, it's beautiful out there, all right. There's valleys, mountains, lots of trees, wildlife. Pretty as a new maiden."

Reuben nodded in agreement. This sudden contradiction was as much a part of Samson's behavior as everyday breathing air. He could be pointing out the deep darkness of a hole one minute, then pointing out the benefits of such a hole the next.

Reuben took a chew of tobacco and handed his plug to Samson. He sat back and looked philosophical.

"Dunno, hoss. I ain't never got as far as Oregon, myself. I've heard folks talk about how the beav almost run right into the traps out there. Always had a hankerin' to go, but the time's never been right," he said wistfully.

"Oh, you'd find it to your likin', all right." Samson nodded.

The two spent the better part of an hour while Samson reminisced about Oregon. Several times, he remembered the excitement and adventure that he and Nancy had shared so many years ago, and he'd almost feel a yearning to return. But then Nancy's face would invade his thoughts, and the yearning would slip away into grief.

They were passing the jug back and forth while Samson talked. Finally, he set the jug in his lap and popped a cork into the opening. He looked hard at Reuben.

"Ah, hell, Reuben! This is just silly talk. I need to do something with myself, all right. But it ain't Oregon. Know where I need to be? Tennessee. Did I ever tell you I've got a mama and sister still living there? Been years since I last saw 'em. By dern, that's what I oughta do. Go back to Tennessee."

Reuben nodded in agreement. "Yep, hoss, a man needs to see his ma every chance he gets. Mine's a-buried on top of a little hill in Kentuck. She died in '29." He looked sad. "I guess I should go back, too. Just seems like I don't ever get the time."

Reuben's words were lost on Samson. He was still thinking back to his days as a boy. Samson's own mother had been a small, frail woman who had never stood up for herself. She had let herself be bullied through life, first by strict, abusive parents, and later by a selfish, neglectful husband. Afraid Samson might turn out to be the same way, she had done her best to build a fierce, competitive spirit in him. She had found her only joy in her son, in watching him grow up self-confident and assertive. Samson felt a shame run through him. What would she think of him now, he wondered, spending his every waking hour in a drunken state, unable or unwilling to face life's responsibilities. It was worse than anything she'd ever feared for him.

Reuben broke into his thoughts with a short laugh. "Hell, Samson, maybe we oughta just go ahead and take those immigrants to Oregon."

Samson's eyes widened, the whites standing out against

the room's darkness. "Are you serious?" he asked, unable to hide the surprise.

"Not for that Mellner feller, you understand," Reuben said quickly. "But hell, hoss! A man needs to do something once in a while. Something different."

"Aw, that's just foolish talk. What would I do when I got there? I sure as hell don't wanta settle down. Give me a pull of that jug, if you don't mind," Samson said.

Reuben handed over the jug of whiskey. He didn't mind, even though Samson had no money to pay, and Reuben made his living by selling. He reckoned he'd always give Samson whiskey to drink, even if he never had any money or possessions to trade for it.

Ever since Samson had come here, following that awful trip a year earlier, he hadn't shown an ounce of ambition for anything other than getting drunk. Reuben felt a deep compassion for what the man had gone through, and didn't begrudge him his misery. Still, he didn't quite know how to take Samson. Surely the man had to be tired of going nowhere on a dead horse.

In a light voice, he persisted. "Well, I think it's a grand idea, hoss. Shucks, you wouldn't have to stay out there if you didn't want to."

"You surely don't think all this talk is serious," Samson said. "I was just running my mouth, is all. Figured you were doin' the same." He waved the jug toward Reuben. "I was serious about going back to Tennessee, though. Do me good to see some family."

The liquor was having its effect. Samson's speech was edged with a fuzziness. The room began to sway before him and the walls seemed to breathe in and out. Samson laid his head back.

"Still, hoss, I think you oughta think about going to Oregon. Heck, that's what we both oughta do. You and me."

Samson tried to nod, but he couldn't lift his head.

"You and me," he mumbled, just before he fell asleep.

5

An old man was standing in front of him, laughing. Samson couldn't hear any sound, but he was sure the man was laughing at him, just the same. Something about the way the aged lips curled up at the edges bothered him. It was almost like a snarl.

The man was bare-chested and dressed in buckskin leggings. His hair was like a woman's—flowing down to the middle of his back and white as the arctic snow with a silver shine to it. His skin was bronzed and leathery from countless days under the sun-drenched sky. A man who had become old and used up.

But the eyes were young. Samson saw how they sparkled, even in the twilight of day. And they looked at him as if they could see way deep down inside a man, to his soul. The eyes communicated wisdom, humor, anger, and sorrow all at the same time.

The voice was soft and rhythmic, yet Samson heard each word clearly and distinctly, without strain.

"You must get up from this place and go forward. It is disgraceful to let the harvest of life pass."

Angrily, Samson reached out and tried to grab the old man, but grasped only air. It always happened this way. He had seen the old man many times before, standing there with the same haunting smile on his face. Samson always tried to touch him, to push him away, and always the man would be just out of reach.

Samson tried to sit up but, like before, he found he

couldn't move a muscle. Everything except his mind was paralyzed.

He was awake. He could see the room and everything in it, all as normal as could be. Yet, he couldn't raise a finger, couldn't will his body to move an inch. The old man started up with his silent laughter again, causing a panic to run through Samson like a hot knife. He tried to scream out, but nothing in his mouth worked.

Suddenly, the old man reached forward. In his hand was a cloth that appeared from nowhere. Ever so lightly, he patted the raised bump on Samson's head. Samson tried with all his might to pull away, but the muscles in his neck contracted and refused to let him move.

"Lie still. Let me dress your head."

The old man had first started his visits shortly after Cordry's death and had been haunting him off and on since, maybe once a month or so. Samson hadn't felt any cause for alarm, at first. The old man had just stood there a while, then floated off and disappeared. It was in the last month or so that the paralyzed feelings had started up. All Samson could do was sit or lie there, wide-awake and able to see what was going on around him, but helpless as a newborn to do anything about it.

Samson's vision began to cloud. The face became fuzzy and seemed to float. Then, suddenly, the vision came back into focus. Only it wasn't the old man.

A beautiful woman was looking down at him. Samson rubbed his eyes and blinked. Was he still dreaming?

His nostrils took in the womanly fragrance. At least this dream had a little pleasantness to it, he thought.

But it wasn't a dream. He realized it when he felt her soft hand touch his face, then the soreness on his head.

"So, you're Samson. You're not what I expected."

Cautiously, Samson tested his body to make sure the paralysis was gone. Slowly, he raised his hand and brushed his forehead. The woman's eyes watched him solemnly. Samson tried to say something, but the words hung in his throat and all he did was squeak like a silly boy. He coughed a few times before he could manage to speak at all. "Who are you?" he asked and coughed again.

"Becky Sinclair," she said, unceremoniously. "And you are our savior."

Samson groaned and rolled his head deeper into the pillow. "Where'd you get such an idea?"

"You shouldn't frown like that. It doesn't do you justice, at all," the woman said. "Why, a handsome fellow like you should keep a pleasant look about him." She leaned forward so that her face was only about six inches from his. He could smell her breath. It had a sweet, pleasant smell to it. Just as suddenly as she had leaned forward, she pulled back, her eyes studying him. With the back of her hand she lightly touched his cheek. "Why, you're as soft as a newborn. I've been told you were married once and that you're thirty-five years old. But you don't look any older than my baby brother, Ralph. He's seventeen."

Maybe he was still asleep, after all, Samson thought. He'd never encountered such strange talk before. That would explain it all. He must be dreaming about this whole conversation, just like the old man.

Her voice was edged with impatience. "I know you aren't a mute. Are you just terribly shy?"

Samson wished he could wake up. This dream was irritating him, and he had enough problems in his waking world. He said, "You've got a lot of sass. If someone sent you here to talk me into taking a bunch of immigrants to Oregon, you can just go right back and tell them the answer is still no. It was no then, it's no now, and it will still be no tomorrow."

She didn't even flinch. "They said you were feisty, but that's a trait I admire in a man. For your information, nobody sent me here at all. I heard you needed tending to. You also need a bath," she added. She stood up. "Get out of those clothes. I'm sure someone in the group has some clothes that will fit you. I'll have one of the men bring some water."

Samson's eyes narrowed. "I'll not do it," he said. Then she stepped back, and he got a better look at her. The anger drained away.

She surely was the most beautiful woman he'd ever laid eyes on. He liked small women. He didn't know why, but

he did. And she was small. Not more than five-two, he
guessed. She had dark eyes that were soft yet probing and
critical. Her hair was pulled back from her face and tied
with some sort of ribbon. He was surprised to see that she
wore britches. Still, he couldn't keep his eyes off her
womanly figure. Even though she was dressed like a man,
there was an amazing allure about her.

She seemed to be amused by his ogling. A crooked
smile crossed her face. Her eyes looked deep into his. It'd
been a long time since Samson had held a woman's gaze.
The remembrance brought back a pleasant feeling.

As the seconds ticked by, they searched each other's
eyes, like two animals. Then, just as Samson's body began
to tingle from the excitement she brought him, she
dropped her gaze.

Samson wanted more, but he knew she wouldn't give it
to him. Her eyes turned disinterested and she looked away
from him to study the room around them.

Samson felt disappointed and a little ashamed. In just a
few minutes, this strange woman had already claimed
something in him. Only a woman could hold such power
over a man.

"If you'll not undress, I'll send someone else to see that
you do."

The words were tossed over her shoulder, and as suddenly as she'd appeared, she was out the door, leaving
Samson hungry for more of her presence.

He was still sitting there, his body filled with her excitement, her scent still in the air, when Reuben entered.

"I declare, hoss! Sometimes these old eyes of mine can
forget how pretty a woman can be!" Reuben grinned. "It's
sure gonna be hard for me to look at that squaw of mine
for a spell."

Samson nodded and sat up. He was wishing Reuben
Cook would allow him a few moments alone to think
about what had just happened. But Reuben didn't appear
to be leaving any time soon. "She's from the wagon train,"
he said absently.

They heard a commotion outside the little window, so
Reuben pulled back the burlap curtain to peer out. He al-

most jumped back when he came face-to-face with about
half a dozen children. They jumped, too, but soon reappeared in the opening. Their eyes widened as they stared
inside at Samson.

"See?" one of the big boys said. "He ain't dead at all."

"Told you so," another one said.

A smaller boy gawked at Samson a while, then shook
his head in disbelief. "Well, I sure thought he was."

A curly-headed girl made a face and said, "Aw, Joey.
You're as dumb as a tree."

One of the children started to chant, "Joey is a liar, Joey
is a liar." Soon the others were joining in, and Joey started
to holler.

"Mercy!" Reuben shouted impatiently. "You young'uns
git! Go on back to your folks!" He smacked his hands together, sending them scurrying in all directions. He turned
to Samson with an apologetic look. "Dang young'uns! To
tell you truth, they're about to drive me crazy!"

Samson didn't appear to have been affected by the
ruckus. He was staring at the door. "Who was she, Reuben?" he asked.

"Oh, just some little young'un from the wagon train.
Couple of them boys were her brothers—"

Samson looked annoyed. "No, no! I'm talkin' about the
woman that came in here. Who was she?"

Reuben shrugged. "Dunno, hoss. I saw her come into
the tavern and say something to that squaw of mine. The
next thing I knew, she disappeared in here with you." He
rubbed his beard in thought. "She sure was pleasant on
the old eyes."

Just then there was a rap at the door and two men entered.

"What's this? Some sort of meeting room?" Samson
commented as he watched them approach. "Didn't know I
was entertaining guests."

One of the men held out a bundle and dropped it on
Samson's lap.

"You must be Samson. I brung you these clothes. Mrs.
Sinclair said I was supposed to fetch your old ones."

Reuben's eyes widened. He looked first at both men, then at Samson.

Samson was wondering if he'd heard right. "Who'd you say?" he asked.

The man spoke up, slowly, as if he were talking to a man who's half-deaf. "Mrs. Sinclair said I was to pick up your dirty clothes and bring you these clean ones. Said we wasn't to leave 'til we got 'em, either."

Samson knew he'd heard the man right. A flash of heat shot through his body and left him stunned. It made no sense at all. He'd just met Mrs. Becky Sinclair, but already she had stirred up a terrible desire and longing. To find out that she belonged to someone else ripped at his insides. He knew it wasn't reasonable to have these feelings, but reason had left the minute she first spoke to him and touched his cheek.

Instead of revolting any further at their requests, Samson sat up and swung his legs from the bed. Without protest, he started to take off his clothes.

The door opened again, and a third man stepped inside with a bucket of water. Two older women in bonnets came in right behind him.

They looked at Reuben in a scrutinizing way. One of the women finally said, "Are you the one we're supposed to bathe?"

Reuben made a small protesting sound. He stepped back, blinking in surprise, and stumbled over a chair. He shook his head and seemed unable to remove his eyes from the bucket of water.

The man who had brought the clothes said, "Nope, it ain't him. It's this one here." He turned to Samson. "This here's Mrs. Head and Mrs. Evert. They're gonna wash you up," he said matter-of-factly.

Samson, who had undressed to the point where his britches were almost down to his knees, was standing with his hands over his manhood. A reddish hue crept from the top of his head and covered his face. "Ain't nobody giving me a bath," he said. His words were soft and low, almost breathless, as he stared at everyone in disbelief. What, he wondered, had he done to turn his life in this direction?

Desperately, he looked at Reuben. "Get 'em out of here," he said.

Still eyeing the bucket of water, Reuben nodded slowly. "You folks better let Samson be. Just leave your water and the clothes and go on."

The man with the clothes stayed put. He set his jaw and glared hard at Samson. "Mrs. Sinclair told us not to leave until we had him bathed and wearing these clean clothes. So that's just what we intend to do."

"I don't give a hang what Mrs. Sinclair said, or any other female for that matter," Samson said, hitching his pants back up. He picked up the bundle of clothes and threw them back at the man. "I've had about all I can stand from you people. Get on out of here and take all these people with you. Now!"

The second man appeared to have more sense. He walked slowly back to the door and pulled it open. "Aw, come on, Alf," he said. "Let the feller be. I reckon a grown man knows how to bathe himself. Just leave the clothes and water and give him some peace."

The man with the bundle held Samson's stare for a moment. It was clear that he wanted to say more in the way of a threat if Samson didn't cooperate. But everyone was watching him. Finally, he heaved a big breath and tossed the bundle of clothes at Samson. Without a word, he turned and left the room. Quickly, the other man and the two women followed him out.

When the room had cleared, Samson and Reuben sat down for a moment. Neither one spoke, and they avoided each other's eyes. The silence was heavy in the room for a long time. Finally, Reuben got up and left the room.

Samson untied the bundle of clothes. He laid them out and stared at them for a long time.

"By damn," he said. "I do believe the world's gone crazy."

6

Samson stepped outside into the brisk air. He felt different. Not good, but not quite bad, either. The fresh air revived him. He gulped in several deep breaths. When he looked up at the sky, the bright sun smacked his face, causing little dots to dance about in the path of his vision for a moment.

The clothes he had on were worn soft, but they were clean. He quivered and wished he had some whiskey. Usually, by this time of the day he'd drunk enough to settle his nerves and push out the bad memories that were always there to haunt him.

All around, he could see wagons. Oxen, mules, horses, and people were everywhere. There was a clanking of tools and voices as men worked to get the wagons ready for their long trip. Down by the water's edge, women were washing clothing and talking in a loud chatter over all the noise. Amongst it all, children ran laughing and playing and getting in the grown-ups' way. Samson felt as if he had stepped into the streets of a big city.

He wandered about. At first, no one noticed him. Before long, a trail of children formed behind him. Soon, they were calling out his name and plying him with questions. Others began to take notice; the men stopped their clanking and hammering and stared at Samson, mumbling to one another. Even the women at the riverbank paused in their scrubbing to take a good look.

Samson heard his name being passed throughout the

crowd. He wanted to scream at them to get on about their business and leave him alone. But he knew they wouldn't.

Realizing he had no other option but to wait until their scrutinizing was satisfied, he began to study the crowd. He searched the faces in the crowd, looking in every direction. She was nowhere to be seen.

It wasn't that he figured on engaging her in any kind of conversation. That would be too much to hope for. The fact was that Becky Sinclair had managed to do something he would never have thought possible. Even though her visit had only been a scant five minutes, she had somehow ignited something inside of him. His body ached for her.

He hadn't moved more than a hundred yards from the tavern when Joseph Mellner approached. "It's good to see you're up and about," Mellner said.

Samson eyed him warily as Mellner stopped in front of him. Mellner looked Samson over like he was a horse for sale. Then he started to walk slowly around Samson, his chin in his hand. Mellner was a tall man; still, he rose up on the balls of his feet and stared down at the big goose egg on Samson's head. He shook his head, stepped back, and stared at Samson, his jaw set and arms crossed. There was no emotion in his voice. "I'm right sorry about your head, Roach, but you left me no choice, man. You were so drunk, it was the only way."

Samson's innocent demeanor suddenly changed. His boyish features turned serious as his eyes fixed on Joseph Mellner. "You did this?" he asked.

Mellner held his ground and stared defiantly back. "I certainly did, and for good reason. You were a drunken wild man, and you couldn't be reasoned with. Now that you're all sober, there's something we need to get straight right now. I'll simply not allow any of your drunkenness during our trip to Oregon."

Under any normal circumstances, Samson would have pounced on Mellner like a hungry wolf on a rabbit. He didn't like Mellner in the slightest bit. After all, Mellner had been the one to put the lump on his head. But even the fact that Mellner was addressing him in such a patronizing and disrespectful manner didn't raise his anger. Instead,

Samson felt impatient. Mellner was merely a waste of his time.

Maybe, he thought, she was watching him. Maybe she was somewhere close by, blocked from his view. He couldn't help ignoring Mellner and peering around him, right, then left, to look for her face in the crowd. He wanted desperately to find her.

The children, who were still milling around, began to press closer, sensing that something exciting was about to happen. They moved in so close that Samson felt himself held captive, with Mellner face-to-face against him.

Instinctively, he gave Mellner a sudden light shove to one side and hurriedly stepped around him. The children quickly parted to let him through, then fell back in behind as Samson strode off, searching throughout the crowd.

He'd gone only a few paces when he felt Mellner's large hand grab him by the shoulder. The grip tightened and tried to pull him backward.

Samson whirled around. Mellner opened his mouth to speak, but before he could utter a sound, Samson had thrust his angry face close to Mellner's. Spittle flew from his mouth as he spoke. "Don't ever touch me again. Other men have tried to touch me, and they found themselves buried in several different places." His eyes were hard and menacing.

Mellner, a big, proud man with callused hands, broad shoulders, and strong arms, blinked in surprise. He took a stumbling step backward. A man who was used to having his way and speaking with authority, he grappled for words.

"W-w-well, we need to work out the details," he said, his voice quivering.

Samson matched Mellner's backward step by moving forward, his face wrought with fury. His jaw twitched. "Mister," he said, "we've got no deal. Not now, not forever. Now, if you want to see your children and their children and live to tell them entertaining lies, you best leave me be."

Mellner's arms hung straight at his sides. His hands

clenched and unclenched as he tried and failed to hold Samson's gaze.

The entire encampment had grown silent, as every eye was on the two men. Samson and Mellner stood there, like two men on a center stage with an audience before them waiting for the next line to be recited. Samson's last words still hung in the air as if they glued the scene together.

Finally, he turned slowly around and started to walk away. He half expected Mellner to grab him again, or for the whole crowd either to jump him or start throwing things. He felt the hair on the back of his neck bristle up. He could feel them all staring. It left him somewhat unnerved, but he knew he couldn't look back.

He tried to divert his thoughts to Becky Sinclair, but it wasn't the same. He was consumed with what had just happened, what all those people had just seen. With each step he took, some of the anger was erased and replaced by feelings of embarrassment. After all, strange as Mellner's methods of persuasion were, it was a fact that Mellner and his people believed in him. Instead of showing them any ability, Samson had only let them see his temper.

By the time he reached the end of the encampment, the children had given up hope for any more excitement and dispersed. Samson had even stopped looking for Becky Sinclair, figuring she must have decided that he was just as disagreeable as all the others must think. He walked to a little clump of trees and stared out into the distance.

What in the world was happening, he wondered? Why had these people decided to make it their business to make him the center of attention? And why couldn't they just take "no" for an answer? Life would be much simpler if they'd listen to what a man said the first time and go on their merry way. He surely didn't like being in this position.

He had no bad intentions in life. It had never occurred to him to want to hurt or disappoint anybody but himself. He preferred to drink away life's responsibilities, to fade into the crevices of the world and go unnoticed. Samson had often thought that if he could have one wish, he'd be invisible. That way, he could sit along the creekbed with an endless supply of Reuben's whiskey and drink and dream, with no one to disapprove or make it their business to reform him.

Samson had held this philosophy for some time and was quite comfortable with it. He'd had no desire to change anything, which was why he now cursed the stirrings of something old and familiar inside him.

Maybe it was Becky Sinclair, or maybe it was that obnoxious Joseph Mellner and his friends. Samson had no idea. But something had unwrapped the cocoon he'd built around himself and dusted off that natural driving force to go forward and succeed in life that a man carries deep inside. The force he had kept buried for so long.

It was crazy, it was. All of a sudden, Samson could hear his mouth saying one thing, but feeling his heart say something altogether different.

He wished he hadn't let his temper get the best of him with Joseph Mellner. He wished he could take back all the drinking. Samson wished he could take on a different personality and release the pride that controlled his life. He wanted desperately to blink his eyes and turn into the man they expected and thought him to be. With all of his energy, he struggled to summon the courage to walk back through the encampment, search out Joseph Mellner, and in a civil way gladly agree to guide them to Oregon.

He had spent years fighting such inner battles. Lord, he thought, it seemed like pride had figured into every wrong turn in his life. Samson sometimes wondered if his hurt over Nancy's and Cordry's deaths wasn't so much for his own sake as theirs. Not that wondering would change anything, but he couldn't help pondering just what his motives were.

It was a burdensome subject. Samson could think about it all day and into the night, but he still wouldn't have the courage to make peace with Joseph Mellner and move his life forward. He'd never have that kind of strength again.

His melancholy turned bitter. The Irish pride rose up inside him. He began to fantasize about seeking out Becky Sinclair's husband and giving him a pounding simply for

his ownership of her. All the contradictions of his predicament ran through him, playing his mood from one ex-
treme to the other.

He was startled by a familiar voice behind him.

"You look nice in the clean clothes."

Samson's heart leaped. A tingling ran through his chest
and all the way down to his fingertips. He felt his knees
quiver at the slight raspiness in her voice.

Unsure of himself, Samson turned to face Becky
Sinclair. He warned himself not to panic or say anything
stupid.

She was even more beautiful in the sunlight. She had a
small face, with a perfectly tilted nose. Her lips were full
and her teeth were like ivory. The sweat on her tanned
face only enhanced her beauty. Samson's gaze moved up
to her chestnut brown eyes. They were large and surely the
most outstanding feature about her. The whites were as vi-
brant as a cloud on a perfect day. When she looked at him,
Becky again took Samson inside her and owned his soul
as only a woman can do.

Without moving a muscle, she spoke to him silently as
their eyes held one another. In a split second, she had
flirted with him, then pulled back without changing a
thing. There was both an allure and an aloofness about her
that troubled and puzzled him. Her expression didn't
change as she spoke again.

"If we wait much longer, wintertime will set in before
we get there. There's a lot of little children, and I'm afraid
the cold weather won't agree with them."

Samson was surprised at her knowledge, but he was
even more surprised at the boldness of her statement. Samson had never encountered a woman who participated in
men's discussions. It didn't particularly bother him,
though.

As she had done in the room in Reuben's tavern, Becky
pulled her eyes from his, leaving him empty. He wanted to
stop her, tell her to come back, but instead he watched her
walk to a fallen tree and sit down, leaving him standing
there feeling foolish and awkward. He took in a deep

breath to calm the nervous energy that ran through his body.

"You're married, then?" he asked.

"That surprises you?"

She was teasing him. Samson knew right away that this was a dangerous woman to have such feelings for.

Becky rubbed her knees. "You might say I'm an old married woman. I married Tom when I was nineteen. In case you're wondering, that was ten years ago. I was going to be a schoolteacher." For the first time, she showed a tender side as she turned her head and stared off in thought.

Seconds passed. Her voice grew soft and the raspiness faded. "I never did become a schoolteacher," she said. "Don't have any children either, for that matter."

Samson could identify with the sudden emergence of pain on her face. She couldn't hide it. Something told him the last ten years had not always been happy ones. He gave thought to her comment about wanting to be a schoolteacher. Somehow he had a hard time picturing her as a schoolmarm. But, that had apparently been her heart's dream, and something had destroyed it.

While he was standing there, mulling those thoughts, she abruptly stood up. Her voice was raspy, and she was teasing him again.

"There's a lot of people depending on you," she said. "Besides, Oregon is a long ways away. Folks might get well acquainted with each other." She tilted her head sideways. " 'Course, what I mean is there's a lot of good men on wagon trains. I'm sure you'd enjoy their company."

Samson held up his hands. He suddenly wanted to be able to tell her differently. "I wish I could help," he said, "but I just don't think I'm the man to lead anybody anywhere. Besides, don't you think I have better things to do with my life?"

Again, their eyes locked. Becky looked at him for a moment, then shook her head.

"No, I don't think you have a single thing better to do with your life."

7

alvin Page stared at the leg. It belonged to a white person, but it was so dirty and covered with scratches and bruises, it was hard to tell.

He picked up the leg and bent it at the knee. It was stiff, and it took some effort. Curiously, Calvin released the leg and watched as it slowly straightened itself out again. He rubbed his big hand down the foot to the toes. They, like the leg, were stiff and cold to the touch. Carefully, he bent each toe and watched them slowly uncurl to their original positions, one by one.

Before he could even think of blinking them back, tears filled Calvin's eyes. He held the immigrant woman's leg in his arms and cried. In his mind, he could hear his mother's voice telling him once again that he should always be a good boy. She must have told him that a thousand times. My God, he thought, what would she think if she could see him now? Her only son, standing out in the middle of nowhere, holding the severed leg of a poor immigrant woman.

He suddenly glanced skyward, a habit he'd taken on when his mother died three years earlier. Calvin wasn't at all sure where a person went when he died, or if he could still see things that went on down below. It ate at him, not knowing, since he often had the feeling that someone was watching.

He had that feeling right now, that some stern, unforgiving eyes were staring down at him in disapproval. Calvin blinked the tears away so he could see better. He stared up at the clouds some more, hoping that his mother wasn't watching him hold the dead woman's leg. It had never occurred to him to look downward. No, if his mother had gone anywhere, it had to be heaven. Why, Calvin had never seen her do anything at all that would cause her to be cast into the pits of hell.

There was nothing overhead but clouds and sky, but Calvin could imagine his mother's face in his mind's eye. His whole body gave an involuntary shudder, and he dropped the leg. It made a loud thud as it struck the hard earth. Calvin jumped, then looked quickly around at the others.

He wished he had the nerve to saddle his horse and leave. Such ideas passed quickly, though, when he looked down at the sleeping form of Dick Carter. Carter scared him, even in his sleep. Calvin thought about the dark, burning eyes, eyes that held not one ounce of humanness in them. He'd cut a wide berth around bad men, all his life, but Dick Carter was no average bad man. He'd come into Calvin's life and stayed there, dragging Calvin along with him. Just being close to Carter's sleeping form made Calvin nearly wet himself. He worried night and day about doing something that might strike the man the wrong way.

Calvin had witnessed Carter's mean ways many times before. He had thought that things couldn't possibly get any worse. That was why he hadn't been prepared for the night before.

It had all started out as a harmless enough plan. Carter had asked Calvin to join him and some others in heading out west, past the settlements, and robbing the traveling immigrants. They set out with Jimmie Rice, Davis Martin, Sal Musso, and Little Larry Hartz and robbed the first immigrants they came to. It was easy work. The traveling families were more than willing to hand over their money and valuables at the sight of six men toting guns. The first couple of robberies had been good ones with a reasonable profit. Calvin had been quite pleased, until yesterday, when things had gone bad. Real bad. He turned away from the sleeping Dick Carter, and let his mind pass back over what had happened.

They had come across a young man and his pretty wife, who were traveling alone in a wagon. The couple was seated on the ground beside a small campfire. The immigrant had smiled at them and offered up coffee.

"You're welcome to join us," he said, and the young wife nodded pleasantly.

The men were just starting to dismount, when Dick Carter suddenly pulled his gun and fired a shot, right into the immigrant's neck. He fell, instantly dead, across his wife's lap.

She sat there a moment, shock filtering out any expression from her face. Then she started to scream and wail at the same time. Her body trembled uncontrollably as she cradled her husband's head in her arms. There was blood flowing everywhere, over her arms and onto her lap, forever staining her light blue dress. The thought passed idly through Calvin's mind that the bullet must have severed an artery. There was so much blood.

Then the woman looked up at him. Her face was soaked in red. Calvin felt his stomach lurch.

"Why?" she screamed. She looked at each of them, her face distorted with agony. Her blond hair was streaked with blood. Calvin thought for a moment that she might have been shot, too. But then, he reasoned, he'd only heard one shot.

The woman repeated her question, not seeming to care that she was screaming at her husband's killer. She cried and sobbed louder, rocking her husband's body back and forth in her lap.

Calvin looked around at the other men, careful to avoid Dick Carter's eyes. Davis Martin, Jimmy Rice, and Little Larry Hartz seemed as stunned as he was. Even Sal Musso, whom Calvin had always considered to be mean as a snake, had a startled look about him.

It was Little Larry Hartz who finally spoke.

"Why'd ya go and do that for?"

Dick Carter raised his head and glared at Little Larry. "I wanted to watch him die," he snapped, "and derned if he didn't die too fast."

Little Larry Hartz didn't have a reply, which seemed to irritate Dick Carter.

"You got some objection?" he asked menacingly.

The tension grew thick, as Little Larry stared first at the sobbing immigrant woman, then at Dick Carter. After much deliberation, he shrugged and said, "What's done is done."

Dick Carter seemed satisfied with that. "Anybody else got somethin' to say?" he asked, his eyes challenging the rest of the men.

There was dead silence around the campfire as the men looked at each other while keeping a wary eye in the direction of Dick Carter. After a safe measure of time had passed, Sal Musso regained his composure.

"Dang!" he commented, pointing at the dead immigrant. "How much blood you reckon he's got? I've butchered hogs that didn't bleed that much."

That struck Dick Carter as funny, which made Calvin feel a whole lot less worried. All the men relaxed somewhat and turned their attention to the immigrants' belongings.

They left the woman to her grief and rifled through the wagon's contents. Jimmy Rice, who was a distant cousin to Calvin, found over two hundred dollars hidden amongst some clothing.

"I told you we was gonna get rich," Dick Carter claimed. He reached out and grabbed the money. Jimmy Rice looked annoyed but said nothing.

The rest of the men were excited at Jimmy's find, but for Calvin, money had suddenly lost its appeal. He hadn't minded robbing the settlers of their belongings and leaving them to fend for themselves. It hadn't even bothered him when they'd left folks with young'uns to feed. But to kill a man was a different matter. He had never taken the time to ponder such a thing, and it made him feel confused.

It helped some when Sal Musso turned up two jugs of liquor. Calvin sat down with the others and took his turn at the whiskey, taking extralong swallows of the burning liquid.

Before the sky had lost the last dim rays of sunlight, the men were drunk. It was then that the horror began.

The liquor had mellowed Dick Carter's anger, but heightened his yearnings. Savagely, he yanked the young immigrant woman by the hair of the head, and dragged her apart from her dead husband's body. Quickly, he covered and took her there on the ground while the men watched. When he had finished, Sal Musso climbed atop her. The woman's eyes had cried themselves dry. She stared off forlornly at some distant object that only she could see or understand. One by one, each had a turn with her.

Calvin had nearly grown ill at the sight of the woman cradling her dead husband in her arms, covered with his blood, and he truly did feel terribly sorry for her. Still, when his turn came, which not surprisingly was last, the desire in his loins pushed aside any guilt feelings he might have had. Not allowing himself to think, he climbed quickly atop her nearly lifeless body. He tried, but she was so used up by the others, he could barely feel himself inside her. He glanced down at her face and into her hopeless eyes. Her feeling for life was gone.

Calvin was again reminded of his own tired mother. She had worked her life away, used herself up, to where she had nothing left to give her son. Calvin had felt used up, too.

His arousal left him completely, and the deed was left unfinished. Slowly, Calvin got to his feet and pretended that he'd had a fine time with the woman.

The two jugs of whiskey were empty and had been tossed aside. Feeling relaxed and full of himself, Dick Carter started a discussion about dressing animals. Why, he said, he reckoned he could dress out a man near as quickly as he could do an animal. Sal Musso, who was feeling his liquor and would get challenging at such times, took out his own knife and stared bravely at Carter.

"That ain't nothin'," he proclaimed. He gathered up the dead immigrant, and as casually as if he were gutting a deer, he made a big cut at the man's throat, then sliced him from neck to the groin and reached inside. He began to pull out the dead man's innards.

Calvin watched through the flickering flames of the campfire. The whiskey had made him numb, but he wished he had more to finish the job and send him into a good hard sleep. For all he had drunk tonight, he still hadn't been able to chase away the guilt that gnawed at his insides. The fact that Sal Musso had gutted the immigrant while his wife lay in a catatonic state just a few feet away had somehow driven Calvin to where he felt a kinship to her. He didn't know how, but he thought he could understand the way she felt at this moment.

Sal Musso stood up and threw his knife within inches of Dick Carter's foot.

"There you go, Dickie. Now, you can skin 'im." Sal Musso laughed at his own macabre joke.

A sneer crossed Dick Carter's face. Sal Musso had managed to steal away the attention of the other men, and he was purely upset about it. He growled.

"Why, you Italian turd! I reckon anyone can skin and gut a *dead* man."

Calvin watched through the thick haze of his drunkenness as Dick Carter grabbed the immigrant woman by the hair. Before she could blink, he slashed her throat, sending a spray of blood into the flames of the campfire and sizzling into the night air.

Calvin retched and threw up the whiskey, while Dick Carter's big knife cut the woman from breastbone to pubis.

Calvin brought himself back to the present and stared again at the leg that he had dropped at his feet. He couldn't remember Dick Carter severing the woman's body into pieces. He must have fainted, or passed out. He didn't know. He had awakened this morning to find her remains scattered all over the ground.

If his stomach had held anything else, he would have thrown up again when he saw the woman's head perched on the wagon seat, staring out at him. Now, there was nothing inside him to throw up, so he just retched dryly and felt the misery. He was trapped, and he knew it.

Dick Carter would kill him for sure if he showed any disapproval. Though not as mean as Carter, Sal Musso would no doubt do the same, he thought. He wasn't too sure about the other men. Even though Jimmy Rice was distant kin, he was still a rough sort. Calvin supposed, or at least he hoped, that Jimmy wouldn't ever kill him. The other two, Davis Martin and Little Larry Hartz, were followers, like Calvin himself. They didn't pose much danger. In fact, if Davis and Little Larry were all he had to worry about, he could just leave.

The thought occurred to him that they were all still sleeping soundly. He might possibly get away, if he took their horses, too. Then he thought about having to sleep alone in the middle of nowhere, knowing that Dick Carter and Sal Musso were after him, and discarded the idea. He was likely to die of fright, he thought, just pondering the idea each evening when the sun went down and the night sounds started.

Forlornly, he took in a deep breath and filled his lungs with fresh morning air. He willed his legs to sit down on his bedroll.

As he waited for the others to awaken, he looked up at the sky one final time.

"Please, mama," he mumbled under his breath. "Don't be mad. It wasn't me that hurt this poor woman."

8

Calvin felt appreciative of life's little blessings. He'd always carried that trait, but never so much as the next morning when he arose. Dick Carter had risen from his bedroll hung over, yet in a reasonably good mood. He didn't waste any time with starting up the campfire, and Calvin was grateful for that, too.

Carter quickly ordered the men to saddle up their horses, and in minutes they were leaving the death camp. Calvin took notice that Carter averted his eyes from the scattered remains of the dead immigrant woman, but he did take a short kick at the dead husband for lying in his way.

Davis Martin grinned at Calvin from atop his horse. "Dickie sure is somethin', ain't he?" he said.

Calvin didn't answer. He just nodded his head and offered a forced grin in return. Such a remark made him angry, especially when it came from Davis Martin. Davis was scared of Carter; Calvin could tell by the way he jumped every time Carter spit out an order. Still, it bothered him how Davis had such a way of patronizing Carter. It wasn't that Calvin and the other men didn't patronize Carter, too—all except for Sal Musso. But Davis Martin played up to Carter all the time.

Davis's comment hung in the air as the men turned their horses west. They rode in silence, each man allowed his own thoughts about what lay behind them. Carter pulled his horse out in front of the others and rode alone, head high and jaw set. Twenty yards behind came Sal Musso, with the other men following. There had been a few other times when Carter had taken himself away from the others. This morning, they all seemed to understand, or maybe it was a sense of relief, but not a word was said about it.

Outside of stopping to eat and rest the horses, they rode steadily all that day and the next. No one seemed to mind the fact that they hadn't run across a single human being in two days. The idea of robbing and looting had lost its spark. The usual nonstop rambling and sharp barbs among the men had quieted to a few stray comments here and there.

Calvin worried over this new situation. He'd never known these men to be so preoccupied in thought. He let his mind stir up recollections of every foul deed this group had committed. No, it wasn't a good sign that they were so ponderous. It wasn't like them to be somber, not for two days, or one day, or even thirty minutes. Men like them didn't think about much, other than what foul deed they could do next, or how they could spend their next cache of stolen money.

That night, they made camp out on the prairie, next to several big rocks. The rocks looked like boulders that the earth had just suddenly spit up out of the ground. They perched there, huddled together in the middle of flat ground, as though they didn't belong. There was a sprinkling of prairie grass.

Calvin tried to find a soft clump of grass for a pillow. The cold night air that had set him to shivering in his saddle made for a cozy sleep as he wrapped himself in his blanket. He burrowed down and closed his eyes appreciatively, but the dreams that came were full of images of the poor immigrant woman. Her head was still perched on the wagon, but her eyes were open and her mouth was moving, as if asking him please to help her, help her husband. And she was crying.

He slept with the dream playing over and over in his mind, until he awoke just past dawn. Calvin felt grateful for the bright daylight, for his dreams had turned into a horrible nightmare that left him scared stiff. He lay there a moment, letting himself relax so the deep pain in his chest would fade away. He looked up at the sky, happy to see it. There'd been many times when he was sure the dreams were going to kill him before he saw the light of day.

He sat up slowly and noticed that everybody else was up. Dick Carter was off with his horse, tending to a sore hoof. Sal Musso was pouring coffee they'd stolen from the immigrants' wagon, and Jimmy Rice leaned over a pan of frying fatback, also taken from the immigrants. Davis Martin had found a hole in among the rocks, and he was picking at it with his knife. Little Larry Hartz sat by the fire, shivering. He was forevermore suffering from the cold. Twice, he'd gotten so close to the flames, he'd set his clothes afire.

Calvin took in another deep breath of the fresh morning air. It felt good to have the daylight chase away the last effects of the dream. He was just starting to feel better when his eyes fixed on Dick Carter, who was still off with his horse. The longer Calvin watched Carter, the sicker he began to feel. Again, the deaths of the young couple haunted his memory. No matter what he did, he couldn't stop the gnawing feeling inside him. It seemed to be growing, chewing up his innards. He wished he had courage like Carter, Sal, even Jimmy. They didn't seem to be sick or brooding with worry.

He examined each of the men, then looked down at himself. Why couldn't a man's strength be judged by his size, he wondered? Why, he was bigger than any of them. He was nearly six feet tall, and weighed over two hundred pounds. Absently, he poked his finger into his sizable stomach. It felt tender and soft.

He remembered back, two summers ago, when they'd all been together. Calvin couldn't remember why, but he'd laughed at something Sal had said. Carter, who'd been standing close by, had thought Calvin was laughing at him. For whatever reason, he'd taken exception to the goings-on and delivered a hard blow to Calvin's stomach. Nothing had ever hurt quite as bad as Carter's fist. It completely knocked the breath out of Calvin. Two years later, and he could still feel that punch.

He looked up from his stomach and stared at Dick Carter. The man was only about five-ten, he figured, and maybe 175. Still, he could fight like a giant.

Then there was Sal Musso. Calvin had never had the occasion to feel Sal's power and had no desire to. Sal was a tall man, at least an inch taller than Calvin, and pretty solid at around 190. He was a vicious fighter and could probably lick Carter in a fair fight. But, then, there would never be a fair fight with Carter. Sal and everybody else knew it.

Jimmy Rice was lucky to weigh 150 soaking wet, but he could fight and had enough dirty tricks to get an upper hand. Davis Martin fit somewhere in the middle of all of them. Little Larry Hartz earned his nickname, standing five-four and 120 pounds at most.

Melancholy filled Calvin up. He had always been big for his age. As a boy, he'd heard the adults talking about it, exclaiming over his size. He knew they expected big things from him, too. Yet, he had never been able to perform like the person that everyone thought him to be. For while he was big on the outside, he had the heart of someone else. Younger boys, half his size, could send Calvin scurrying at a run.

A knot formed in Calvin's throat as he remembered a time when he was nine years old. His father had died when he was five years old, and his mother had remarried shortly after. Calvin's stepfather was a mean-spirited man, who had never cared for Calvin or his siblings.

One summer, there had been a big family picnic. There were maybe a dozen children there, and Calvin had towered over all of them. Calvin couldn't remember exactly what had caused the disagreement. In all likelihood, it had been mostly one-sided. His cousin, Jimmy Rice, a year younger and much smaller, had punched Calvin in the nose.

Calvin had run to his mama and hugged her around the waist, crying into her side. His stepfather, who had never had a kind word for Calvin, made fun of the boy. Angrily, he'd pulled him away from his mother's side and held his face out for all the family members at the gathering to see. Calvin could still remember the harsh statement, and the note of genuine disappointment in his stepfather's voice.

"I told you we had us a girl in boys' clothes," Calvin's stepfather had sneered at Calvin's mother and at the crowd. Then, with a vicious jerk, he'd turned Calvin toward his mother and forced his face into her breast. "Suckle! Suckle your mama like I tell ya, boy. Why, you can't even stand up and account for yourself with a boy half your size! Only a girl or a suckling would cry like that."

Calvin could still recall the incident like it was yesterday. Again, he touched his soft stomach, then absently ran his hand up and down his arm muscle. It was soft, too. Calvin had grown from a scared young'un into a weak, spineless man.

Right now, he hated his stepfather. He hated Dick Carter and Sal Musso and Jimmy Rice. He hated little Larry Hartz. Calvin looked off to his left. Davis Martin was still kneeling on the ground, digging in the rocks with his knife. He hated Davis Martin the most, he thought, for Davis was just like him. Weak. Calvin suddenly felt like picking a fight with Davis and considered the idea, but he didn't really have the nerve, even for that.

He closed his eyes and swallowed hard, trying not to cry. Inside, he offered up a prayer for his mother to come and lift him up to be with her. But even as he knew she couldn't answer, it occurred to him why he had gotten himself into this current mess. The very reason why he was crying inside, feeling so terrible. It was his weakness again, his fear to take hold of himself and answer for his own manhood. That weakness had driven him straight to Dick Carter, Sal Musso, and Jimmy Rice. Once again, he had hidden from his own failings in life by surrounding himself with the toughest renegades he could find.

Calvin had run with this group before. By the time he was a teenager, back home in Ohio, he'd been deeply involved with his companions. They had terrorized every neighborhood boy within miles. Calvin had been guilty himself for some of the terror inflicted on his fellow adolescents, although he always managed to hide his actions behind Dick and Sal and Jimmy. That was the source of his anger with Davis, he supposed. Whereas Calvin had only occasionally done it, Davis had been particularly abusive to the other town boys back home, as long as he had one of the others to protect him. Davis disgusted him, Calvin decided, because he had no honor. But then, he knew, neither did he.

"What in hell are you diggin' at?" Sal said to Davis.

Davis's head had disappeared and his voice sounded muffled. "There's a hole. Looks like an entrance to a cave here amongst the rocks." He pulled his head out and dug some more.

He was joined by Little Larry. "He ain't lyin'," Little Larry said. He stared at the hole. "Why, I reckon I could get down in there."

"You find your own hole," Davis said. "Soon as I git it dug out, I'm goin' in myself."

"Goin' into what?" Sal said. "I reckon you just found some varmint's hole. Probably a badger. That's right, a badger. Go on in there. He'll eat your ass alive." He laughed.

By now, everyone except Dick Carter was standing around, peering into the hole, which Davis had managed to open to about a foot across.

"You ever et badger?" Little Larry said to no one in particular.

After some thinking, one by one, they all agreed that they hadn't. Davis said, "I've et many a groundhog, though. I'll bet it tastes just like groundhog."

Sal Musso pointed at the campfire. "Git me a piece of that burnin' firewood," he said to Little Larry. "I'm gonna dig down in there and find mister badger and shoot 'im. Git that hole bigger," he said to Davis.

It wasn't long until Davis had dug out an entrance big enough for a man to squeeze his shoulders through. Sal took a torch of burning wood, shoved it inside and peered down. He stood back up. "Hell, boys. That badger's buried himself up under those rocks. I reckon you'll have to crawl on in there, Davis."

Davis, who had been all prepped and excited at first, had suddenly lost his enthusiasm over crawling into a dark hold under the rocks. "I don't know if'n I can get down in there or not," he hesitated.

"Sure you can," Sal said. He stuck the burning wood back into the entrance. "See there? It opens up, back toward that rock. Take this wood with ya. You'll be able to see fine."

Davis's eyes grew wide. "W-w-well, what if that badger's down in there? I mean, lookee here, I don't know about messing with no badger."

"Well, that's the whole purpose," Sal said. "How else we gonna eat 'im if we don't go down in there and fetch 'im up?"

"What if he ain't down there? What if I get down in there and don't find nothin'?" Davis said, hoping his rationale would convince Sal that the whole idea was useless.

"He's in there, all right. Ain't none of ya seen a badger runnin' around during the night, did ya?" Sal asked the others. They all shook their heads.

"I-I-I don't know," Davis said. "Why, one of them animals is likely to get ahold of a man down there 'n' kill 'im!"

"Naw, just shoot 'im," Sal said. "Lookee here. Calvin and I'll hold on to your feet. Take hold of the fire in one hand and the pistol in the other. When you see that badger, just shoot 'im in the head. Then, we'll pull you 'n' the badger out."

Davis stood there, his eyes blinking rapidly. Absently, he reached for the burning stick that Sal held out to him. He swallowed hard, his Adam's apple bobbing up and down. Finally, a look of resignation crossed over his face.

Little Larry suddenly stepped forward. "Aw, hell, give me that fire," he said, glaring at Davis. He bent down on hands and knees and crawled into the hole with ease. Sal and Calvin grabbed his feet as the rest of him disappeared.

"You're right!" he hollered back at the others. "It opens

way up, under these rocks. Let go of my feet. If there's a badger in here, he's back under a ways."

Inside the cave, Little Larry held the torch out in front of him. What had been a small hole in the rocks now opened up into a large area at least six feet wide. As far as the torch would show, he could see about ten feet inside. The only problem was that the area was only two feet high. He worked his way slowly, with the torch held out before him. Soon, he had crawled at least fifteen feet into the earth.

He saw the cave narrowing to a small hole to his right. He eased toward it, his heart racing, wondering what he might find. He'd heard stories about caves full of gold left by the Spaniards. Then again, he thought, this cave looked like no other human had ever been here before, like maybe nature had simply belched it up without anyone ever taking notice. Still, one couldn't be sure about such things. He felt excited as he crept farther into the earth's cavity.

He put his torch into the opening. It was sort of a tunnel that ran down a few feet, then curved. *No problem,* he thought. He could easily back out if he had to. Little Larry was almost a mole. He always had been. Back in Ohio in his youth, he'd loved nothing more than cave exploring, pressing his tiny body into any opening he could find. He'd never found anything worth finding in his exploring, but it had been a thrill just to be able to do it. Crawling into tiny places had been about the only worthwhile thing about being small.

Little Larry eased down into the rock tunnel, his shoulders scraping against the sides. Again, his heart pounded in his chest as his mind conjured up all kinds of possibilities. Was he the first human ever to see this? Or was it some long-lost hiding place for some ancient Indian tribe? What if he found a dead body in there, or an animal? What if he came face-to-face with a badger?

He stopped. Little Larry had almost forgotten why he'd crawled into this hole to begin with. The realization hit him that a badger could very easily rip him to pieces, especially a trapped badger. He could back out easily enough, he thought, but not with a badger on the chase. He put the torch in his other hand and worked his right arm down to his pistol, then pulled it out of its sheath. He crawled farther on. To his relief, he didn't come face-to-face with a badger. Instead, the tunnel began to widen somewhat. Five feet farther, it was nearly three feet wide.

Sweat flowed down his forehead and stung his eyes. It was cool inside the cave, almost cold, but he felt clammy. He breathed in the stale air. If a badger were here, he reckoned, it wouldn't be this deep. He knew he might as well turn around while he had the room and start on his way back out, but curiosity pushed him forward.

A few feet farther in, Little Larry saw the thousand eyes. The flames of his torch caught their glow and they shone back at him like stars.

From nowhere, a rope shot out at him and stung his cheek. Little Larry yelled out. Then, a noise commenced. It echoed through the cavity, filling his mind and all his senses. The rattling came from everywhere, off the walls, above and behind him, as if someone had opened up the top of his head and poured it inside. The snakes were everywhere, piled on top of each other, writhing and slithering and rattling their tails in alarm.

"Oh my God!" Little Larry cried. He grabbed his cheek. It was throbbing. He could feel the holes. His hand came away bloody.

"Help! Help! Oh my God, help me!" he cried, only half realizing that no one could hear him. Again, he grabbed at his face. The sudden movement brought another strike from a big rattler that had been curled not more than two feet away, perched up on a little ledge. Its fangs went deep into the side of his hand, the one holding the pistol. He dropped it.

"Oh my God! They're killing me!" He screamed in terror, but it was lost in the din of the rattling tails.

Another strike caught him on the shoulder. He started to bawl like a baby as he struggled to crawl backward, barely aware of the rocks' jagged edges ripping into him, tearing clothing and hide alike. His head swirled in panic. He could feel his cheek swelling. His hand throbbed and burned and ached from fingertips to elbow. His shoulder was on fire. The delirium grew inside him.

When he reached the part of the tunnel that widened, he threw away all caution and flipped his body around. His head slammed against the overhead rock, ripping off a chunk of his scalp. He dropped the torch, and it fell under him. He didn't even feel the hot cinders burn his flesh.

Now, he was in total darkness. The rattling still ringing in his ears, all Little Larry knew to do was crawl, his mind struggling to remember how. Forward he went, constantly scraping against the jagged edges of the rocks. He'd lost his sense of direction. He felt almost dreamy, as though he were in space. Up was down. Right was left. Still, he crawled.

Finally, he made it to the narrowest part and pushed himself painfully through the small opening. Far up ahead, he saw a tiny shaft of light.

He made his way toward it, weakly. It felt as if he were moving in slow motion. He wondered if he was moving at all. Was he dying, he thought, or already dead? Was this how he was meant to leave the world?

Suddenly, as his body spun and reeled with pain, everything in life came down to reaching that shaft of light at the opening. He didn't want to die underground like some varmint. In a split second, his mind put together the scenario of his body lying there dead, with rattlers crawling all over him. He could see the big one crawling through his chin and up through his eyes. Little Larry started to scream, the sound bouncing from the walls and traveling out through the small opening.

"What in the heck's goin' on down there?" Sal hollered.

"Badger must've got 'im for sure," Davis said.

Just then, Little Larry's head popped out of the hole. Blood ran from the top of his head in streams down his face.

Calvin jumped back. The sight of Little Larry sent a shock of pain through his chest.

"My God! What'd you run into?" Sal said.

Little Larry gasped and cried. "They kilt me, Sal! They've kilt me for sure!"

"What?" Even Sal's eyes bulged. He stepped back in horror.

Calvin was surprised at his own actions as he pushed past Sal. He grabbed Little Larry by the shoulders and easily pulled him out of the hole. By now, Dick Carter had joined them. He stood and looked down at Little Larry, curious, like he was looking at nothing more than a rock on the ground.

"Snake," he said. "Got him right on the face. I'll be damned."

"Rattlers. Got my hand, too." Little Larry barely managed to hold up his hand.

"Well, I'll be damned," Dick Carter repeated. "Git ya anywhere else?"

"I don't know." Little Larry tried to search his mind, but all he could see were hundreds of snakes, crawling all over him. His body started to shake. There wasn't a part of him that didn't ache. He tried to think about where else he'd been bitten, but he couldn't remember.

"Git him on up here, boys," Dick Carter said. "Might as well lay him out comfortable. I know a man that got bit on the toe by a copperhead. Had to cut his leg off. I think the only thing that saved him was the fact that he got bit so far from his heart." He paused and stared off toward his horse. "I don't think Little Larry's gonna be so lucky. Can't cut a man's head off."

They laid Little Larry in his bedroll. Dick Carter poured himself some coffee. One by one, the others joined him. Little Larry's sobs soon became part of the background noise, much like the wind. Dick Carter talked about which direction they should head in.

Calvin's mind was totally fixed on Little Larry and his predicament, but he was afraid to mention the fact. No one said another word about Little Larry, until finally Sal said, "How long you think it'll be 'fore it kills him?"

"Dunno," Dick Carter said. "Don't know much about rattlesnakes. I think they're a lot more powerful than copperheads, though."

"Well shit," Sal said. "I hate to see the man suffer."

"You're right," Dick Carter said. "Calvin, you shoot 'im."

Calvin was looking over at Little Larry when Dick

Carter gave him the order. He wasn't sure he'd heard right. "Shoot him?" he repeated in a weak voice.

Dick Carter nodded. "That's right. Shoot 'im. Hell, I'd want somebody to take me outa my misery if'n I was layin' there, sufferin' like that. 'Sides, we need to git movin'. I'd like to fill my bags up and git out of this god-forsaken country with its cussed wind. Get back to where they got trees."

A dread went through Calvin like he'd never experienced. His heart pounded so loud, it sounded like it was sitting right up there in his head instead of his chest. He could barely speak. "I can't, Dick."

"Can't what?"

Dick Carter was grinning at him the same way his step-father had grinned. Calvin wished he could think of something clever to say, something bold, that would take Carter's mind off of another killing. But no words came to save him.

Carter was still grinning. "Well, go on," he said. "Shoot 'im."

"I can't," Calvin said again. His voice trembled.

"Why not?"

"Shoot Little Larry? Why, I've known him all my life. 'Sides, I ain't never . . . kilt nobody before. You know that, Dick." Calvin stared at Carter with pleading in his eyes.

"Well, I'll be damned," Dick Carter said, disgusted. "If that don't beat all. I guess you want me to shoot 'im for you. Do I need to wipe your ass, too? What did you think this was, a pleasure trip?" Carter blew out his breath. "You've shot animals before, ain't ya, Calvin? Or don't ya got the stomach for that, either?"

Calvin said timidly, "Sure I have, Dick. I've kilt deer and turkey. I've kilt beef, chickens, squirrels, lots of varmints. But that ain't the same, can't you see that? I just can't shoot Little Larry."

Dick Carter looked over at Little Larry. "Hell, he's almost dead anyway." He stared hard at Calvin. "You go over there and finish the job, and I mean it, Calvin, unless you want me to shoot you. I'll not have a man ridin' with me that's gutless. You ain't gutless, are ya, Calvin?"

Calvin felt as though he must weigh a thousand pounds as he tried to stand up. His legs shook so badly, he wasn't sure they'd hold him if he did make it up. "Please, Dick, don't make me do this," he tried again.

Suddenly, Dick Carter jumped to his feet and clenched his teeth. He pulled his pistol and rammed it into Calvin's stomach. "Here, take my gun. Maybe it'll make you feel better. Now, go shoot 'im, Calvin. Right now."

Calvin knew there was no use talking with Carter. He'd seen him like this before. Where sympathy could get to most men, it only seemed to drive Carter into a rage. Before he turned, he looked at Sal and Davis. They sat there watching, expressionless. Calvin looked at Jimmy. He could read the pain in Jimmy's eyes. It was a small comfort, but it gave him some relief to know that Jimmy felt for him.

It took all of his strength to walk over to where Little Larry lay. He was breathing in rough, jagged breaths.

Tears ran down Calvin's cheeks. He was glad he hadn't started crying until his back was turned on the others. He stood there, nearly frozen as he stared down at Little Larry.

Little Larry quivered and shook. His eyes seemed to be glazed over. Calvin wished that Little Larry would die, right now. He started to pray, harder than he had ever prayed in his life. "Please Lord, please! Let him die 'fore I have to shoot 'im."

He prayed it over and over, but Little Larry continued to lie there and shake. Calvin could feel the other men's eyes, watching him silently. He could almost imagine the expressions on their faces. He didn't know how long he would have stood there if Dick Carter hadn't called to him.

"By damn, Calvin, you shoot 'im before I shoot you!"

It occurred to Calvin to wonder why Carter was so anxious to get Little Larry shot, since he was going to die anyway. Why didn't he just do it himself?

But wondering was going to get him shot, too. Calvin could feel Carter's impatience rising. Slowly, he raised the pistol and pointed it at Little Larry's forehead. His legs again began to tremble wildly.

Involuntarily, he barely swung his head around, as the contents of his stomach came lurching forward onto the ground, not a foot from Little Larry's head.

As Calvin stood there regurgitating, Carter started laughing uncontrollably. "Why hell, Calvin! You're gonna piss me off in a minute! Can you believe this?" he asked the others. "Some desperado, huh?" Getting no response from them, he shifted to a somber tone.

"Now, Calvin, when you get done gaggin' yourself, you shoot Little Larry, or else I'm shooting you. This is my last warnin'."

Calvin could barely see for the tears that clouded his eyes. He gripped his pistol and pointed it at Larry's chest. His hand shook so, he had to steady it with his other hand.

He closed his eyes and gave a low groan as he pulled the trigger. Little Larry grimaced. His body shook a time or two, then went still.

Calvin opened his eyes. His legs felt so weak, they nearly gave way. He took in a deep breath of cool air. He could still breathe. Suddenly, a relief came over him. The deed was over and done with. Little Larry was dead, but *he* was still alive. He knew that was no small matter.

9

It was still an hour before dawn when Samson set out walking. He went through the encampment and all the way to the little grove of trees where he had met with Becky Sinclair. There in the trees, he stopped, tilted his nose up the way a dog would, and sniffed. He was hoping that he'd catch some of her fragrance, still lingering. It was a fool notion, he knew, but he tried anyway. All that came to him was the smell of wind and dried prairie flowers, but he could remember well enough how good it had been to stand there and enjoy the air around her.

It felt crisp and cold in the early morning. Last night had been the first time Samson had gone to bed without a drink for longer than he cared to recall. His body shivered unmercifully, but not from the cold. He knew that part of the trembling was the effects of all the whiskey he'd been drinking the last year. The rest was caused by the sudden lack of the stuff, plain and simple.

He sat down on the same fallen tree where Becky had rested. When he'd first gotten out of bed, he'd nearly hyperventilated. He was still feeling short-winded and dizzy, and his stomach had gone sour. He had to fight the urge to give it up, to head for the tavern, grab up a jug of whiskey, and wash away all these aches and pains. He felt like an old man this morning, and that troubled him. His body felt stiff and cold.

It wasn't that he didn't feel happy with the victory of his abstinence. He just didn't know how long he could hold out. To be honest, he wasn't sure how much he *wanted* to hold out.

As Samson sat there, he thought back over his life. It seemed that he'd been born outdoors and right in the middle of adventure. He'd been barely fourteen when Davy Crockett had taken him under his wing, back in Weakley County, Tennessee. Crockett, who was thirty-six at the time, had taught Samson the ways of the woods. Samson had never been happier than when he was hunting or exploring with Crockett. He reckoned that between them, they must have killed more bears than anyone in the history of Tennessee.

Though he admired and looked up to him, Samson had never shared Crockett's inclination for politics. In fact, he often thought that Crockett might still be alive if he hadn't lost his last election and made that fateful trip to Texas. Samson had agreed to go along with Crockett, but Nancy had pleaded him out of it, insisting that Samson had a son to consider. To this day, Samson carried a bit of guilt for not having been by Crockett's side when he died.

In the end, Nancy had been right. His yearning for excitement was a selfish and trite thing, next to being near to his son. Samson, himself, couldn't remember anything of substance about his own father. He'd heard rumors and stories about his parents both coming from Ireland. In fact, Samson had been born during the crossing. His father had been described as of average size, with a terrible temper. Samson's mother had never had much to say about her husband, except to fly into a tirade about his fondness for liquor and her intolerance of it. Samson was left with little to work with in formulating any kind of opinion about the man. He pictured him as a terrible businessman who had tried three or four times to establish taverns, but had failed because of his tendency to drink too much and start fights with the customers. One day, when Samson was three years old, his father had just up and disappeared, never to be heard from again.

Samson looked back at the encampment. He could hear the faint voices of the people as they stirred from their sleep. The flames of fresh fires began to flicker in the

morning darkness. Even though he'd told himself otherwise many times, he really did wish he'd known his father.
Maybe then he wouldn't be sitting there on the dead old
tree, suffering from the miserable want of liquor and fighting a guilty conscience. Maybe Cordry would still be
alive, so Samson could look into his smiling face and hold
out his arms for a big hug. Maybe it would be Nancy he'd
be thinking about this morning instead of a married
woman.

Except for his marriage to Nancy, it seemed to Samson
as if he'd felt empty inside all his life. Maybe that was
why he'd taken to Davy Crockett. In some ways, Crockett
had been like a father figure to him. Crockett was surely
the only adult male who had tried to teach Samson in the
ways of life. He still grew amused when he thought about
Crockett's braggadocious ways. The man had loved to
talk. In fact, Samson figured Davy liked talking better than
anything, and talking about himself, at that. During their
first few hunting trips together, Samson had decided that
Crockett had to be all hot air for the number of bears he
professed to killing and the Indians he claimed victory
over during the big war. No man, he thought, could face
that many bears and Indians and live to tell about it. But
it hadn't taken him long to see that Crockett was, indeed,
an extraordinary man, whether hunting or tracking in the
woods, or in a tavern holding center stage and telling his
wild and unbelievable stories.

All his reminiscing made Samson sad. That made him
feel even older. He sniffed hard and wiped his face with
his palm. The noise from the early risers in the encampment was starting to break his concentration. He stood up
and started walking aimlessly toward the west, chewing on
a twig he'd pulled from the dead tree.

He's always liked to get off by himself like this, even
when he was married. He enjoyed reliving some of those
pleasant days with Davy Crockett. Sometimes, he'd recite
one of Crockett's stories to himself. Samson had the ability to recall anything he heard, almost word for word. Often, his thoughts would take him back to San Antonio and

Crockett's death at the Alamo, or his father and mother would come to mind.

He needed to go see his mother. It had been far too long and she would be an old woman by now. But that would have to wait. He glanced back toward the encampment.

It would have suited him fine if he could just gather up his few belongings and be on his way from this place and Joseph Mellner, the children, Becky Sinclair. But the more he tried to push their faces from his mind, the more they kept coming back to him. It had even gotten hard to bring back his old remembrances for thinking about the people who demanded that he take them to Oregon.

Samson walked a couple of miles, to where the darkness was being pushed from the landscape. Again this morning, everything was frosted over. He stopped and took a longing look toward the vast, empty west, free of wagon trains and folks and pretty married women ...

His body shook for a drink. He watched a coyote in the distance, loping along with its nose sniffing the earth. He was like that coyote. His nose wasn't to the earth, but he was searching this morning, too, and neither one of them knew exactly what they'd find in life. Samson felt sure, though, that Becky Sinclair and the immigrants back at the encampment would all figure in there somewhere and become a part of him, one way or another. The idea scared him, but not without a small touch of excitement.

The sun was just reaching over the horizon when he turned back. The sudden brightness made him close his eyes, and when the spots cleared, he envisioned the face of Becky Sinclair.

He slowly made his way back to the encampment, and instead of seeking out Joseph Mellner or Becky Sinclair, he headed straight for the east side of Reuben's tavern.

Gertie was frying fatback over a fire out front. Reuben stood barefoot in the doorway, his wiry gray-brown hair all pushed up to one side and sticking in the air. He rubbed the sleep from his eyes and blinked at Samson. "Damn, hoss. Is that you?"

Samson nodded. The smell of the frying fatback eased up his nose with great pleasure. It'd been a long time since he'd eaten breakfast. He'd always either been drinking whiskey, if he was up early enough, or been too hung over. Gertie also had a big pot of coffee boiling, and the mixture of aromas was overwhelming.

Reuben stepped out from the doorway with his bare feet on the nearly frozen ground. His big toenails had turned black and looked as though they were going to fall off. Samson had never noticed them before, but now the sight caught his eye.

"Say, Reuben, it looks like a copperhead done bit both of your big toes," he said.

"Shucks, hoss. Wasn't no copperhead at all. They just stared turning that way four or five years back. First the right one and then the left one." Reuben wiggled the toes on his big feet for emphasis. "I wish the dang things would just fall on off. The way it is, they give me nothing but misery every time I bump into something." He walked over and rubbed his hands over the fire, then reached for Gertie's ample backside. Giving Samson a wink, he patted her the way a man would his dog.

"I don't want you burning my eggs this morning. Hear me, woman? I like 'em where the yeller still runs a bit." He gave her behind one last squeeze and turned his own backside to the fire. "I declare! It's something seeing you up and around this time of the morning. Where you been off to?"

"Just walking," Samson said.

"You're gonna take those folks to Oregon, ain't ye?"

Samson stared at the fire so long and hard it burned his eyes. The bluntness of the question surprised him. Without looking at Reuben, he asked, "What makes you think that?"

"Dunno, hoss. Just have a feelin', is all. Look, it ain't none of my business, but that ain't such a bad idea," Reuben said.

Still with his eyes locked on the cooking fire, Samson said, not unkindly, "You're right, it ain't none of your business." He rubbed his eyes. "But I reckon you're smarter than most men. That is, I am kinda leanin' that way for sure." He paused. "You must think I'm crazy."

Reuben stretched and rubbed the heat from his backside. "Ain't nothin' crazy about it, a-tall. Once this bunch pulls out, won't be nothin' left but me and the squaw here 'til another wagon train comes along. No sir, ain't no future here, and a man's gotta have a future."

He disappeared into the tavern and returned carrying Samson's rifle, pistol, knife, and saddle. "You'll be needing these, hoss," he said and set them on the ground at Samson's feet.

Samson shook his head at the charity. "No sir. I can't take 'em," he said. "At least not unless I get some advancement from those immigrants. We traded, fair and square. It just wouldn't be right for me to take 'em back."

"Done been paid for. Right handsomely, too." Reuben said with a grin. "That Sinclair woman come last night and paid for 'em."

Anger shot through Samson. He hadn't told anybody until this very moment that he intended to go. What gave her the right to make such bold assumptions? He thought back over their conversations. He was sure he hadn't said a thing to let her believe that he'd decided to go.

Suddenly, his heart started pounding. It scared him to think that anyone held such power over him. Almost sheepishly, he stared down at the saddle and his weapons. He had a mind to go seek her out, take her by the shoulders, and shake some sense into her. Becky Sinclair didn't know a thing about him, he thought. None of them did. Where did they all get such a nerve, to come along and dictate a man's life to him?

But it was only wishful thinking. By the time Samson laid eyes on Becky, her beauty would sweep through him like a prairie fire, and he wouldn't be able to say an angry word to her. He wouldn't be able to say a thing to any of them. No, he'd just make a fool of himself one more time. He was sure of that.

Still, he was resentful. He had a mind to trade the saddle and weapons right back to Reuben for more whiskey. And he would, if only he could get up the nerve to do so.

Reuben rubbed his beard and studied Samson. There was an edge of sympathy to his voice. "How 'bout some breakfast, hoss?" he invited. Without waiting for an answer, he said to Gertie, "Fix Samson some eggs to go with his fatback, and don't burn 'em."

Feeling meek as a lamb, Samson sat down to breakfast with Reuben and Gertie. He tried to hold his pout and feel sorry for himself. He wanted to be angry and strong against these people. He didn't want to like any of them.

But, off in the distance, he heard them. The camp was again full of activity. The children were noisy and the people talked and laughed like they were happy with life. They had an exciting new place to go and a chance to make their dreams come true. The possibilities were endless.

And Becky Sinclair was so beautiful.

10

❦

Once Samson had made up his mind to accept their offer, he was ready to move. It was his way, almost as if he feared something would catch him from behind if he didn't get started. It was a complete contradiction to his nature, because he could mull something over in his mind for so long, he'd start getting a headache and his stomach would churn and twist until it burned. It was a difficult and painful process, but once a decision was reached, Samson couldn't wait to see it acted on.

One thing troubled him deeply. This wagon train was too big and he knew it. Eighty wagons was going to be a chore, and they seemed to have a surprisingly high number of children. The migration to Oregon had started in 1841, when a hundred folks made the trek. Samson had led part of that first group. Then in '42, the number had doubled to two hundred. It was estimated that more than a thousand folks had made the journey last year. On Samson's own fateful trip, just one year ago, there had been thirty-five wagons and only a couple of dozen small children. Even so, several of them had died along the way. That was what frightened Samson the most: the thought of the children. He had heard talk among the immigrants about traveling conditions and weather and Indians and such, but he gave those little thought. No, it was the little children who worried him the most. He prayed that God would protect them.

Samson had sent Reuben to tell Joseph Mellner that he had agreed to lead them, and it wasn't long before Mellner and several others appeared at the tavern. Mellner still carried the scar from yesterday's exchange between Samson and himself. There was a difference in his eyes in that they didn't seem nearly as bold and forthright.

They all welcomed Samson like a new son in the family, but not without some trepidation. One man muttered something about Samson's drinking; another wanted to be assured that Samson wouldn't take them partway and then quit. One man even questioned, in a kind way, the fact that Samson was so small and looked so young. All in all, though, they seemed more than grateful that he had agreed to their offer.

Samson called a meeting right after the noonday meal. He told Mellner that he wanted to speak to the entire group, which Mellner thought was a splendid idea. That way, he said, the immigrants could ask questions and Samson could explain everything to them. Some of their worries would be put to rest. Mellner nodded in agreement, but Samson knew he had called the meeting just as much for himself as for the rest of them.

After the men left, he set off for another of his solitary walks. Finally, something had come along to push aside all the bad thoughts that he'd been dwelling on during the past year. He walked along in high spirits, concentrating on what kinds of wisdom he might impart to the immigrants.

It was nearly an hour before his old insecurities came back. Suddenly, a dread filled his body as the unpleasant memories returned. This was a big responsibility, all those people. If anything bad happened along the way, it would be on his shoulders. Yet, it was impossible for tragic occurrences not to take place—it was the nature of the trail and he knew it. Why couldn't this group be just him and a bunch of bawdy men who would be more or less the victims of their own miscues? Samson tried telling himself that he wasn't responsible for each and everyone's personal safety. He was just supposed to be their guide, to lead them along the right pathways, to make arrangements at the trading areas, deal with Indians, instruct them at river crossings, and the like. It was not his responsibility, he tried to reason, to keep up with straying livestock, or to stop a little one from catching his death of cold or drowning in a river . . .

Such thoughts would surely drive him crazy. Before any more could occur, Samson turned and headed back for camp.

At precisely one o'clock, he was standing on a wagon seat, looking out over a huge throng of people gathered before him. He was surprised at the number, estimating there to be three or four hundred people. As he was gathering himself to speak, he thought of Davy Crockett and what a fine time he would have had, addressing such a crowd. Whereas Samson was nervous and hoped he didn't sound silly, Crockett would be licking his chops at such a grand opportunity.

Just as he was about to open his mouth to speak, Joseph Mellner stepped up next to him and held out his arms.

"Hear ye, hear ye!" he yelled. "Let me have your attention. We need silence!" He lowered his arms and gestured toward Samson. "Now unless you've been asleep somewhere for the past few days, you know that this here is Samson Roach. He's agreed to lead us all the way to Oregon." He raised his hand to quiet a few cheers that sounded through the audience. "Now it's important that you hear what the man has to say. You womenfolk, keep those young'uns quiet."

A hush fell over the crowd. Mellner nodded solemnly and turned the stage over to Samson.

Samson took a deep breath and stepped forward. Once again, he thought briefly of Davy Crockett and tried to draw strength from the memory of his late friend's speaking abilities. *Just say it like Davy would,* he told himself.

When he spoke, his voice sounded high-pitched and quivery, but he knew he had no say over his vocal cords.

He licked his lips. "First of all, I think we've got too many wagons," he said. He looked sheepishly at Mellner and then mumbled to the crowd. "But I don't guess we can worry about that."

A man from the middle of the crowd hollered, "Louder!"

Samson coughed into his fist and started again, as loud as he could.

"I guess the first thing," he began, "is to be prepared. I don't need to tell you folks that it's a long journey, full of hardships. There's always the problem with the weather. There'll be times when we'll get bogged down so bad, we'll be spending more time digging out of mud than anything else. You've got to be well supplied. Anybody that don't have three to six hundred dollars per family, well . . . Unless you've got a way of borrowing money, you'd just as well not even think about making this journey."

A heavyset middle-aged woman with a bonnet and a red-cheeked baby in her arms asked him why the need for such a large sum of money.

The woman's ignorance irritated Samson. He looked scornfully at her. "Why, any number of things," he said. "There'll be times you'll need money for the ferry. You'll need money to buy supplies along the way. You'll need money once you get to Oregon." He stopped and stared at her. *How could anybody wonder about such a thing,* he thought. He grew more angry. Suddenly, he wished he could back out. It really wasn't the woman's fault, he knew that. It was that old fear of accepting responsibility that had started gnawing again at his insides.

He shook off the troubling thoughts, tried breathing evenly, and began again. He was careful not to look at the woman with the baby. "You'll also be needing some of the following items." From his pocket, he pulled a piece of paper where he had made notes. "You'll need cooking kettles and frying pans, a coffeepot, plates, cups, knives, and forks. You'll need lots of dried beans and dried fruits. You'll need a goodly amount of saleratus. You'll need vinegar and pickles along with mustard and tallow, and chipped beef. Rice is a good thing to take along. I would suggest that you outfit yourself with at least ten pounds of salt, twenty pounds of sugar. Two hundred," he emphasized the amount, "pounds of flour wouldn't be too much. And, maybe the most important thing is at least ten pounds of coffee."

He paused and studied their faces. No one seemed surprised or concerned over anything he'd said so far. They just looked excited and somewhat relieved.

"I spoke with Reuben. Seems you people have already bought him out of most of his supplies, but twenty miles west of here is a trading post. The last time I was there, which was about this time last year, they had plenty of everything. You can finish stocking up there.

"You menfolk, you'll need some good, dry gunpowder and bullets. There ain't been a lot of trouble with Injuns that I've heard of, but that's not to say we shouldn't be well armed, just in case. We'll leave first thing tomorrow."

Several of the men nodded, and Samson looked the crowd over one final time. He turned and shrugged at Mellner. "I guess that's about it," he said. He paused and dug for courage. It bothered Samson to have to ask a man for anything. "You said something about a horse?"

The superior look had reappeared in Mellner's eyes. He once again had his shoulders pulled back and carried an air of importance about him. He nodded, closing his eyes in doing so. "I'm a man of my word. You will have a fine horse to travel on. You keep your nose clean and get us to Oregon, and you'll be well taken care of." He spoke in the manner of a man who was not to be questioned.

Before Samson stepped down from the wagon seat, he took the opportunity to glance through the crowd. He scanned the faces, looking for her.

She was nowhere to be seen. Samson had to wonder if she was real or just a figment of his imagination. he laughed at himself for being so foolish, but still there was a mystery about Becky Sinclair that only added to her powerful allure. He had never seen her among ordinary folks, yet she would suddenly show up out of nowhere and find him when he was all alone. Again, she was curiously missing. Disappointed, he jumped from the wagon seat and headed toward Reuben's.

Tomorrow, he would begin a new life.

11

S amson awoke early and sober. It was some time before the light would be cast upon another cold and frosty morning. He thought it felt colder than usual as he arose and went outside. After he relieved himself, Samson threw his saddle on the bay mare that Mellner had given him the night before. So far, Mellner had been a man of his word. The bay was a fine horse, with good muscle tone and a spirited nature. The young man who had delivered the horse to him had looked down at the ground and made the comment that he was sorry about the bay's rebellious nature, but Samson had just laughed and told him not to worry. The fact was, he was quite pleased that the bay was spirited. Riding and handling a horse were second nature to Samson, and to his way of thinking, horses with lots of spunk came in real handy in times of trouble. They were a natural to go to full speed when it was needed.

Excitement was flowing through Samson's veins as he took his new horse on a solitary ride through the dusky countryside. Not only did he want to break in the bay a little, he was also trying to burn away some nervous energy. He noticed the horse was just as skittish as he was, and that gave him a feeling of comfort. They'd make the journey together, he thought.

By the time he returned to camp, people were up and busy with packing their wagons and horses. He was happy about that. He wanted to get moving as soon as possible. There was no use in losing good daylight.

At Reuben's, Gertie was frying breakfast outside over a

fire. Even from behind, Samson saw a sadness in her, the way her shoulders drooped and she kept her head down low. It was odd that he would even notice a difference about her; in the year he'd known Gertie, he'd only seen her use two expressions. One was no expression at all. Samson marveled at how she could walk around and even engage in conversation and never move a muscle in her face. Then, on occasion, she would work herself into a smile. It was a big smile that pushed her chubby cheeks up against her eyes to where they would become little slits. This morning, though, he could tell that something was troubling her.

Samson eased down off the bay, which skittered about nervously. He intended to try to calm the horse down some, but no sooner had his feet hit the ground than Reuben came bounding out the door of the tavern, fully dressed except for his bare feet. He seemed as though he was in a big hurry, carrying as many jugs of whiskey as his fingers and arms would allow. He gave an excited nod to Samson, stepping lively with his long legs, and set the whiskey in the back of a wagon that was parked next to the tavern. As soon as he put the whiskey inside, his long legs hurried back into the tavern.

Samson stood there holding the reins of the bay and watched Reuben, wondering what in the world he was up to. Soon, Reuben came out again, carrying the same number of whiskey jugs.

"My, someone's got a powerful thirst," Samson commented. "Must figure on doing a fair bit of drinking on the way to Oregon." He frowned. "That's where these immigrants ain't got a lick of sense. Reuben, they ought to be worrying about buying your bacon and flour, instead of all this." He watched as Reuben passed him and hurried back into the tavern.

Again Reuben returned with an armload of whiskey. He was breathing hard, but wasn't slowing down any. "Ain't no immigrants' whiskey, a-tall," he said. "I'm goin' with you."

Samson quickly tied the reins of his horse and followed after Reuben. "You're what?" He fully intended to stop him from running back into the tavern, but this time, Reuben paused and rubbed the sweat from his brow. He nodded his head. "Yep, hoss, I'm goin' with you for sure. Traded this feller and his wife from Virginee the tavern and half the whiskey for his wagon and furniture. Of course, I ain't got no need for furniture. I reckon I can get me some when I get to Oregon."

For the first time, Samson paid attention to the wagon. Beside it on the ground lay a bed and several odds and ends of furniture. He peered inside. Besides the whiskey, there was a rocking chair, a couple of old satchels that had been tied with a rope, some cooking utensils, a coffeepot, and a bedroll. Samson turned his gaze back to Reuben, who was already headed back into the tavern.

He was stunned at the thought of a man leaving his business. Reuben seemed like a happy man with his tavern, and Gertie did most of the work while Reuben spent his days drinking with anybody who happened to stop by. He was virtually free to pursue his favorite pastime of chewing the fat at his leisure. Once in a while, he'd pour a drink or two, but that was only when Gertie was occupied with another customer.

When Reuben returned from inside the tavern, he was carrying a few last jugs in his left arm. In his right was a sack of flour. He dropped them into the wagon, leaned against it, and sighed. "Gonna miss Gertie," he said.

"What? You mean she's not going with you?" This confused Samson even more. He looked over to where she stood, still leaning down over the frying pan. She didn't seem to be paying any attention whatsoever to what Reuben was doing. But Samson could read the pain in her, just the same.

"It ain't none of my business, Reuben, but Gertie don't seem none too happy with the situation."

Reuben nodded sadly and wiped his brow. "Shucks, hoss. She's happy. That's just an Indian for you. Not much emotion in 'em. I asked her to come along with me, but she starts talking about how this was where her life got started in the white man's world, and this is where she'll die." He saw the puzzled look on Samson's face and shrugged. "Didn't make no sense to me, neither. That couple from Virginee was happy to have her. So you see, everything works out in the end, I suppose." He took an admiring look at Gertie's backside. "Still, I'm going to miss the old gal, 'specially on those cold nights," he said forlornly.

After some of Gertie's breakfast, Samson made another inspection of Reuben's new wagon. Why, he figured, there was enough whisky for a man to stay drunk all the way to Oregon. He reached down and absentmindedly rubbed his hand over one of the jugs. He could almost taste the contents. It seemed like years since he'd had a drink.

Then Reuben was standing beside him. "I always wanted a good rockin' chair, hoss. That Virginee woman's pap made that one for her." He pointed to the front of the wagon, where the nicely built rocking chair sat. "I'll get lots of use out of that."

Reuben had added a few other household items, but mostly the wagon was loaded with supplies and whiskey.

Samson still couldn't help feeling that Reuben was making a mistake. He thought of the sadness in Gertie. "You sure you want to do this?" he asked. "I know it ain't none of my business. I surely don't care what a man does with his own life. And I'm happy to have your company, to be sure. Still, Reuben, something about this just doesn't seem right."

"Hoss," Reuben began as he looked philosophically off into the distance, "I ain't a young man no more. I could live out my years right here, for sure. But I guess I got a hankering like everybody else for something new. Why, if it's as beautiful and fertile out there as they say, and if they truly do have those beav that run right up to a man's doorstep, I reckon I want to be a part of that too."

Samson could certainly understand Reuben's thinking, but he still found it hard to rationalize a man's leaving his wife behind. Gertie seemed like a right hand to Reuben. And he surely seemed to like her.

"Well, I imagine it'll take some getting used to, not having Gertie around."

Reuben put a chew inside his mouth and offered some

to Samson. "She ain't very much to look at. Can't get her to bathe but once, sometimes twice a month. She don't say much, but that ain't all bad. She don't complain any, neither." He turned and spit, then wiped his mouth with his sleeve. "But that backside of hers can sure keep a man warm on a cold night. I'm gonna miss her all right, hoss, but I reckon there'll be other squaws along the way." He winked at Samson, and that was that.

Where Samson had had visions of getting started right after breakfast, the situation dictated otherwise. It was well past noon when he finally got the wagons all lined up and headed west. But even then, new hitches got thrown into his plans to make a lot of distance the first day.

He spent the first two hours riding back and forth from one end of the train to the next. The immigrants became restless. Dogs were yelping and children were noisily running after the cattle that had started to scatter. To make matters worse, two of the wagons had already broken down. One had lost an axle, and the other had broken a wheel. By the time they made camp, Samson's chest was burning from worry.

Alone, he sat down under a cottonwood tree and pulled a small book and pencil from his pocket. He opened to the first page and wrote,

"First day—traveled 6 miles."

He was going to write more about their first day out, when he heard the voice that he'd been listening for.

"I haven't had a chance to thank you personally," Becky said. She was standing not more than five feet away. The late-day sun filtered through the top of the tree and danced across her face.

He jumped to his feet, the paper and pencil spilling onto the ground. Suddenly, the burning sensation that had plagued him for hours disappeared from Samson's chest. All the worry over the day was gone. It dawned on Samson that he hadn't thought about her all day, he'd been so busy on other things. He couldn't believe he hadn't seen her during his many trips up and down the train. Was she really here now? he wondered. Was she real, for that mat-

ter? Or was his mind playing tricks on him? He held his
eyes tightly on her, just in case she might try to disappear.

"Joseph Mellner said to tell you they'll set you up a tent
for sleeping and there will be a different lady bringing you
your meals each day."

Samson heard what she said. He even nodded. But his
mind wasn't on her words. Their eyes locked.

Samson had loved Nancy, but never had Nancy caused
these stirrings inside. It had been a love that grew in a
gradual way, but his body had never ached in her presence
the way it did right now, standing there in front of Becky.

This time, he wasn't surprised when she pulled her eyes
away from him and turned. Though he wanted more of
her, he was already beginning to understand her ways.

Still, once she was gone, he stood there dumbly for several minutes, until Reuben came along, rubbing his back.
He broke Samson from his reverie.

"Damn, hoss. I'd forgot how painful travelin' could be,
and I don't even have Gertie to rub the soreness out of my
back."

Samson pulled his gaze from where Becky had been
standing. "What's that? Your back? See, I was worried
about that, Reuben," Samson lied. In truth, he hadn't given
one thought to Reuben's back on the journey. He was hoping Reuben couldn't guess his thoughts.

Reuben rubbed his back one last time and shook his
head. "No cause to worry, really. I've had this bad back
since my twenties. Worked on a boat and tried to lift too
much. No, the back's just fine. Come on over to the
wagon a spell," he said. "I got somethin' that'll warm both
of us up real good."

They spent the time at Reuben's wagon drinking and
reminiscing. It took lots of fortitude on his part, but Samson was careful not to drink too much. The whiskey had
a nice, soothing effect, like an old friend. As the evening
wore on, he found himself wanting to drink more heavily,
but he dodged the temptation well, which pleased him. By
nightfall, Samson had a fine fire going. One of the women
had brought him enough food to feed a family. He eagerly
shared it with Reuben.

Reuben was just pushing the last bite of biscuit in his mouth. He rubbed his belly. "If I eat like this all the way to Oregon, I'll be as fat as Gertie."

"I eat too much myself," Samson confessed.

"Shucks, hoss, you didn't eat half of what I et. I'll make a deal with you. As long as they bring this much food every night, you can drink all of my whiskey you want, and I'll break bread with you in return." Reuben was feeling good at this point. The only worry he had was over food. He'd gotten used to Gertie's cooking and he'd mourned over how much he was going to miss it.

Samson leaned back and put his head on his saddle. Joseph Mellner had set up a tent for him up at the head of the wagon train, but he'd just as soon stay right here. His eyes grew heavy. He was used to sleeping out under the stars, even on cold nights. His thoughts turned to Oregon. He said, "What you going to do when we get there, Reuben? Think you might open up a tavern?"

Reuben had to admit it was a fair question. He couldn't see himself as a farmer. All that solitude would be more than he could stand. He took a big drink of whiskey and shrugged. "Well, there's a lot of people here, hoss. They may act like Sunday preachers around the womenfolk, but once they get to Oregon, they'll want a tavern. I guess ol' Reuben may as well supply 'em one." He grimaced in thought. " 'Course, I sure do wish Gertie would have come along. She's right good for business, you know."

"She's good for taking care of you, Reuben. But she don't talk enough to attract business."

"She's quiet all right," Reuben said. "Like all Indians, she never said much. But the customers took to her well. She kept their glasses filled, which in turn kept my pockets filled." He smiled.

Samson was pleased at the thought of a tavern. He was thinking about it when he fell asleep, leaving Reuben talking to himself.

Samson had barely crossed over into slumberland when the old Indian with the flowing white hair sat down next to Reuben. It puzzled Samson that Reuben paid no attention to him whatsoever. Samson tried to sit up, but once again he was paralyzed. The Indian's eyes sparkled in the firelight. They smiled pleasantly at Samson. He nodded, and his voice soothed the panic from Samson's paralysis.

"It is good," the old Indian said. "As rain soothes the parched earth in the dry season and brings forth new sprouts, the same will be for you. For you are like the parched earth. The rain shall come, and there will be much seed to come forth from you and grow."

Samson's eyes fixed on Reuben, who was drinking whiskey and talking as if the old Indian wasn't there. It was strange, but Samson couldn't hear a word Reuben was saying. He studied Reuben's face, tried to read his lips, but still he couldn't make out anything. Confused, he turned back, and the Indian was gone.

All through the night, the words about the rain and the parched land swam in and out of his dreams. At one point, Samson could see himself standing in a field. Corn started sprouting and growing out of every part of his body. Samson grew afraid. He tossed and turned and called out in his sleep. Once, his goings-on even woke Reuben, who had crawled, half-drunk, under his wagon, fully clothed except for his bare feet, which were now sprinkled with frost.

12

Calvin couldn't get Little Larry Hartz off his mind. He was riding with the rest of the men, back a few paces, letting his thoughts toss and worry over his companion. It wasn't just the actual killing that had Calvin so occupied. It was the knowledge that he was now and forever a part of Dick Carter and his gang. He still felt the longing to turn away and ride off from the rest, but where could he go? He wondered if he would be wanted by the law for killing Little Larry.

As he rode along, lost in his thinking, it was no small wonder that his horse, Knight, didn't walk him right into some low-hanging tree limbs. Knight had a propensity for doing such things, and Calvin was too distraught to have the ability to react. It was a running commentary among the men that Knight would have been pleased to kill Calvin with the aid of any available tree limb. Of course, the main reason Calvin hadn't been knocked silly this morning was the fact that the trees in these parts were scrawny prairie trees, few and far between, and so small as to not have many good, low-lying limbs. The ill-intentioned horse had too few pickings to find a good choking tree limb for Calvin.

Calvin opened and closed his eyes several times, trying to erase the image in his mind of Little Larry, lying there stone-cold dead, with Calvin and his smoking pistol standing over him. Dick Carter had reminded him that Little Larry was going to die anyway from the snakebites.

Calvin was doing him a favor, Carter had insisted. Still, it failed to give Calvin any comfort.

He felt a tremendous guilt riding on his shoulders. The truth was, he felt responsible for Little Larry's departure from this world. It didn't matter that the snakes had bitten him. Calvin felt deep down that Little Larry had been the kindest member of the group. Not that he didn't sometimes do or say things that got under Calvin's skin. Still, Little Larry was the best of the lot, in Calvin's opinion. For one thing, he hadn't made fun of Calvin as the others had, and at times he had even been the one to openly question some of Dick Carter's meanness. Little Larry had never actually stood up to Carter—no one had ever done that. But at least he wasn't afraid to offer an opinion. Not even Sal dared to contradict Dick Carter, and Sal was the only man in the group who could ever seriously hold his own against him.

The day wore on and the men's restlessness grew. Davis finally broke the silence and started talking about Little Larry. He reminisced about their growing-up years and recounted every bad deed they had accomplished together. Calvin began to wish that Davis had been the one who'd crawled into the hole and gotten bitten by snakes. Little Larry had never gone on like this. Besides, there was a tone to Davis's voice that struck a raw nerve. Calvin knew that Davis was surely trying to say things that were pleasing to Dick Carter's ears.

This irritated and angered him. Davis Martin wasn't talking about Little Larry in a sorrowful, regretful way at all. He might have wished Little Larry was still alive, but that wasn't why he was carrying on this way. No, Calvin thought, Davis was playing up to Dick Carter, just as he always did.

Calvin turned his attention inward and tried to rethink the situation. Try as he might, he couldn't determine any way to get away from this group with his health. Now, thanks to his own hand and gun, he was more entangled with them than ever. These thoughts reminded him of the dead immigrant woman. Had anyone come along and found her scattered remains yet? Or were she and her husband still lying there, being picked clean by the buzzards?

In private, Sal had told him that it would most likely look as though Indians had done the killing. No one, he said, would suspect a white man of such a terrible thing. Calvin tried to believe him, but the idea didn't hold much validity. For one thing, they hadn't run across many Indians at all. Calvin had expected to see them everywhere, out here past the settlements. Instead, all they'd seen were poor Indians traveling in small bands. This struck Calvin as curious. All his life, he'd heard stories about the treacherous ways of the red savages. The stories had been full of looting and burning and killing, and Calvin's biggest fear going out west was of being tortured and scalped by Indians. He'd listened to the stories and envisioned some great red man, a brave warrior who would fight to the death. One who could scalp a man without a thought, then burn him alive. In Calvin's mind, the warrior stood at least seven feet tall, with rippling muscles and a fierce nature. When Dick Carter invited him along to rob the white travelers, Calvin had agreed, but he'd lost plenty of sleep worrying over Indians and killings and such.

Now it was almost disappointing. The only Indians they'd encountered were fretfully hungry-looking and dirty. Calvin was sure that the mean, murderous ones were out there someplace, and he was still wary of them, but he surely hadn't had any of his expectations met. No, instead of bold, angry warriors, the last two males he'd encountered were poor and pitiful. Instead of being tall, they were of only average size, with arms that held no more muscle tone than those of a woman. One of them was old, probably forty, and the other was maybe in his teens. Surely, Calvin had told himself, there were more hearty Indian males than those they'd seen out here.

The Indian women had been disappointing, too. They'd been nothing like his imaginings. Calvin didn't totally understand it, but Indian women had always caused an arousal inside him. He thought about them often. It had started back when he was younger—fourteen or so. Always the same image of a young Indian woman riding a big horse would appear in his mind. Her long hair blew straight behind her, ruffling in the breeze. Slowly, his mind's eye would travel down to her bare legs, pressed tightly into the horse's sides. Her dark skin would shine in the bright sun. And Calvin would feel a stirring deep down inside. He enjoyed the feeling, and at the same time he wondered about it. Maybe, he thought, it had something to do with those stories he'd heard.

The storyteller had been his mother's older brother, Uncle Harvey McDaniel. Uncle Harvey had been a trapper, until the day he'd met the company of a mother grizzly and had come away from the encounter missing one leg, part of a hip, his right eye, and a sizable piece of his scalp.

There was hardly a day went by that Calvin didn't replay each of Uncle Harvey's stories in his head. He especially liked the ones about the Indian woman Uncle Harvey claimed to have lived with. According to Uncle Harvey, he had bedded down with many others as well, and he had much to say about the qualities of the red woman.

Calvin had thought a thousand times since about Indian women, wondering if all of Uncle Harvey's stories were true. He was sure they must be. It had given him pleasure to take off by himself and ponder the subject in private, even daydream about being with an Indian woman himself. Eventually, his excitement over the idea had grown to the point where he could scarcely do his thinking in front of anyone, for fear of their noticing his bodily reactions.

That brought up another thing that troubled Calvin. Being with Dick Carter and his group, he'd never had the opportunity for privacy. They hadn't allowed him to drift off by himself where he could enjoy his speculations about Indian women.

As Calvin was mulling this over, a cold thunderstorm set in. He pulled up his collar and tugged on his hat. The wind followed, picking up speed. Soon, the rain was coming down hard and at a slant, like icy needles. It wasn't long before the ground was soaked.

The men rode on silently, left to their own thoughts about the events of the last two days and the sudden turn in the weather. Underneath Calvin, Knight shook his head and snorted in protest at the cold drops that stung his face, one right after the other. Calvin, too, felt as if a thousand little pins were piercing his skin as the rain bounced off his red cheeks. His eyes were watering, and he could barely manage to see.

The air was filled with the sound of thunderclaps that seemed to shake the earth under them. Calvin was scarcely aware of the other men riding ahead. He had no concerns about how miserable they might be. He was too deep in his own thoughts, too uncomfortable and forlorn to care. If anything good had come from the situation, he guessed it might be the fact that the drastic weather change had turned the earth a thick dark gray, and it seemed to insulate him from the world and the other men.

The horizon was dark as charcoal. It looked like late evening, yet it was only around noontime. Calvin might have been satisfied, riding along in the cloak of the dark sky and the falling rain, for a long time. Dick Carter, though, soon spoiled this welcome solitude.

"We need to stop!" Carter hollered out. "Make camp." He was rubbing his cold hands together.

Sal's voice called out from somewhere in the gloom. "Make camp? Just where do you figure we can do that? By damn, we're in the middle of nowhere!"

Dick Carter didn't like cold weather. He never had, and cold rain was even worse. Back home in Ohio, he'd always cussed the winters, but this was more than he'd ever bargained for. It was ridiculous, the likes of what they were experiencing.

"I don't give a damn," he said irritably. "Let's stop and get underneath our blankets, or something."

Calvin could hear the conversation through the sounds of the wind and storm, but he tried not to let the words reach his brain. He wanted to keep riding. He couldn't bear the thought of stopping with these men, being close to them and their voices and interruptions.

Maybe, he thought, he could just keep on riding. Maybe they'd think he couldn't hear them and got lost in the darkness. Why, he could just ride on throughout the day and into the night. He could put a safe distance between himself and the others. They'd never find him. . . .

But he knew better than the folly of his thoughts. As much as he hated the situation he was in, he couldn't fancy himself sleeping out there all alone at night. He was too afraid that one of those seven-foot Indians might appear and do horrible things to him. Or maybe he'd encounter a grizzly, just as Uncle Harvey had. He hadn't seen any grizzlies, but he was sure there were some out there someplace.

Besides all that, one of the other men would most likely notice him riding away and come after him. Reluctantly, Calvin pulled rein on Knight and joined the others.

They climbed down off their horses, quickly pooled their blankets, and soon were huddled all together on the wet ground. Above them, the thunder and lightning filled the sky as the storm raged on.

13

Samson spent a fitful night, tossing and turning through a series of bad dreams. A thunderstorm developed and rolled over the land, and he managed to incorporate the thunder into his dreams, until one monumental boom shook him from his sleep. He'd been at the Alamo, and Santa Anna was dropping shells right into the middle of where he fought next to Davy Crockett and the Tennessee Volunteers. All around them, Tennesseans were falling. Then Crockett himself fell, only he didn't die. He just got up and started shooting again. This happened over and over. Crockett would get shot, then rise up as though he'd just been tapped on the shoulder. Once, a shell went right through Crockett's midsection and out his back, creating a large hole—so large that Samson could see through it. But Crockett just sat there and reloaded. "Like killing bears," he was saying as the huge thunderclap vibrated through the earth.

Samson suddenly sat up. His body was bathed in a cold sweat. He hated dreams. Ever since childhood, he'd been plagued by nightmares. Some mornings, they distorted his reality for a while, until he could reassure himself that they were just dreams.

To the west, lightning illuminated the skies and the thunder cracked loudly. The temperature was just above freezing. By the time the rain reached them, he and Reuben had just settled into breakfast. Soon, the rain got so heavy that everything became soaked. It came through the tents and the wagon coverings. People were hollering at each other. Mothers huddled their littlest children under blankets. The sheep and cattle were bawling. Samson and Reuben had to abandon their breakfast and take refuge under his wagon, but the winds came and whipped the rain around to where they got just as wet under the wagon as they would have outside of it.

"Damn, hoss, this looks like a bad one," Reuben said. He crawled to the end of the wagon and looked up at the sky, squinting as the big drops of rain pelted him in the eyes. He crawled back underneath. "It's a bad one, all right. That sky looks dark and unforgivin'."

Reuben's assessment had been right. By ten o'clock in the morning, it was still raining hard. The water had etched its own series of pathways in the earth, and streams flowed all throughout the camp. The winds had picked up and whipped the covers from wagons. Tents had blown away and the ones left standing sagged from the weight of the water.

Samson crawled out from the pool of water under the wagon where he'd been lying. He looked up and down the wagon train, then started walking up the line. He felt so cold he was sure he'd catch his death of pneumonia. But thoughts of his own health were brief. His main concern was for the children.

The rain was blistering his face with its severity, yet he sloshed from wagon to wagon, barking out instructions. It was pretty much a waste of time, but it would have been hard to convince Samson of that fact.

To many, Samson Roach was a selfish man, but those were folks who couldn't see inside his heart. The truth was, Samson had always carried a deep concern for children. Maybe it stemmed from not having a relationship with his father. He didn't know, himself. Whatever the reason, Samson had an overprotective nature when it came to young'uns. He had felt the same over Cordry, only ten times stronger. After Cordry died, his worries had seemed to get worse. He began to worry about everybody around him except himself.

During the past year, there'd been times when he would sit for hours, out by himself somewhere, and spend the whole time worrying about Reuben and Gertie, or maybe some travelers whom he'd met just briefly at the tavern. Samson might notice that their wagon was overloaded, or maybe they didn't have enough provisions to keep them alive. Or the children weren't dressed warmly enough. It didn't matter what the situation; he would find something to worry over.

The drinking helped. It wasn't that he didn't like caring about other folks. Worrying about other people just carried too big a risk of getting hurt again. Samson felt like he'd had enough hurt to last a while.

Each of the wagons was soaked clear through. The children stared out at him miserably. The families were huddled together for warmth, but no one seemed to be sick. That cheered him a little.

It was noon by the time he'd completed his rounds. Several head of cattle and some horses were reported missing. Samson threw a saddle on the mare, and he, along with some other men from the group, went about the task of finding the strays in the rain, which was still coming down at a steady pace.

By the time they had gathered up the last of the livestock—a little bull that had tried to charge Samson and the mare—the rain had finally slowed to where just a light drizzle fell. Water covered the earth. The little streams had become bigger streams, and ponds had formed in the low-lying places. Samson cursed the weather. The heavier wagons would sink fast after this kind of downpour.

It wasn't until Samson sat down with Reuben that he got the shakes. There was nothing dry left to wrap up in, so he just had to sit there and shake. His chattering teeth drowned out nearly every sound in his head and made talking nearly impossible.

He looked down at Reuben's bare feet. As cold as he was, there was Reuben sitting around with no shoes on, as if it was a normal day. He couldn't help being annoyed. He looked like a wet hen, Samson thought, with the head of a grizzly bear. Reuben's thick hair stuck up in all directions and his beard hadn't been trimmed, and now water was rolling off both onto his shoulders.

"Why don't you put something on your feet? You're gonna catch a cold," Samson barked out between his chattering teeth.

Reuben grinned and shook his head. "I'm used to it, hoss. Been barefoot so long, it don't seem to matter whether it's cold or hot. 'Course, Gertie used to squeal out at night when I put my feet up under her nightshirt. Always complained they were too cold. Tell you the truth, I can't see no difference." Reuben uncorked a jug of whiskey. "This will do something for that shivering of yours. I swear, you ain't gonna have a tooth left in your head if you don't stop clanking them together like that. Here, take a big long drink," he instructed.

Samson was still irritated at Reuben's lack of respect for the elements, but the whiskey jug held a stronger appeal. He took a long drink, then another. It felt warm and satisfying going down. He was about to tip the jug again, when a voice made them both jump.

"I warned you not to drink on this trip."

Joseph Mellner's voice sounded disappointed, but there was anger in his eyes. Samson looked up and saw him standing there with his hands fisted on his hips. The sight irritated him.

"Now lookee here, Mellner. I told you I wouldn't get drunk, and I won't. But that's not to say I won't partake at times."

Mellner's face grew red. His jaw twitched, as though he truly wanted to express himself, but he wouldn't do that. He had learned enough about Samson to know it was better to watch his tongue. After several calculating seconds, he said in a voice that didn't match his demeanor, "Just can't tolerate drinkin'. It weakens a man and harms others around him."

Reuben stood up and jovially held the jug out to him. "Why shucks, hoss, there's your trouble! You need a drink to quiet down your nerves some." He smiled in a friendly way.

The veins in Mellner's neck popped out. His mouth drew down into a snarl, and he angrily shoved the jug back into Reuben's chest. Reuben lost his balance in the slick mud and plopped back down into the water where he'd been sitting, sending a spray into Samson's face.

Reuben flung aside the jug of whiskey and started struggling to get to his feet. There was a wild look in his eyes, but Mellner didn't seem to care. He just stood there and waited for Reuben to come at him.

Seeing what was going on, Samson grabbed Reuben's buckskin shirt and held him back. Reuben slipped again, but this time more gracefully. He sat down and stared hard at Samson.

"Let it be," Samson said simply. He turned his attention to Mellner. "You just don't learn very easily, do you, mister? Well, I don't know how you folks do things in Pennsylvania, but a man out here can get himself buried for less than what you just done."

Joseph Mellner was trembling with anger. He was being pushed to his limit, but he knew he didn't have the fortitude to match Samson's ferocity in a fight. He stood there, wondering what to do with the man whom he and the entire wagon train now depended upon. Finally, he waved his hand at them and stomped off, mumbling to himself as he disappeared.

For supper, one of the women brought him some dried fruit and a kettle of cold beans from the night before. She seemed embarrassed and explained how they weren't able to get a good fire going. Samson told her not to worry. In fact, the cold beans tasted just fine, as he had a hunger like he hadn't felt in a while. His shakes had gone away, too.

That night, Reuben got drunker than Samson had ever seen him. Samson didn't mind; he figured Reuben had been embarrassed by what had happened with Mellner. Even though Reuben was as easygoing as a man could be, Samson knew him to be a proud man. There'd been other men like that, men who were pleasant and quick-witted, but whom others would judge to be silly and foolish. Samson carried an uncanny knack for seeing to the root of an individual, and he'd come to the conclusion that, if the need ever arose, there was a hell of a fight stored away inside of Reuben Cook.

He was too wet and cold to relax into a decent sleep.

Once, when he dozed, the old Indian showed up. This time, there were no words. He was sitting in a tree, watching Samson as his old eyes glistened. He wasn't moving or speaking, but the longer he sat there, the more Samson felt comforted. Finally, Samson's mind watched as the old man faded from sight.

He slept deep and hard the rest of the night.

14

amson slept past daybreak. Something inside told him
there was no use in getting up early. It was cold, and a
slow, steady sprinkle had started up again.

When he sat up, he banged his head against the bottom
of the wagon, just hard enough to cause him to grimace in
pain. He held his head in his hands for a while and cursed
his fate. It didn't seem like many of his latest decisions
had been wise ones, and the fact that he was sitting there
in a puddle under a bogged-down wagon with a bump on
his head pretty much gave those feelings credibility.

There was a movement in front of him. Samson peeked
through his fingers and saw a pair of man's legs standing
at the end of the wagon. He groaned at the intrusion, then
crawled out to meet the man.

He was surprised to see a boy in his midteens.

"Are you Mister Roach?" the boy asked.

"I'm Roach." Samson rubbed the tender spot on his
head and studied the boy. "Are you with the wagon train?"

"Yes, sir, I'm William Knox, but everybody calls me Willie," the boy said. He talked fast, his words almost running
together. "We're from New York. Besides my parents, I got
three younger sisters. Patricia, she's eleven. Betty is mine.
And the baby's three. Her name's Karen."

The boy finally stopped talking and just stood there,
looking at Samson. Samson didn't know what to reply. He
didn't appreciate early-morning conversation, never had,
especially when it started the instant he woke up. He
looked back at the wagon and felt angry that he'd bumped

his head. Unable to show his normal diplomacy, he looked impatiently at the boy.

"Well now, Willie, what's your problem?"

Willie, who was just about Samson's size, with light sandy brown hair and freckles, grinned broadly. "No problem, sir. I was wanting to ride with you."

Samson looked perplexed. "Ride with me? Why, hell, you are going to Oregon, aren't you? I reckon we'll be ridin' together for a long ways," he said.

Willie twisted around like he was about to wet himself. "Shoot, mister, I don't mean like what you're thinkin'. I mean, I'd like to ride up at the head of the train with you. Go out scoutin' with you and lookin' for Indians. Mister Cook told my pa that you used to hunt and fight with Davy Crockett. Why, I don't reckon there was ever a man alive that had as big a name as Davy Crockett! I've read all about him. I might even have read about you." He thought a moment, then his face grew apologetic. "But I can't remember whether I have or not."

Just then Reuben came up, walking barefoot and carrying a small sack. He looked hung over, but still managed a big smile. "Got a poke full of breakfast, here," he said with a satisfied look. "A Missus Harms sent it. Got preserves and old biscuits." He took a bite of one he'd been carrying in his other hand. "Missus Harms apologized about 'em bein' dry, but she didn't need to."

Samson ignored the sack of biscuits and frowned at Reuben. "What are you doing, feeding this boy's pap full of stories?"

Reuben paid no attention. Instead, his eyes fell on Willie. "Good mornin'," he said.

The boy nodded, but Samson spoke again.

"This boy says you was telling his pap about me and Davy Crockett," Samson said, still irritated at having to carry on a conversation this early in the day.

Chewing on a biscuit, Reuben calmly handed the sack to Samson. He eyed the boy. "Who's your pap? What's his name?" he asked.

"Aaron Knox," the boy replied.

Reuben tilted his head upward in thought, rubbing his

fingers through his beard. There was a big dollop of fruit preserves dangling from the tip of his beard. "Aaron Knox," he repeated. "Aaron Knox. From New York?" He looked at the boy.

Willie nodded. "Yes, sir. We're from New York."

Reuben took another bite of biscuit and thought again. He nodded. "Yes, I may have said something to that effect. But I can't remember every conversation I have."

Samson gave up trying to make any kind of point with Reuben and dug two biscuits out of the sack. He offered one to Willie. "You shouldn't be tellin' stories about me, Reuben."

"Weren't no story, hoss. You *did* know Davy. Hunted with him. Ain't that a fact?"

Samson gave Reuben an impatient look. "I knew him back home in Tennessee. We hunted together some, but we didn't do no fighting together. I'd appreciate it if you wouldn't tell people otherwise." He turned to Willie. "Now lookee here, boy. Ain't nothing exciting about what I do. You best run on back to your folks. They're gonna need your help on this trip more'n I will."

Willie went to squirming again. His hopeful face fell to a look of consternation. "Please, Mister Roach. I won't be no trouble at all. Besides, how's a fella to learn things?"

Samson looked the boy over. There was something about him that reminded Samson of himself. He wasn't a very big kid, with small features. His eyes were blue, like Samson's, and their hair was just the same sandy brown shade. He carried an easy smile. Samson wished *he* still had that easy smile in life, himself. Once, his smile and optimism had been as big a part of his personality as anything else. But the years had hardened him, made him suspicious. Now, folks told him that he frowned too much. "How old are you, boy?"

"Fifteen. But I know how to shoot straight," the boy said, like he had to apologize for his youth. "I've been huntin' since I was eight."

"Did your pap teach you?"

"Yes, sir."

Samson nodded vaguely and stared off. At Willie's

mention of his father, the old melancholy settled back in. Samson found it hard to listen to anyone talk about sons and fathers and how close they might be. It made him angry at first, then envious. But then his thoughts would turn to Cordry, and the sadness would engulf him so hard, that he felt as if he would suffocate. How he longed to see his son again. Samson would give anything to go back to one of those bright, sun-filled days when he and Cordry had trekked off hunting in the woods by themselves. He had made Cordry a crack shot and an independent lad. Sometimes Samson wondered if he wasn't the cause for Cordry's drowning. After all, if Samson hadn't made the boy so confident, he might not have wandered off by himself to go swimming. He might even be alive today. . . .

Samson had gone through many jugs of whiskey over such thoughts. It hurt to think that he might have led his own son to his death; still, Samson realized that it was important for a man to teach his son the ways of the world.

These contradictory thoughts had nearly driven him to insanity. "What if" was the single most common thought that ran through his mind, but it was a powerless thought that took a man nowhere in his musings.

Right now, he was thinking about how he would love to jump on his horse and ride to his mama in Tennessee. He was sure that she would take him in her arms and tell him everything was all right. She'd talk some sense into him, make him see that it wasn't really his fault. There was a little voice inside him that told him that he wasn't to blame, that life just sometimes worked out that way. But he didn't trust the voice, or anything or anyone around him. He couldn't.

Willie and Reuben were waiting, expecting an answer. Samson nodded like he'd just been pondering Willie's shooting expertise.

"You sure your pap would agree to this?" he asked the boy.

A big grin crossed Willie's face. "Yes sir!" he said excitedly, then glanced away and sort of shrugged. "Well, I'm sure he'd approve."

Samson felt surprised at what he was getting ready to

say. It wasn't his desire to get close to anyone. He liked those times by himself, where he could think for long spells without interruption. The truth was, he was a selfish man, and he knew it. But much as he enjoyed his privacy, a sudden urgency rose up inside him to take his boy under his wing. A brief battle started up inside him. One part of his brain was saying "take him," while the other part was telling him he was surely going to regret it. Samson looked the boy in the eyes.

"You go talk to your pap and tell him about our discussion."

Willie was ready to take off at a run, but Samson stopped him. "Listen, boy. We're gonna do this on a trial basis only. Now, there's gonna be times when I won't want you around, understand? You're still gonna have to be helping your folks out. I don't want you to be neglecting your chores . . ." He intended to say more, but Willie looked so excited he was about to bust. And he clearly wasn't listening. Samson waved his hand and said, "Git," and Willie disappeared.

Reuben had forgotten about eating his biscuits and preserves and was staring wide-eyed at Samson.

"What's wrong with you?" Samson said, glaring.

"Well I declare, hoss! Are you sure you want that pup hangin' around you all the time?"

"No." Samson stared off, thinking about what had just taken place. He took a bite of his cold biscuit. "No," he admitted, "I'm not sure at all. But then again, I'm not sure about a whole lot of things."

Reuben didn't seem to feel the need to analyze the situation any further. Satisfied the subject was closed, he settled down to finish the cold biscuits and preserves.

Samson was nervous. He saddled up the mare and rode slowly across the grassy patches in the soggy earth, thinking. This sitting around and waiting for things to dry out was about to drive him crazy. Several times, he thought about a jug of whiskey and wished he'd taken one along with him.

That afternoon, the dark clouds lifted somewhat, and the wind picked up a little. Samson's spirits lifted, too. He reckoned it would take a lot more than one afternoon of sun and wind to dry things out enough to move the wagons, but this was a favorable start. He studied the sky overhead. It looked forgiving. He felt hopeful.

As he turned the mare back toward camp, he decided that, muddy or not, they were moving out first thing in the morning. Even if they only made five or six miles, even if they had to spend the day digging the wagons out of the mud, anything would be better than the boredom of just sitting there with nothing to do but wait.

Besides that, Samson knew he didn't have any choice but to get his mind off the troublesome thoughts that filled him up, be it the sad remembrances of Nancy and Cordry, or his troublesome lust for a married woman.

15

An easterly wind rose up, whipping the travelers unmercifully. It was bitter cold as everyone packed away their sleeping gear and prepared to move on.

They hadn't seen the sun for so long, folks were starting to comment that the wind must have blown it away. A dampness lingered in the air, in their hair and clothing and everything else.

Samson was dressed as warmly as he could, but still the cold cut right through. There were goose bumps all over his body and he couldn't help shivering.

He had little time to think about his misery, for no sooner had he finished packing up, than he was greeted by Willie's smiling face.

"Mornin'."

Samson wanted to be cordial, but he couldn't move himself to speak. Early-morning talk was the last thing he wanted, particularly social conversation. And he had the unsettling feeling that, once Willie got wound up, he'd keep up a chatter all day long. As with many of his decisions, Samson wished he hadn't made the one to invite the boy to ride with him. He surely had no intentions of victimizing himself on this trip any more than he had to.

Samson's silence didn't register with Willie in the slightest. The boy had too many questions about too many things. Samson wondered if Willie had dreamed up all these wonderings in one night, or if he'd accumulated them over the years. There were questions piled on top of questions, which was bad enough without Willie's high enthusiasm.

Samson offered only a grunt here and there. It wasn't
that he didn't know the answers to Willie's queries. He
just figured the boy could learn them somewhere else, or
at least at a more convenient time. Which wasn't now. The
one thing that Samson had always demanded for himself
was time alone when he first started the day. But now Willie was demanding that. The sound of the boy's happy
voice began to gnaw on his nerves.

When he finally couldn't take any more, he spoke up in
a loud voice, "Lookee here, Willie. You go around and
check on everybody up and down the train. Make sure
they have their tents put away. See that the livestock is together. Tell them we're moving in thirty minutes."

Willie started to open his mouth to say something, but
Samson stopped him. "Hurry, now. Make sure you check
every wagon."

Willie nodded solemnly and took off. As soon as the
boy was out of earshot, Reuben, who'd just returned from
walking up and down the line, wishing for a cup of coffee,
shook his head and said, "I dunno, hoss. I knew a feller
once had this bird from South America. That danged bird
talked all the time. Used to give me a headache. Folks
took to avoidin' that feller, every time he came around
with that dang thing. I think Willie's gonna be like that
bird."

Samson's chest felt heavy at Reuben's words, for he
knew them to be true. Grimly, he reached for the little
mare's saddle. "Well, let's enjoy our little moment of
peace and quiet until the little bird flies back," he said.

As daylight completely illuminated the earth around
them, the winds whipped up harder than ever. Deep rivu-
lets ran through the standing pools of water. Trees that
knew it was time to begin the process of spring blooming
were bent over at awkward angles. It was hard for Samson
to fight the urge to grab up a jug of Reuben's whiskey and
take a sudden turn, away from the train.

They had gone a little over a mile when Becky appeared. She rode up beside Samson on a palomino horse,
so quietly he didn't even hear her coming.

She didn't say anything at first. She just rode there beside him, looking straight ahead. Samson had a hard time keeping his eyes from her. Her face seemed pale and her nose was red, but even with the cold wind whipping her hair into her face, she was still the most beautiful woman he'd ever encountered. Even Willie was struck silent by her presence. The howl of the wind and the sounds of the horses and wagons grew louder around them.

"You look cold," Becky finally said.

Samson had been thinking about that very same thing, but hearing her mention it made the cold suddenly disappear. He felt touched at the thought that she cared enough about him to mention his comfort.

"I'll be all right," he said. "You shouldn't worry about such things."

"Do you mind if I ride with you a ways further?" she asked, locking her eyes into his.

"It's a free country."

"That's not what I asked."

Samson glanced quickly at Willie, who was all eyes and ears. Without ceremony, he said, "Well, I reckon that would be all right."

To Samson's surprise, Becky rode beside him the whole morning. She rarely spoke. It would have been difficult to carry on a conversation with the howling wind, anyway. But just the same, Samson wished he could think of something clever to say to her. He wondered if he'd lost some of his social skills over the past year. Then again, she wasn't talking, either. It dawned on Samson that Willie's conversation had stopped altogether. He felt gratitude over that, but her extended presence was enough to make him start yearning for a jug of whiskey more than ever. She was making him tingle all over, riding so close beside him. He knew he was surely going to say or do something stupid if he didn't get his nerves calmed down.

Finally, the sun found an opening in the clouds and perched almost directly above their heads. They rode up on a little creek.

Samson told Willie, "Go back and pass the word. We got a creek to cross. Tell them to latch everything down."

Willie surveyed the creek for a moment. He said, "Why,

that's just a little creek. We won't have no trouble crossing that."

Samson's ill humor rose. "I didn't ask for no opinion," he said. "Just tell them to secure everything. Tell them the creek's running pretty rapid, what with the rain. And, Willie, tell them to be extra careful with the little ones."

Once the irritation of Willie was gone, Samson turned his attention to Becky.

"Shouldn't you be with your husband?"

Becky turned her head sideways and looked at him out of the corner of her eye. "Why," she said, "you sound just like my father."

"Well, I ain't your father, but still I gotta wonder what your husband must think about you riding up here with me."

Becky's features softened. A hint of pain appeared in her eyes. "To tell you the truth, I don't imagine he knows or even cares what I'm doing."

Samson had to ponder that. It amazed him that a man might think so little about such a beautiful woman as Becky Sinclair. The tingling spread through his body. He wished he had the nerve to reach out and hold her in his arms, but he knew he couldn't, even if he did. In fact, he was afraid if he was to move at all, he'd do something to make himself look foolish. "Why, I find that hard to believe," he finally said.

"Well, I guess you can believe what you want."

Samson noticed that her eyes once again sparkled with confidence, more confidence than he'd ever seen in a woman before. And they were teasing him. He said simply, "I guess."

"Does my riding up here bother you?" she asked politely.

"Like I told you, it's a free country."

She smiled at him then, and her face lit up like a harvest moon. Samson swallowed hard. He was starting to feel overpowered by her again. Becky had a way of rendering him speechless, to the point that all he could do was sit there and stare at her and wait for some kind of inspiring words to appear. But nothing clever came to mind. He had to admit he felt a terrible relief when Willie finally rode up.

"That was awfully quick," Samson said. "You sure you told everybody about the creek?"

"Yes, sir," Willie said. He glanced nervously at Becky. She smiled at him, and he quickly snapped his mouth shut and turned two shades of red.

Samson could see that she was having just the same effect on Willie as she was having on him.

The creek caused little problem as the wagons made their way across without incident. The water was only about a foot and a half deep, but it still took nearly the whole afternoon before the last wagon had crossed. Samson was anxious as he watched the wagons carrying children enter the water. He held a post at the water's edge, checking each wagon to make sure they were all either safely inside or riding atop an animal that was big enough to wade through. He even went so far as to have Willie stand downstream, in case one was to fall in.

They made camp on the other side. Becky had gone back to her own wagon, and Samson and Willie made another quick round to check on the train. Several folks had managed to find some dry wood and had fires lit. They were hurrying to get supper fixed before the colder night wind blew in. Everyone seemed happy enough. Samson sent Willie on to spend the night with his parents, and surprisingly, the boy didn't protest. It was turning into a most pleasant evening, in Samson's viewpoint. He was especially pleased to see that Reuben had put on a pot of coffee and had supper laid out when he returned.

They had just sat down to relax and eat when four men approached, led by a tall man with handsome features. They stopped short of where Samson sat. Samson put down his fork and looked up at them. The tall one spoke.

"Name's Tom Sinclair. I want you to know I don't appreciate the attention you've been showing my wife, Becky."

He waited for an answer, but all Samson did was stare back. Samson's heart was about to leap from his chest. He was dumbfounded and unable to utter a word.

Off to his side, Reuben, who had been eating away, laid his plate on the ground and slowly wiped his hands on his pants. He was studying Samson's face, hoping for some kind of reaction to this man's challenge. But all he could see was that dumb, bewildered look.

Tom Sinclair hovered over Samson. His eyes were cold and confident. Finally, he said, "We've got a long ways between here and Oregon, and if you know what's good for you, you'll stay away from her."

Samson still didn't answer. He was struck powerless. Something inside made him want to jump up and get in the man's face, but something else wouldn't allow it. Instead of anger, he felt guilty as sin.

Tom Sinclair took a deep breath. He obviously hadn't gotten the fight he wanted, but he had won, nevertheless. He looked proudly at his three companions and they snickered. As he turned to leave, he repeated his threat. "Remember what I said, Roach. Stay away from her."

Heat flooded through Samson's veins as he watched the four men until they disappeared. His face was flushed red as a rose. He sat there in stunned silence, barely able to pull his thoughts together.

Reuben had stood up and was angrily pacing back and forth. "By damn, hoss!" he said, "Who does that feller think he is, walkin' up on a man and talkin' like that?"

Samson just sat there and felt the guilt stretch heavily over him. He'd felt this way once before, a long time ago.

He'd been sixteen years old the day his mother had come upon him and Lillian Ward swimming naked together. She had been out picking berries when she just happened to see them. Samson could remember like it was yesterday.

Lillian was fourteen and he'd known her most of his life. One day, they'd been on a walk together and had come across the little pond. Being an impetuous sort, she had teased him about going swimming, until before he knew it, they were both in the water together. It had been the first time Samson had seen a naked female. At first, he'd been embarrassed, but then a new sensation had come over him. A very pleasing sensation.

But then his mother had appeared. She stood there and watched Samson with a strange look on her face. Samson had known it to be disappointment. In him.

Samson had been struck dumb back then, too. Even though nothing of an intimate nature had ever happened between him and Lillian, he'd felt just as guilty as if it had.

He'd never forgotten that day and the look on his mother's face. He'd never forgotten the words she'd said to him, later.

"You shamed that Ward girl," she'd said.

To this very day, Samson still didn't understand how he had shamed Lillian Ward. After all, it had been her idea to go swimming in the first place. Still, when he occasionally thought back on the incident, that same old feeling would come back. He still felt guilty over hurting his mother and shaming Lillian Ward. It was that exact same feeling running through him right now over Becky Sinclair.

Reuben, who was never one to contain his thoughts, stayed silent as long as he could. Finally, he sat down next to Samson and leaned close. "What'd you do with that Sinclair woman, anyway?" he said in a low voice.

Samson gave a slight shrug. "Nothing, really. Just talked, is all." His voice trailed off and the guilt came upon his face. He had to blink and turn away.

"Dunno, hoss, but I'd say that Sinclair feller is gonna have to be dealt with sooner or later. He don't remind me of a feller that lets something lie. I've seen his type before," Reuben said. Getting no satisfactory response, he said, "I thought that Mellner feller didn't allow no drinkin'."

"He don't. Why?"

"Those boys were drinkin'," Reuben said. "That's interestin'." He paused a moment, rubbing his beard in thought. "Some men can tell a woman from her smell, others can tell ya what's gonna be on the supper table before they get in the house. Me, I can smell whiskey on a man twenty paces away," he said proudly. "Those old boys been drinkin'."

"No sin in that," Samson said. "Give me some whiskey, will you, Reuben?"

Reuben shook his head and went to fetch a jug, muttering to himself about the confusions life could hold.

Some time later, Samson made his final rounds quickly, hoping he wouldn't come across Becky. He felt every eye was watching him, making sure he wasn't shaming any other women. His paranoia got so bad, he was afraid to look at anyone head-on, for fear they might read his thoughts wrong.

That night, he went to bed with the jug of whiskey by his side. He fell asleep half-drunk, the guilt filling him up and spilling into his dreams.

16

J ory Matlock pulled his collar up around his chin and looked up at the sky. The wind was picking up.

He looked back down and studied the woman's head. The easterly wind caught in her hair and it was whipped up and about. If the head wasn't so large and covered with dried blood, it would look like a doll's head, sitting there on the wagon seat. He shuddered. She'd been a young woman, and evidently pretty.

He'd gone through some articles in the wagon and found papers that carried the names Jim and Hazel Street. They'd traveled out here from Indiana. Indiana was a far piece away, and Jory reckoned there'd be nobody he could notify of the death. He'd give them a decent burial.

The earth was soggy. He decided to dig just one grave and bury the dead man and the pieces of his wife together. It took most of the afternoon. He could have made a shallow grave, but that wasn't Jory's way. He remembered burying his friend, Oliver Worthington, back in '36. The ground had been frozen hard. Jory had dug just enough to cover the body with a thin layer of earth, only to cross back by the grave two days later and find the coyotes had dug Oliver up and fed on his carcass. He had made an effort from that day forward to be sure and bury a person properly, even if it took some time to do it. No, he thought, a decent burial was little enough respect, even though he had never known Jim or Hazel Street.

By the time Jory packed down the last shovelful of dirt, the temperature had dropped considerably. He went to the wagon and tore a board from its side, then took out his knife and carved the names of the couple, where they were from, and the date. His hands felt stiff and awkward as he worked at the wood.

He was just finishing when he noticed a horse and rider at the edge of a little grove of five trees that stood out on the prairie. Quickly, he eased over to his horse and pulled his rifle from its scabbard. Then he walked leisurely back to the grave and erected the head marker, all the while taking glances back at the rider. Once the marker was firmly planted in the ground, he casually walked to the rear of the wagon and fiddled with a rope while he took his first long look at the man. There was something familiar about him.

The rider was slow coming in, so Jory reached into the remains of the campfire and pulled out the coffeepot that had been left behind. He shook it out, then scooped up some of the spilled coffee that someone had dumped on the ground. He found water in the barrel, filled the pot, then set the coffee aside to build a fire.

The ground was wet and there wasn't a dry stick of wood in sight. Jory looked at the wagon. It was still a good one, and it bothered him to vandalize it, even if its occupants were dead. Still, it was wood and he was cold. He circled around and found that the boards on the south side were still dry. He pulled a few away and busted them up on a rock that jutted out next to one of the wheels. He found some rags and got them burning, and soon the wood had caught into a nice fire. Jory looked up and motioned for the rider to come on in.

The rider picked up his pace, and as soon as Jory could see his face, he relaxed. It was Standing Bear, a Pawnee whom Jory had known for at least ten years, ever since he'd come west. Jory was surprised. It had been four years this very month since he'd last seen him. Standing Bear had been old even then, and he'd been very sick at the time. Jory had figured him to be dead. But here he was in the middle of the prairie. Jory was very glad to see him.

"Git on down, my friend. We'll have some coffee as soon as this fire gets it hot enough to boil."

Standing Bear gladly obliged. There were no hellos or other amenities. "You got tobacco?" he asked simply.

"Yeah, I got tobacco, but not for smokin'. I got a twist for chewin', in my bags, there." Jory walked over and fetched a chew, then tossed it to the Indian. "I thought you was dead or somethin'. I ain't seen you for a spell."

"No, I am not dead," Standing Bear said. He bit off a big piece and chewed a while, then added, "I am without woman, but I am not dead." He looked at the grave. "Who did you bury in the ground? A friend of yours?"

Jory shook his head. "Naw, I found 'em. Man and his wife. He'd been shot, and the woman . . ." He paused a moment. "Butchered like some kind of animal."

Standing Bear was not impressed by the gruesome details. He wasn't surprised, either. He didn't understand people who came out past the settlements, especially those who traveled alone. He, himself, had no desire to kill any of the immigrants. In fact, he rather selfishly enjoyed them, because he could usually get a handout of some sort, whether it be whiskey, food, tobacco, or whatever. But there were others, even some of his own people, who hated the immigrants who made the westward journey. They wished to see all of the immigrants dead.

"White men did this," he said.

"You know who?" Jory asked, surprised at this news.

"I do not know who. I only know it was a white man who did this."

"I've known Indians to butcher folks before," Jory said. "Butcher and scalp 'em. What makes you so sure it wasn't Indians?" There was an irritation to his voice.

Standing Bear looked off into the horizon with his unblinking eyes. He got up and walked around the campsite, studied the ground and peered into the back of the wagon. His old eyes glistened as he looked at Jory.

"Indian would not be so foolish to leave behind such useful things," he said. He bent down and picked up two tin plates and a fork. "You will see that whoever did this took only food." He looked at the spot where Jory had scooped the coffee from the ground. "They left waste of good coffee. No, Indians would not do this. Indians think of their bellies like the white man, but Indians would also take these plates. They would take the water barrel and pot for coffee. If they didn't take the wagon, they would burn it." His old body was stiff as he walked away from Jory. He turned around. "No, it was white men who did this." He spit, dismissing the subject. "The tobacco is good. Jory Matlock always carries good tobacco and good whiskey."

That evening, Jory shot a rabbit and they fried it up. The winds refused to let up, and brought cold temperatures with them. The men tore more boards off the wagon and huddled near the fire. It did little to keep them warm, but they didn't complain.

They ate mostly in silence. Jory watched Standing Bear with curiosity, as he always did when they broke bread together. The old man didn't say much, but he didn't miss much, either.

"Why are you always alone when I see you?" Jory asked again.

"I have no woman," Standing Bear said with little emotion.

"Couldn't you find you one if you wanted?"

"Perhaps," the old Indian said. His eyes took on a sparkle as he stared into the fire as if the flames held some deep answers for him.

He gave thought to his life. There had been three squaws, five sons, and three daughters. All were dead now, save two of the daughters, and they had both gone to live in the lodges of men whom he cared little about. His shoulders drooped a little. A man without sons had little to be happy about in his old age, he thought. It bothered him to hear others, spending hours around the fires talking about the brave deeds of their sons. It bothered him so much, he'd taken to going off by himself for days and weeks at a time. Finally, he'd left his tribe for good. It was true, he thought. Many times, he didn't miss having a squaw to warm his bed at night, to skin his kills and make him fine clothing. But he was getting older. Such comforts might be needed. He knew that if he was to take another squaw, she would most likely be old and used up, too, and would not want to warm him at night.

They were thoughts that gave him little hope and filled his heart with sadness. He was old, but his mind could still entertain thoughts of frolicking with young squaws.

"Why do you have no woman?" Standing Bear asked Jory.

"I don't reckon no woman would put up with me," Jory said truthfully. "Never could stand to stay in one place for too long. White women like security," he added. "They could never live like your people, moving around with the weather and following the herds. No," Jory sighed, "white women like a house with frilly things in it. They like soaps and lotions that smell pretty."

Standing Bear only nodded. It was true, he knew, for he had observed white women on the wagon trains that he traded with. They were foolish, more interested in what was inside bottles than the sparkling bottles themselves. But they were pretty, and a curiosity to him. Even if Standing Bear did think them silly and spoiled, he had often entertained the thought of lying with one.

He pulled his eyes from the fire. "You, Jory Matlock, lay with Crooked Tree's daughter. There have been others." He nodded. "They like to lay with you. It is said among the people. Tell me, Jory Matlock, is it different?"

"Is what different?"

"White women. Are they different? I myself have thought of laying with white women, but I do not know any that I could ask this of."

Jory laughed out loud. "There are some you could ask, Standing Bear, but you sure might get shot if you ask the wrong woman in the wrong company."

Standing Bear pondered what Jory had said. He wondered who these women were that he could ask. From the way Jory laughed, Standing Bear thought perhaps he was not telling the truth. Still, he intended to pursue the subject further, if they should see any white women. Maybe Jory would show him the woman whom he might ask. He wished that a white woman would come along, right now. Not just any white woman, but one whom Jory would say it was all right to ask.

The next morning, the prairie lay still and cold. Jory felt

relieved that the wind had finally died down. He hoped it would warm up some. The cold made his joints ache. His fingers were so stiff, he could barely move them. At forty-seven, he felt both young and old. Mentally, he couldn't see where his thinking had changed much at all since his youth. It was his body that was slowly beginning to betray him. For one thing, he had once been able to drift off to sleep the minute he closed his eyes, and he usually didn't wake until morning. Nowadays, he'd been having trouble getting to sleep at all, and found himself waking up several times during the night.

It left a man tired and worn. The cold weather, which once hadn't bothered him much, now made his hands and feet swell. His back ached most of the time.

But none of those inconveniences worried him as much as the fact that Jory had started having trouble making water. Night or day, he'd go off to relieve himself, and once his stream would start, it would suddenly stop, then dribble for several minutes. He was always leaving himself wet. This was especially uncomfortable on such cold mornings.

He rubbed his numb hands together over the campfire, getting so close he managed to sear the hair on the back of one. He drew back and uttered a curse, then glanced at Standing Bear.

To his chagrin, Standing Bear was watching him wordlessly, holding his coffee cup in his hands. The old Indian looked to be at least twenty years older than Jory, but he seemed to be taking the cold in stride.

As they drank coffee, Jory made his decision. It wasn't anything of a surprise. He had known from the moment he'd ridden up on the death scene. He would have to track down the men who had killed the young traveling couple.

He looked at Standing Bear. "So, you say white men did this," he said thoughtfully. Standing Bear was right, he knew. If anything, Indians would have killed the man and taken the woman. Even from her scattered remains, Jory had known that she was a handsome woman. Her face had still shown a classic beauty. The kind of beauty that men thought about when they were alone.

"Yes, white men," Standing Bear said. "Six white men."

"Six?" Jory said, surprised. "Did you see 'em?"

The Indian shook his head. He paused to take a drink of his coffee. "No. I have seen their tracks. Out there." He pointed west. "Horses' tracks. There were six of them."

"Fresh tracks? How fresh?"

"Two, maybe three days. They were not in a hurry," Standing Bear added. "You are going after these men?"

"Yes. Someone has to. We can't have people going around killin' folks," Jory said grimly. "There's enough problems in life as it is."

Standing Bear stared back into the fire. He nodded his head. "You are a brave man, Jory Matlock. Six men against one. Those are not good numbers, even for a brave man. Do you have lots of good tobacco and good whiskey?"

"I've got some."

"I will go with you."

Jory stared at Standing Bear and the Indian looked back at him. There was a certain look in the old eyes that settled him. Jory was grateful for the offer, for it was not a favor that he could have asked. Whoever had killed the Streets were evil to the bone. It would be dangerous, and Jory had no idea what he would do when and if he caught up with them. It was just something he had to do. But old as he was, Standing Bear was a keen tracker, and efficient tracking came in handy during a manhunt.

Jory nodded. "Much obliged. I must warn you, though. Six against two still ain't very good odds."

Standing Bear said nothing. The warning didn't bother him. He liked this white man. They would travel well together and find the men.

Besides, Jory Matlock always had good tobacco and whiskey.

17

Jory and Standing Bear headed west. Jory's hands still felt stiff. He looked up at the open sky, hoping for a few rays of the sun to appear and bring him some relief. He took to riding with his hands tucked alternately under his armpits to warm them. Underneath the men, the horses' hooves made loud sloshing noises as they tromped through the water and mud that covered the ground.

Jory felt an unusual urgency about him. He had to find the killers. Mixed and various thoughts raced through his mind about the faceless men he and Standing Bear pursued. He wondered what kind of man would mutilate another human being. Jory had known plenty of men out here on the mountains and prairies west of the Mississippi who were mean enough to kill over a wrongful glance. He'd seen those who would kill a man for his furs or money, or to take his women. *Still,* he thought to himself, *to kill and mutilate?* It was a vicious and evil deed that chewed at Jory as they rode silently along.

No, these men he was tracking were less than human, he decided. And those who killed once would surely think nothing of killing again. Jory gave thought to the fact that he and Standing Bear had best be alert and, above all else, ready to kill. And fast.

The idea held little appeal—it wasn't something he felt particularly inclined to do, unless it was a matter of self-defense. Whatever the case, Jory knew that a man rarely had time to think about such things when the situation came up. Even in this country, where hostile Indians could be found roaming freely and a man had to be on his guard at all times, there was still a chance of avoiding trouble just by being cautious.

This, though, was altogether different. These were white men. Cold, vicious, unmerciful killers.

Jory decided to try to get this thought out of his mind. He asked the one question that had always come to him when he'd met up with Standing Bear.

"Do you miss your people?"

Jory offered up some tobacco. As if the tobacco were his own, Standing Bear took a big chew and stuck it happily in his mouth. He liked working it around, the flavor singeing his taste buds. It rolled over his tongue, sending different tastes all around.

"What is there to miss?" he finally said. "I see my people when I want to see them." He stopped talking to work the tobacco some more. It was getting moist and more flavorful. He didn't like to think about such things, anyway. It had entered his mind to wonder why he'd taken to roaming about by himself. It was sometimes lonely, he had to admit. He wished there were more willing young squaws about. Each time he returned to his people, he found he'd aged to the point where fewer and fewer of the squaws paid him any mind at all. Only a few old ones with half their teeth rotted out showed any interest, and they held little appeal for him.

When he thought back over his life, he remembered he'd always favored the young ones. As a very young brave, he had felt a particular liking for those who had barely crossed into puberty. He still had pleasant thoughts about such young squaws, but now he preferred those who were a little older. Someday, he would go to the north, where there was much snow and many animals, men who trapped and lived in the mountains. Jory had told him of many such things that stuck in the back of his mind. He'd often heard of the beauty of the Sioux squaws. He'd seen a few in his travels, but none the likes of which he'd heard about, for sure. Someday, he would make the trip north and find out.

"You, Jory Matlock, have good tobacco, but you, too, have no woman. Why do you have no woman?"

It wasn't that he cared about Jory's welfare. Rather, it had suddenly occurred to him that Jory might have or know of a white woman who would lie with him.

Jory thought about the question. There were times when he would, indeed, like to have a woman. Since coming west, his standard fare had been simple, one-time frolics. There'd always been a whore to find at the rendezvous. The French traders usually seemed to have one or two. Mostly, though, during the last two years, his frolicking had been with Indian women.

Until lately, Jory hadn't missed being domesticated, but now, something was starting to change that, little by little. At night, thoughts of his parents back in Massachusetts came to him. He'd see visions of his mama taking care of his papa through the illnesses. Jory could never remember his papa not being sick, or his mama not taking care of him. Maybe, he thought, that image of his own upbringing had driven him away from a domesticated life. Maybe he was afraid that if he ever slowed down, some woman would have to take care of him, too.

As his body ached and the nights grew colder, good sleep was getting harder to come by. Jory often wondered if he might not have been mistaken, not finding a good woman to take as his own.

He then thought back to the small wagon train he'd encountered last summer. It was easy to wish for last summer again. Agnes Perring was a pretty widow woman from New Hampshire, and she'd caught his eye right away. He'd ridden with the train for over a week and enjoyed Agnes's favors. She had tried to talk him into joining the wagon train and going on with them to Oregon, but he had argued back that the train was too small and he'd best head back east, or at least stop and wait for additional wagons to join them. He had approached the wagon master, Vernon English, and tried to share the rumors he'd heard about warring Cayuse Indians. He'd spoken to the men on the train as well, but everyone had dismissed his advice as foolish. Besides that, they said, joining up with a larger train would only slow things down.

The next winter, a trapper friend named John Tallman told Jory about an Indian attack on a seven-wagon train with just over fifty people. All had been killed.

The way Tallman had described it, Jory knew it was Agnes's party that had been attacked and murdered by the Cayuse. He felt guilty for not taking a stronger stance with Vernon English. He should have persuaded the man to turn back and abandon the idea. Or, he thought, maybe he should have stayed with them. Maybe he could have fore-seen the attack and helped them prepare to defend them-selves.

He hadn't been able to get the pretty widow out of his mind. He had let her get away, and now she was dead. Jory doubted whether such an opportunity would ever arise again, but if it did, he intended to let his feelings cul-tivate themselves. He sighed.

"I do not have a woman. I'm just like you, Standing Bear. We're a couple of old fools out here. If we had any sense a-tall, we'd be snuggled up right now with our women," he added.

Standing Bear was still preoccupied with his desires to sample the wares of a white woman before he died. He said, "If I ride with you and we catch the six white men, will you find me a white woman that I can ask to lay with me?"

"Why hell, Standing Bear! We're apt to get killed! Six against two. But if we don't, I'll do my best to oblige ya," Jory said.

They came across the bleached skull of a buffalo lying in the low grass. The sight made Jory hungry for a good buffalo steak. He reckoned he enjoyed the taste of buffalo better than anything. Maybe it was because he'd eaten more buffalo in the last fifteen years. He liked the outside fried near crisp and the inside pink and moist. He'd get the fire really hot and sear the outside good. His mouth began to water, just thinking about it. Instantly, thoughts of killer men and frolicking women were put aside. He forgot about his stiff, cold hands and wished for a fat young buffalo to wander by so that he could shoot it for their supper. In fact, in the back of his mind, he'd been thinking about his empty stomach ever since they'd broken camp.

They rode in silence for over an hour. Standing Bear tried to picture in his mind just what it would feel like to lie with a white woman. Would it be different? Would she be happy with him when they'd finished? He was comforted in the fact that he spoke such good English. As a child, he'd developed a fascination for the traders and had learned a great deal of French from them. He'd stayed close to the missionaries who visited his camps. He was sure the white women would find pleasure in his fluency. He wished he'd been more inclined as a younger man to find one. The truth was, though, that the only whites he'd come in contact with had been the wives of the missionaries. He remembered the great Bible man, Joshua Whittingham, and his wife Kathleen. He'd spent considerable time in their company. Once, when Kathleen was bathing in a creek, he'd stood in a bush and watched her. Over the years, things had fallen from his memory: the names of family members, great hunts and battles, but he could still see Kathleen's milky white body as if he'd looked upon her only the day before. Sometimes when he was alone, he would scan her entire body in his mind. The details of her facial features had dimmed over the years, but he could remember every line of her body. In his mind, he still saw her large breasts with tips as pink as prairie flowers, and her round backside. He could still recall that her secret hair had been a light red. He would get so caught up in his daydreaming, he could almost reach out and touch Kathleen with his fingertips, stroke her smooth skin. He searched through his memory for some small remembrance of her face. She had been a handsome woman, he knew, but all he could conjure was a body with a face that was void of eyes, nose, and mouth. It bothered him some. He wished he could see her smiling at him.

They must catch the killers quickly, he knew, for only then would he have the opportunity to ask Jory Matlock to find him a white woman to ask his question of.

When Jory saw two black specks in the distance, excitement stirred inside, for he could not get the longing for a buffalo steak out of his mind. In fact, even a rabbit would do right now.

"Standing Bear, look! Buffalo!" He pointed to the north.

Standing Bear looked off and studied the dark specks. Soon, another one appeared. He seemed unmoved.

"It is only white people," he said. "Two men and a woman."

Jory snapped his head back around to stare hard. Even though he still couldn't make out any more than spots, his spirits sank. Soon, the outline of riders and horses became clearer. Standing Bear had been right. In spite of his disappointment, Jory felt amazed at the old man's eyesight.

When the riders drew near enough to see Jory and Standing Bear, they put their horses into a hard lope. Jory pulled his rifle up over his saddle to where he could aim and shoot fast if need be. He still couldn't tell if it was two men and a woman riding toward him, or if they were white or not, but he figured Standing Bear was likely right as not.

He thought of the dead immigrant woman and her husband, and his stomach churned with anxiety. Were there three more riders out there? He looked around, but could see no one else.

The three were approaching hard and fast, and Jory could now see a woman's long hair blowing as she rode. Standing Bear had been right, but that still didn't change anything. The six killers could include a woman.

He glanced quickly at Standing Bear, but the Indian appeared nonplussed. The riders came to within thirty yards before Jory could make out their faces.

There was an urgency about all of them. Jory wondered for a minute if they were being chased. As far as he could see, they were riding alone. He kept his rifle ready to swing into action. Were the six killers just out of sight, chasing them? The waiting almost unnerved him.

The three rode right up between them, causing Jory's horse to spin around and do a side step.

"Whoa!" he said loudly and lifted his rifle. "You folks crazy, ridin' up on a man like this?"

The woman didn't even seem to hear his complaint. Almost before the words left his lips, she shouted at them.

"Please! Have you seen a baby girl? We've lost our baby!" she said, her eyes wide with fright.

"We ain't seen no one. Not a soul all day," Jory said in surprise.

The woman let out a large sob, and one of the men spoke up.

"You sure you ain't seen a little girl, 'bout three years old with long dark hair?" he asked in a worried tone.

Jory was still staring at the woman and the pain in her face. He shook his head and said softly, "I'm right sorry, but we ain't seen no one. Is it her young'un?" He nodded at the woman.

The crying woman looked at him through her tears. "My sister's girl. Little Louisa Pickett. She wandered off this mornin'. We can't find her nowhere. Please help us find Louisa!" she pleaded.

"Ma'am, we'd be glad to. Where 'bouts did you lose her?" Jory said.

The man pointed back toward where they'd been. " 'Bout three miles back. Got six wagons in a small train, headin' for Oregon. We was all eatin' breakfast, and the little one wandered off. Been lookin' for her all morning."

Jory looked nervously at Standing Bear. He had no desire to insult him, but he had to ask the question.

"Any sign of Indians?"

The man shook his head. "Ain't seen any for more'n a week."

"Did you pick up any tracks? Any idee which direction she might've taken off in?"

"No tracks, no trail," the man said. "We just been lookin' in all directions."

"You say you've got others lookin' for her, too?" Jory said. "Well, I sure don't mean to alarm you folks, but several miles east of here, we found a man and his wife murdered. We picked up the trail of six riders."

"Oh my God!" the woman squalled. She covered her mouth with her hands. "Oh God, please no!"

Jory questioned his own wisdom at mentioning the murders, but it was too late. Besides, he told himself, it was best that folks be forewarned. "Ma'am, I'm sorry as can be," he said, "but you need to be aware of it." He turned to the men. "You could wander out here on the prairie for days and never find a single jackrabbit. Now, the best thing to do is take us back to where you started from. Standing Bear, here, is a good tracker. He'll try to pick up some sign of where she could of headed off."

As Standing Bear listened to the plan, he grew melancholy at being included in the search. He'd made his decision to ride with Jory Matlock, in the hopes of enjoying some good tobacco and good whiskey and finding a white woman to ask his question of. Now, he must help look for a white man's child. He hoped they would find her soon. Then he could think once again about how to fulfill his great desire.

A sudden thought came to him that gave him new hope and cheered him considerably. Maybe this lost child would bring him new opportunity. Maybe he would find the little girl and return her to her family, safe and unharmed. There would surely be many white women who would be grateful to him. Perhaps one of them would want to answer his question. Perhaps she would lie with him.

18

Half a dozen wagons were pulled into a semicircle. The small group of travelers had come west from Virginia. There were thirteen men, six women, and eleven children, counting the lost little girl. They had all come from the same area of Virginia. Jory found out that the names of the three who had ridden up on him and Standing Bear were Molly Jackson, Noah Bayh, and Clark Van Dorn. According to Molly, they had been eating breakfast that morning, when little Louisa Pickett had told her mama, Bertha, that she was going to her auntie's to play with her doll. Bertha, being busy with her morning duties, hadn't paid much attention. Molly said the child had never shown up at her wagon. That was the last anyone had seen of Louisa.

All the men, save the two with Jory, were out looking. They had dispatched themselves in every possible direction.

Jory and Standing Bear accepted cups of coffee and sat down to wait with the others, hoping someone would return to the camp with the girl.

But no one found her. One by one, the men came back, shaking their heads and wiping their eyes in frustration. Bertha was no help to them. The grieving mother had gone into hysteria. She couldn't remember anything.

Jory was sorry he'd mentioned the six killers in front of Molly. He hoped she wouldn't mention them to the mother. Even though he wasn't sure she could comprehend, she surely didn't need another burden added to her heart. He did feel, however, that he should caution the men, and he dispatched Noah Bayh and Clark Van Dorn to tell them.

Another search was begun. Standing Bear and Jory did a slow look all around the camp, moving outward, searching for tracks.

It was over an hour before Standing Bear picked up the small footprints two hundred yards to the south. Jory wasn't completely satisfied that they belonged to little Louisa, but it was the best they had to go on.

They took off immediately, following the tracks. As they carefully made their way, Jory thought about the small child. He had never had children, a fact he sometimes pondered. Still, even though he had no young'uns of his own, it didn't diminish the awful fear that gripped him. Suddenly, he was more aware than ever of the cold. His hands had ached and bothered him this morning, and he had selfishly cursed the cold for his own aches and pains. Now all he could concern himself with was the little one. When last seen, Louisa had been wearing only her shoes and nightshirt, her doll clutched in her arms. Jory couldn't erase the picture in his mind of the child out there somewhere, cold and frightened, wandering around all alone.

They hadn't traveled very far when they lost her trail. Jory wondered how much a three-year-old child weighed. Thirty pounds? Forty? The tracks they'd been following were barely deep enough to recognize, even with the melting ice wetting the ground. He looked around. There were long stretches of thick prairie grass that covered any prints that might have been made. He sighed to himself. If they didn't find her soon, it would be hard to pick up the trail again.

As they rode farther, it became apparent they had indeed lost the trail. He and Standing Bear split up. They would try to stay within a couple of miles of each other. Jory's eyes felt strained and he had a headache from looking out over the endless prairie. Every so often, he stopped to listen for a sound, but nothing came to him but the empty hum of the wind. By late afternoon, he decided that she couldn't have made it this far. He turned around and headed back north in a serpentine sweep, hoping to cover every inch possible. He rode that way until dark, twisting back and forth over and over, his eyes sweeping over the ground to the horizon and back. Still, there was no sign of little Louisa Pickett anywhere.

By seven o'clock, it was pitch-dark on the prairie. He returned to the wagon train, hoping that good news awaited.

It didn't. Most of the searchers had returned and were drinking mugs of hot coffee. Their long faces showed their pain and desperation. Jory grabbed some bacon, chewed it down, and drank his coffee. Then he noticed his hands. They had grown stiff since the sun had gone down and the night cold had set in. He'd been so concerned about the child, he'd forgotten about the pain.

Standing Bear had not yet returned. Jory inquired about his old friend, but no one had seen the Indian. Jory hoped that held a positive meaning.

"If I could switch horses," he said, "I could go back out."

A fresh horse was quickly offered. Noah Bayh looked thankfully at Jory, but there was also resignation in his eyes. "You can use one of mine," he said softly, "but I'm afraid it's no use. There's no light out tonight. Such thick cloud cover. I'm afraid a man would just get lost out there. We appreciate your efforts, though, more than you'll ever know."

"I don't have any children of my own, Mr. Bayh," Jory said, "so I can't know the pain her people are goin' through. Still, I couldn't live with myself to think that she's out there somewhere and no one's tryin' to find her. I appreciate the use of the horse."

Bayh nodded. "Of course, you're right. I'm sorry. It's . . . it's just been such a trying time. Look, I'll come with you."

Jory had already swung himself up in the saddle. "I don't need nobody to go with me," he said. "Last I saw him, Standing Bear was headed southwest. I'm goin' to the southeast. If you're goin', I suggest you go due west. Others can go east, northeast, or northwest. It's hard to tell where she's at. I'd imagine it would be easy to walk in circles out here."

This time, as he headed out into the night, Jory thought of the six killers. Had they plucked the child up? Had some Indians taken her? He found it hard to believe that a little one could vanish, or that her little legs could carry her so far on the plains that a man couldn't find her.

All night he rode, stopping now and then to listen. He was grateful there wasn't much wind, but the damp cold was bitter. As he rode under the dark sky, searching for a little girl he could only imagine in his mind, his hands grew so cold he couldn't ignore them anymore. Soon, he lost feeling and he wasn't sure whether he still held the horse's reins or not. The wetness in the air grew thicker, seeping inside his clothes and sending chills through his body. Above his own misery, Jory started praying for this little girl he didn't know. As the night wore on and dawn approached, he felt the emptiness of failure.

Failure was a familiar old friend to Jory. He'd battled to prove himself a worthwhile being all his life. As a child growing up in Massachusetts, he'd been forced to carry a heavy load in looking after his father, a heavy drinker who often put the family into debt. More often than not, Jory would be dispatched to work off what his father owed to this man or that.

He remembered his thirteenth birthday, the fifth of January. The day had passed without mention, as he'd spent the entire winter working for Mr. Asa Tillary, feeding and tending to his stock. Jory had not allowed himself to think about it much, but he couldn't help longing to be with his mother and little sisters. Elizabeth and Sarah Jane, who were two and four at the time, had always looked up to him instead of their own daddy, and he sorely missed having them fight over a position on his lap.

Jory had spent another nine months working for Mr. Benjamin Worthington. Like before, it had seemed to last forever. He remembered the times he'd come home, after the long absences, hoping for a small bit of welcome. Instead, his father would seem angry at him. He'd berate Jory and demand to know what kind of job he'd done for the men. There'd never been a word of how his father had missed him. Never been a word of affection.

Jory had a great love for his mother and little sisters. He had an older brother named Jack and an older sister, Kara, but it was the little ones that he was fondest of. It seemed to Jory that Jack had escaped their father's constant criticism, but looking back, he wondered if maybe Jack hadn't gone through the same things he had. Maybe he just hadn't been old enough to realize it. He guessed he never would know, since Jack had drowned at the age of eighteen, when Jory was fifteen. Though nothing had ever been said, Jory always felt as if his father blamed him for the drowning. He hadn't spoken to Jory for weeks afterward.

Just before Jory's sixteenth birthday, his father and another man had sneaked off to a neighbor's barn and gotten so drunk that they somehow managed to burn the barn down. Once again, Jory was dispatched to the neighbor's farm to work out the loss. This time, it was to be for one year. Not only had his father destroyed the barn; he also owed the man a considerable sum of money.

That was when Jory left home for good. He never set foot on the neighbor's farm. Instead, he'd headed south to New York. From there, he'd gone to Virginia, then to Ohio. He had been drifting westward ever since.

He often wondered about his family. He felt guilty for having left his mother and little sisters, but he knew he couldn't have lasted much longer, being peddled out to pay for his father's mistakes. The resentment had started growing inside him to the point where it was eating him up inside.

It had been over thirty years since he'd seen any of them. Elizabeth would now be thirty-six. Sarah Jane thirty-eight. Where were they living now, he thought. He wondered whom they had married and how many young'uns they had. He hoped they'd married good men. Sometimes he missed them so much, he could hardly stand it. When he'd left, they'd been only five and seven. Just little girls. He wondered what they looked like now. Sometimes he would wake up in the middle of the night, all alone, and weep. He felt guilty for leaving them and never going back. The plain truth was, Jory felt guilty about most things in his life. The questions ran over and over in his mind. He wondered about his older sister, Kara, too. He hadn't thought about Kara as much as the younger girls, and that bothered him.

And his mother. Jory had to swallow a lump in his throat. She would be seventy-three years old, one year younger than his father, if she was still alive.

Sometimes he wondered if any of his family was still living. Life was hard, and he considered it pure luck that he was still here himself.

It was the deep emotion he carried about his father that spawned the guilt, but it was also his father who had caused him much of his pain. All through his youth, he'd craved his father's love and attention, only to be spurned and made to feel he wasn't good enough. Jory flopped from sorrow to anger, and back again. Over and over.

Jory had decided he didn't dislike his father. He'd just never been able to understand the different feelings his father had seemed to show toward him. If he'd wanted to, he could have pitied the older man. Even after all these years, those feelings still surfaced, almost every day.

As he rode in the predawn in search of Louisa Pickett, she suddenly took on the faces of his little sisters. He could recall how frightened they had become when the sun went down. The sounds of night animals or storms approaching would scare them. They often looked to him to hold them and assure them that everything was all right.

Louisa didn't have anybody's lap to climb into. She was all alone with the night sounds. Jory felt a desperation to find her.

His rambling thoughts were interrupted when he saw a silhouetted figure on a horse. He could tell that it was Standing Bear. He loped toward him.

"Seen anything?"

"No. I have not," the Indian answered.

"Have you talked to any of the other men?"

"Two, but that was hours ago. You got some good tobacco?"

Jory handed him a chew and said, "I think someone

would've found her by now. Do you think maybe someone kidnapped her? Maybe the six that killed them immigrants?"

Standing Bear took a big chew and rolled it around in his mouth until it was full of the juice. He liked the taste and the way it stung his throat. It made his mouth feel alive. "No one took the little girl," he said. "Maybe someone found her, but she was not stolen. There would have been signs, tracks." He gestured around them. "But there are no tracks."

Jory nodded and studied the situation. "You go on back, Standing Bear," he finally said. "I wanta look some more. There's a wooded area a couple miles east of here. I wanta look at it in the daylight. If anyone's found her, have 'em fire off a round."

Standing Bear nodded wordlessly and turned back toward the wagons.

It was getting light as Jory rode to the edge of the small grove of trees. Suddenly, a coyote emerged. It was dragging something. Jory's heart jumped into his throat when he saw the head and the legs dangling from its mouth.

His hand shook as he reached for his rifle and aimed. He took in a deep breath to calm himself. He couldn't miss, and he knew it. He fired and felt grateful to see the coyote jump, run a short way, then flop around like a fish out of water. He waited a moment, then rode in.

He thought for a moment he was going to be sick. He thought of Louisa's mother and the news he would have to take her. He thought of Elizabeth and Sarah Jane.

In the grass, next to where the coyote now lay dead, he saw a doll. It had been chewed and ripped apart by the coyote. Relief swept through Jory, but only briefly. This was the same doll that had been described by Molly. Louisa's doll. Jory gathered up the tattered remains and turned his horse toward where the coyote had been.

He tried to brace himself, but he knew that no matter how hard he tried to feel indifferent, he would not be prepared for what lay ahead.

19

Jory found his first tracks of Louisa Pickett at the edge of a small creek. He also saw the tracks of the coyote, and the sight made his heart sink a little.

Louisa's tracks went into the water. He led his horse in and waded across. The water was at least two feet deep. On the other side, there was no sign of a footprint. He rode back and forth and searched until he was sure, then went back to the tracks and headed west alongside the water.

A quarter of a mile west, he picked up her tiny tracks again. He followed for a short distance and found where they once again went into the water. He stopped and studied the situation. She had entered the water here, all right, but the water was more shallow, no more than eight or ten inches deep. He crossed, and there were her little footprints on the other side.

Jory let out a sigh of relief. For one thing, he couldn't see any coyote tracks, only Louisa's. For another, the child had known enough to cross where she wasn't as likely to get drowned. He wondered if it was wisdom on her part, or just pure luck.

As best he could, he followed the tracks to the south, but quickly lost them in the prairie grass. He turned and rode back toward the creek, studying the ground, but it was no use. Her trail had disappeared again.

It was good and daylight when he stopped. He was failing in his search for Louisa Pickett. The word struck him, sending a familiar old sinking feeling to his stomach. He rubbed his eyes. They felt tired and strained and his head hurt. He was stiff from riding all night in the cold.

Sighing to himself, Jory once again took up a serpentine sweep, back to the spot where he'd found her tracks by the creek. By now, the hope of finding her alive had passed. He started to wonder if the coyote had left anything of her remains. He wasn't sure whether he wanted to find her body or not; still, he knew he couldn't stop looking until he knew something, one way or the other.

Every so often, he would stop to listen, hoping against hope that he would hear a gunshot. He kept an eye on the horizon, watching for someone to ride out and tell him to come back in, that she'd been found safe. So many thoughts and feelings had run through him, his tired mind began to feel confused. Had he been riding forever? What was he doing out here in the cold, going around in circles? He began to question his thinking abilities. Maybe he was losing his mind in the howling prairie.

He barely heard the trembling whimpers above the wind. At first, it didn't register in his head what it was. *It's a puppy,* he thought. *Sounds like it's just about given out from crying all night over being separated from its mother.* He shook his head and listened closer. How'd a puppy come to get lost way out here, he wondered. Probably got left by one of the passing immigrant families. May have gotten separated from the litter and not even noticed.

Jory moved slowly, listening for the faint whimpers to guide him. Then he saw the little girl in the deep prairie grass.

She lay in a fetal position, pulled tightly into herself. Her shoes were muddy and her nightshirt torn. The long dark hair was matted and wet, giving her the appearance of a tiny old woman.

Jory gave a start at the sight. His body began to tremble, and when he climbed down off his horse, his legs shook. He had trouble keeping his balance as he bent down to pick up Louisa.

In his arms, she felt as cold as death. He pulled her close to him. Her eyes were closed. She gave no sign of realizing that someone had picked her up. Quickly, Jory shrugged off his coat and pulled his shirt open, then pulled her body into his warmth and wrapped his coat around her.

A fear and urgency more terrifying than he'd ever experienced came over him. She was so cold, surely she was near death. At best, she would probably die before he could get her back to the wagon train.

He pulled her tighter. Visions of his own little sisters came to him. Elizabeth and Sarah Jane hadn't been much bigger than this when he had left. Even though he'd missed them, he'd let their youth pass by. Guilt swept over him like a dark cloud. Tears ran from his eyes and he began to pray, begging for the life of Louisa who, before this moment, he'd never even laid eyes on. Yet, she was more precious to him than anything he'd ever known.

Louisa's breath felt cool against his chest. Expecting her to die any second, he grew angry at himself that he hadn't found her sooner. Though it was agony for him, he couldn't stop his mind from reflecting on her ordeal. He could see her in his mind's eye, walking alone, carrying her little doll. His body shuddered and shook when he thought of what must have gone through her child's mind when darkness came and she was all alone, scared to death, her little feet and hands so cold they hurt. He started bawling. She couldn't have understood why her mother wasn't here, taking care of her. Again, he thought of Elizabeth and Sarah Jane and how easily they had been frightened. He fell to his knees, holding her, and buried his face in her hair, unable to chase away the images.

It startled him when she began to babble. Her little voice quaked and shook, but he understood.

"M-m-mommy. I want mommy." She tried to wiggle in his arms. Jory felt surprised at her strength. "Brrr! I cold! Louisa cold, Mommy!" She began to whimper, a little stronger this time.

Jory smiled through his tears. "Yes ma'am," he said hoarsely. "Let's go find your mama."

Clutching her little body next to his, he climbed atop his horse. He prayed harder than he'd ever prayed as he rode back to Louisa's family.

Slowly, some warmth began to return to her body. She was a chubby little girl, and she felt soft against his skin.

"You can't let her die. Not now, God," he pleaded. "Let her make it back to her family."

Her breathing deepened against his chest. It was warm. She had fallen asleep.

When he returned to the immigrants' camp, all was quiet and still with the spirit of despondency hanging overhead. Jory and Louisa rode right up to Bertha's wagon. When Bertha looked out to see her daughter, her cries were loud enough to alert the rest of the party. Soon, everyone was there, transformed from a group of mourners into a camp full of joy.

Jory himself, after riding through the dark night, tired and cold, suddenly felt young and alive. He ate a much-needed meal, then climbed up inside one of the wagons and closed his eyes. To the best of his knowledge, it was a dreamless sleep.

When he awoke, it was dark outside. He felt disoriented, almost as though he was still asleep as he rose and left the wagon to look around. There were folks huddled around campfires, talking in low tones. Jory watched them. He felt strange, like he was there, yet not there. There was something wrong about the place.

He stood there several minutes before he felt fully awake. Molly Jackson noticed him and brought coffee.

"You are a hero," she said, smiling at him.

Jory tried to rub the sleep out of his eyes before he accepted the cup. As he nodded his thanks, he looked back at her.

It was the first he'd noticed that Molly Jackson was a handsome woman. She was tall—as tall as he was—with large features, but she definitely possessed soft, feminine qualities. Her mouth was soft and full, the eyes were a deep brown, sympathetic but touched with humor. He noticed the hints of aging that showed at the corners. She was older than he'd realized. It surprised him, for Louisa's mother appeared to be in her late twenties at most. Molly looked to be at least fifty. He tried to pull his eyes off her face.

"How's Louisa?" he inquired hoarsely.

Molly frowned. "Not so good, I'm afraid. Taken ill with a fever." She sat down and motioned for him to join her. "Poor Bertha. This morning she was overcome with happiness to have Louisa back, and now—" She shook her head. "It's just so cruel, to have lost the girl, then got her back, and now . . ." Again she shook her head.

Jory, who had just had the best sleep he could remember, suddenly felt tired again. The news hit him like a mule kick. True, he hadn't expected Louisa to live when he had first found her. But as he carried her, he'd felt her small body turning warm against his, and it had been so easy to get caught up in everyone's joy and hope for her recovery. He remembered his fervent prayers for her safety. "It would be a terrible tragedy," he said honestly.

Molly got up to refill their coffee mugs and returned with a plate of food.

"You must be starving," she said. She watched him wordlessly gulp down the food. He was like most men, she thought. Unceremoniously selfish. But then, it was hard to harbor such bad thoughts toward Jory. After all, he had brought Louisa back.

Molly's own kids were all dead and gone. She'd given birth to four. Jonathan and Seth had died as infants. Eleven-year-old Helen had died of a broken neck after falling from a horse, and Clement had been struck by lightning. Molly had been alone for the last six years. Louisa was Bertha's only child and had become like the granddaughter Molly would never have. Yes, she was grateful to this Jory Matlock. Still, he was a man, and she'd had her fill of worthless men.

Her first husband had left behind nothing but memories of beatings and tongue-lashings. She had not mourned the day he died of consumption. Her second husband, Lucius Jackson, was the father of her four children. Lucius had been a sour man, lacking in affection for her or any of the children. The marriage had lasted fifteen years, which was about fourteen years too long in Molly's estimation, until Lucius had been killed in a shooting accident. Over the years, after losing the children and enduring her husband's selfishness, she'd finally grown sour. There was no spot left in her heart for a man. Nevertheless, from time to time she still felt the urge to be with one. It wasn't an emotional need. It was more like a brief physical want.

Right now, in this solemn time, she felt an overpowering urge for Jory Matlock. She'd watched the way he walked and how he sat in the saddle. She imagined what he would feel like atop her. Once, two years before, she had felt the same urges for a widower back in Virginia named Samuel Pridemore. One afternoon at a church picnic, she had had him. It had been terribly disappointing when, after a mere couple of minutes, he had spent himself, leaving her as empty as before. Samuel had professed that he had fallen in love with her and had nearly pestered her to death to repeat their encounter. Three times, she had agreed, and was sad to say that each had been a repetition of the time before. Samuel would quickly satisfy himself and leave her empty.

After that, Molly had decided not to give in to her urges so readily. There had been several opportunities with some promising men, but she was too convinced that all men wanted only one thing, whether they were married or single. It didn't matter that many came to her under the pretense of wanting to help her, a woman alone. Men's loyalties lay in their loins, she reckoned. They only lived to fulfill themselves.

She had virtually given up the idea of finding another husband. For one thing, she needed someone who enjoyed talking, going to picnics and such. Someone who offered a strong shoulder to lay her head on after frolicking. She wanted a man who could be tender and keep his mind fixed on her needs, too. There were a few men out there who were like that, she was pretty sure, but her chances of finding even one who was available were slim.

She pushed the words out of her mouth. "Do you have a family?"

Jory was taken by her abrupt question. Not that it wasn't a fair one. It was the look behind it. A look that caused a quivering to run through him.

"Not a wife and young'uns, if that's what you mean," he said.

"That's too bad. You're a handsome enough sort," Molly said. She got up with a sigh and left him there with his coffee.

That night was filled with anxiety. Little Louisa was eaten up with a fever. She tossed and cried out all during the night. Jory joined the family in their vigil. He, too, was caught up with her life-and-death struggle. An awful fear gripped at him as her little body lay there, racked with sickness.

All throughout the ordeal, the one bright spot for Jory was Molly. He enjoyed her frequent company as she served up his food and kept his coffee cup full. Molly wasn't alone in her kindness. In fact, all of the immigrants couldn't seem to do enough for Jory. They even invited him along on their trek to Oregon.

Jory remembered the similar situation he'd faced a year ago. Agnes Perring's train had seven wagons, while this one had six. Close to the same number of men were traveling in both wagon trains. He recalled John Tallman's relating the story of the brutal murder of Agnes and her party by the Cayuse. He had felt a terrible guilt for not going with them, even though he knew he'd likely have been killed too.

Now he was faced with making the decision again. Agnes Perring had been a younger, smaller woman, but he had developed deep feelings for her. It felt as if he was reliving the same experience all over again—he'd heard it called déjà vu—the way Molly Jackson and her handsome face lay heavily on his heart. He couldn't understand it; she was bossy and outspoken, and there was a bitterness about her general nature. Still, something was drawing his feelings toward her.

Louisa's condition teetered on the brink of danger for several days. They could only force tiny sips of water into her mouth, and it was a common belief that she wouldn't survive the ordeal. But, as one pointed out, even though she didn't seem to be getting any better those first few days, she didn't get worse, either.

Then on the fourth day, Louisa woke up hungry. The fever had turned into a terrific head cold, but people lived through head colds, and the immigrants were elated. Louisa was tired and her voice was raspy, but her eyes took on a new spark and there wasn't any visible sign of damage to her small body.

Jory visited her several times each day. Louisa's own father was usually there, but he was a solemn and quiet man who had only managed to shake Jory's hand weakly in way of thanks. Louisa, as if bonded in some mysterious way to him, would light up when Jory came near. As she gained her strength, she took to sitting on Jory's lap and hugging him frequently.

A good feeling had returned to Jory. He thought such love had been lost to him, but Louisa had brought it back. He couldn't describe it in words, but the sensation speared through his body. He pretended he was young again as Louisa sat and chatted on his lap. He pretended it was Elizabeth and Sarah Jane, or one of their own children, coming to sit on Uncle Jory's lap. It gave him a terrific urge to go back and find his family.

The longing in his heart to return to Massachusetts became overwhelming, but so did the idea of staying with this little immigrant party and joining their adventure to Oregon.

Spending such time with Louisa, Jory managed to catch her cold. It first hit his head, then spread into his chest. It was one of the worst colds he could remember. Molly ordered him quarantined to Louisa's wagon, which he didn't mind, and continued to serve him his meals, which he didn't mind even more.

As the days passed, Jory remained torn between his options. His mind reluctantly returned to his original mission. Surely, the six killers had a great distance on him by now. Still, that didn't change the fact that they were out there, and the chance that they would prey on someone else was likely.

Decisions had always caused Jory grief. Now, he was faced with one of the toughest in his life. Though he wanted to stay with the group, he knew he could never live with himself if he didn't track down the six killers.

Finally one day, he got out of bed and announced to Standing Bear that they must go and find the six men.

The news wasn't received well at all. Standing Bear again mulled over the question that had occupied his mind for so long. Surely, he thought, he could now ask one of these immigrant women to lay with him. He had a particular fondness for Molly. In his mind's eye, he could see her as he had seen the missionary women. But now it was too late. Standing Bear would again have to wait for another white woman to come along.

It was with sadness that he left the camp with Jory.

20

The wagon train woke to a calm, peaceful day. There was a light wind. It was the first time in days that the dark clouds didn't threaten.

As Samson was readying himself for the day, he was approached by several of the travelers. They wanted to take this opportunity to dry a few things out, they said. Their bedding and clothing were still damp and uncomfortable. Besides that, some wagon repairs were needed.

Reluctantly, Samson agreed. He would much rather have gained several miles that day. He'd planned to ride out a way in front, get off by himself, and do some thinking. He needed to get Becky Sinclair and her husband out of his mind. Otherwise, he was going to have a long and painful trip all the way to Oregon.

He ate breakfast with Reuben, then saddled up the mare and explained that he was going to ride up ahead, do some scouting. He still felt the sting of embarrassment, and he wasn't sure how many people knew about his one-sided conversation with Tom Sinclair. Reuben just nodded at him wisely and said nothing.

He'd ridden just out of sight of the wagon train, when he heard the sound of horse hooves behind him. He groaned. He'd been so careful to sneak out of the camp quietly. Willie was the last person he wanted to see right now. He fully intended to tell him so, too. He stopped the mare and turned around, but before he could speak, he saw it was Becky.

She was riding toward him at a hard lope. Samson's

heart raced. Was she crazy? He had figured her to be a dangerous woman, but this was just too much.

Just as she drew close enough to make out her features, he spotted the black eye.

She rode right up to him. "I hope you don't mind, but I need the company this morning." There was a softness in her voice that he hadn't noticed before.

Samson was taken aback. Her left cheek was swollen. Under and above her eye, it was all covered with purple. There was a tiny cut at the corner of her eye that was crusted over. "He ... your husband. He did this to you?"

She shrugged. "It's nothing. I fell off my horse, is all," she said.

"Ordinarily, when folks fall off a horse, they land on the other end," Samson said. "You didn't fall off your horse. Your husband did that."

Becky forced a painful grin. "Don't call me a liar. I guess I know what happened to me. I must look awful," she said as she reached up and lightly touched her damaged face.

"You shouldn't be here," Samson said sternly. "You know your husband came and talked to me last night."

She look puzzled. "You must be joking," she said. "Tom talked to you? About what?" Her face grew more serious.

"Now, what do you think? He doesn't really appreciate you and me meeting in private. In fact, I don't think he wants us talking at all." Samson reached forward, tracing his finger over her swollen face, barely touching her skin. "Still it would take a dog of a man to do something like this." he said. For the first time, Samson didn't have that little quiver in his voice when he spoke to her. Gone was the guilt and anxiety. His face was serious. "Look," he said, "you best ride on back. I'm sorry for what happened to you, but he's your husband. I guess he feels he has the right to protect what's his."

Samson knew his words didn't match what he felt inside. His anger at Tom Sinclair filled him up. He ought to kill the man, he thought.

But no. That would be a huge mistake, and he knew it.

During the long hard months of travel on a wagon train, peace and harmony were a "must." There were plenty of things that could happen, all on their own, to stir up trouble. Fraternizing with another man's wife was just not tolerated. It was an unwritten law, but still everybody knew about it. Samson again felt himself having one of those inner struggles. "Look here," he said, "we're going to buy ourselves a whole lot of trouble if we're not careful. I believe your husband meant what he said, or elst he wouldn't have come and talked to me last night with his friends." He paused and looked softly into her eyes, then shook his head. He nearly choked on his words. "He wouldn't be beating around on you if he didn't care."

Becky laughed. The sound that came out was short and harsh. "I guess I should expect that kind of thinking from a man. A woman gets beat on, so you figure the man must care, huh?"

Samson nodded as he made a point of staring at her battered face. "Yep, I knew he did that to you. What'd you lie about it for?"

"What if he did do it? I didn't think it was any of your business."

"I reckon it's my business if I caused it."

"You had nothing to do with it."

"Not according to your husband. He thinks we've been seeing too much of each other. That's what he said. He's concerned."

Once again the teasing note returned to her voice. A cruel little smile played around her lips. "Tom didn't do any of this because he cares for me," she said. "It was his pride. He was just showing off. Tom has not been a faithful husband to me. He's always preferred the company of his drunken friends." She shook her head. "No, this was just a show he put on to impress them."

Samson felt confused. He couldn't deny the attraction he felt toward Becky Sinclair. Why, if he were ever to have a choice between Becky and any other woman he'd known, the waiting and wondering could stop right then and there. But he also couldn't deny the fact that she was married. And it really didn't matter what kind of marriage she had. Good or bad, she was tied to another man. He took in a deep breath and made what he knew in his heart to be the right decision.

"Well, show or no show, I think you'd best ride back there and stay with the others. It's a long ways to Oregon, and none of us can afford any trouble. We all have to share each others' company for a long, long time." He softened his words a little. "Besides that, you've only got two eyes."

Becky sat there on her horse and looked deep into his eyes. Her face lost its attitude of lightheartedness and spirit. She was suddenly sad, like a person who'd given up hope of ever being happy again. Samson thought he must be seeing the real Becky, and it tore at his heart. Then, without another word, she turned away from him and left.

Once she'd ridden off, Samson felt about as desolate and alone as he'd ever been. No matter how many opportunities life seemed to provide, he just couldn't seem to get things in order. Just when he had the chance to start a new life, in came new problems. And he didn't really feel like he was entirely to blame. He'd had a hard time pushing Becky out of his mind, ever since that first moment he'd laid eyes on her. But he'd tried. He really had. Why was life so complicated, he wondered again. Why couldn't she have been a single woman? That would have made everything so simple. But, Samson told himself, why had all the other events of the past year happened as they did? He sighed and wished he could go back and change it all. Then maybe life would be less complicated. Then maybe he'd be sleeping better at night, without a bottle tucked under his arm.

Samson stayed away from camp all day. He finally returned at dusk. Reuben was leaned up against the wheel of his wagon, while Willie sat nearby. They both stood when Samson rode up. He could see the concern in both of them.

"Dern, hoss, where you been all day?" Reuben asked.

"Just lookin' around."

Samson could tell that Reuben wanted to ply him with questions, but he yawned really big and made a show of being too tired to talk. He needed to think, and he had to be alone to do that. The only way to find privacy was in his own bedroll, with his eyes fixed shut. Reuben and Willie said nothing as they watched Samson crawl up under the wagon and pretend to fall asleep quickly.

He was grateful when the darkness soon covered the earth. He could hear Reuben and Willie talking in soft voices over the campfire, but not loud enough to disturb his thoughts.

Another cold day greeted them. After a fairly tolerable day previously, everybody woke up to wintertime temperatures once again. Samson had spent a fitful night, dreaming and tossing himself awake. The cold wind blew in just a little after three o'clock in the morning, rousting many from their beds early. Calves were bawling, and the ewes were crying their misery. People moved around as fast as they could, hurrying to get their families and all of their livestock fed. Breakfast was a bleak affair, as the wind howled out of the east and attacked their campfires.

The wind, in fact, howled all day long. But with it, the travelers found a new energy and sense of urgency. With a strong determination, they moved along at their best speed since departure. They kept a steady pace from sunup to sundown.

By day's end, Samson calculated that they'd made twenty-two miles. It had been a good day for him as well, except for the times when Becky would flit in and out of his thoughts. Which was often. He could see her face everywhere, in every tree, every creekbed, every bush. He would think back to how her voice sounded. He remembered her lovely face, and the sadness he'd last seen in her eyes. Samson was truly thankful that she had heeded his advice and stayed back with the others. It at least gave him a fighting chance to get her out of his mind. That night, he was so tired and hungry, for once Willie's constant chatter and Reuben's observations didn't bother him. On the contrary, they were a fairly effective diversion from thoughts of Becky Sinclair. Not altogether effective, but fair. At least, he thought, he'd made it through one day.

Reuben's offer of a drink of whiskey was tempting, but Samson refused the offer. He had a feeling that drinking might cause him to do something foolish. For Becky's safety, he knew he didn't need that.

The long cold day and the bitter wind seemed to have the same effect on everyone. The camp went to bed early that night. Even the livestock were worn out from the day's pace. There, among all the people and animals, the place where they'd made camp became strangely quiet and still. Samson felt grateful for the small pleasure.

21

The lower temperatures lingered like an unwelcome guest. Black clouds reappeared and settled overhead, as if they had spotted the wagon train and decided to move to that exact spot. The immigrants began to mumble and comment that they surely couldn't have much worse weather to deal with.

So many people were sick, and there was still so far to go. Becky was tending to a little brother and sister, ages five and three, who belonged to the family in the wagon behind hers. It was funny, but she hadn't even been able to make their acquaintance before the children went down ill. Over their sickbeds, their mother had absently told her that they were from Delaware and that their name was Johnson. The babies had suddenly become sick with fever after the first rain. Noticing that Mrs. Johnson had seven young ones to tend to, Becky had offered her assistance, which was readily accepted.

Her husband, Tom, was in a surly mood. He brooded all through breakfast, barely speaking. He would glance in annoyance at the wagon, but say nothing, just to let Becky know how unacceptable it was to have two strange, sick children there. Finally, he got up to leave the camp. He had lost some cows during the night and had to go out to retrieve them. As he mounted up to leave, his only words to Becky were to be sure those damned children were gone when he returned.

She knew he wouldn't be back before bedtime, if he returned that night at all. Tom was in one of his moods, and finding the cattle was just an excuse to go away from her. He'd started running off soon after they were married, occasionally at first, then more and more often over the years. Back in western Virginia, he'd sometimes been gone for days at a time. She eventually grown used to his absence. In time, she'd even grown grateful for the days when he'd run off with his men friends to drink and gamble. She'd learned to relish the peace and quiet.

This morning, she knew he was off to do some hard drinking. Joseph Mellner had been to their wagon just the day before and talked to Tom about the evils of whiskey. Tom had just hurled insults at him, until Mellner went away and Tom fell into one of his angry sulks. Becky didn't mind it, much, as long as he didn't take anything out on her.

"You want me to saddle your horse, Mrs. Sinclair?"

It was Jeremy Price. Tom had hired him to drive the wagon and help with the trip.

"No, Jeremy," Becky said as she rubbed a rag over three-year-old Claudia Johnson's face. "I'd better ride back here with the babies today. They are so sick." The pain went through her. She'd always wanted children of her own, but hard as she and Tom had tried in those first two years of marriage, she'd never been able to conceive. Though she didn't think about it much now, she'd wondered in the early years if her barrenness hadn't driven her husband away from her emotionally. He'd come from a large family with seven brothers and five sisters, all of whom loved to brag about their fertility and dote on their young. Tom always seemed to hate their family get-togethers. He brooded over such talk about children. After that, he'd started to drink more. Then he'd become more and more abusive. Becky had worried herself sick at first, wishing there were something she could do to make him happy. But over time, she had grown cold. She'd had to.

Now, there was no longer any romance in their lives. Their occasional frolic only happened when he was heavy with liquor and forced himself on her. It sickened Becky to have him come barreling in and mount her like an animal, huffing over her with his putrid whiskey breath. She nearly gagged when he tried to kiss her. But she endured it, fearful of what could happen at his angry, drunken hands.

Jeremy stood peering in at Becky and the sick children in the back of the wagon. He was extremely nervous in Becky's presence. When she talked to him, he answered with his eyes flitting about, never once settling on hers. Jeremy had decided that Becky must be the most beautiful woman who had ever lived. He thought about her constantly, and sometimes at night he'd let his mind make up stories about him and her together. It was a dangerous thing to do, he knew, because he didn't dare show any kind of feeling. He was deathly afraid of Tom Sinclair.

"Would you wash out these rags in fresh water?" Becky said, looking at him. "Hurry, please. We've got to make these little ones as comfortable as possible."

Jeremy swallowed hard and kept his eyes glued on the rags she handed to him.

The Johnson boy, Lucas, slept hard most of the morning, but little Claudia tossed about and cried for her mama. They both grew so hot, Becky was consumed with worry. Outside, it was dark. The winds were cold and made an eerie howling noise. Becky washed the children's bodies with the rags, over and over, hoping and praying their fevers would break. She'd heard so many horror stories about the fate of children on these journeys. She gazed down at their small, innocent faces. Her heart yearned for their safety.

When the brief storm came, it was late afternoon. Becky instructed Jeremy to build a little canopy inside the wagon with a few pieces of wood that Tom had brought along. As she expected, the rain still managed to dip and swirl inside. Becky still felt grateful for the extra wood. There had been times when she'd almost tossed the little pile out the back of the wagon; it had seemed like excess baggage. Now, she was glad she hadn't.

She had stayed in the wagon with the children all day. That night, she stepped out to relieve herself and check on Mrs. Johnson and her other children. What she found there only frightened her more. All the other children were still as sick as ever. They were laid out in the wagon, side by side, packed tightly together. A couple of them were moaning lightly, but the other three were too sick and hot to do anything but stare at her with their red, puffy eyes. Mrs. Johnson hovered over them, fetching cloth after cloth to lay on their burning faces. She seemed to be in a daze as to what to do next. Becky's heart cried out for the big, stout woman, whose face was masked in fear like a child's.

"Mrs. Johnson. Are you all right? How are the children?"

Mrs. Johnson looked at Becky. Her face was flushed. She looked sick, too, but it was from exhaustion. She tried to speak, but a single tear rolled out of her eye and down to her trembling lips.

"My babies—" she whispered.

Becky nodded and touched her hand. "It will be all right," she said. It was all she could say. She left the poor woman and returned to her own wagon.

All through the evening and into the night, Becky cared for the little ones like they were her own, but nothing seemed to help. They needed liquid, but were too weak to raise up. Becky opened their little mouths and squeezed water from the rag, drops at a time. Still, the fevers held on.

Sometime before midnight, Lucas fell asleep. He seemed to be somewhat better. At least he didn't feel as hot as he had during the day. He slept peacefully, but little Claudia still tossed about. She would sleep restlessly for a few minutes, then open her eyes and cry out for her mama. Finally, Becky took the small, hot body and held her in her arms. Claudia felt like she was on fire, lying next to Becky.

She must have dozed. Off in the distance, Becky heard a faint voice. It was calling for water. She slowly pulled her eyes open and let them shut again. She felt cold. So cold, in fact, she was shivering. The voice came louder, asking for water. Becky's brain cleared, and she finally realized that the voice was real. It was Lucas, asking for a drink.

It was early morning. Becky blinked the sleep from her eyes and peered through the bright light at the boy. He was lying there, staring at her. In her arms, Claudia felt cool.

Their fever must have broken, she thought as relief flooded through her. Her grogginess lifted.

She smiled at Lucas, and then rubbed Claudia's forehead. It was cool and dry. But something was wrong.

It hit Becky with the force of a heart attack. She shifted Claudia in her arms, tried to rouse her. She shook her lightly by the shoulder. But the eyes were shut for the final time. The lips were still and her tiny chest was no longer heaving for breath. Becky knew the girl was dead, but still she tried desperately to wake her up.

Lucas sat up and watched, wide-eyed, as Becky pulled Claudia's lifeless body so close that their faces were touching. "No, no, Lord, don't let this be," she cried out. Tears ran from her eyes.

Jeremy appeared. He looked into the wagon at Becky and his concerned expression turned to worry. "What's wrong?" he asked.

Becky didn't answer. She couldn't. She didn't know what to do. Her grief was suddenly so powerful, she couldn't move from that spot. It was almost as if she had given birth to her own child, watched the child grow, and then witnessed its death, all in a matter of a few hours. She cried some more and held Claudia against her breast, feeling like a little bit of herself was dying inside, too. It was an awful, wrenching feeling like she'd never had before.

Lucas moved over and laid his head on her knee. "Can I have a drink? I'm thirsty."

Becky sniffed hard. He was well, she told herself, and that was important. She had to be strong for Lucas now. She mustn't let him be scared. Relaxing her grip on Claudia, she reached out and gently rubbed his dark tousled hair. His face felt cool and damp. She tried to sound bright, but her voice was shaky. "All right, honey. We'll get you a drink."

She looked at Jeremy, and he understood the deep anguish that was passing through her heart. "I'll get some water," he said softly, and hurried away.

Samson dug a small grave, and Claudia Johnson was buried. With his knife, he carved out the particulars on one of the boards that had been used for shelter inside the wagon. Everyone from the wagon train attended the simple ceremony. Joseph Mellner read from the Bible and recited a prayer, then led the group in the Lord's Prayer. Mrs. Johnson stood there with her husband, holding a tiny infant in one arm and a two-year-old in the other, both still sick with fever. Slobber ran from her mouth as the tears streamed from her eyes. She tried to join in the praying, but she was crying too hard to speak. Mr. Johnson appeared to be grieving in a quiet way, but his eyes showed his pain.

It seemed that children all throughout the train had taken ill during the night. A strange hush fell over everything, as folks huddled in their wagons, tending to the sick ones. Gone were the adults' constant chatter and the nuisance of the children's shrill shrieks of laughter that seemed to fill the air all during the daylight hours. Instead, the thin, wailing moans of the sick could be heard all along the train.

Becky was glad that Tom had stayed gone all night. But, like an old shoe, he turned up not long after they had buried Claudia. He was full of liquor and oblivious as to what had happened. He just gave a sheepish half grin at Lucas, who sat in the back of the wagon, before he crawled in and passed out.

Becky eyed him. She'd made up her mind to split Tom's skull if he said one word. Later, she was grateful that he hadn't.

The much-needed easterly wind had died down, and the immigrants were left to find other ways of drying out. They pushed on slowly through the damp cold. Becky had offered to keep Lucas for a while, and Mrs. Johnson had been so grateful, she'd kissed Becky on the cheek. Now, as sick as Lucas had been only twenty-four hours earlier, he was up playing. The only reminders of his fever were his chapped lips and chafed cheeks.

Tom had only given them both a cross look before he'd ridden off again. Becky had avoided him and refused to respond to any of his attempts at conversation. When the irritation grew in his voice, Becky hadn't shown any concern. Tom's sulking and brooding were of little importance to her now. It had come to her when Claudia died, like a thought that had been there all along, only locked up like a puzzle. She hadn't understood, before. But with little Claudia's passing, everything suddenly became clear to Becky. Her own thoughts, her own feelings, her own emotions. What they really were. It was obvious that she hadn't loved Tom for years, but she'd always felt it was her duty, her place to make the marriage work, even if it was as hollow as a dead tree. But she wouldn't put up with his ways anymore. She couldn't, even if she wanted to. Life was too short, and she'd already wasted so much of it, feeling alone and desperate.

As the day wore on, Becky left the job of handling the wagon to Jeremy and spent her time playing with Lucas. She tried to keep him from being too lonesome for his family. But Mrs. Johnson had her hands full with the others, and she still hadn't had a chance to pass through her grieving. Becky offered to take care of the other children, but Mr. Johnson politely shook his head. Lucas, he said, could stay.

Becky tried to remember all the little games that she had played as a child. She tried them all on Lucas. Anything to keep a smile on his face. Seeing him happy cheered her up, too.

The passing of time eased her grief and allowed her thoughts to return to Samson. It scared her. Becky couldn't explain what had happened back at the tavern. It made no sense at all that she'd started falling in love with him at their first meeting. Though she had loathed Tom's drinking, it hadn't seemed to matter at all when she had been warned that Samson himself was a drinking man. There was a difference in him, something that she could see, deep down inside, whenever she looked at him. Something that was missing in Tom. It was a core, a center that gave Samson meaning.

Her mind fought bitter battles. She tried insisting that she was just having motherly concerns. Maybe she was trying to save Samson from himself. Maybe, then, her feelings for him would change, and she'd feel nothing.

But there wasn't a shred of truth in it. The fact was, all during those long, cold years with Tom, there had been men who had tried to catch her interest. And, strangely enough for a woman who had never received love from her husband, she had felt no interest at all. She had worried that something must be wrong with her. Why hadn't she taken a fancy to any of the other men? When she did dream about leaving Tom, she had never once dreamed of going to anyone else.

Until Samson. Ever since that day at the tavern, it had taken all of her willpower to think a single thought that didn't involve him. As she had stood, holding Lucas close to her hip and watching Samson dig the little grave for Claudia, she had felt like walking up and putting her arms around him and letting him share her grief. It had seemed like the most natural thing in the world at the time. She had had to grapple hard with herself to keep from doing just that. Only some hidden small speck of reason kept her standing where she was, clutching Lucas in her arms.

She wondered just how long she could hold on to that rationality.

22

The sun seemed to be taking an extended holiday. The sky was a dark gray. Everyone was miserable. Talk was sparse, with only an occasional complaint for conversation.

Samson went about his duties faithfully, though he often wondered what had motivated him to sign on with this train. In a way, he took some solace in everyone else's misery. It gave him a chance to be alone, without having to talk about subjects that he cared little to converse about. Not that Willie didn't talk his ear off, but after a while the cold had even Willie subdued.

The train moved slowly during those dark days, but even in the midst of such terrible weather, it soon took on its own gait. The immigrants, like it or not, started to become more proficient at digging themselves out of muddy creekbeds and tending to their chores. The trail was a hard life at best. One either learned it quickly or got swallowed up in it.

Even though Samson had little, if any, regard for most of the immigrants, he was starting to appreciate their toughness. Even as axles would break or canopies would blow off and be hurled away by the wind, even as wagons would occasionally be completely blown over, they rallied. No matter how big or small the problem, the immigrants would quickly fix it and move on without a word.

Feed for the stock was becoming increasingly scarce. The immigrants went to feeding them flour and meal, something Samson knew would come back to haunt them later. In his travels last year, he'd noticed there had been corn for sale along the way. So far this year, none was to be found. Small creeks that had given little challenge last year were now crested over and full. Wagons and people alike were challenged at each crossing.

After a spell with scarcely any dry wood for campfires and everyone chilled to the bone, the worst threat of all hit the group. Sickness had first struck the children and old folks, but now it began to spread like a grass fire throughout the train. Strong, healthy folks went down with colds and high fevers. In some cases, whole families were laid sick. And the black, nasty skies showed no signs of breaking up.

Samson had talked with Mellner and some of the other leaders. It was decided that they would push forward. Those who had folks to spare would take over the wagons for the sick families. There was no time to waste.

Samson himself felt lucky. Reuben teased him often that it was all the whiskey he'd drunk, but he seemed to be the only one in the whole wagon train who had escaped getting sick.

Others weren't so lucky. Besides the little Johnson girl, they'd buried two other children. A man named Tillis, who seemed as healthy as an ox, took sick and died. Samson dug their graves and wondered what drove people to uproot their families, to put them in such a perilous position.

But he knew the answer. He remembered his and Nancy's excitement. He remembered how nothing on this earth would have stopped them from seeking a life in the rich Oregon territory.

There was little chance to find fresh meat. Wolves and coyotes were the only living things to be found. Samson, who had killed an abundance of game on his other trips west, managed only a few rabbits, a doe deer, and nothing more. There on the prairie, he saw buffalo bones, scattered about. He knew there would be big herds farther west, but still the sight of those whitened bones gave him a depressed feeling.

At night, more guards were posted over the livestock, as

several of the sheep had already been scavenged by wolves.

Samson saw very little of Becky during those days. He'd hoped it might give him some relief. But it didn't. He still thought about her, night and day. He could handle his emotions, most times, but on those few times he saw her, caught a glimpse of her, an overwhelming feeling would hit him.

Near the end of the week, the sky turned a lighter gray. The air felt heavy with moisture and the threat of sleet still persisted, but Samson thought he could feel a change coming. True or not, he felt his hopes rising.

One day, he was riding along by himself, with the wagon train a mere speck in the distance behind him. He was thinking about Oregon and Becky Sinclair and feeling optimistic about the weather, when something caught his eye.

There, up ahead and directly in Samson's path, sat a lone, silver-haired figure atop a beautiful white horse.

Samson squinted and tried to better focus his eyes. The man seemed to have appeared right out of the air. Even with the darkened skies, Samson could see for miles, out across the prairie. He'd seen no sign of the rider before.

He felt a chill. The hair on the back of his neck bristled up. Maybe he'd been there all along, he thought. But how could that be? Samson had noticed the tree, miles back, and there hadn't been any horse with a man sitting under it. He was sure of it.

He glanced back at the wagon train. It was still there, still real, lumbering slowly toward him.

He turned back around. The man was still there, too. Sitting there on his horse, unmoving, watching.

Samson's hand absently fell on the stock of his rifle. He rode on forward, his eyes never moving from the man.

There was something vaguely familiar. As Samson drew nearer, he could see that the man was bare-chested, yet he didn't appear to be cold. His long white hair lay across his shoulders as a woman's does when she lets it down. And the eyes, steady and serious. Unblinking eyes.

Samson's chest flushed with heat. The hair stood up all

over his body. Recognition came upon him in a split second. He'd seen this man a hundred times before, but only in his dreams. *Why, I must be asleep right now,* he thought, though he surely knew the difference between being awake and asleep. He looked skyward, then all around. He touched his horse, anything to reassure him that he was indeed awake.

Samson's mare walked straight up to the magnificent white stallion and nuzzled at its nose. The stallion snorted softly and returned the favor.

But Samson wasn't paying any attention to the horses. He was gazing into those deep, penetrating eyes. He knew those eyes so well from his dreams. They were the eyes that had robbed him of sleep and caused countless hours of pondering. Now, they gazed right back, and Samson felt weak and powerless.

He waited for the man to speak, but nothing was said. Samson wanted to say something, to ask a question or two, but he couldn't force his throat muscles to work. Unlike in his dreams, his hand and arms worked just fine, but his voice was frozen shut. Meekly, he sat there like a schoolchild waiting for his teacher to speak.

Several long, silent minutes passed without a word exchanged. Nothing else in the world seemed real, outside of that small circle under the tree. The old man gazed unblinking at Samson, his weathered old face still strong and his hands steady.

Samson knew this was not completely real. At least, there was no logic to what was happening that he could figure. Still, he noticed that his fear had gone. Instead, a nice peaceful feeling had come over him.

Finally the old man's eyes looked past Samson into the distance behind him, back toward the wagon train.

"It is good."

The old man's voice was as smooth as the world's finest silk and seemed in perfect harmony with Samson's hearing.

Samson swallowed hard. The paralysis still had hold of his throat. He didn't know what he would say, even if he could speak, but he felt that a few words were in order. He opened and closed his mouth a few times, then gave up trying to say anything.

Once again, the old man's eyes fell upon Samson. Even under the gray sky, they sparkled. He spoke again.

"Take the people to the rich, fertile land. In their harvest, you will find your own."

The old man beckoned toward the wagon train, again looking past Samson.

Samson turned around to study the wagon train. Suddenly, he felt his voice relax. He could talk. "If you mean taking them immigrants to Oregon, I've already agreed to it," he said politely. Glad that he could finally converse with the old man, he turned back around.

"Who are—"

The old man was gone. Samson looked all around, even rode behind the tree. Again, the hair bristled all over his body. A tingling went through his scalp and down his back. In his chest, Samson could hear his own heart pounding. He instinctively looked down at the wet ground. But he knew what he'd find. There wasn't a track to be seen.

23

Dick Carter was as unpredictable as the weather. Most often, he was moody and standoffish, but there were other times when he liked to stand up and voice his opinions. It was as if he'd been bottling up words for a while and had to spill them out on occasion. He played the orator, starting off slow and measured, then building up the excitement until his speech became rapid and his voice so high-pitched that it took on the tones of a woman.

Today, he was in a talkative mood. They had killed a buffalo nearly a week before, and had settled down for a spell to enjoy the meat before they headed on. Now they were just finishing up the latest meal, and Carter had taken a stand on a cluster of rocks and was enjoying being the center of attention. Foremost on his mind was how they could make enough money to retire. The more he talked, the more he stirred himself up.

It seemed to Calvin that the more excited Carter became, the more distraught he felt himself. He'd been hoping that they would all grow tired of this western venture. Maybe then they could take what booty they had and return to Ohio, or better yet, go their separate ways. Listening to Carter, though, Calvin knew it was just wishful thinking. There was no doubt that Carter had more hold-ups in mind for the future, and Calvin would be a part of them.

Suddenly, the monologue was interrupted by the sound of a horse's hooves. Sal appeared. He'd left the day before to scout around, and was just returning. Carter often sent

Sal ahead, since he was the best horseman and finest shot in the group. Even Dick Carter admitted that fact.

Sal rode up in the middle of Carter's oratory and pulled his horse up short. His face was flushed. "Boys!" he said as he dismounted.

The interruption irritated Carter, but Sal didn't seem to notice.

"We've hit easy pickin's!" he went on. "About eight miles north, maybe twenty miles east of here. There's a little group of immigrants, six wagons. Been camped in the same spot for a few days. Just sittin' there. Got some fine lookin' females among 'em, too."

Dick Carter stared hard at Sal. "You ain't tellin' us nothin'. Shit, there's immigrants all along the trail."

"That may be so," Sal countered, "but all we've run onto is great big outfits that's too big to mess with, and only a couple travelin' by themselves. I'd say this here is easy pickin's," he repeated. " 'Sides, that ain't all I know. I run into a feller that told me about another train, thirty miles or so east of here. Got more'n seventy wagons."

Carter still looked steamed over Sal's breaking into his talk. Whatever excitement he may have felt about Sal's news, he didn't show it. He stared in silence as Sal turned to the rest of the men, hoping for a little more interest from them.

Jimmy Rice began to ask all sorts of questions. Davis Martin's eyes lit up, but he kept a leery eye on Carter and said very little, lest he show too much enthusiasm.

Calvin kicked a stone into the fire and cussed under his breath. He couldn't hide his irritation at Sal for bringing up this new opportunity for more robbing and, possibly, more killing. Ever since Little Larry's death, there hadn't been any discussion at all about killing and such. Even though that didn't mean much with this group, Calvin had hoped maybe they were all growing tired of their adventure together.

"Well, what do you say?" Sal said directly to Carter. "That little bunch o' wagons is just sittin' there, ripe for the pickin's."

Carter scowled at him. "That's just like you to think of

the small money. That's what's wrong with all of ya. Why, if it weren't for me, you'd all just stumble through life." He paused a moment to let his insults sink in. "But," he went on, "that big train's got to be loaded down with treasure. We'll go after that one."

Sal looked around at the group and said, "I don't know, Dick. We're down to five men. And that man said there's at least seventy, maybe even eighty wagons!" He shook his head. "That's too many guns to go up against."

Carter clearly didn't like Sal's questioning his authority. "What's wrong? You scared, Sal?" he sneered.

Calvin looked up at the two men for the first time. Though Carter was mean as a snake, it was a rare thing when he and Sal exchanged hostilities. They almost seemed to share a mutual respect.

Sal said, but with less authority than Carter, "I ain't scared, Dick, and you know it."

Seconds passed as the two men stared at each other. "We'll see," Carter said. "We'll stay here tonight and leave at first light in the morning." He walked back to his solitude.

Calvin awoke long before daylight. He was surprised at the stillness of their camp. Someone had added wood to the fire, and its steady blaze felt good. He looked around at the others, sleeping soundly. Why, they were easy pickings, he thought, lying out here with nobody on guard. He could see the silhouette of Carter, still sleeping soundly off by himself. Calvin grew suddenly bitter at his arrogance. He wished he had the nerve to bash Carter's head in. *Why, the man must be crazy,* he thought. *Trying to overtake a big wagon train would be next to suicide.*

As Calvin sat there feeling sorry for himself and worrying over his terrible situation, he did as he had so many times before. When life seemed hopeless, he let his mind drift off into a daydream.

He thought about the Indian woman that he'd envisioned so many times, sitting on the big horse with her bare legs. She stared off into the faint glow just over the horizon, then turned her face toward him.

As he sat in the predawn stillness of the prairie, the picture became so real to Calvin, he felt a warmth spread over his midsection. Absently, his big hand started rubbing against his member. Soon, he saw the beautiful Indian maiden slide down from the horse's back. She moved closer, then methodically stripped off her buckskin clothing. She slowly removed her beaded shirt, keeping her face turned toward him. Her breasts were full, her skin glistening. Calvin strained his mind's eye to make out their points. He envisioned them to be large and dark. His breathing grew heavy.

The maiden smiled at him invitingly. She licked her lips. Calvin's right leg started swaying back and forth with his hand's movements. His eyes tightly shut, he pulled his member free from his britches. Teasingly, the maiden put her thumbs inside the waistband of her short buckskin skirt and slowly inched it downward over her hips.

The skirt fell to her feet. She rubbed her hands over her naked body, her smile inviting Calvin to come and enjoy himself.

Calvin's hand moved rapidly up and down, up and down. He groaned and gritted his teeth as a dam began to burst below.

"What in the hell are you doin', Calvin? Chokin' your chicken?" Davis Martin said in a loud voice.

Calvin jumped. His right leg snapped shut like a clam's shell. He growled, but he couldn't stop. He tried to still his hand, but instead it continued as the waters surged.

In spite of his pleasure, Calvin wanted to die, to flow away with the river. A deep flush of embarrassment went through him as the water from the dam inside him spewed forward, a small ripple sizzling as it shot into the campfire. He gasped. The Indian maiden, who had stood there so beautiful and inviting, disappeared.

"What's going on?" Sal said, as Davis Martin broke into wild laughter.

"Hell, Sal! Look at Calvin! He been sittin' here, chokin' his chicken, and I think he mighta just kilt it!" Davis roared.

"I'll be damned, Davis! Is that somethin' to wake everybody up about? Chokin' his chicken?" But before he could finish, Sal, too, was laughing.

Calvin was so ashamed, he wished he could find a rock to crawl under. In fact, if his rifle had been lying beside him, he swore he'd be putting it right up against his own face and pulling the trigger. He looked around for it. It was leaning up against a rock, and he'd have to get up from his bedroll to fetch it. Miserably, he hunkered down where he was and let the others have their laugh.

He cursed himself for his own stupidity. Calvin had taken to fantasizing about the Indian maiden a long time ago. He'd almost been caught several times, even by his own mother. It was dangerous, taking such risks, but no amount of thinking had been able to keep him from the pleasures of his dreams.

Even Dick Carter had his laugh at Calvin's expense. "I'll tell ya one damn thing, Calvin. You better keep your chicken chokin' to yourself. I don't know about a man who'd be doin' such a thing with others present. You better not get close to me at night, neither." He couldn't hold his grave tone any longer and joined the others in hard laughter.

Calvin couldn't bring himself to look at anyone. His skin felt hot from embarrassment. He moved himself off and away from the others. Tears tried to run down his cheeks, but he rubbed them roughly away. He bit down on his lip so hard, drops of blood formed on his lip. He'd never faced such humiliation in all his life. He felt grateful when Carter finally gave the order to mount up.

Apparently, Carter had lost his feelings of bravado. Instead of hitting the larger train, he announced that they would head back east to the smaller group of immigrants.

Calvin didn't care one way or the other what they decided to do. He let his horse trail way behind the others. They'd been riding almost an hour when his cousin Jimmy pulled up beside him.

"Don't let it bother you, Calvin," he said sympathetically. "I reckon we all choke our chicken at times. Even Sal and Dick. Quit frettin' over it and come on up with the rest of us."

Calvin's eyes just barely met his. He was grateful for
Jimmy's kindness, but he couldn't join the others. Not yet.
He only nodded.

Jimmy's words might have given him some momentary
relief, but it wasn't about to last. Much to Calvin's chagrin, Davis decided to keep his shame alive with occasional looks and snickers. Calvin wished he had the nerve
to shoot David, but he didn't. Feeling so low and miserable, he wondered if he had the nerve to do anything manly.

Then something caught his eye. It was off to Calvin's
left, in a stand of trees. Something had moved out of
place. Seconds later, some men emerged on horses.

Indians. At first, there were two, then more appeared
from among the trees. Calvin felt his shame turn quickly
into anxiety. He nudged his horse forward, catching up
with Jimmy.

"Look! In the trees over yonder. Indians," Calvin said,
nearly breathless.

The other men heard, and they all stopped to look.

"What do you make of it, Dick?" Sal said.

Carter stared into the trees wordlessly.

"Looks like more'n a dozen of 'em," Sal said.

"Don't look none too friendly," Davis Martin added.

"There you go! If you ain't a bunch of crybabies,"
Carter said. "Just what did you ladies expect to see out
here, anyway? Jimmy, you ride on over there and see what
they're up to."

Jimmy glanced at him quickly. "I don't know, Dick," he
said. "If they ain't up to no good, I reckon I'd be a dead
man."

"He's right," Sal added.

"Why hell, if'n you're afraid to ride over there, let's
just shoot 'em then," Carter said, irritated.

Calvin started trembling. It started in his hands, and
then he could feel it everywhere. He'd known it would
come to something like this. Maybe, he hoped, Carter was
just agitated and saying words he didn't really mean. He
had a tendency to do that, to spit out threats whenever he
got riled up or confused. But Carter was also an unpredictable sort, given to doing outlandish things. Calvin sud-

denly had the greatest fear that he would be too paralyzed even to aim his gun if Carter ordered them into an attack.

"Aw, lookee here, Dick," Sal said. "I'll ride over a little ways."

Carter didn't answer one way or the other, so Sal loped over toward the stand of trees. He pulled up about twenty-five yards short of the Indians and waited. Shortly, one of the Indians rode out to meet him and stopped a few feet away.

Calvin's heart pounded inside his chest as he watched the goings-on. He was thankful that Carter hadn't sent him and even more thankful to Sal for volunteering. His trembling subsided somewhat over the fact that Sal and the Indian seemed to be conversing and no one had been shot as yet. He was relieved even more when Sal returned.

"Didn't understand a whole lot," Sal said. "But they're hungry. I did get that much out of the conversation."

"Hungry, my ass!" Carter said. "Let 'em go kill somethin', like we did. I hear savages are s'posed to be great hunters." He spit and stared angrily at the Indians, who still sat on their horses by the stand of trees. "Well, I ain't givin' them what meat we got left. Hell, I might be hungry myself in a day or two."

"Look, Dick," Sal said in a serious tone, "I counted 'em, and best I can tell, there's thirteen of 'em. That ain't no odds to be fightin' against over some damn food. Hell, let's give 'em what buffalo meat we got. We can catch up with that party of immigrants and get somethin' to eat there."

Dick Carter shook his head. "Now you're expectin' me to give all the food I got to them savages. I'll give it to 'em all right." He started nodding rapidly. "I'll give 'em that and somethin' else for their dinner."

"Don't, Dick," Sal said. "You'll get us all killed."

"What are they gonna kill us with? Bows 'n' arrows? Hell, I figure we can shoot 'em all easy enough."

"I don't know," Sal said. "Could be bitin' off more'n we can chew here. I say we give 'em the meat and go. Who knows, there may be more of 'em around the next turn."

"By damn, that's just my point," Carter said. "We feed 'em here, and what are they gonna want next time? Our horses?" He spit again. "Go on, Sal. Tell 'em we got food, but tell 'em they gotta come and get it."

Sal looked hard at the dark shine in Carter's eyes. He seemed to resign himself, then turned and rode back toward the Indian.

"Listen up," Carter said to the other men. "Calvin, get on over here. Gather up what everybody's got and put it right out there, on the ground."

Calvin, who just minutes before was wondering if his legs would operate, quickly got down off Knight and collected what buffalo meat was left. It amounted to about twenty pounds. He laid it out on the ground in front of the others, then crawled back atop his horse.

"Jimmy, you know what to do," Carter said. "The rest of you boys be ready. Do what I do."

"What's that?" Davis asked excitedly.

"Just have your gun ready, Davis. You got that, Calvin?"

Calvin nodded dumbly and fumbled for his gun.

"Tell you right now," Carter went on, "you two better not mess up, 'cause if them Indians don't kill ya, I will."

When Sal and the Indian started toward them, the others slowly pulled out from among the trees and followed. Calvin was shaking so hard that Knight started fidgeting under him. The horse swung his big head around and looked back at Calvin with a wild eye.

It surprised Calvin to see that the Indian was much older than he'd looked from a distance. He was upwind of the men, and Calvin's nostrils took in a foul odor. The Indian sat silently on his horse, looking tired but proud.

Soon the others had ridden up. Their faces were solemn, their eyes piercing and guarded. Still, there was a weariness about all of them.

Sal motioned to the meat on the ground. The older Indian motioned to the others. Two Indians jumped down from their ponies and grabbed up the meat.

"Whiskey," the older Indian said and nodded. He said

something else that Calvin didn't understand, then nodded again and waited.

"You want whiskey?" Carter said with a big smile. He pulled his pistol and aimed it at the Indian's head. "Then take a drink of this!" The gun went off.

No sooner had the Indian been felled than Sal began to fire his gun. Then Jimmy started shooting. The Indians, surprised, started scattering. Most of them headed back toward the trees.

Calvin hesitated a moment. Dick Carter's words rang in his ears. Grimly, he lifted his gun and squeezed off a round, making no effort to aim at anything in particular.

Three Indians lay on the ground. That left ten of them still alive. Carter's voice called out.

"Let's go get 'em!"

He took off with his horse at a run, followed by Sal and Jimmy.

Davis looked back at Calvin. "You comin'?" he asked.

Calvin noticed the uncertain look on Davis's face. He was sure it matched the look on his own, and that angered him more than anything else. "I reckon I am," he yelled. "What the hell do you think?"

They raced toward the trees, firing their guns like wild men. Ahead, Calvin saw Jimmy stiffen in his saddle, then lean forward, grabbing desperately for his horse's mane. Over the sounds of battle, he let out a bloodcurdling scream.

"I been hit, Dick! I been hit bad!"

The Indians had found refuge behind the trees. Suddenly, arrows were whizzing all around them. Several cut through the air on either side of Calvin's head. Sal's horse took two arrows in its rear flanks. It reared and went to bucking, sending Sal flying to the ground. To Calvin's amazement, he came up firing. He turned around and hollered to Calvin.

"Come here, dammit! Give me a hand!"

Leaning low in his saddle, Calvin nudged Knight over to where Sal crouched on the ground and pulled him up behind him.

"Come on, let's get out of here," Sal panted in his ear. "They're gonna kill all of us."

The men all went into a retreat. They raced for their lives across the prairie, while the arrows still came at them. Jimmy barely hung on to the neck of his horse. Calvin and Sal lagged behind as, under the extra weight, Knight began to puff hard. Calvin expected to die any second.

They rode hard for several minutes, then Carter began to slow his horse to a lope. Shortly, he pulled up.

"Well hell! What're we runnin' for?" he said, looking back. "They ain't chasin' us."

Calvin pulled Knight to a stop and turned around. Sure enough, there wasn't an Indian in sight. He let out a deep breath of air and was just about to feel good again, when he noticed the bloody arrow sticking out of Jimmy's back. Jimmy was barely in his saddle, draped over his horse's neck.

Calvin thought of Jimmy's folks. They had been kind and gentle people who loved their only child deeply. Calvin never understood how Jimmy had gotten so wild, the way his daddy doted on him and the way his mama had seemed to worship the ground he'd walked on. Right now, he could see them back on the farm in Ohio, worrying over their son. And here Jimmy was, riding with an arrow in his back.

Sal slid down from behind Calvin and went to Jimmy. He helped him from his horse and laid him on the ground.

"I believe he's done for, boys," he announced. "I think they've done kilt him. Get on down and give me a hand, Calvin."

Calvin thought his words sounded cruel, but he wanted to do just what Sal said. More than anything, he wanted to go and embrace Jimmy. Even though Jimmy had dealt Calvin a lot of misery over the years, they were still blood kin, and that counted for something. The only trouble was that Calvin had wet himself during the battle with the Indians. Even if Jimmy was dying, it was more embarrassment than Calvin was willing to face. He sat there atop his horse, dumbstruck by this new situation.

"Damn it, Calvin, didn't you hear me?"

Reluctantly, Calvin eased down off the right side of Knight's back, keeping the horse between himself and the other men. He stole a glance at them. They were sure to notice. Stiffly, he walked toward Jimmy. It took everything inside of him to make his legs move.

Though Calvin had no desire to die, he would gladly have traded places with Jimmy at this moment and been grateful for the trade.

24

The immigrants woke up to a cold, clear day. It seemed odd to them, and there were mumblings about whether or not some kind of trick was being played. Surely more gloomy gray clouds were lurking over the horizon, waiting for the wagon train to roll in under them. But despite their suspicions, the nice weather held. Their shaky spirits were warmed even more when they came upon a trading post and found fresh corn. Not just a little corn, but a wagonload. They bought it all, enough to feed all the immigrants and the stock. That day they made twenty-one miles.

Becky dragged herself from her bed and listlessly prepared breakfast. She felt tired and melancholy. The Johnson family had rallied back to their healthy selves, and she had finally given Lucas back to his parents. It had broken her heart. The mere fact that she had never even seen the boy until just a couple of weeks before didn't change the huge loss she felt, not having him under her wing anymore. They had spent such a short time together, yet they had experienced so much, going through the death and burial of little Claudia, Lucas's separation from his family, long hard days of travel. A bond had formed between them quickly, and Becky found herself nursing a powerful hunger inside for a child of her own. The day Mr. and Mrs. Johnson came for Lucas, and she handed him over to them, an emptiness came upon her that she could neither understand nor handle. She didn't shed any tears on the outside, but inside she cried like a baby.

Tom awoke in a foul mood. There was nothing surprising

or unusual about the fact; Tom had spent a good part of the past several years in a foul mood. Becky had learned to put up with it, going about her life and preferring to live in her own mind with her own thoughts. Usually, he just seemed to find her presence annoying. This morning, though, there was something different about the way Tom looked at her. It was a purely hateful look that unnerved her.

"Pour me some coffee," he said.

Eyeing him carefully, Becky reached over the fire for the coffeepot. Suddenly, she felt a sharp jab on the back of her thigh.

Tom was leering at her. "You're slower'n an old woman," he said and pulled back his boot to kick her again.

Jeremy jumped up from where he'd been eating his breakfast and moved between them. "Please, don't do that," he said nervously.

In one motion, Tom grabbed his hat and slapped Jeremy across the face with it.

"You shut up and mind yourself, boy, or I'll run your ass all the way back to Pennsylvania."

Jeremy, who had a powerfully deep feeling for Becky, had an even deeper fear of Tom. He retreated like a scared cat and went off away from the wagons. When he'd found a secluded spot where no one could see, he sat down and wept.

He wasn't crying from any physical pain. Tom's hat had only stung him where a piece of rawhide strip caught him in the eye. He wept from shame and embarrassment. He wished he could have stood up and fought Tom like a man. He had a pretty strong idea that Tom would have killed him, or at least broken him up really badly. But that didn't matter. A real man would have tried anyway. In any case, Jeremy knew he didn't have the courage to pursue the matter. So, with great shame, he sat and cried.

Becky paid little attention to Tom and his boot. The kick had hurt a little, but she gritted her teeth and tried to act as if nothing had happened. She wasn't about to give him that satisfaction. If his intention was to rile her this morning, then he could just go and rile someone else.

Tom usually chose one of two ways of dealing with Becky when he was angry. One option was to get up and leave for a while. Maybe he'd show up again that evening, or maybe the next day, or in a week or two. He'd still be angry, but the anger would have simmered down into a brooding mood. Or he might decide to attack Becky with a putrid mouthful of foul words. Today, he chose the latter.

"You been dallyin' with that boy?" he asked nastily.

Becky acted as if she didn't hear.

" 'Cause if you are, you best tell him he's lucky I didn't kill him. Ain't nothing a man hates worse than having somebody sticking their nose where it don't belong, 'specially where a man's wife is concerned."

Becky leaned over the fire to pour more coffee. Tom studied her backside. "Yeah, I imagine you must look awful inviting to a half-wit like Jeremy," he went on. "He's just about that age where a woman's bottom looks more inviting than a piece of apple pie."

Becky handed him the coffee, then backed away from him. Her face looked pinched. "For God's sake, Tom!" she said. "Are you listening to what you're saying? Why, we've known that boy since he was a baby! He's never even said a disrespectful word to me. Besides that, why, he's still just a young'un!"

Tom was taking a drink of coffee when Becky spoke. He listened to her words, heard her voice rise, and grew angrier. The line of reason was crossed. Becky had barely shut her mouth, when Tom's coffee cup went hurtling through the air. Becky tried to jump out of the way, but the cup struck her shoulder and the hot coffee splashed in her face. Startled, she sucked in her breath and the tears that had been held inside all morning started to run down her cheeks.

Her crying only made Tom angrier. Inside, he knew she hadn't done anything wrong, but he could no more prevent his own anger than a man could fly.

"You whore!" he said through clenched teeth. "You can just dry those eyes up right now, 'cause it ain't gonna do you any good. Just 'cause we've known that boy since he was a baby, that doesn't mean a damn thing. Why, I caught him pulling on his turkey the other night when he thought everybody was asleep. That's right! Lying right there under the wagon, right under you. Had his eyes all closed." He gave a harsh laugh. "I'll be damned if that boy's a young'un. I imagine all he was thinking about was you while he was lying under there."

"Tom, please!"

Becky couldn't believe what she was hearing. She couldn't believe that Tom would embarrass Jeremy by telling such a personal thing.

She wasn't stupid, nor naive. She'd noticed Jeremy looking at her. She'd noticed him all swollen on more than one occasion when she went to wake him up in the mornings. But he was just a curious boy, and she knew he was too terrified of Tom ever to be disrespectful.

Tom was glaring at her. "Well, he'd better keep pulling his turkey under the wagon, 'cause if I ever catch him trying to fool around with you, I'll cut that turkey of his'n off. 'Course, I guess if I went to cutting turkeys off, I'd have to cut on that Samson Roach, too."

Becky had tried to ignore Tom and let his ravings just roll on by, but instead his words pounded away at her like hailstones on a roof. He had won, again. Dropping her head, she started to sob, her shoulders quaking.

She felt so weak and tired and hopeless. Through her fingers, with her blurry vision, she saw Tom's hand reach toward her. It was shaking, as if his hand were angry, too. He took hold of her face, squeezing her with his thumb and fingers. They bored into her cheeks, deeper and deeper. She felt his thumbnail cutting through the skin on her ear as he turned her face toward him.

His lips were pulled back from his teeth and his eyes were wild. "Shut that crying up."

Her crying was driving him crazier. Violently, he shoved her to the ground. Becky could almost see the evil force taking over his thinking. She felt like screaming for it to release him, but from the past, she knew that it was there to stay. At least, for the time being.

He stood over her, breathing in short, ragged breaths. "Whore, I told you to quit that crying. Shut up! You want everybody to see you crying like some loony?"

Neither of them was aware that several people had

stopped their morning chores and were watching the goings-on. Suddenly a man stepped forward.

Joseph Mellner had always been a man who believed in standing up for another's rights, no matter what the consequences or the danger. He had been dreading this day, but he had known that it was coming. Tom Sinclair was a dangerous man, to be sure, but Mellner knew he couldn't live with himself if he just stood by and watched something like this happen.

He grabbed Tom in a bear hug from behind. "I'll not have this," he said breathlessly. His words lacked the authority that he had hoped for, but he squeezed even tighter with his arms.

Tom grunted and tried to spin around and pull loose from Mellner's grasp. Both were big men, and strong, but soon Tom's anger won out. He wrenched himself free and punched Mellner flush on the cheek, raising an instant wait.

"I'll kill you," Tom growled. Suddenly, from nowhere, a knife appeared in his hand. He drew back and started forward with it. He would have driven it straight into Mellner's heart, but then he felt something crash into his side, hurling him to the ground. The knife flew through the air, end over end, and fell harmlessly to the earth.

Stunned, Tom tried hard to regain himself. He mumbled that somebody was going to pay. He started to rise up, when a man's foot appeared, slamming him in the shoulder and forcing him down on his back.

This time, he didn't have to wonder what was happening as he looked up into Samson Roach's eyes.

"Stay right there 'til you cool off," Samson warned. The pressure of his foot grew heavier on Tom's shoulder.

"Why, you little son of a bitch! Who do you think you are?" Tom said. He scooted backward, out from under Samson's foot, and got to his feet. He looked at his knife, lying about six feet away.

"I wouldn't advise that," Samson said. "I think you'd best take yourself off a spell and cool down."

Tom let the knife be. He didn't need it anyway. He reckoned he could whip a man no bigger than Samson with one arm. Quickly, he shrugged off his woolen coat. There was a sneer across his face as he removed his hat. He almost looked like he was enjoying himself. The adrenaline raced through him.

His eyes were on Samson Roach as he began to move about. "You've had this coming for a long time," he breathed. He began to roll up his sleeves.

Joseph Mellner had little use for either of them. Most times, Samson seemed to be a fairly decent sort, but nevertheless he drank like a heathen, and Mellner couldn't stand that. Tom Sinclair was just plain evil. Mellner had known men like that, and he'd never trusted any of them.

But the truth was, like him or not, he needed Samson. And though he could see the fire in Samson's eyes, he remembered very well the strength of Tom Sinclair. He had wrestled against Mellner's grasp like a wild animal. He reached up and touched his cheek. It was throbbing. No, he decided, Sinclair was surely about to hurt Samson, maybe even hurt him so bad he couldn't take them to Oregon. And that was a chance Mellner just couldn't take.

He stepped forward and raised his large arms into the air. His face was stern. "Now look here. There will be no more of this, and I mean what I say. I'll not have any fighting." The indignation had returned to his voice, a fact that surprised him and gave him back some of his pride.

Tom Sinclair glanced briefly at Joseph Mellner, then looked around at the crowd. "I don't see how you or anyone else could dare stop a man from defending his wife's honor," he sneered. He motioned toward Samson. "I suspect everybody here knows how he's pawed and chased after Becky. Now, he's gonna get his comeuppance. So, Mellner, if you know what's good for you, and everybody else or that matter, you just stand clear while I give it to him."

Mellner didn't like what was happening. Not at all. He took in a breath and stepped closer to where Tom was standing. He shook his head. "I reckon you'll have to go through me, and I promise it won't be as easy as the last time," he said, not altogether sure of his own words.

An unmistakable click sounded through the crowd. Joseph Mellner turned to see the Tennessean, Ralph Nixon, pointing his Kentucky long rifle at Mellner's chest. It was cocked and ready. Nixon had taken up with Tom several days before, along with another Pennsylvanian named McCord. Trouble had been brewing ever since, and Mellner had known it was only a matter of time. He had dreaded the moment that was happening now. He froze.

"I'll shoot you, old man," Nixon said. He spit tobacco juice, with more spittle dripping into his beard. He grinned at Tom and said, "He's all yours."

As if Nixon and his Kentucky long rifle weren't enough persuasion, McCord came out of the crowd and moved to the other side of Tom, his rifle aimed and ready.

All this time, Samson had let the men do their arguing while he stood back to study the situation. He surely did welcome the opportunity to get hold of Tom Sinclair. In fact, he itched for such an occasion. He'd seen the looks on the immigrants' faces when Tom accused him of being with Becky, and he'd realized then that many believed him.

Samson, himself, had nothing to lose, nothing to gain. But what about Becky? If he were to lay a licking on Tom, it could come back to haunt her. He had no idea what limits there were to Tom's brutality with her. And how would the other immigrants react? He surely didn't want to make her pay for a fight that really didn't involve her at all.

Tom Sinclair was a big, powerful man with an athletic build and a cocksure attitude, but Samson had no intention of taking a licking from such a man if he could help it. On more than one occasion, he'd seen men beaten to death by less-physical specimens than Tom Sinclair. He suddenly wished the circumstances were different. He wished he hadn't drunk so much for so long. But even more, he wished Tom Sinclair didn't exist.

He took on Tom's sneering gaze and matched it with his own. "Now, lookee here, Sinclair," he said. "I've got no quarrel with you, and you're wrong about your wife."

"Shut your mouth," Tom snarled as redness crept up his face. "Everybody here knows how you've eyed her, like some big prize. We've seen you ridin' off together. You ain't foolin' nobody," he added, his anger rising.

Samson stood stock-still, glaring calmly back. "Part of

what you say is true. We have talked. But that's all. Now, let's just leave it at that."

"I've seen your kind before," Tom went on. "Men with bad reputations. They walk around, all full of themselves, like they're some kind of evil mean. Until they face someone that's just as mean as they are. Or worse. Then they wither away like dying flowers. Well, Roach, you ain't gonna talk yourself out of this one, 'cause you just met somebody meaner. All that matters now is I'm gonna whip your ass and whip it good."

Before he'd finished talking, Tom suddenly stepped forward with his left foot and threw a right from way down in the country. He put every muscle he had behind it.

But his hand never connected. Just as Tom had taken his step to throw his lethal right-handed punch, Samson let go with a kick that startled every pair of eyes in the crowd. His right foot left the ground and went higher and higher in the air, over his head, and caught Tom Sinclair flush on the chin. Tom's head snapped back and he fell to the ground with a terrible thud, as if he'd been hit by a heavy club. He lay there, looking surprised and befuddled.

The immigrants' eyes widened and people gasped with both excitement and disbelief. Some looked scared, but no one backed away. If anything, they crowded in closer.

Samson stepped over Tom, whose glassy eyes tried to focus on his attacker. With blazing speed and an uncanny accuracy, Samson unleashed a left-right-left. Tom Sinclair was out cold.

McCord had raised his gun and held Samson in his sight. Samson wasn't even looking at him. But McCord couldn't pull the trigger. Something in the man's actions had terrorized him all the way to his heart. He hovered there a moment, then slowly pulled his finger back from the trigger. His breathing was heavy and his eyes wide. He shook his head and lowered the gun to his side.

The unexpected turn of events and the unbelievably quick dispatch of Tom Sinclair at Samson's hands distracted Ralph Nixon to the point where he'd forgotten about shooting anybody at all. He stood there, with his mouth open, watching until Tom was done for. He stared at Tom a moment, then seemed to realize what had happened. Quickly, he yanked the Kentucky rifle to his shoulder and had Samson dead to rights, not ten feet away. Another voice spoke.

"I knew of a chicken once that lived three weeks after his head got cut off. But you know what, hoss? I ain't never knowed no man that lived without his head for more than a blink of an eye. Oh, his body might jerk a bit, but he's dead, right away, once his head's gone."

Reuben Cook was behind Nixon, reaching around his neck and grabbing hold. One hand held a razor. He edged the sharp blade up close, tight against Nixon's Adam's apple, and said, "Just twitch wrong, and I'm gonna show this crowd just how a man dies without his head."

Nixon's rifle fell to the ground, but Reuben still held on to him, just for fun.

Samson slowly backed away from Tom Sinclair. He wished the man had more fight in him, because Samson still felt a lot of fight inside himself. He'd tried to avoid this, but he guessed he'd known all along that it was impossible to avoid. Now that it had happened, he wanted more. He wanted the no-account to get up and try his mighty right-handed punch some more. More than anything, he wanted some of Tom's blood for the black eye he'd given to Becky.

Becky, he thought. Anger and frustration filled him. He bit hard on his bottom lip, causing it to turn white under the pressure of his teeth.

By now, every immigrant in the wagon train was there, still crowded tightly around. The latecomers were so far back, some couldn't even see what was happening and had to ask others to relay what had just been done or said. Those who had seen still carried looks of disbelief. Many stared at Samson with a new kind of respect.

From amongst the crowd, a man's voice was heard.

"Just goes to show ya, you can't always bet on the big dog."

25

As it happened, the little train of immigrants that Dick Carter was so anxious to seek out and plunder found him first.

Jimmy was badly wounded. He was surely going to die, in everyone's estimation. Calvin was making himself sick, worrying over whether Dick Carter was going to make him shoot Jimmy, too. It had been bad enough having to shoot Little Larry, but there was something extra disturbing about killing your own cousin. He was glad when Davis Martin called out that wagons were approaching. They all got up to watch.

A man on a horse was out ahead of the train. He saw the men and rode toward them. When he had gotten close, he noticed Jimmy.

"By damn!" he said. "Looks like that feller's in bad shape." Then he saw the arrow, still protruding from Jimmy's back. His face turned pale. "Indians? Good God," he said, unable to pull his eyes away from the arrow.

"That's right," Dick Carter said. He stepped closer to the man and watched him warily. "We were attacked. Them savages got Jimmy here and killed Sal's horse. We sure could use somethin' to eat, and maybe some doctorin' for our friend, here."

"Certainly, of course."

The man, who gave his name as Noah Bayh, rode back to the train and led the wagons to the men. The immigrants welcomed the gang with open arms. A tall woman immediately stepped forward and introduced herself.

"My name's Molly Jackson. Reckon you can put him in my wagon, right there."

She directed them to lay Jimmy down on a blanket, then looked him over.

"When did this happen?" she asked, without looking up.

"A few hours ago," Sal said.

"What in the world were you boys thinking?" Molly said with an air of sarcasm. "Surely you weren't gonna just leave the arrow in there?"

"We didn't figure he was gonna make it," Sal said weakly.

Calvin just nodded dumbly, wondering himself why they hadn't at least tried.

Molly's forehead wrinkled as she cut away Jimmy's shirt and looked him over. There were beads of perspiration all over his face. His eyes were only half-open, and he stared off somewhere in the distance. He was breathing heavily through his mouth as blood rose up between his teeth.

"This isn't a good situation, but that arrow's got to come out. What we need is a doctor, but there's none here. I got a brother-in-law who's a doctor and I helped him some." She paused to examine where the arrow was lodged in Jimmy's chest. "That arrow goes right through this poor boy's lung. When we pull it out, the lung might fill up with air and kill him. But, I reckon that's a chance we have to take."

With hands as big as most men's, she touched the tip of the arrow that protruded from Jimmy's back. "We're lucky it went through," she said. "Otherwise, we'd have to push the tip on out. First thing we're gonna do is break the tail off here at his chest." She looked at Sal and Calvin. "You look like pretty strong fellas. You two hold him still."

Quickly, Molly grabbed hold of the end of the arrow and snapped it off. That done, she laid the palm of her hand against the stub. She looked at Dick Carter. "Now, when I push, you pull on the other end."

Carter glanced at her, then looked at Davis and motioned for him to do it.

Davis's eyes went wide. "I-I-I don't know, Dick. I ain't never done anything like this," he said.

"He's my kin," Calvin spoke up. "I'll pull. Davis, you hold him still. Is that all right, ma'am?" he said to Molly.

"Lord a mercy, it don't matter to me," Molly said. "Long as somebody does something." She looked at Calvin. "Take a few deep breaths, then we'll do it. I'll get it started, and all you hafta do is pull."

Before Calvin could even think about what he was doing, Molly nodded and pushed hard on the arrow. It came a little, and Calvin started pulling.

"Now!" Molly said. "Pull hard. Try to get it out as straight and as quickly as possible."

Calvin pulled harder. He was surprised at the effort it took. Sweat began to drip from his forehead, stinging his eyes. Finally, the arrow came out. He looked down at Jimmy, whose eyes were still only half-open.

"He's out," Molly assured him. Immediately, she cleaned and covered the entry and exit holes.

"What's gonna happen to him?" Calvin said in concern.

Molly looked at Calvin and forced a smile. He was so young, she thought, with his cheeks still somewhat chubby. She studied his chin. He didn't even shave yet. There was a tenderness about Calvin that she didn't see in the others.

"Only time will tell," she said softly. "He could bleed to death. Choke on his own blood. But there's a funny thing about the lungs. Sometimes, they have a way of somehow stopping the bleeding, better than any other part of the body can do. Unless he's had a blood vessel busted. Our biggest worry right now is if too much air gets in the lung. That could squeeze the heart off."

She finished bandaging Jimmy, then looked again at Calvin. He was staring down at Jimmy with such a sad expression, Molly reached out and touched his shoulder. "Only time will tell," she repeated. "He can stay here as long as need be. Why don't you get somethin' to eat? I'll stay here and watch him."

Calvin nodded and left the wagon, promising to come back shortly.

Molly studied the young man who lay there, near death, in her wagon. Something was eating away at her. It wasn't the fact that he was there, nor was it the fact that Indians had done this to him. She thought back to what Jory had said about the six men he was chasing. They had murdered an immigrant family. It was strange, but here were five men, out on horseback, with no families and no provisions. Five men, and one was wounded. Maybe one of the six men had been killed by the Indians in the same raid. She wondered if the chubby-faced one would talk to her. She'd try.

She turned away from the sick man and went to her trunk. She'd carried it with her all the way from Virginia and it was precious to her. She bit her lip as she looked inside. There lay all of her life's possessions. Not much to show for fifty-three years, she thought.

A baby quilt lay on top. She reached down and took the soft material in her hand, squeezing it gently as she pulled it to her chest. When she lifted it, a tiny bootee fell out onto the floor. Molly swallowed hard, trying to force back the lump. A sharp pain pierced the back of her throat. It seemed like all she had left in life were the memories of dead babies. She picked up the tiny bootee, lifted it and the blanket to her lips, and cried silently.

Her babies. The bootee had belonged to Seth, her youngest. He had been born premature and had hung on to life for three weeks. Now all that she had left of him were the bootees. Jonathan, her second born, had been a chubby little baby with big features like her own. He'd taken sick just before his first birthday and died. She had been especially close to Helen. Her only daughter had been a pretty little girl, Molly remembered, and headstrong like her mama. But of all her tragedies, it was the death of her oldest, Clement, that had been hardest for her to bear. She'd had him for so long, nursing him through childhood illnesses. He'd been so close to her, so loyal, always with a smile and laughter to go along with it. He had almost made it to adulthood.

Molly could remember like it was yesterday. She had been the one to send him out into the storm to check on the milk cow. She would never get that night out of her mind. When he'd been late in returning, she'd gone out into the night and found him. Lightning had hit a tree that Clement and the cow were passing under, killing them both. Molly wasn't one to harbor guilty feelings, but she couldn't help putting the blame on herself. She also couldn't stop the anger that welled up inside, every time she remembered Clement and that horrible night.

A rattling sound snapped her out of the reverie. It was the man, trying to breathe. A bubbly noise came from his mouth.

Molly remembered then why she'd opened the trunk. She dug down deep, past the quilts, clothes, toys, and dishes, until she located the pistol. It was clean and loaded. She quickly hid it amongst the sacks of flour and beans. Then, with one last sweep through her memory, she fixed the precious things neatly back and closed the trunk.

Jimmy hung on that evening and through the night. Molly and Calvin took special care of him, one taking turns while the other rested.

He died early the next morning. Molly was with him. She watched as he took a long, deep breath. His body rose a little as he let out some of the air. He lay still for a second, then the rest of the air left his body.

She was glad Calvin hadn't had to watch Jimmy die. She felt the urge to mother him. He seemed like such a troubled young man. There was a thread of decency in him that didn't show in the others.

Calvin had told her the dead man's name. Jimmy Rice. What about him? What had he been like? Were he and Calvin both nice, innocent boys who had fallen in with killers?

Molly sat next to the body, waiting for daylight. She cried a little, something she didn't allow herself to do in front of others, but it wasn't this strange young man that she'd just met causing her tears. She was crying for Clement, Helen, Jonathan, and Seth. She cried because death always brought her back to their passings.

Molly wiped her tears. She hoped Bertha would bring

Louisa by this morning. It was wonderful that the little girl was up and around again. Not even a hint of the head cold was left. Her fondest times were spent holding Louisa. She'd pretend it was Seth, or Jonathan, in her arms.

At daylight, she climbed out of the wagon and gently woke Calvin.

"He's dead," she said.

Calvin sat up slowly and blinked his eyes. "Oh," he said. "Oh my goodness."

"I thought you might like to come in and have some quiet time with him before the others come," Molly said.

Calvin nodded his head, taking the news in slowly. "Yes, I should," he said. He looked into Molly's face. "He was my cousin, you know." He got up and walked to the wagon.

Molly felt a deep compassion well up inside. "No, I didn't know. Where were you boys from?" she asked.

"Ohio," Calvin said as he stepped up inside.

A long period of time passed, and Calvin still hadn't emerged from the wagon. Every so often, Molly checked in on him. Calvin remained sitting in the same way, staring at Jimmy.

Molly had always been a student of people. It was funny, she thought, how even folks who were total strangers would eventually give away something inside themselves. She had only to watch them long enough.

She could tell that Calvin was scared and lonely, giving the impression of a man who'd just lost his only friend in life. Of course, she could be wrong. It was possible that she was just witnessing a true, heartfelt pain over losing a relative. But she didn't think so. There was a depth to his pain that she could sense, and she doubted if that pain was new.

Calvin sat there for nearly an hour before he got up and came back outside.

"I appreciate your takin' care of Jimmy," he said softly. "His mama and papa would've been grateful for what you did."

"Didn't do anything any decent person wouldn't of

done," Molly said. "Here, I brought you some breakfast. My sister Bertha made it."

Happy for a diversion, Calvin dug into the food. Molly watched him eat.

"So, Jimmy had folks?"

"Yes'm. His mama was my own ma's sister. Jimmy had good folks," Calvin said between gulps. "They were right proud of him."

"You all were close then, I take it," Molly said.

Calvin stopped eating to look at the wagon for a moment. "Yes'm, I guess you could say that," he said. "Jimmy was my first cousin, ya know? We was close to the same age, Jimmy bein' a year younger." He shook his head and sighed. "I know this is gonna grieve his ma and pa to death."

"They'll be hurt. That's a fact," Molly said. "I been through a lot of painful things in this old world, but ain't nothin' compares to buryin' a young'un. And it don't matter how old they are, either," she said sadly.

"Yes'm."

Molly got up and poured Calvin more coffee.

"I'll bet it's a pretty place, Ohio."

"Yes'm. It's real pretty," Calvin said with feeling.

"Tell me about it. What's it like there?"

Calvin stopped eating again, but only momentarily. "Hills," he said. "That's what I remember most. Little rollin' hills and playin' in the creek. We did a lot of that. Me and Jimmy and the others."

"The other men you're ridin' with? They're from Ohio, too?" Molly asked.

"Yes'm. We're all from the same part of Ohio."

"All five of ya, huh?"

"Yes'm."

"Oh," Molly said in a casual tone. "Where are you all headin'? Oregon? California? Or somewheres in between?"

The question seemed to confuse Calvin. For the third time, he stopped eating, glanced at the wagon, then looked off into the distance. He shrugged slightly and said, "Oregon, I guess."

"You mean, you boys just took off from Ohio without even knowin' where you're goin'?"

Calvin hesitated with the last bite of food, started for his mouth, then pulled the food back again.

"Oh, we was goin' to Oregon, all right," he said.

Molly stared intently at him. "The five of ya?"

"Yes'm," Calvin said. He pushed the last bite of food in his mouth with his finger and looked down at the empty plate. He was still hungry, and the food was mighty good. He wished he could be a part of this immigrant train. The people were nice, especially Molly.

"There was six of us, once," he said, barely audibly. "Little Larry Hartz, he was with us, too. But he got all snakebit and died."

"Snakebit? Well, I declare! I ain't seen no snakes, and I'm glad I haven't."

"I wish we hadn't, either," Calvin said honestly. Little Larry and Jimmy had been the most kind to Calvin. The fact that both were dead put him into a gloomy state. Of the others, only Sal was apt to show him any kindness at all, and that was only on occasion.

Molly's stomach churned, and a little chill ran up her spine. These were the six men that Jory had warned her about. She was sure of it. The six murderers, and here she sat, with one of them not more than two feet away.

In her heart, she didn't believe that Calvin was a killer, but instincts could be wrong.

She had to warn the others, and she knew she had to do it in a sensible way.

A sudden panic came over her. She felt an urge to jump up and run away from Calvin, to grab up Louisa and hold her in her arms. She wanted to take up her pistol and protect the little girl from these men.

At the thought of Louisa, Molly's sympathy toward Calvin faded into anger. It didn't matter what she thought about Calvin or anyone else. It didn't matter who had done the killing and who hadn't. He was riding with those men. As far as she was concerned, anyone who tried to raise a finger toward Louisa would have to kill Molly first.

Unable to control herself, she blurted out, "Did you all kill that immigrant couple?"

Calvin's mouth dropped open as his face flushed a deep red. He blinked his eyes rapidly. Inside, his heart began to race. "W-w-what immigrant couple?" he stammered.

He knew she thought he was lying. Involuntarily, his body began to rock slightly, back and forth. "Who are you talkin' about?" he asked again.

"Did you kill 'em, Calvin? Tell me!" Molly's jaw twitched as she spoke.

"What immigrant couple?" Calvin repeated. A humming noise started up inside his head. He was barely aware of it and had no control over it. "I didn't kill no immigrant couple."

"I know you didn't, Calvin, but they did, didn't they? The men you're ridin' with. Which ones did it? Was it your cousin, Jimmy? Was it the handsome one, Sal? Or was it Dick Carter? Who killed them, Calvin? Who took the lives of that poor man and woman?" Molly stopped, feeling breathless.

"You must be crazy," Calvin said. "What man and woman are you talkin' about? We ain't kilt nobody."

Molly, her mind full of Louisa and her own dead children, felt even more anger come over her. She gritted her teeth and grabbed Calvin by the shirt over his stomach.

"Look, Calvin," she said. "No one's gonna hurt you. I don't believe you're a killer, but I believe you were with those who killed them immigrants. Look at you, Calvin. Look at you! You look like you've seen a ghost."

Calvin tried to pull back from her. His eyes were wide. "No! You're wrong. Nobody's kilt nobody! It was Indians that kilt Jimmy. We ain't kilt nobody!" His breathing picked up. His eyes darted about.

Molly let go of Calvin's shirt. He was about to panic, and she knew it. She backed off a little and tried to calm herself. "Look," she said slowly and evenly. "You need to think about all this. You done lost your cousin and another man. Who's gonna die next, Calvin? You? What about your own ma and pa? What's it gonna do to them, hearin' that you're runnin' with killers?"

Calvin sat there, silent, but there was a sorrow in his eyes. Encouraged, Molly went on.

"I want to help you, and you've gotta help me, too. Maybe we can help each other." Molly forced a small smile. "Yes. Maybe we can help each other. I know what it's like to be scared, and who could blame you. I promise, Calvin, the other men don't have to know a thing about our talkin'."

Another man's voice cut into their conversation as Sal approached.

"How's Jimmy?"

Molly jumped and grabbed her chest. "You startled me," she said to Sal.

"How's he doin'?" Sal asked again.

"He died, right before daybreak," Molly said. "Calvin and I was just discussin' his mama and papa." She patted Calvin's leg.

"I'm sorry, Calvin," Sal said. "They were cousins, you know," he said to Molly.

Calvin nodded his thanks and stole a nervous glance at Molly. She said nothing.

"If'n we can borrow a shovel, ma'am, Calvin and I will bury him," Sal said.

Molly expected the other two to come along and help bury Jimmy, but they didn't. When she went to check on Louisa, Davis and Carter were nowhere to be found. She inquired and were told that they'd gone hunting with Clark Van Dorn.

Molly waited for the men to return, keeping close to her pistol and an eye on Louisa and Bertha's wagon. She thought about telling her sister, but Bertha wasn't as strong as Molly and was apt to panic, and panic was one thing they didn't need to do.

Once Calvin and Sal had buried Jimmy, Noah Bayh got the wagon train moving again. Molly, whose wagon usually rode second behind Bayh's, dropped back to the fourth spot, just behind her sister Bertha and Louisa. That way, she could keep a close eye on them.

If those men planned to do anything to this train, and especially to Louisa, they'd have to kill Molly first.

26

Samson rode along a mile ahead of the nearest wagon. Willie had protested when Samson had told him they couldn't ride together, but the plain truth was Samson didn't want him, nor Reuben, nor anyone else for company. It was a time that called for reflection and deep thought.

There was something odd coming over the wagon train. It was a mood or an attitude. Samson couldn't quite pinpoint what was going on, and that was why he needed to get off by himself and think.

Something had happened yesterday. It wasn't just the fight with Tom Sinclair. Normally when a fight occurs between two men, they just have their words, take to their fists, then go on their way. Yesterday, though, it seemed as if the whole camp had somehow become involved. It wasn't just a disagreement between two men, or three or four.

Samson felt like a huge split had been formed. He'd heard once about how a person could suddenly start acting like two people. The folks in the wagon train seemed to have split down the middle, too. He could feel it all around him. Some folks still smiled and nodded his way and talked to him like everything was normal as could be. But others had started giving him unsettling looks. Samson could feel disapproval in the way they pulled their eyes quickly away from his. There was a disdainful sound to their voices when they spoke to him, if they spoke to him

at all. The two sides seemed to be evenly matched, both
for and against him.

His two greatest fears in facing off against Tom Sinclair
had been Becky's safety and the immigrants' reaction.
Now, he had to worry about both. He felt no shame for his
behavior with Becky. He couldn't think of anything he had
done wrong as far as she was concerned; he certainly
hadn't let anyone know about his feelings for her. Still, he
understood and accepted the way folks felt about the sanc-
tity of marriage, especially on a wagon train, where everyone develops a special closeness, almost like family.
Samson knew there would be rough days ahead; he saw in
people's eyes what little esteem was held for a man who
would "lure" a married woman away from her husband for
private interviews. And how could they know any better?

An even worse concern was over Becky. Yesterday's
meeting with Tom Sinclair certainly hadn't made her look
any less guilty herself. He wondered how Tom had dealt
with her, after all was said and done and everyone had finally gone away.

No, things were in a pretty bad stink right now. Samson
thought a while longer and decided that his best bet was to
try to stay away from everybody. Maybe he wouldn't be
on their minds as much, and maybe then things would settle down some. Nonetheless, it hurt and confused him that
he now had enemies that he hadn't had before. He couldn't
deny his feelings for Becky, but in truth, he hadn't made
one move toward her, and even though he still cared
deeply for her, he had no intention of doing anything about
his feelings.

At midmorning, Samson rode up on a small band of Indians. There were five of them. He cautiously let them approach and found them to be friendly. Samson remembered
meeting a couple of them the year before. They were harmless sorts of the Pawnee tribe. They were clearly wanting to
do some bartering.

They rubbed their bellies and motioned toward the wagons behind Samson's back. Times hadn't changed over the
past year, Samson thought. They were still begging for
something to eat.

One of the Indians was tall and thin. He was sitting atop a spotted horse that looked too small for him. His long legs dangled off the sides of the skinny mare, almost touching the ground. He made a comical picture as he held up some pelts, laughed, and nodded. All of his teeth were gone, save one right up front. He held up his furs and rubbed his belly.

"You are hungry," Samson acknowledged. From his saddlebag, he gave them what he had, which consisted of three biscuits and some cured ham. He declined the furs.

"You keep 'em," he said.

The Indians stayed with the train all that day. Several people offered them food. Samson tried to warn them not to be too generous.

"Food's scarce," he told them. "And them Injuns are just like strays. Start feeding them, and they'll be at your back door every night. You got something to trade, fine, but you best keep your food for your own families."

Again, he noticed several of the immigrants giving him resentful looks. Around dusk, the Indians left. They were happy and laughing. The tall Indian with one tooth stayed longer than the rest, but finally left carrying more food than the little pony could handle. Samson saw him dismount and walk alongside the animal.

That evening, as he made his usual ride up and down the train, he noticed that the Sinclair wagon had some unusual activity. There were at least two dozen men and women gathered around it. They ate supper together and then spent the evening talking in hushed tones. Samson didn't know what they were talking about and couldn't guess. Reuben had his own ideas.

"You know, hoss, I've knowed men like that Sinclair feller," he said. "Snakes. But for some reason, they always locate people that'll foller 'em around. Every one of 'em I ever knowed was up to no good. If you ask me, I'd say that's the start of a bitter brew over there."

"I didn't ask you, Reuben," Samson said as he lay back with his head against his saddle. He didn't want to talk about it. He'd already discussed it with himself. Inside, though, he knew Reuben was most likely right in his prediction.

"I know you didn't ask, but we got a long road ahead of us, and that Sinclair feller ain't gonna let yesterday's whippin' lie. No sir." Reuben shook his head.

"Just what do you expect me to do?" Samson asked, half-angry. "I'm not the law. I'm just a feller that's been hired to show these people the way. Do you want me to go over there and say something? Is that what you want?"

Reuben wrinkled his brow. He wished Gertie were there right now. His loins had ached all afternoon, and it took considerable effort to push her out of his mind. Funny, but he'd barely thought about her at all until today. Now, it was about to overwhelm him. He wished he'd never said a word about Tom Sinclair, so he could still be thinking about his wife.

"You're right, hoss," he said. "I was just sorta speculating, is all. You want a drink?"

Samson shook his head. It surprised him that he didn't fancy a drink, after all he'd consumed the past year. Drinking had done a good job of helping him dodge life's problems.

But now he just wanted a clear head, to think about Becky Sinclair. He wondered if she, too, was in that crowd of people. Was she a part of their conversations? Had she turned against him, too?

It was troubling for Samson to do such wondering. Right before dark, he pulled out his pad of paper. He sat there a long time with his pencil. Finally, he wrote: "19 miles."

It was a beautiful morning. The weather was pleasant and warm enough for things to thaw. Samson tried to dispatch Willie to the rear, but he put up such an argument that Samson told him to ride on ahead and hunt for deer. He'd seen a couple just before Willie had ridden up. In fact, he was feeling a little mad at himself for not having shot one himself. The pure fact was, he'd been riding along, chewing on a cracker with no thought in the world as to shooting deer. When two fat does had suddenly appeared, it had taken Samson a moment to jerk himself out of his thoughts and reach for his gun. By then it was too late. The wary deer were gone.

Willie was glad to be given such an important assignment. Samson was glad to have the solitude.

They had traveled eight miles when they broke for the midday meal. The weather was so nice, they decided to make camp there for the rest of the day. Everyone needed the time to take care of some much-needed chores. A good-sized creek afforded the women a chance to do their washing. The men turned their cattle out to graze and relax. A blacksmith by the name of LaMunyon from New Jersey shod several oxen and a couple of horses.

Nearly all the children were bathed in the creek, while some adults bathed. To Samson's surprise, some of the ladies walked a way upstream, took off their clothes, and waded in to wash. Except for a few straggly bushes, they were in full view. He was impressed by the immigrants' honor system, as most of the men turned away respectfully. He wondered how such behavior could be passed on to the younger men, until he spotted some of the older boys, planted in some of the straggly bushes, spying on the women. The women seemed not to notice. Samson waited to see if Becky was going to bathe, too, but there was no sign of her.

There was so little time to cook while they traveled that the women took the opportunity to make up large quantities of food for the days ahead. Several boiled big pots of beans. Cobblers and corn bread were made. That evening, for the first time since they'd left Reuben's tavern, they seemed to relax. Gone were the deep lines of strain from the hard cold and icy travel. Mothers played with their young'uns. Three brothers from South Carolina entertained with songs. They had amazingly clear voices and harmonized. Someone pulled out a fiddle and played along. Soon, there was dancing around the campfires.

Samson had climbed up on a little ridge that looked down over the mass of wagons. Outside of the trepidation in his heart over the lines he could see forming for and against him, he could still feel a peace inside himself.

There was a serenity that he hadn't known for a long, long time. Maybe, he thought, he was becoming useful to himself again.

Samson lay on his back, closed his eyes, and listened to the pleasant sounds of the immigrants below him. It brought back memories of Nancy and Cordry. In his musings, Nancy looked the same, but he could see Cordry bigger and heavier, grown taller by the day. In his mind, Samson somehow managed to add the year since Cordry had died. He could picture his son, sitting right there beside him, asking Samson questions that little boys only asked their daddies. A longing came over him and a lump formed in his throat. His daydream became so real, Samson caught himself reaching out and patting a rock that lay next to him. In his mind, it was Cordry's head that he touched so lovingly and gently. He tried to swallow the lump, but it was useless.

He let the tears come. They ran, unchecked, from his eyes and down into his hair. He looked up at the wide, expansive sky. It made him feel small and suddenly very alone.

The old, familiar urge for a drink came over him. It was times like these when Samson felt powerless and nearly desperate. He knew he wouldn't make it through the night without the soothing oblivion that whiskey gave him. He sat up and rubbed his eyes, then saw the silhouette standing directly in front of him.

The flowing white hair lifted and fell gently in the breeze. Samson was gripped with fear. Was he going crazy? Even though the old man seemed real to him, he had always appeared in Samson's dreams. Samson knew he was awake. He was sure of it. Was he going crazy? Then the figure spoke.

"It's a good thing I saw you walk up here before dark, otherwise I might never have found you," Becky said.

Samson blinked and rubbed his eyes. He jumped to his feet. "What are you doing here?" he asked, ashamed that she might see his tears.

"It's a free country," Becky said in her own independent

way. It was a trait that scared Samson, but that he also found oddly appealing.

"Becky, don't be crazy," he said, not unkindly. "I'm afraid of what might happen to you if you're seen with me."

She stepped toward him, and he looked quickly all around them.

"I don't care anymore," she said simply. "Haven't you ever been at a point where you don't care anymore?"

In the dusky light, Samson could just barely make out her features. Moonlight glinted in her eyes, and they sparkled. *What a question,* he thought.

He could certainly understand someone giving up and not caring. That was exactly what he'd done. He knew what it meant to see no tomorrows in life, and to give them no thought. He'd accepted that about himself, once, but this was Becky talking. Samson could see her dilemma more clearly than he could accept and understand his own. Folks like Becky Sinclair shouldn't have such depressing thoughts.

"Why in the world did you come on this trip?" he asked, surprised by his own question.

She walked around him and sat down next to where he'd been sitting. She stared at the same things he'd been staring at: the encampment, the immigrants. Their voices and laughter drifted up to them, sounding thin and weightless. Scattered fires flickered in the night breeze.

Without moving her eyes from the scene below, she said softly, "To tell you the truth, I can't answer that. Oh, I thought I knew, at first. Maybe I hoped things would get better for us. But some things just never do change. . . ." Her voice trailed off.

Samson had a terrible urge to sit down beside Becky and pull her body close to his. In the pale light, he could see her biting down on her bottom lip. Her misery was becoming his own misery, and he knew that was the worst thing that could happen. He'd never been apt at dealing with his own situation in life. How could he expect to help anyone else? Desperately, he wished his thinking was more clear. He wished he could think of something magical to say to her. But there was nothing to be said. Instead, he turned his back to her. "You'd better go. Someone's sure to miss you."

"Why?" Becky asked, her voice trembly. "I don't really think anyone cares."

"You're wrong on that one," he said, remembering all the unfriendly stares he'd gotten from the immigrants after his fight with Tom. "Oh, they'll notice, all right. They'll notice that we're both gone. People are like that. Some people spend their whole lives worrying about what others are doing."

"Do you want me to go?"

Samson turned around. "Yes and no," he said truthfully.

She was looking up at him with such a longing, it shook his senses. All of his thoughts about what was right and wrong started to backslide. Reason began to flee from his thinking. A selfishness came over him. He shook his head. "This is crazy. I mean, we both know that this can only lead to a lot of problems."

She stood up and came near him, so close that her face was not more than a foot away from his own. He felt her sweet breath when she spoke.

"I'm attracted to you," she said.

Samson was taken aback by her boldness. He stood there, his body turning warm and flushed with excitement. He'd thought she was attracted to him, or maybe he'd just hoped it. He'd never been eaten up inside over a woman the way he was with her. He'd pondered over what her feelings must be, over and over since that very first day. It had nearly sent him out of this wagon train, worrying about what it all meant. But she did care. She wasn't just being friendly or bored. She really cared. His voice was quivering. "I know," he said slowly. "I have feelings for you, too. But that doesn't change the situation any. We can't sacrifice all these folks for what we feel between us. We have to think of them. Now, I think you'd better go."

The words nearly hung in his throat. It was the last thing he wanted her to do.

She stared at him for a long time, then took in a deep breath. "I suspect you're right," she said finally.

Becky didn't want him to be right. For such a long time, life had been no more than a living hell. Her marriage to Tom had been a cruel joke, but she had long since come to the conclusion that this was how her life was meant to be. She'd always figured to live out her life, right by Tom's side, accepting his abuse and pulling into herself for what comfort there was to be had there. But Samson had changed all that. He had put a spark inside her.

But there was nothing she could say, really. What good would it do to spill out the feelings that were swirling around inside her? What could Samson do or say that would change things? What could either of them do? As her good sense returned, Becky resolutely reached out and took Samson's hand, squeezing it gently, then released it. Quickly, she slipped past him and disappeared into the night.

Samson stood there, frozen in place and helpless as a schoolboy, unable to stop her. His hand tingled where she had touched him. He stayed there, in his spot on the little ridge, savoring the feeling long after Becky had gone.

27

Samson awoke, feeling no more rested than he'd been the night before, when he'd finally drifted off to sleep. It had been nearly two o'clock before he'd been able to turn his thoughts of Becky into dreams. And wonderful dreams they'd been. Samson tried to remind himself that that was all they had been: simple wishes that showed no hope of coming true. Still, he found a pleasure in them.

He enjoyed his thoughts about Becky all through the morning. Riding at the head of the wagon train, Samson let his mind create visions of her, pretending he was holding her in his arms, her body pressed tightly against his. He thought about what she must look like underneath her clothes, with her long hair flowing down her back. He could almost smell her fragrance and hear her soft laughter.

It was having an effect on him, and a time or two he could feel himself start to swell. These occurrences brought him out of his daydreaming just long enough to realize how foolish he would look if Willie were to notice. Quickly, he'd snap something at Willie, ordering him to ride on ahead or back to check on the wagons. It left Willie a bit confused, but he did as he was asked, only to return a short time later and take right up with his chattering again. For the most part, Samson had learned to block the boy's words out of his mind and keep himself to his own thinking. It worked, until his thoughts would warm to the point where he'd have to send Willie off on another mission.

Samson was just about to send Willie away for the fourth time, when he spotted two men, off in the distance. They were afoot.

Samson studied them for several minutes. It was a strange sight given the fact that the settlements along the trail were starting to become more scarce with each passing day. Samson knew that they would soon reach a point where they saw no settlements at all, and the only human contact would be an occasional trading post or army fort.

There was a weariness in the men's gait. Sternly, Samson ordered Willie to stay put, and put his mare into a lope to meet the two.

Samson rode right up close and stopped. The man appeared disoriented and paid him little attention at first. Then, finally, one man looked up at him with a blank stare. Both continued walking straight forward, until the other man stumbled into Samson's horse.

"Where you fellers headed?" Samson asked, looking them over curiously.

The second man blinked hard and backed away from the horse. Samson noticed then that he was barefoot. Both men wore clothes that were ripped and tattered.

"Could you spare a drink?" the first man said in a ragged voice.

Samson slid down from the mare's back and offered his canteen. The men grabbed for the water as though they had a powerful thirst and drank without speaking.

"Where you fellers headed?" Samson asked again.

The first man paused from his drinking. Water ran down his chin as he looked past Samson at the wagon train. "Turn back, mister," he said softly and gestured over his shoulder. "Back yonder, there's lots of warring Indians. More'n you can count. You gotta turn back quick-like."

"Is that what happened to you?"

"Hundred of 'em, maybe two," the man went on. "There was ten of us. We was camped along the creek." His voice trailed off and he began to weep. "Bean 'n' me, we're all that's left," he managed to say.

"Indians?" Samson repeated with a frown.

"That's right," the man nodded. The water seemed to

help revive him somewhat. He took in a deep breath. "Me and Bean McCloud, here, was off a-huntin', or we'd be dead, too." He took another drink from Samson's canteen. "My name's Ross Gibson. Whole group of us came over from Kentucky. When me 'n' Bean came back, we rode up and found 'em all dead. Our friends and family." He started to cry again. "Some of the Indians saw us and gave chase. Shot Bean's horse from under him. I pulled him up on mine and we rode together. Damn near rode my horse to death. Had to leave 'im back a ways. We're lucky to be alive, mister."

Samson nodded in sympathy. "Well, you fellers are safe now."

Ross Gibson shook his head. "Ain't nobody safe in this forsaken country. Turn your wagons back, mister. Them Pawnee devils will kill all of ya."

"Pawnee? Are you sure?"

"They's Pawnee all right." Ross Gibson said. "I've been through here a couple of times. Ain't had no trouble before, 'cept for some horse thievin' they did three year ago. But it was Smoke. I seen 'im with my own eyes."

Samson started at the mention of the Indian's name. What the man was saying was true. The Pawnee had begged for food and other things, and they had a penchant for stealing livestock on occasion, but they had been peaceful for the most part. Smoke was another matter. Samson had heard tales about the Indian. He'd even looked into those cold dark eyes once himself.

Yes, he thought, he could believe this story about Smoke. Still, it surprised him. He had figured the only trouble they'd possibly have would be with the Blackfoot or Sioux farther on west. Now he felt a chill going down his spine.

He quickly helped Gibson mount up on his own mare, then he and Willie set the barefoot Bean McCloud atop Willie's horse.

Samson gave Willie orders. "Take 'em to Mellner," he said. "Get 'em some food and decent clothes. Then tell Mellner to ride on out here and meet me. Find somebody to look after Reuben's wagon and send Reuben back here with my horse."

Willie nodded and started to leave, but Samson stopped him.

"And listen, Willie. Keep your mouth shut about them Indians. Not a word."

When the three had gone, Samson stood there for a long time, rooted to the spot, letting his mind dance back and forth from one direction to the next. His main priority, he knew, was the safety of the entire wagon train. Still, it was Becky who concerned him the most. Try as he might to concentrate on how best to defend the needs of nearly eighty wagons, his mind kept straying back to Becky. It was a bit unnerving to think that a woman had taken such control over his thinking and feelings, especially under what could be very dangerous circumstances.

He was about to give in to his heart's desire when the old man appeared. Samson looked up to see the soft white hair, flowing silvery and expansive down the aged shoulders. The eyes were filled with a timeless knowledge as they bored into Samson's own. Samson strained to understand the wisdom they conveyed.

The beautiful white horse was prancing about, each movement causing the man's hair to ruffle delicately. Instinctively, Samson reached out to touch the horse's nose, but the stallion jerked its head away.

Suddenly, Samson had the urge to climb up behind the old man and ride off with him. It didn't matter where he had come from or where he was going. He couldn't imagine anything bad ever happening, as long as he was with this strange old man and his white horse.

He tried to speak, but his lips wouldn't move. Instead, Samson tried to speak his mind with his eyes. He was staring up at the old Indian when the sound of horses approaching broke into his thoughts.

He turned to look. It was Mellner and Reuben. When he turned back, the Indian was gone. Again. Samson frowned in disappointment. He grew suddenly angry at the two for interrupting the feeling of peace he'd been enjoying. He longed for more of the comfort that the old man brought to him.

Joseph Mellner was frantic. Even though Samson was in charge, he still felt an obligation to the folks back in the wagon train. After all, he'd been the one who'd convinced so many of them to make this trip to Oregon for a chance at a new life. It was a responsibility he refused to take lightly.

"Indians!" he exclaimed. "What are you going to do, Roach? I don't need to remind you that we have women and children back there!"

Samson looked into Mellner's bouncing eyes and grew more agitated. He'd always considered himself a compassionate man, but he had little use for the likes of Joseph Mellner. The man spent more energy running his mouth than looking for solutions.

"Relax," was all he said.

"Relax?" Mellner's voice rose to a high pitch. He stared at Samson. "Is that all you can say? Why, those two men said Indians killed everyone in their party but them! Is that your plan of action, Mister Roach? To relax?" He shook his head in disbelief.

"I'm aware of what the men told you," Samson said bluntly. "But the truth is, we don't know the whole story yet. Maybe those men done something to rile the Indians." He looked at Reuben. "What do you think?"

Reuben looked thoughtful. He rolled a chew around in his mouth, spit, then took off his coonskin cap and rubbed the sweat from his head. Finally, he said, "Well, I'd say there ain't no doubt the Indians got 'em. We just don't know for sure why. You're right about that."

"You figure they was Pawnee?" Samson asked. "After all, one of them said something about Smoke."

Reuben replaced the coonskin cap on his head. "Pawnee are mostly thieves," he sighed, "but that Smoke is a real turd. I reckon he might've upped his ambitions from thievin' to killin'."

"Why, I've always heard the Pawnee were friendly Indians," Mellner said. "I was told that we only had to worry about the Sioux."

Samson ignored Mellner's remark, but Reuben didn't. He shook his head. "No hoss, Indians are about as agreeable as most other folks, less'n they git riled or they git hungry. The Sioux ain't no worse'n the others. Pawnee ain't no less ornery. But that's only if'n you rile 'em. 'Course, now," he went on thoughtfully, "you can't say that about the Blackfoot. You want to take an Indian who's pretty much troublesome all of the time, it's them Blackfoot."

Mellner grew irritated listening to Reuben's carrying on about Indians. He didn't give a hoot as to what Reuben thought. Why, a person could just look at the man and tell he was a heathen! No, it was Samson's opinion he wanted to hear, not that of some scraggly barkeep like Reuben Cook. He waved his hand impatiently and turned to Samson.

"Now see here, Roach. We've got to have some kind of plan. We've got women and children to think about."

Samson looked weary. "Just what do you want me to do?" he asked.

Mellner's eyes blinked rapidly, and the indignation returned to his face. "Why hell, man! That's what we're paying you for!" He failed to hide the panic in his voice.

"You're paying me to take you folks to Oregon," Samson corrected him. "I told you there would be hardships along the way. Surely you knew enough to expect it." He sighed. "Go back and gather up the livestock. We're going to make camp right here. Post double guards and tell all the men to get their weapons ready. Try not to panic everyone. Reuben and I are going to scout ahead. And Mellner, try and keep those two fellers isolated if you can. We don't need them upsetting everyone. I'll be back directly and talk to them."

Mellner seemed satisfied with the confidence in Samson's voice. He hurried away to ready the wagon train for camp.

Samson and Reuben followed the two men's tracks westward. After an hour, Samson was sure that the Pawnee hadn't been tracking the two. They traveled on for another two hours, but still they saw nothing.

"I reckon we best get back," Samson finally said. He looked surprised at Reuben's silence. "You've been awful quiet, Reuben. That ain't your nature."

Reuben pulled out a chew and took a mouthful. He worked it in his mouth a while, then spit. He was frowning.

"There's something wrong, hoss," he said. "I can't put my finger on it, but something's upset those Pawnee. I've dealt with 'em many times and I ain't never heard tell of 'em killin' folks for no reason. Outside of bein' thieves, I've known 'em to be a peaceful lot." He paused a moment. "I just got a feelin' these men done something to 'em."

"I have a feelin' you're right," Samson agreed thoughtfully.

When they returned to the wagon train, the wagons were circled out. It looked like a fortress. Everyone who had a gun was set into position.

Samson and Reuben were immediately set upon by Mellner and a group of men, Tom Sinclair among them. There was a wild look about them that Samson had seen in men like this before. Their earlier fears had put them into a frenzy. They crowded aggressively around and stared up at Samson.

"Did you see anything?" Mellner demanded.

Samson just shook his head, "Where's Gibson and McCloud?"

"They're at my wagon," Mellner said. "I got their whole story. Their group was camped for the night, when they were viciously attacked with no warning. I say we go find those Indians, before they do the same to us." The other men started nodding their heads furiously.

Samson couldn't believe what he was hearing. "Have you lost your mind?" he demanded. "Why, if that war party's as big as they say it is, you'll head out there and get yourself killed as easy as pickin' off a herd of buffalo."

"I told you there wasn't no use talking to him," Sinclair said to Mellner.

Samson glanced at Tom Sinclair. The man had wild eyes, he thought, like the caged tiger he'd once seen in a traveling European circus that had come to Tennessee. Samson had known a few other men with eyes like Sinclair's, and most had been crazy men. It surprised him somewhat that Sinclair was so bold, in the wake of the ass-whipping that Samson had recently administered to him. What's more, Sinclair was staring menacingly at Samson, holding his gaze with an open stare that showed the craziness in his eyes. It didn't bother Samson, except for the fact that it caused more worry over Becky.

Samson turned his gaze from Sinclair to Mellner. "I'm tellin' you right now, you don't want to go off half-cocked, lookin' for trouble. It's too risky. We'll stay right here the rest of the day. In the morning, we'll head out."

Mellner's jaw twitched, his face flushed red. "I just don't see where that makes any sense at all! Why, we'll be like sitting ducks on a pond!"

"That's a chance we'll have to take," Samson said. "This way, we'll be expectin' them. We'll be ready. If nothing happens, we can load up and be on our way tomorrow. We can't stay in any one place for long. There's not enough grass for the animals to graze on, and we're already running low on supplies." He looked at all of the men hovering around him. "You men knew from the beginning that starting out on this trip was the easiest part. Getting there is the hardest. There's gonna be hardships every mile of the way, and this is just one of them." With that said, Samson pushed his way through the group and walked away. They stared at him silently.

Samson went to Mellner's wagon to see Gibson and McCloud. He spent the next hour talking with them. Both men were still visibly shaken by what had happened, but they held to the same story. No one, they said, had done anything to provoke the Pawnee attack.

Samson took Reuben aside. Whereas Mellner had little respect for Reuben Cook, Samson placed a great deal of trust in Reuben's knowledge of Indians.

"What do you think now, Reuben? What do you really think?"

Reuben shrugged. "If I'd have to guess, I'd have to say

they're tellin' the truth. Those men are scared, hoss. Too scared to be makin' up any stories."

"That's my feeling," Samson said. "I always knew that Smoke was a bad one."

"Bad to the bone, hoss. Gives me the creeps just bein' on the same plains with him." Reuben had known Smoke for many years. He'd watched him rise among the Pawnee and gain leadership within the tribe. So far, his band of followers was fairly small. Reuben had always felt a fear of what might happen if Smoke ever got a true rein on things. He added, "He's crazy enough, hoss. Got enough hate in him to do about anything, I 'spect."

Samson thought about Mellner and Sinclair and the frenzy they'd created among the men. He almost felt like letting them go, patting them on the back and telling them to have a go at the Indians. It would serve them right, he thought. But it would also drastically cut back his supply of available men to guard the wagon train. He sighed and excused himself from Reuben and set out on one of his solitary walks.

Rifle draped across his shoulder, Samson enjoyed the feel of the night air. It helped, being able to look up at the sky and feel like a part of it. The earth let him be. It was still and quiet and allowed a man to think clearly.

He hadn't been gone but a few minutes, when he could feel another presence. It annoyed him to think that he was being followed.

He half expected to turn around and see the Indian with the flowing silver hair and the prancing white stallion. But, he thought, he'd never heard the man approach before, or even sensed his presence. Slowly, he eased the rifle from his shoulder and cocked it.

Nightfall had set in, and everything had turned into dark shapes and silhouettes around him. Ahead, in the waving prairie grass, was a small clump of bushes. Quickly, Samson made his way toward them and eased around to where they were at his back. He dropped to his knees.

It had been foolish, he thought, to come away from the safety of the wagon train. He might at this very moment be in the thick of a Pawnee raiding group, lying in wait for the time to strike. He strained his eyes as he peered out. He looked behind him through the small openings among the bushes. Nothing. He was just about to kick himself for being so jumpy, when he saw the silhouette of a person.

The walk was familiar. The shape was definitely feminine. It was Becky. Samson grew angry that she would do such a foolish thing, but he also felt an excitement that he couldn't push away.

He waited until she was right beside the bush, then reached out and grabbed her by the coattail. In one motion, he yanked her down and quickly cupped her mouth with his hand. He kept it there until he was sure she recognized him. Slowly, he eased his hold on her.

There was a tremble in his voice. "You shouldn't be here," he said.

"I know," she said, barely above a whisper. Her eyes were open wide, the whites glistening. Her warm breath and womanly scent instantly filled his nostrils. It was soft and sweet, and he had an overwhelming urge to pull her lips to his. Instead, he stared hard into her face, unable to kiss her, but also unable to let her go.

The words came out of his mouth before he had a chance to think. "I've got deep feelings for you," he said in a gruff voice.

"I know," she said. "What are we gonna do about it?"

A tingling ran through Samson with such force that he felt his body tremble. His loins were hot as a brushfire, raging out of control. He was in love with Becky Sinclair. She made him feel like no woman had ever made him feel. But even that knowledge couldn't prepare him for the way his body reacted to her nearness.

She reached up and, ever so gently, rubbed the back of her fingers against his cheek. His face burned at her touch. He turned weak inside. She had fallen into his lap when he pulled her down, and she still lay there against him. As she continued to stroke his cheek, a swelling started down below, pressing into her side. Embarrassed, Samson tried to speak, but the words stuck in his throat.

Samson's growing manhood continued to develop on its own, and to his surprise, Becky squirmed and dropped her elbow to rub against it. Samson shuddered and closed his eyes. He could feel her warmth, feel her move forward. Her hair brushed against his cheek and her lips came gently to his. Her breath quickened, and Samson felt his head reeling. She nibbled at his lips, and slowly the nibbling turned into a kiss. Samson couldn't hold back any longer. He put his arms around her and pulled her closer.

Their lips bathed each other as they kissed long and deep. Becky maneuvered to where she was now straddling him, holding his head in her arms, her fingernails digging into his scalp. Below, Samson nearly exploded when she pressed herself against him. The words of protest that had been running through his head suddenly disappeared completely, and he could only think about the want that he'd been carrying inside for so long.

Without a word, their hands started undressing each other. Samson took in a deep breath as her soft breast touched his face. For the first time in so long, all of his worries were forgotten as they came together in the darkness of the prairie.

28

Jory and Standing Bear left the immigrants and resumed their business of picking up the killers' trail. Jory's heart felt heavy. Molly Jackson had done things to him that no one had ever done before. Even Agnes Perring hadn't touched his heart the way Molly had. He had left her with a deep feeling of trepidation and already yearned for her presence.

Standing Bear, too, felt unhappy at their departure. He'd grown fond of the little wagon train and the immigrants. Ever since Jory had ridden into the camp with Louisa, the immigrants had treated them both like European royalty, and Standing Bear had basked in their generous treatment.

He had wanted so desperately to ask his question, or better yet, to have Jory ask it for him. There were some fine white women in the group. Molly would have been a perfect choice, but he would have been happy with Louisa's mother, Bertha, too. She was young and tender. He liked the way she walked. Besides, Bertha's man seemed to be an unpleasant sort and not interested in her at all. Yes, Standing Bear thought sadly, Bertha would have been a fine choice.

There was yet another woman who had caught his eye. Mary was dark-complected and about thirty years of age. She would have been acceptable, also.

But, it was Molly who crowded his thoughts the most. She was pleasing in all aspects, outshining the other women like a bright star. Molly often reminded him of the missionary woman. He could close his eyes and envision her milky white thighs wrapped around his body. They were full thighs, but not like those of a fat squaw. Once, he had caught a glimpse of Molly bathing her feet, and although he could only see to her knees, it stirred great emotions in him. Yes, he reckoned, Molly would be the best choice in the whole world. Still, he would be satisfied with Bertha or the dark-complected one named Mary.

Standing Bear had noticed that Jory also held a particular fondness for Molly. He found this curious, since Jory seemed to have a way with all women but showed an interest in few. Never before had Standing Bear seen in Jory Matlock's eyes such longing and affection as he showed for Molly Jackson. Standing Bear suspected that Jory, too, held great visions of feeling Molly's milky white thighs wrapped around him. That was all right, he decided. Jory could have Molly. One of the other women would suit him just fine. Then again, maybe Jory would show his appreciation to Standing Bear for helping him hunt for the killers. Maybe he would let him sample Molly when he was finished with her. This new thought gave him a good feeling inside.

It took the two men some time to pick up the killers' trail. No sooner had they located the tracks than they came upon a dead man. He was lying face up in his bedroll near an outcropping of rocks.

They dismounted and stood over the body.

"Snakes," Standing Bear said. "He has been bitten many times."

"I don't think it was snakes did it," Jory said. "There's a bullet hole in his chest."

"Yes, but he was bitten." Standing Bear pointed. "His neck and face. Snakebites."

"Whoever heard of snakes out crawling around in the wintertime?" Jory wondered.

Standing Bear straightened and went to look among the rocks that jutted from the ground.

Jory stared at the marks on the man's face and neck. They were twin puncture wounds, all right. He shuddered and looked quickly around for any snakes that might be crawling around on the cold ground.

It was then that he spotted a horse, standing all alone, off to the west. It didn't appear to be going anywhere in particular. Jory looked back down at the body.

Standing Bear returned, carrying a saddle.

"This man rode with the killers," he said. "And that is his horse." He nodded toward the west.

Jory nodded grimly. "And I'd say he got killed by one of his own party."

"Yes, after he was snakebit," Standing Bear said. He led Jory to the cluster of rocks. "See this entrance? The snakes that rattle live deep in the earth in the time of winter. This man went down into the snakes' hole. This man was very foolish."

Jory stared. He looked back at the dead man. He was young. Even in death, Jory could see the tenderness of youth about him. He almost felt a stirring of pity.

These were ruthless men that they were after. They hadn't even bothered to bury their dead. The fact that they had left a good horse and saddle behind told Jory that they were traveling light, on horseback, and not with any group of immigrants.

A heaviness crept into Jory's heart. In Molly's presence, he'd been able to put his thoughts of the butchered immigrant woman aside. His attention had turned to other problems and concerns in life. Things had almost turned to normal for him. He was merely on a hunt for outlaws whose victims had faded from memory. Now the haunting sight of the woman's head on the wagon seat came back all too clearly. Jory knelt down and looked the dead body over.

"What's your name, feller?" he whispered softly. "Where'd you boys come from?"

Standing Bear's voice surprised him from behind.

"It is sometimes good to talk to the spirit of the dead," he said. "Many of my people say they have conversed, but I have not had a spirit ever answer me. Not that I could hear."

Embarrassed, Jory quickly stood up. "We have to hurry and find them," he said, "before they hurt anybody else."

He couldn't help thinking of Molly and the rest of the immigrants.

Standing Bear fetched the saddle. "I will catch the horse," he said. "They will make for good trading."

Jory took the man's blanket and wrapped the body, then dug a shallow grave. He said a word over the man and they left. Standing Bear showed pride in his new acquisitions. He had saddled the horse, and led the riderless animal alongside him by the reins. He pointed out many times to Jory what a fine mare it was, and the saddle was nearly new.

The trail was days old, but the men's tracks were easy enough to follow. Still, it soon became a wearisome task, since the trail had no apparent direction. They had continued to ride west, but kept turning back and forth to the north and south. The only direction they hadn't taken was back to the east. Jory wondered if they had any particular destination, or if they were just wandering outlaws. Maybe the dead man had been their leader. He thought again of the snakebitten face.

It was late afternoon when Indians appeared, almost out of nowhere. Soon, they were all over the landscape in front of them and to the west. Jory figured there were a hundred, maybe more. They rode their horses into a semicircle about seventy-five yards away, to where Jory and Standing Bear were surrounded on three sides. It was Standing Bear who finally spoke.

"They are Pawnee. My people."

"Well, what in hell are they doin'?" Jory asked. "Ain't no huntin' party. Not this many braves," he added.

Standing Bear looked grim. "It is a war party. Come, we must ride to them. I will speak with them." He began to ride slowly toward the line of Indians.

Jory hesitated. He had dealt with Indians countless times before and found them to be mostly misrepresented in lore. In some ways, he saw little difference between them and the white men. They desired to be left alone with food to eat, water to drink, and good shelter from the cold. Jory had always kept plenty of tobacco, and sometimes carried whiskey, to trade with them. Outside of a couple of isolated incidents, he'd had very few problems with Indians.

But he'd never seen this many gathered together before. Trouble was brewing. He felt sure of it. Even though he rode with Standing Bear, one of their own, that still didn't mean that Jory was safe. And Standing Bear's nervousness didn't help matters any. Reluctantly, he urged his horse to follow.

There was a tension in the air. Jory was barely close enough to make out their faces, but he could tell they had an angry look about them.

When they'd gone within twenty yards of the semicircle, Standing Bear turned to look at Jory over his shoulder. "You stay here, Jory Matlock," he said. "Let me speak with them."

No sooner had Standing Bear spoken than half a dozen Indians rode briskly toward them. Jory recognized one of them as Smoke, an ornery sort whom Jory had never found to be anything other than quarrelsome, even when accepting Jory's gifts of tobacco and whiskey. Jory had little use for the man, but right now he felt a genuine fear.

His mouth felt dry as cotton. Smoke's piercing gaze locked onto Jory's as recognition flickered in his eyes. Jory started wondering if he was still going to be alive five minutes from now. He'd never trusted Smoke under normal circumstances, and now Smoke was traveling in a war party. Jory tried to swallow, but his tongue had enlarged in his throat.

Different thoughts started to swirl in his brain, centering and stopping on Molly. Would he ever see her again? He wished with all his heart he hadn't left her. He wished he'd accepted her invitation to ride to Oregon with the wagon train. He longed for her company and her reassuring ways.

Standing Bear positioned himself in front of Jory and guided his horse forward to where Smoke waited. They spoke in the Pawnee tongue. Jory strained to recognize bits and pieces of their conversation and drew from it that four of the Pawnee people had been killed by white men while offering them their hand of peace.

Jory nervously looked around at all the braves. Their
jaws were set and their eyes were cold. Even if he hadn't
understood a single word of the Pawnee tongue, Jory
would have known all too well that something was wrong.

Standing Bear turned to Jory. His face was solemn. "My
people were three, maybe three and a half days from here.
A hunting party was sent out, and they were attacked by
white men. Four of my people were killed. I think it was
the men that we now follow." He paused a moment and
motioned toward the Indians. "Now, Smoke is going to
hunt for these men, too. He will kill all of them. He will
not sleep until this is done."

Jory nodded.

"He wants to know if Jory Matlock has tobacco."

Jory's eyes were watching Smoke and the others closely.
"You know I got tobacco," he said.

"I know, but it is not good that I reveal these things. It
is better if you give your tobacco freely to Smoke. He is
crazy, you know." Standing Bear nodded.

Jory tossed the tobacco to Smoke, who caught it and bit
off a chew in one motion. With no sign of appreciation, he
stuffed the rest inside his shirt. As he turned his pony, he
spoke to Standing Bear in an angry tone, then rode away.

"What did he say?" Jory asked.

"He said some day he will kill you. But not today."
Standing Bear stared after Smoke with an irritated look.
"He will not kill you today, because you ride with me. His
mother would like for me to share her lodge."

Jory couldn't help being amused in spite of the situation. "Well, I'm glad for small favors," he said. "Maybe
you oughta just go ahead and make her your squaw. Then
you wouldn't have to wander around all the time, thinkin'
about white women."

Standing Bear grimaced and spit on the ground. "I will
not share any lodge with Smoke's mother. She is too old,
and fat as a buffalo cow about to give birth. Be happy,
Jory Matlock, that Smoke does not know how I feel, or he
surely would have killed you."

They waited until Smoke and the Pawnee had ridden
away. Standing Bear, who watched them leave in silence,

seemed burdened by something else. Finally, he spoke with reluctance.

"Smoke is going to make war on all white men. He is going to hunt down those we follow and kill them. And then he will attack the immigrants."

Jory stared at Standing Bear as the words soaked in. He thought of Molly. He felt a rise of panic in his chest.

"We have to go back to them," he said.

"We are not going to hunt the killer men?" Standing Bear asked.

"What would be the purpose now?" Jory said. "I reckon Smoke will find 'em soon enough. I'm sure he'll take care of 'em. We have to return to the immigrants." Without waiting for an answer, he turned his horse and headed back east.

Standing Bear, who was still suffering over the repellent idea of lying with Smoke's mother, felt his spirits lift. The wagon train. Maybe this time, Jory Matlock would help him. He pulled his horse in a trot behind Jory, thinking about milky white thighs.

29

~~~~~~~⟡~~~~~~~

D avis Martin had gone out with Noah Bayh. They were
tending to a calf that had wandered away from the
wagons and fallen sick. Bayh was an agreeable sort
who didn't ask questions, but liked to talk about all sorts
of interesting things that Davis had never given thought to.
Davis was enjoying himself. He liked being among the
people in the wagon train and listening to their stories,
hearing their plans. Even the children were an amusement.
It was a pleasant break from robbing folks and watching
men die. He almost wished he could join this group and
travel with them to Oregon.

They were working on a plan to haul the sick calf back
to the wagon train. Bayh was bending over the animal, and
Davis had just straightened up to go to his horse, when
Davis suddenly felt a terrific pain engulfing his entire
body. He thought at first that his horse must have kicked
him, but the horse was too far away.

Davis looked vacantly around him. Everything seemed
still and quiet. He jerked involuntarily and grabbed his
stomach when the pain grew more intense. In his confu-
sion, he stumbled away from Noah Bayh and the calf and
looked out across the prairie. Little white spots appeared
before his eyes and swirled everywhere. A funny rushing
sensation ran through his head, causing him to feel faint.
Nothing seemed real. In the distance, he thought he could
see Indians. They seemed to be riding toward him, but he
didn't feel at all afraid. In fact, he began to stumble toward
them.

His head felt so light. He reached up to rub the sweat from his eyes, but his hand bumped into something. He tried again. What was it that kept getting in his way? He needed to clear his eyes. They were burning and dripping and he just needed to rub them to make them feel better. Again, he tried to lift his hand to his face, but was stopped by a dull pain.

It occurred to him then to look down. Slowly, Davis dropped his head. At first, it didn't register. He stared at the shaft of the arrow that had lodged in his sternum. His eyes widened in horror.

Away in the distance, Davis thought he could hear someone crying out. Noah Bayh was calling for Davis to run, to get away. But Davis couldn't run. He couldn't move.

The Indians were now all around him, fuzzy colorful images that seemed to dance and sway on their horses. He stood there, his quivery legs barely able to keep him upright. Suddenly the face of an Indian loomed before him, close enough that it came into focus. The face was brightly painted and made Davis think about the ghost stories he'd heard as a young'un back in Ohio. He cocked his head a little to the left to take a better look, just as the Indian with the macabre face raised a club high above his head.

Davis didn't notice. He was in his own world, dreaming about the pleasure of his youth. Even as he watched the Indian swing his arm downward and the club crashed against his skull, he felt nothing.

The Indians took their time in killing Noah Bayh, carefully surrounding him as he desperately tried to run back toward the wagon train. They enjoyed themselves, laughing and taunting, forcing Noah to run and dodge among their trotting horses. They let him amuse them in this way for several hundred yards, until one of them lost his humor and buried an arrow in Noah's back. It was enough to kill him, but a second Indian shot an arrow into Noah's neck. Before the lifeless body had tumbled to the earth, a third arrow struck.

Ten-year-old Roger McIntyre was the first to see the Indians approaching the wagon train. He jumped up from the ground where he'd been playing, and barely got out the word "Indians," when an arrow severed his windpipe.

Reese Patterson was not far away. He was thirty-six years old, had a wife and four children and had brought them from their home in Virginia. Barely an hour went by in his life that he didn't think about Oregon and the new start he was going to give his family. Back in the States, times were hard, and bank failures were a common thing. He had heard stories about Oregon's rich soil and the great opportunities that waited there. He'd saved for three years for this trip, and then sold everything they owned. A carpenter by trade, his assistance had been invaluable to many of the immigrants. Reese was a generous sort, always lending a helping hand to fix anything broken and always doing so with a smile.

Reese heard young McIntyre's distressful cry and turned to look. His eyes suddenly filled with horror. Indians, their faces painted, were everywhere, filling the landscape.

His thoughts flew to his wife and children, and his heart filled with love. Mae Belle was a good woman, he thought. More than he deserved. And his children. Martin, the eldest at eleven; Richard, who was nine; Tommy, six; and the pride of his life, three-year-old Dianne.

A deep anguish came over him. His body took on an offensive posture, as he hurled his right shoulder back toward the wagon like a mother hen protecting her chicks. He tried to pray, but the words scrambled in his mouth. He grabbed up his long flintlock rifle and, despite his feeling of desperation, calmly squeezed off a shot.

An Indian fell dead from his horse. Reese gritted his teeth and began to reload, but it was the only shot he was to fire. An arrow pierced his heart, killing him instantly.

Soon, a fierce battle was under way. The Indians swept down on the train with a vengeance. The immigrants, vastly outnumbered, swung into action with a quick aggression. They managed to drive the Indians back momentarily, but once the Indians regrouped, it was just a matter of time. The immigrants still fought valiantly, killing two

Indians for each immigrant, but the numbers where overwhelming and the immigrants began to fall, one by one.

Sal Musso was with fifteen-year-old Sadie Andrews. The girl had held a grip on him ever since he'd first laid eyes on her. They were off riding. Sal was showing her how to handle a horse, or at least that was what Sadie's parents thought. She was the only child of the Reverend Maynard Andrews and his wife, Harriet. Reverend Andrews felt a deep calling from God, and he couldn't wait to reach Oregon and start a new congregation. Even though Sal and his friends seemed to be rough young men, the Reverend was impressed with Sal's manner. The missus was simply charmed by Sal's handsome face and athletic build. They agreed that it was good for Sadie to learn how to handle a horse. After all, Oregon was sure to be a primitive place in the beginning.

Sal was riding along close to Sadie, looking into her deep brown eyes. She took his breath away. He was thinking about such things as settling down and giving up his wild nature. A woman like Sadie would be well worth the effort it took.

The six Indians were nearly upon him before Sal realized what was happening. He quickly shot one with his pistol and had another in the bead of his other pistol when an arrow went deep into his horse's neck. As the beast was falling under him, Sal dived for Sadie's little mare.

With his agility and strength, he landed perfectly behind her and quickly shielded her body with his. He grabbed the reins and swung the little mare around, kicking her sides hard in an effort to outrace the other five Indians.

Quickly, the Indian ponies were on all sides. Sal dropped one with a gut shot, but not before the Indian buried his hatchet in Sal's shoulder. Bravely, Sal fought on. One Indian tried to grab Sadie, but Sal shoved him aside, and together they fell to the ground.

Sal's right collarbone had been shattered by the hatchet, but Sadie was there, and he had to save her. Savagely, he buried his knife in the Indian's groin, then jumped up to face the remaining three Indians.

A tall Indian was grinning as he pulled Sadie from her

little mare. She was crying and screaming Sal's name. Sal grabbed his knife and raced toward her. He yelled and screamed his rage, but before he could reach her, an arrow entered his back and cut through his lung.

He stumbled and fell to his knees. He managed to glance up and saw her, clutched in the Indian's arms, struggling to get away. He called out her name, and their eyes met, briefly, just as a hatchet nearly severed his head. He died with only her innocent eyes to comfort him in the hereafter.

Dick Carter had been mean and evil as the devil in life, spitting his wicked bravado in all directions. He snarled at the Indians as they rode in, shooting the first Indian he saw in the thigh. He emptied his gun and felled another, but they soon had him surrounded. An arrow cut off the top of his right ear. Carter screamed out in pain and threw down his weapons.

He fell to the ground on his knees and raised his hands high above his head. Blood trickled down his neck.

"Please, please!" he called out. "We ain't with these immigrants! Me 'n' my boys, we'll help you rob em! Please don't kill me!"

He started bawling. A big Indian on a well-muscled pony spit at him, then buried a hatchet deep in his skull. Carter's body twitched and jerked a few moments, then he was dead.

Molly shot the small Indian that was trying to unhitch her oxen. Before he died, he directed a stunned look at the woman who had felled him. It almost unnerved her, but then she thought of Louisa and screamed out the little girl's name. She threw down the rifle and hopped back into the wagon to grab her pistol.

Just as she was turning to hurry outside, a big head popped through the wagon's opening. Molly's heart jumped and she pointed the pistol. Her hand started to shake. It was Calvin. He held Louisa in his arms.

"They killed her pa, and a couple of 'em grabbed her ma," he said. Blood dripped from Calvin's scalp and ran down his face, falling in big drops from the end of his nose. She took Louisa gently from him, and was about to say something, when Calvin suddenly flung her aside with his big arm.

An Indian had appeared at the wagon's entrance. Calvin shot him, but two more appeared. Calvin screamed like a panther in the night and dived at the two with his knife drawn.

Molly could only sit there with Louisa, clutching her pistol. She needed to go to Calvin, to help him, but Louisa was clinging to her, pushing tightly against her breast, silent with fear. Molly started praying aloud.

Calvin's size easily took both of the Indians down as he jumped at them. His knife flashed as he buried the blade deep into the heart of one. The other Indian lay next to him, dead. Calvin jumped up and ran around the side of the wagon.

Molly quickly crawled to the front of the wagon, Louisa moving with her. Calvin was being attacked by three Indians at once. Molly shot into them, but missed. She cursed herself for not aiming better. She could smell the gunpowder burning the air. Fighting was going on all around them. Molly felt almost insane with fear. She glanced down at Louisa, then looked at Calvin, who was bleeding from several wounds, fighting for all of their lives. For an instant, she was overcome by his savagery.

She had thought him to be soft and cowardly.

He was fighting them hand to hand. Calvin killed one of the three, then another, but other Indians arrived. They jumped from their horses, slashing at Calvin with their knives and hatchets.

Molly felt as helpless as a person could feel. *Poor Calvin,* she thought. He had saved Louisa for her. She wished she could reach out and help him. She began to rock back and forth with Louisa and pray for Calvin, for all of them.

Someone grabbed her from behind with such force she nearly dropped the child. Molly felt her hair being ripped from its roots as Louisa was pulled from her arms. Her neck snapped and something crashed into her head. Louisa cried out, and then there was a deep, black silence.

Calvin knew his life was over. He thought about his

dead mother. He tried to glance upward and tell her he was sorry for running off with Dick Carter and the boys, that he really wasn't such a bad person and that he loved her.

He didn't know it, but he was the last male left alive on the wagon train. He kept waiting to die. He'd been chopped and stabbed more than a dozen times, but for some reason he was still alive. The shooting had stopped, and someone was laughing. His attackers had backed off from him and formed a circle. He could barely see. His eyes stung from the blood that covered his face. He rubbed them on his shoulder, then looked down to see the bone sticking out from where his elbow should have been. His left forearm had been nearly severed. It was hanging from his elbow at a twisted angle. Calvin couldn't remember when it happened.

A horse whinnied off to his right, and Calvin swung his knife in that direction. This brought a loud roar of laughter from the Indians. He wiped his eyes again on his right forearm. It was blurry, but he could make out some of the faces around him. Some sat on the ground, some were on horseback, but most of them were laughing. His body trembled. What were they waiting for? He managed to ponder why, for the first time in his life, he wasn't afraid.

His eyes fixed on one big Indian, sitting atop a spotted pony. As he stared, he could suddenly see the Indian maiden, full-breasted, her legs glistening under the sun. He stumbled toward the Indian and the spotted pony and reached out with his knife still in his hand. Calvin touched the pony's nose, leaving a smear of blood.

One of the Indians on the ground stepped close and drew his hatchet for a final blow, but the big Indian stopped him. He looked down at Calvin and their eyes met. The Indian spoke in words Calvin couldn't understand, then one by one, the Indians all pulled back.

Calvin's body hurt all over. He shivered once, then passed out.

30

❦━━━━❦

When Molly opened her eyes, she was blinded by the sun. She felt disoriented at first. Then, she remembered.

She felt surprised more than anything else. Surprised that she was still alive. Slowly, gently, she ran her hand over her lips and touched her nose to confirm the fact.

Then she thought of Calvin, and wondered if he was dead. Calvin had turned out to be a brave man. He had fought for her and Louisa—

Where was Louisa? Molly tried desperately to get up, but she was so weak, she could only lie back down. The air felt thick, and Molly started to cough. She opened her eyes and looked into the thick black smoke that permeated the air. When her head cleared somewhat, she managed to sit up slowly.

Several of the women were sitting around her. They were in a group, off a way from what remained of their small wagon train. Molly grimaced as she gazed through the drifting smoke. Four of the wagons were smoldering; two others were being ransacked by the Indians. The immigrants' precious possessions lay broken on the ground.

A big Indian atop a spotted pony rode up to the group of women. Molly remembered seeing him earlier, just before she was knocked unconscious. She could tell by his manner that he was a chief. Something bloody was dripping from his lance. They were fresh scalps. Molly grabbed her stomach and nearly vomited. She screamed out Louisa's name.

"What have you done with her, you bastard?" she cried. She half expected to be killed, but she couldn't help showing her anger.

The big Indian only smirked at her. Molly felt her anger rise. With a great effort, she pulled herself to her feet. Ignoring the Indian, she began to look around her. She moved among the women and children, frantically searching for Louisa.

A neighbor girl from back home, eleven-year-old Christine Hackman, grabbed at Molly's legs as she walked by. "Your sister, sh-sh-she's dead," she whispered, and started to bawl.

Molly reached down and rubbed the girl's head, then hugged her against her leg. Tears welled in her eyes. "Christine," she said gently, "have you seen Louisa?"

Christine shook her head. "No," she sobbed. "I can't find my baby brother, Arthur. None of the babies are here, and none of the boys, neither. Do you reckon they killed 'em, Molly? Do you reckon?"

Molly didn't know exactly what to say. She shook her head gently at the girl and was about to offer a word or two of comfort, when the big Indian suddenly rode up through the group of women and grabbed her by the hair. He yanked her head back and grinned as he said something in his strange language. Molly heard the laughter of his companions as they rode up to join him.

"Where are the babies?" she screamed at him.

Her anger brought a bigger laugh from the Indians. Frustrated, she reached up to where his hand still clasped her hair and dug her fingernails in, raking them down into his flesh. Blood began to flow, and the Indian roared with laughter. Looking down at her with eyes as cold as steel, he gave her head a violent jerk, tossing her to the ground.

Molly wet herself. She couldn't help it. She'd had an urge to relieve herself before the Indians had even appeared. It made her feel so helpless, so out of control, she started to cry. All this traveling had gotten to her. She'd had a bad bout with diarrhea—one day, she'd had to run to the bushes more than twenty times. She guessed she must have lost ten pounds during the ordeal. Then her oxen had become tired and hungry. A couple of their hooves had split. She had packed tar in the splits and wrapped tarred string around the hooves to hold them together. It had left her tired and weakened. Several times, she'd thought of giving up this impossible idea of going all the way to Oregon. One man, who had joined them at Independence with his young wife, had already died of cholera. This had added to her fear, for he'd been only twenty-three years old and seemed as healthy as a horse.

But it was Louisa who kept her going. Molly couldn't stand the thought of not being a part of her niece's raising. Sitting there in the stench of her own urine, she cried. She remembered the day Louisa had been lost. It had seemed like the world was coming to an end. Then Jory had come along and saved the girl, bringing joy once again to her life. Now Bertha was dead and Louisa gone.

Hope was like a bouncing ball, she thought. It came to her and left again. Back and forth. Up and down. Molly didn't know what her capabilities were anymore. How much pain was a person expected to bear? Her emotions ebbed, and she lay there where the big Indian had thrown her, letting her sorrow center on herself.

The Indians had found Noah Bayh's wagon, stocked full of whiskey and other spirits. It had been Bayh's intention to open a tavern in their new settlement in Oregon, and he had spent his life savings to buy up a sizable supply of the better-quality stuff. Now empty jugs lay on the ground where the drunken Indians had tossed them. They were a loud and argumentative bunch, and several small fights broke out.

In late afternoon, several head of cattle were rounded up and butchered. After skinning the animals, the Indians gathered up the women to do the cooking. They couldn't communicate in words; instead, they told the women what they wanted by grabbing their hair or poking them with their lances.

Molly's legs stung where she had wet herself. Her eyes burned from the smoke. Her fingers soon became blistered from handling the hot meat. She would have liked to have gotten some cooking utensils, but none were offered and she surely wasn't going to try to find any. The other women were gasping and whimpering as they cooked bare-handed over the fires. No one protested, for fear of a jab in the ribs or backside from one of the sharp spears.

When the meat had been well singed on the outside but was still mostly raw inside, the Indians ordered the women to serve them. Molly was told to feed the big Indian who had flung her to the ground. Carefully, she gave him the food, trying not to touch him. He ignored her as his hunger overtook his interest in the white woman.

Molly turned way from him and looked at the scene around them. Scattered all about were the bodies of friends, loved ones, companions, some with their scalps missing. Molly had known some of them since childhood. Others were folks she had bonded with since their journey had begun. She bit her lip as she noticed the other women. They were all deep in sorrow for their dead ones, too. Her heart cried for them.

She heard a sharp cry, as Sally Lang began to run hysterically toward the body of her fourteen-year-old son. He had been scalped, and his body lay tortured and twisted next to their burning wagon. Sally didn't make it far before an Indian raced toward her and buried a hatchet in her skull. As if pushed forward by a mother's love, Sally stumbled forward, blood running down her shoulders and back. She groped along, reaching out with her hands, until she reached her son's body and fell dead next to him. Molly stared. Sally's hand was touching his. A sob caught in her throat.

Others who had longed to go to their dead kept still, learning the lesson that Sally Lang had taught them. They cried out loud as they sliced off chunks of meat and fed the ravenous Indians.

Molly knew that all hope was gone for these women. Angrily, she took a big piece of sizzling meat and slung it into the big Indian's lap. "You putrid animals!" she screamed into his face. "That was her son, for God's sake!"

The big Indian seemed amused by Molly's anger and frustration. His mouth curled into a broad smile, but his eyes were cold and serious. He picked up the hot meat and held it in his teeth while he sliced off a bite with his knife. A stream of blood ran down his chin as he chewed. Molly started to say more, but the Indian reached up and slapped her, like he was swatting at a fly.

When the Indians had finished eating, some of them lay down, right where they had sat, and went to sleep. Others formed groups and began playing some sort of game. A few started arguing over the immigrants' possessions.

Several approached the women. They yanked them up by the hair, pulled them a little way off from the others, and had them there on the ground. Molly sat down wearily. She put her head between her legs and squeezed her eyes shut. She wished she had been killed during the attack. She waited grimly, expecting any second for someone to grab her and yank her to her feet. But no one did, and Molly heard no more commotion around her.

After a while, she ventured a look around. Some of the women were not more than twenty feet away from her, still being raped by the Indians. She watched as one young Indian climbed off an older woman, and another Indian quickly took his place. Molly swung her gaze back to the left, following the sound of muffled screams. It was little Christine Hackman, who looked much smaller and younger than her eleven years, being held down while another Indian had his way with her. Christine's mother, Gloria, was being covered not ten feet away. Her face was turned toward her daughter, and her eyes were filled with a mother's grief.

It was a murderous orgy, taking place there on the prairie. These poor women, who had sold everything in good faith and left the States with their husbands and families, now had nothing left. They had seen their husbands and sons killed and butchered, and some, like Gloria Hackman, were forced to watch helplessly as their own precious little daughters were savagely raped, again and again. It was a fate worse than death for these women.

Molly couldn't help seeing the mental pictures that ran through her head. It was back in the States, during the late thirties. A big depression had swept the young country, caus-

ing great hardship. Many of the immigrants had lost businesses. Some had even lost their homes. Still, they had survived. They had held on and worked hard, making plans for
setting off to Oregon and a new life. Rather than live under
the threat of failed banks and depression in the States, they
would open new banks in the west. They'd been a proud and
ambitious group, full of excitement and adventure. Now here
they were. All of the men were dead, and the women were
now slaves to the Indian savages. Molly figured they'd be
dead soon enough themselves. Right now, she longed to be
back in Virginia, failed banks or no. If only they'd stayed,
little Louisa could be coming over to spend the night. They
could be baking cookies together and telling stories. No,
Molly thought. They'd all been fools. Now, they were receiv-
ing a fool's bounty.

She glanced around again. She couldn't understand why
she was the only woman left. Why weren't the Indians attacking her, too? A cold premonition came over her, and
she jerked her head up to stare at the big Indian. He was
still sitting in the same spot where she had fed him.

Their eyes met, his cold and serious, hers angry and wet
with tears. She knew then why she hadn't been taken and
raped yet. She was his.

It brought a mixture of emotions to her. Outside of fear
and anger, Molly found a bit of solace in the fact that
maybe she wouldn't be shared, even though the thought of
having him touch her was so repulsive that she felt sick inside.

Molly quickly looked away. Her time would come soon
enough, she knew, and she didn't want to encourage it to
happen any sooner. She could feel the big Indian's eyes
still watching her, and it made her skin crawl.

They stayed there through the afternoon. The poor
women lay in the same places where they'd been ravaged.
A couple were still being covered. Several of them looked
nearly dead. Molly began to feel guilty. She had been left
alone, untouched, sitting with her arms wrapped around
her legs, her chin tucked against her knees. She knew it
was an unreasonable guilt to place on herself. None of this

was her fault, but she still felt uneasy, sitting there all afternoon while the others were brutalized.

That evening, the routine started all over again. Two more of the cattle were butchered, and the women were forced to cook. Some of them could barely walk from their ordeal. Molly took more meat to the big Indian for his supper, but this time she didn't fling it at him or say a word to him. In return, she got only a cold stare from him. There was a deep hatred coming from those eyes. Molly had never seen the likes of such hate, not even among the savage Indians who had destroyed all the immigrants.

Once Molly had satisfied the big Indian's appetite, she decided to test her value at being the big one's property. Slowly, she walked around through the groups of Indians as they sat and ate. Some of them stared at her and a few made comments and laughed, but no one made a move toward her. No one stopped her or sent her back to her place beside the big one. She had been right.

This might be her chance to find Louisa, Molly thought. Maybe they were holding the children somewhere close. Maybe on the east side of the burned wagons. She had noticed some Indians off in that direction, and she hoped and prayed that the children were among them. Trying to be as casual as possible, she made her way through the remains of the burned wagons. Pain shot through her when she looked down at all of the family heirlooms and treasures scattered about on the ground like junk, broken and trampled. She passed by her own wagon, then came to Bertha's. There was little Louisa's cradle. It had been smashed into pieces. Molly nearly doubled over in her agony. Louisa's father had made the cradle and, even though the girl was past the cradle stage, they had packed it for the future children they dreamed of having.

Feeling sick and tired, Molly scanned the dead bodies. She didn't want to find Louisa among them, but she had to know. Half-relieved, she realized that Louisa was nowhere to be seen. Resigned, she made her way back to the women and sat down among them.

Darkness fell on the prairie. The women seemed to have settled into shock. They sat quietly, and as the night tem-

peratures dipped, they huddled closer and closer together
to draw warmth from one another. The Indians kept the
fires stoked with broken furniture and wagon parts, and
the women did their best to benefit from the fires while
still keeping a distance. Molly lay down next to Christine
Hackman, while her mother took the other side, and wordlessly they both tried to keep the girl warm.

Molly didn't remember having fallen asleep. When she
awoke, she felt colder than she ever remembered being.
Her body shivered uncontrollably. Somewhere close by,
someone was weeping. She sat up and looked around. It
was still dark, but she could see the horizon. Morning
wasn't too far off, she figured.

The black silhouettes of the sleeping women had all
gravitated during the night into one large group. They
pressed against each other, wanting warmth and comfort
but having little left to give one another. Some cried out,
even in their sleep. And they were nearly frozen. Molly
heard coughing and hacking among them.

Is this how they would die? Molly wondered. Would the
Indians kill them with their cruelty, or would they simply
freeze to death against the hard, cold earth? What would
the next day bring? Or would they even live to see it?

Molly gave thought to trying to sneak away, but only
briefly. Where would she go, and how could one woman
outrun vicious savages on horseback?

Her mind was worn out from worry, and thinking no
longer seemed like a constructive thing to do. Molly lay
back down and drew herself closer to Christine and Gloria.
She'd have plenty of time to think about it tomorrow.

31

Samson woke up feeling refreshed and mindless of the morning cold. There was an excitement in his body that he had never felt before, a deep satisfied feeling. He yearned for Becky. He'd slept by the clump of bushes, and now he looked around, still in his reverie, hoping that maybe she had stayed with him and was close by. It was impossible, he knew, but still he let himself think about it.

He remembered her sweet scent. Dreamily, he lifted his arm and sniffed at his sleeve. He pulled up his buckskin shirt and held it to his nose, hoping for the faintest fragrance of her. All he could smell was the pungent leathery odor of his deerskin clothing.

He stood up and stretched. Already, campfires were glowing in the dawn. He pulled his thoughts away from Becky. The immigrants were up early. Samson knew it was their fear over the Pawnee that had made them restless.

He needed to take charge. These people had put their trust in him to get their friends and loved ones safely to Oregon. They had paid him good wages, and even promised him first choice of the land in the Willamette Valley. Before, the promise had meant nothing to him. He'd spent most of his thoughtful moments feeling sorry he'd ever made this agreement. Now, as Samson stood there, watching the immigrants hurry through breakfast to make ready for their next instructions, their orders from *him*, he realized with some surprise that he had changed.

There was a new meaning to the promise that Joseph

Mellner had made him. Samson pictured a large stretch of land with rich grazing grasses and fertile black soil. He could do it, he thought. He could farm that land and make it prosper.

A moment of sadness filled his heart when he thought about Becky being married to a turd like Tom Sinclair. He supposed nothing would change that. It would have been nice to have her alongside him on that new Oregon farm.

He started walking back toward the wagons. He had only gone a few paces when Mellner noticed him and headed his way. Samson dreaded the intrusion on his morning, but Mellner had such an eager look about him, Samson cussed himself for his attitude. After all, the man had hired him. He had every right to his expectations of him.

"Mornin', Mellner."

Joseph Mellner looked surprised. He blinked his eyes, trying to get a fix on Samson's pleasant exchange.

"Good morning," he said stiffly, then hesitated, rubbing his big hand across his mouth. "Have you given any more thought to those savage Indians?"

Samson filled his cheeks with air then blew out. Thoughts of Becky's love the night before still clung to him. He lied. "Yes, I have. I reckon I'll head out this morning. Look around. You and Reuben take over here. We'll move out right after breakfast."

"Do you think that wise?" Mellner asked.

"I do," Samson said. "We surely can't stay here. We gotta keep movin'. We've got animals to graze, and they've damn near et up everything here already." He paused and looked at the concern on Mellner's face. "You know that's true, Joseph," he said softly. "We can't sit around here. Surely you've thought about that."

Mellner studied Samson for several seconds, then he squatted down and pulled up a piece of prairie grass. He rubbed it with his thumbnail. "I know you don't care for me, Samson Roach. I must seem like a hard and stubborn man to you."

Samson looked at the top of Mellner's head. Then he, himself, squatted on his haunches and pulled a blade of prairie grass to chew on. "We all got our ways," he said to Mellner. "I reckon you have your reasons."

Mellner worked his thumbnail on the blade of grass until it slivered apart. Then, he pulled up another blade and began the same ritual. His eyes were fixed on his hands, but his mind was far away. Without looking up, he began talking.

"A lot of us, myself included, lost just about everything we owned, back when the banks failed in '37. I tell ya, only by the grace of God did I keep my family from starving. A lot of folks lost their farms and businesses. A lot of them fell prey to sickness. I lost a sister to typhoid, and I've got a brother nearly eat up with tuberculosis." He shook his head at the blade of grass. Finally, he looked up at Samson. There were tears in his eyes. "Back home, in the States, a farmer can't even etch out a living—not with that confounded slavery business going on. These folks here, Roach, they haven't got anything. Their homes, their farms, most of their livestock. All lost. Well," his eyes squinted, "I'm not going to allow that in Oregon. No sir! No nigras are going to be doing the work of white folks. Everybody's going to get an equal opportunity. We're going to have the best churches, schools, and businesses. And the land's going to be worked into some of the finest farms you've ever seen."

Samson nodded his head thoughtfully. He, too, had once held great visions about Oregon. Now, for the first time since the death of his wife and son, he was hoping for something in life. He caught himself listening to Mellner with a positive ear.

Mellner's face had taken on a glow of excitement. He went on. "Did you know that we have a lot of businessmen with us? Why, we have a hatter, and Joel Perkins is going to open a gristmill. Absalon Turner and his sons plan to operate a sawmill. Jeremiah Hooley and Dan Palmer will open up stores. We have two tailors with us and several cabinetmakers. Gene McCray is a silversmith. We have Methodist and Baptist preachers, and I know there are already Catholic missionaries established there. We've got some cattle, horses, chickens, and seedlings. I hear the soil is so rich, it will grow the best turnips and onions. We ought to put out boom crops of barley, oats, and rye, as well as wheat. My goodness, a man ought to eventually have strawberries, even peach and apple trees."

Mellner sighed and allowed himself a small chuckle. "I guess it sounds crazy to you, Roach. But you see, these folks are my friends and neighbors. It was me who started this dream, and I've got to get them to Oregon and a new beginning in life. I can't let them down. No sir," he said, shaking his head. A frown wrinkled his brow. "I'll die before I let them down."

Samson stood up and stretched. "Nothing wrong with dreams like that, Joseph. But, as far as our situation right now, you gotta go about it the right way. If we go off half-cocked, we'll play right into the Indians' hands."

With the feeling he had Joseph Mellner's ear, Samson seized the opportunity to try to talk some sense into him.

"If you want to make Oregon to see those dreams of yours fulfilled, we best keep moving. Think about it, Joseph. There was only a dozen or so men that the Pawnee attacked. We've got a little different situation here. These Pawnee would rather steal a meal from you than kill you for it."

Mellner looked confused and a bit angry. He stood up. "Can you guarantee us that the Pawnee won't attack, just because we are large in number?" he asked.

Samson shrugged. "I can't guarantee anything. All I know is, something had to set those Pawnee off. There's been Indian problems in the past, that's true, but it never came from the Pawnee. Now, if this were Sioux or Blackfoot on the warpath, I'd say you had more to worry about." He stopped and looked down at the ground then back at Mellner. " 'Course, I guess anything's possible," he said, barely audible.

Mellner was staring at him doubtfully.

"Look," Samson said, "let me scout ahead, and you bring the wagons along. Either that, or you can take things over yourself," he added, more bluntly.

"Well," Mellner said, still staring, "I guess we did hire you to take us to Oregon. Mind you, I still don't agree with everything you say. Nevertheless, we'll try it your way."

Samson half expected to catch sight of Becky when he entered the camp, but he didn't. He walked among the immigrants, feeling self-conscious that somebody might know about what they'd done the night before. His worry was unfounded, for nobody seemed to be giving him any knowing or disapproving looks. Instead, they still seemed jittery about the thought that there might be wild Indians attacking them at any moment. Samson avoided Willie's wagon, knowing that the boy would be eager with questions about how to fight Indians.

After a quick breakfast, he set out on his own to scout ahead. He kept a sharp eye for any sign of the Pawnee, and a watch behind for signs of Willie. His mind, though, was fixed on Becky. She had occupied his mind ever since the day they'd met, but nothing could match the way she consumed him now. He had lain with her, and now his every sense was filled by her smell, her touch, her feel. It distressed him to know there were warring Indians to worry about. He needed the freedom to think only about Becky Sinclair. It had been so long since he had anything but sorrow to fill his heart.

Why couldn't life be different? Samson wished Becky's marriage could just fade away and disappear, as if it had never been. Her marriage to Tom Sinclair was an obstacle that couldn't be dealt with. He knew he would always be plagued with social guilt if he caused her to leave her husband, even if it was a bad marriage to begin with.

Samson remembered how it was back in Tennessee, how people had gossiped and carried on about divorced women. No, that was a burden he could never lay upon Becky. Yet, Samson didn't know if he wanted to live life without her.

He should have killed Tom Sinclair when he had the opportunity. After all, the man had started the fight in front of everybody, and even though it would have been wrong to kill a man, Samson would have been justified. . . .

It was wrong, and Samson knew he could never have brought himself to do such a deed, but he still couldn't help thinking about it. He cursed himself unjustly that he hadn't found Becky in the first place. Things would have been a lot simpler if *he* had just met and married her before Tom Sinclair came along.

Then Cordry entered his mind. No, he thought, that wouldn't have worked, either. His son had meant life itself to Samson. Even though he'd never felt as strong a love for Nancy as he did for Becky, he reckoned he still wouldn't have changed anything about Cordry for any other experience in his life.

He grew melancholy at life's funny ways. It just didn't make any sense to him at all. The two things he loved the most—his son Cordry and now Becky—could never have happened together. There might have been another child, but it wouldn't have been Cordry.

Life was too complicated for folks' minds, Samson guessed. He glanced skyward, as he sometimes did, wishing he could make God reveal himself and explain why life was the way it was. He'd always felt a kinship to God. In his head, he communicated his thoughts to the Almighty. *Am I wrong about my feelings?* he asked. Why couldn't He have put things together differently? Why, Nancy would most likely still be alive and happily married to somebody back in Tennessee, while he, Becky and Cordry could be all together as a family and traveling west on a wagon train.

Samson realized that God had nothing to do with such trivial things as the women in his life. But right now he needed questions answered. Questions that were too big for his mortal thoughts and understanding. "What am I supposed to do with these feelings I have?" he asked the sky out loud. "What's Becky supposed to do?"

He had ridden more than two hours without a sign of Indians. He had come to a little plateau that rose up on the prairie, when the realization struck him that he couldn't remember riding his horse to that spot, or anything else about the countryside, for the last two hours. Why, if any Indians had come along, he reckoned they could have killed him while he was sorting out his personal life. It gave him a bit of a chill, thinking about how he had ridden along so deep in his thinking. He looked back over the path he had ridden. At least his horse had had the presence of mind to dodge the holes in the ground that the varmints had dug to raise their young in.

Where had the time gone? Had something spirited him away and set him two hours up the trail? This wasn't the first time such a thing had happened to Samson, and it always spooked him a bit how he could be riding along, then suddenly find himself somewhere down the trail, wondering how he had gotten there.

A hawk was making long, low circles overhead, looking around for a meal. Seeing the hawk got Samson to watching the clouds. It seemed like the sky was filled with white puffs of cotton, mixed into the deep, rich blue. He and Cordry had played a game of watching clouds and pretending they were giant animals and people. Now, Cordry was watching the clouds from the other side.

Samson felt a little guilty, wondering if the boy had seen what had happened with Becky. He wanted Cordry to be pleased, if that was possible. He wondered exactly where Cordry was at this moment. In his mind, he asked the question, *Are you there, son? Can you see me now? I know it was wrong in a man's eyes, son, but I needed her. You understand that, don't you?*

In among the cottony clouds was a larger one, grayish white in color, floating toward the western horizon. It made him think of Nancy. If it *was* a fact that the dead knew what was going on among the living, then she had seen, too. He wondered what she must have thought. Suddenly, some of the stirrings that had stayed in his body since the night before lost their spark. Samson had always had a problem enjoying the things he liked the most for worrying over them. "Do you think I'm awful, Nancy?" he said aloud.

The sound of his own voice surprised him as it broke into the silence of the prairie. He talked to Nancy some more, but not aloud. He tried to explain about how he needed to get on with his life and how Becky—married or not, socially accepted or not—was possibly the only person that could fill the void in his life and give him the strength to go on. *You do understand?* his mind asked the cloud.

If he was looking for some sort of answer, he didn't get one. All he got were burning eyes from looking into the bright sky.

Finally, he pulled his eyes away from the clouds and studied the land around him. Everything seemed peaceful and in a sort of harmony. This surely didn't seem like the proper place for marauding Pawnee to be out killing people. But, Samson reckoned Indians didn't think about such things as peace and harmony when it came to the white man invading their land, even if it was a wagon train traveling through.

If the Indians were still around, he might be getting close. Samson pushed all other thoughts from his mind and tried hard to concentrate on the business at hand.

He rode all that day. Toward sundown, he came across a grave marker that wasn't any more than a flat rock stuck in the ground with carvings on it. It simply read, "D. Park, 26 years."

Samson made camp there. He went to sleep that night thinking about D. Park, wondering if it was a man or woman, and what had caused his or her demise. Dozens of theories went through his mind before he went to sleep.

32

Maybe it was the dread of leading a wagon train through land running with angry Pawnee, or maybe it was the remembrance of his time with Becky. Whatever the reason, Samson woke up several times during the night. Something was troubling him, and if he'd given serious thought to it, he could have come to many different conclusions. He didn't think about it, though. He didn't want to, not consciously, anyway.

Twice, he came awake with thoughts of Becky. Both times, he was swollen, but he couldn't remember having any dreams about her. Other times, he just woke up and stared at the dark sky above. There was no movement, no sound around him.

When morning finally came, Samson woke up feeling tired. His eyes were watery. He wiped at them, but they watered up again. His mouth was dry and his tongue felt parched. Maybe, he thought, he had caught some sickness.

The morning was bright. Samson got up to relieve himself, then sat back down on his bedroll. He wished he had a drink. In fact, he wished he had a whole jug of Reuben's whiskey. His head felt like lead, and his body was tired. The more he sat, the worse he felt. Samson knew he needed to get up, but his ambition level had dropped from the high he'd experienced the day before. It filled him with self-pity.

There was no telling how long he would have sat there. The morning sun was warm, and the prairie around him seemed too big for one man alone to find a band of Indians. Samson pushed aside the urgency that gnawed inside him and let his body sink deeper onto his bedroll.

He felt the presence of someone else before he saw. Samson turned his head. The man with the silver hair and the big white horse stood there along the trail, not more than ten feet away. Samson closed his eyes and rubbed them gently. He knew he had no control over the old man's appearances. After his initial fear, he hadn't much minded the intrusions. This morning, though, he was in no mood for such a visit.

When he opened his eyes, the old man sat cross-legged, facing him. Samson peered at him angrily. He knew he wouldn't be able to speak. *I don't need you this mornin'! Can't you see I'm preoccupied?* he thought.

The old man didn't speak, but smiled softly at Samson. His kind eyes sparkled and, though Samson didn't notice any transformation, he suddenly felt himself begin to relax. He gazed into the beautiful inviting eyes, unable to help himself, and soon his aches and pains were gone.

They sat there wordlessly for close to half an hour. Though Samson was no longer agitated over the old man's visit, he still missed his solitude. He felt grateful to the man for making him feel better, but he wished he'd leave.

He passed the time staring out across the prairie, only occasionally letting his eyes meet the old man's. Each time he saw kindness there and, even though he couldn't have explained it, he felt a forgiveness in those eyes. Samson thought about this for a bit. He knew the man was a vision of some sort. He didn't think he was God or an angel, but he knew that the old man held certain powers over Samson's feelings. He could look at Samson a certain way, and Samson would somehow just know that everything was going to be all right.

Finally, Samson got up to saddle his horse. When he looked back, the old man sat atop the white stallion. The beauty of both the man and the well-muscled stallion nearly took Samson's breath away. He climbed atop his horse and turned it west. The old man and the stallion fell in beside him.

From the corner of his eye, Samson stole glances at his

riding companions. Somehow, their majestic appearance gave him a prideful feeling. Just being in their company, he felt like he was handsome, too, even as he sat there in his dirty buckskins. His face was unshaven and his head itched under his coonskin cap, but none of that mattered as long as he was in the presence of the old one.

They rode until the sun was high in the sky, then the old man pulled rein. The big white stallion pranced about, pawing the earth and snorting. Samson pulled up, too.

The old man spoke for the first time. His voice was deep and commanding, yet gentle and pleasing. His words seemed to penetrate Samson's body, and he absorbed them with more than just his ear.

"You must go there." The old man pointed in a north-westerly direction. "You are needed."

Samson stared off in that direction. He studied the area, all the way to where the blue sky and the prairie became one. He could see nothing unusual. When he turned back around, the old man and his beautiful stallion were gone.

Samson sat there a couple of minutes, then turned his horse off the main trail and headed northwest.

He rode a long time. The sun began to burn his eyes, and he wasn't sure if he was really seeing the rabbit that bounced across his path. He shot at it, anyway, and was pleased when he saw the animal leap once in the air, then fall. He quickly had the rabbit skinned and cooked. His intentions had been to carry it with him until he made camp, but he was too hungry to wait. Besides, a campfire would stand out too much in the open prairie at night. As he chewed on the rabbit, enjoying its taste and wishing he'd brought some salt along, he thought of the old man. *I must be crazy,* he thought. He had a great uncle who had lost his mind. Samson remembered hearing people telling stories about how his uncle had seen imaginary people. He'd used to walk along, carrying on conversations with these imaginary folks. A fear struck Samson as he sat there enjoying the rabbit. Maybe he, too, was going insane, just like his uncle.

He quickly finished the rabbit down to the last bite, tossed the bones aside, and wiped his hands in the prairie grass. He mounted his horse and cursed himself as he turned back toward the trail. If he was going crazy, he wasn't going to do it sitting out there, all by himself.

He hadn't ridden but a few minutes, when a burning smell began to fill the air. Samson stopped and sniffed. At first, he thought it was the smoke from his own campfire, clinging to his clothes. But that wasn't it, he thought. His clothes were a little smoky, but this was a different smell.

It was up ahead of him, definitely coming from somewhere to the northwest. Samson thought about the old man and his instructions, but only briefly. Tugging his coonskin cap down securely on his head, he leaned down low and gave the horse spur.

It wasn't long before he could see the faint pillars of smoke lifting over the horizon. Samson rode for what seemed like more than an hour, following the smell and watching the cloud of smoke. It was funny, he thought, how the prairie made a man misjudge distances. As much time as he had spent out here, he could still be fooled by how close things looked, when they were actually several miles away.

He had ridden up onto a small rise, and was still thinking about how far away those fires might be, when he spotted Indians. He jumped from his horse's back and tied the animal to a bush, then walked forward to get a better view.

Off in the distance, maybe six hundred yards, were a few small rolling hills with trees scattered sparsely about. There, Samson saw the burned-out wagons, some of them still smoldering and smoking. Next to them, Samson guessed there to be a hundred or more Indians camped.

Samson studied the situation, trying to put it all together in his mind. This didn't look at all like the configuration of the group that Gibson and McCloud had described. He counted six wagons burning below. If he remembered right, the two men had told him there were only two wagons full of supplies. They hadn't mentioned anything about stock, whereas Samson counted about forty or fifty head of cattle, herded together.

Mellner had been right in his worry, and Samson had

been wrong in taking it so lightly. He studied the prairie some more. It could fool you. To the eye, it would look flat forever, where in truth it would roll at times. When you rode to the bottom of a little drop, it would still look flat to the eye. A man's own mind could fool you, too, he thought sadly. He wished he'd brought some help along, but he'd been too busy thinking Mellner was overreacting.

The Indians were located in the bottom of a shallow valley. Samson knew he could easily have ridden right into their view. Whether the land looked flat to his eyes or not, he felt grateful to it for giving him cover.

Samson backed out of eyeshot, mounted up, and rode to the north, where he could get closer for a better look. He rode cautiously. The horse under him was a good one, but tired. Samson held no illusions of outrunning a party of Pawnee on rested-up ponies.

It was late daylight, and the sun was quickly disappearing into the western horizon. Though there was still good visibility, only a giant circle of pink was left behind by the falling sun. In a way, Samson was glad that evening was approaching. He was less likely to be seen that way. Still, he needed to get close enough first to get a good look at the situation below.

He carefully moved in as close as he could and tied his horse. From there, he started crawling.

It seemed like he crawled forever. That misjudgment of distance again, he thought. His thighs burned and sweat dripped from his face.

Then, just as suddenly as he had seen them the first time, the Indians appeared below him. His breath caught in his throat as he dropped to the ground. He lay there as the minutes ticked by, hoping that he hadn't been spotted. Slowly, Samson raised his head and crawled on until he found a vantage point that suited him.

He had been right in his assessment. There were a great number of them—at least a hundred, maybe 150. They were passing jugs of whiskey around, and most more obviously drunk. He tried to make a count, and then he noticed the women, sitting together in a group. His heart nearly stopped when he saw that one woman was being covered, just a few yards away from the others. He immediately thought of Nancy, the rape she'd had to endure, and then her murder. He felt a strong urge to shoot the Indian, right then and there, but he couldn't.

Nighttime was beginning to come to the prairie, and Samson was grateful for the opportunity it would offer. Even before the darkness was complete, he started to belly-crawl toward the camp. It was foolish on his part, moving closer without good cover, but he had to get a better look to see if there was anything he could do to help the women.

He also thought about his own group of immigrants, still waiting for word from him. If he got himself killed, they would be left with no one to warn them. Samson wrestled with these thoughts as he inched down the little hill. Several things ran through his mind, back and forth. Nancy's rape and murder. The immigrants. Becky. He wanted more than anything to protect her. But these women needed him now. Samson felt so torn in two, he lost any fear for his own safety.

He crawled to within twenty-five or thirty yards of the women and stopped. It was now dark, and he was in a patch of thick prairie grass that gave him good cover.

Off to his right and ten yards above the women, sat a lone Pawnee. Samson could see he was dozing from too much whiskey. It surprised him that the Pawnee hadn't posted any sober guards. They were overly confident, all right, and careless in their drinking. It was also good that they were out here on the prairie, away from their own camp. Indians always had many dogs in their camps, and the animals surely would have been barking their heads off by now.

It was quiet. A few fires burned low, and the Indians were sprawled out, drinking. The women stayed huddled together, while the one who had been covered still lay on the ground, drawn up onto her side.

Samson lay there in the earth's darkness and examined his situation. It was all laid out in front of him, the captive women and the Indians. He had stopped at a good spot, he realized. He was close enough to see what was going on, but in total cover.

More than likely, this was a futile situation, one man against so many. Besides, these were women he'd never met and felt no ties to, other than the fact that they shared being a part of the human race. Samson fought to keep the doubts from pressing in on him, pushing away any thoughts of giving up and leaving. He longed to be back with Becky, protecting her, even if he couldn't do it as her husband. Then, there was Joseph Mellner, his employer. He had an obligation to Mellner and all of his people to get back and give word of what he had found. They needed his advice and leadership. At the very least, a clearer-thinking man would have gone after help, since the Pawnee had no fears of an ambush.

Still, way down deep inside, Samson knew it wasn't in him to crawl back up the hill and leave these women, no matter what the odds. He decided to wait a while longer. Then he would try to crawl in among the women and get them out. Maybe then he'd find some inspiration as to what to do next.

He waited, whiling away the time with his thoughts. They came and went like a million stars swirling through the night sky. Once he dozed off and dreamed he saw Becky falling from a cliff. He rushed over to grab her, but he couldn't quite reach her. Becky was holding her arms out to him, begging him to help her. But he couldn't. All he could do was watch her falling, headfirst, her mouth opening wide in a terrified scream . . .

Samson came awake, the scream still echoing in his mind. He raised himself up to where his head and shoulders were clearly visible and looked around, wild-eyed, until he found his bearings.

He quickly lay back down, cursing himself. If anyone had been looking in his direction, he would have been easily seen by the Indians, and too dead to be of help to anyone. He got up again to look at the drunken guard, whose head was now dropped low, between his legs. Samson thought he heard snoring. His hand gripped the bone handle of his hunting knife. He took in a deep breath and started making his way toward the unsuspecting Indian.

Samson had always been a contradiction, smaller than the other children and easily mistaken for a much younger child. As an adult, he looked puny and soft. But that was a deadly deception to all but those who really knew him.

The Pawnee was breathing heavily. The uncorked jug between his legs captured the drool that ran from his open mouth.

Before the Indian could awaken, he was dead.

33

Molly was drifting in and out of sleep, with short nightmares playing through her mind. Once she dreamed she saw a two-headed Indian standing over her. He was holding a big hatchet, waving it above her face. One of the warrior's heads had large bulging eyes and flopped back and forth against his shoulder. The other head was bloodred and smeared with war paint. The man-thing sneered at Molly and raised the hatchet. It was so large, it blocked out the sun. Slowly, it began to move downward, toward her.

Molly jerked, and woke herself up. It took a moment to remember where she was and the predicament she was in. She thought about her lost family and wondered about little Louisa. It tore at her heart.

Shortly, she dozed off again, only to wake up in a cold sweat, her heart pounding in her chest, as some other bizarre dream ran through her unconscious mind. This happened so many times, Molly soon wasn't able to separate her waking times from her dreams. Was the two-headed Indian real, she began to wonder? Was she really there in the darkness among a group of women, held captive by savages? Or was the entire wagon train just a dream?

Molly thought she was once again dreaming when the hand cupped her mouth. She gasped and the hand tightened. This was real. It was the big Indian, coming finally to take her. Molly wet herself.

"Don't scream, I'm here to help you," a voice whispered.

Molly's eyes widened, but she nodded. The hand slowly relaxed. Molly turned and looked into the face that hovered above hers. At first, she thought it might be Jory Matlock. But, even though it was too dark to see clearly, she knew it wasn't Jory. This man was much too small. Molly had never seen him before. He leaned down, so close she could smell his breath.

He whispered, "Is this everybody?"

Molly whispered back, "I think so. Who are you?"

The man touched his finger to her lips. "Shhhh. We haven't much time. We need to wake the others."

The man moved to where Christine lay and cupped his hand over her mouth. She jumped, but he pressed himself down against her and whispered into her ear. Quickly, she moved over next to Molly.

"That way," the man said. He was pointing toward the little hill. "I'll send the others behind you. When you get over the top, stay quiet and wait."

Molly, her body trembling, got up stiffly and started crawling, with Christine just behind her. They crept through the prairie grass up toward the little hill, past the sleeping drunken Indians. Her heart pounded so loud in her chest, she was sure it would wake them up. Every few feet, she would turn to make sure Christine was still behind her.

She wondered who the stranger was and how many men were with him. Several times, she tried to look back and see if others were following. From her position on her hands and knees, though, there wasn't much to see but waving prairie grass and the dark sky above.

They had gone seventy or eighty yards, when Molly's knees began to ache. Already, her hands were cut and bleeding. She cursed her body for not being stronger.

"Are you all right, Christine?" she whispered.

"Yes," came the faint answer behind her.

The girl's courage helped Molly keep moving. They continued to crawl slowly toward the hilltop. Molly tried not to think about how badly her hands were stinging. The muscles in her thighs were straining, and her knees felt so sore, she wasn't sure if she could make it.

These weaknesses angered her. She had to stop and catch her breath and let her aching thigh muscles relax. Sweat was running down her forehead and into her face.

Meanwhile, Christine crawled past her. Molly had to grab her foot. "Let's stop a minute," she pleaded, and the girl nodded. This was having little effect on Christine, but then Molly guessed the girl couldn't weigh more than eighty pounds, whereas she herself had to be somewhere between 150 and 155. That was according to the market scale back in Independence. Molly had never considered herself to be a dainty woman. She'd always been big-boned and fleshy. It had been accepted as her lot in life. Now, though, she felt big as a fat-legged boy, trying to crawl up a small hill on her raw hands and knees. Molly asked the Maker why she, too, couldn't have been born small and lithe, like Christine.

More by will than anything else, she forced herself to keep on crawling. The short rest had done her no good at all. Her joints felt stiff and swollen. Her legs were cramping. Tears mixed with the sweat that ran down her face. She puffed and cursed under her breath—cursed her body for letting her down at this time of need.

But Molly just gritted her teeth and pushed on. The pain and fatigue became so intense, she couldn't think of anything but putting one hand in front of the other and pushing forward with her throbbing knees.

She began to wonder if she was moving forward at all, or just stuck in the same spot. Maybe the hilltop was pulling back, moving farther and farther away, always out of reach. Molly gently touched the ground with each knee, and her hands dug at the shafts of prairie grass, over and over again, making herself believe that it was doing some good.

She knew she had to stop again. There was a soft rustling behind her, and Christine's mother appeared. Molly tried desperately to keep up, but her stops became more and more frequent, and soon Christine and her mother had passed her completely. Two more women passed her. By the time Molly reached the top of the hill, three more women had gone around her.

Molly let her body roll down the other side of the hill
to a point where she was finally out of sight of the camp.
She lay on her back, taking in deep, long breaths. Her
body hurt everywhere. Surely, she thought, there couldn't
be any skin left on her knees, and the flesh underneath was
torn ragged. Her hands had swollen to the point where she
could barely close them. Her thighs stung from a mixture
of sweat and urine.

As she lay there with her eyes staring skyward, her
body cold and totally exhausted, Molly thought death
would surely be a satisfying experience. She felt little self-
regard for her weakness and poor physical condition, but
she couldn't help it.

To make matters worse, she started wondering about
Louisa. Where was she? Louisa had meant everything to
her. She began to weep, softly at first, then her body
started shaking uncontrollably. She bit her lip until it hurt,
trying to suppress any sounds from her crying.

What was left in life to live for? She had given occasional thought to getting married again. It would have
been nice to settle down with a good man in Oregon. Jory
Matlock was such a man. There was a toughness about
him that she admired, yet he was gentle and full of decency. She could tell that. And he was considerably handsome. Molly reckoned Jory was about the most handsome
man she'd ever laid eyes on. Just days before, she had
been consumed by thoughts of him, allowing herself to
think such pleasant thoughts as growing old in Oregon
with a man like Jory to spend the cold nights with. She'd
imagined herself in her nice new home, baking pies and
cookies with Louisa. Those thoughts and visions had made
the hard journey an acceptable thing to endure.

Now here she lay, her body screaming in pain, her heart
empty for Louisa, and Jory a million miles away. It occurred to her that Jory might be dead. Maybe the Indians
had killed him, too.

But little Louisa. Even Molly's own love desire was
trivial when compared to the loss of the little girl. The
more she thought about her, the harder she cried. It was
just too much for one soul, she thought. To lose her, get

her back, and then lose her again. Her arms ached to hold
her niece and keep her safe.

Thinking back, she reckoned her whole life had been
one of misery and loss. Her own babies. She had carried
them inside her, given them life and loved them so much,
only to have them taken from her. It seemed like everything she'd treasured in life had been snatched away, like
some thief in the night. She tried to hold to reason, but she
couldn't help but question God's mercy, or maybe His lack
of it. Sobbing, she looked up through her tear-filled eyes
into the night sky, *Where are you?* she screamed silently.
*Where is your mercy? Your loving hands? And where are
my babies? Oh, what did I do wrong, Lord? Why did I
make you angry?* She was still talking to God when she
saw a shadow block out the sky.

It was the man. He bent down close and whispered, "I
think everyone's here. We've got to move on now and be
quick about it."

Molly was brought quickly out of her melancholy. She
sat up and looked. The women were all around her, surely
every one of them. She felt shocked that the man had gotten every single female out of that camp and up the hill.
Even in the dark, she could tell that they were all in a state
of shock. Their clothes were ripped and torn, and their hair
hung lank and dirty like windblown weeds. Some stood
there weeping openly, while others just stared at the
ground, shivering. No one seemed to believe that this was
really a rescue, and that the Indians wouldn't come riding
up on them any minute to take them back.

It was then that Molly realized that she was in a better
mind than most of these women. They, too, had a tremendous pain to bear. It filled her with shame that she had
been so selfish. She glanced at Christine. The girl stood
only a few steps away, clutching at her midsection and
crying softly while her mother held her and gently rubbed
her head.

Wordlessly, the stranger gathered them up and they all
started out on foot. He walked his horse alongside them.
Molly expected to be surprised by the savages any second.
Maybe this time they would just kill them all. Maybe the

big Indian would decide not to wait any longer and take her to use for his own. That would be worse than death. Her legs continued to shake and quiver, but somehow they managed to carry her onward.

The group walked until the dawn. Molly was glad that this stranger had come in the night and led the women out of the darkness of hell, but her sadness overtook her. As she walked, there was time to think, and the heavy burdens that weighed on her heart were too powerful for her exhausted mind to ignore. Her sister, her brother-in-law, many friends, some of whom she had known all her life. How could they be dead? It was too sudden and painful to fully understand. It was even harder to have to wonder about Louisa. Molly's mind took on the cruel bent of imagining all sorts of horrible deaths for the tiny girl. She pictured her skull being bashed in, her body pierced by arrows as she tried to run away. She could see them chopping the little one up, or throwing her from rider to rider. Molly visualized all of this, and though it filled her with horror, she couldn't help it.

When daylight came, Molly noticed that the stranger was constantly looking over his shoulder. Once, he walked among them and softly gave instructions for everyone to walk as fast as they could. When he passed by, Molly said, "They'll be coming for us, won't they?"

Their eyes met briefly. His face was young, a baby face, yet Molly could see a maturity in his eyes. At first, she had guessed him to be barely past twenty, but the pain he carried in his gaze told her that he was much older. He was handsome and yet frail. Molly felt even more surprised that this man could have come in amongst those Indians and gotten the women out.

There was a kindness in his voice, yet it was steady and unwavering. "Don't you be thinkin' about that," he said. "Just think about movin' on. Don't worry."

Molly didn't mean to be rude, but nonetheless, she snapped back at him. "What do you mean, don't worry? We haven't got anything else to do, but worry!"

The man didn't respond. He just looked away and

moved on through the women, offering words of encouragement.

They walked deep into the morning. The cold of the night was easing off somewhat. Molly was surprised that there'd been no sign of the Indians. She wanted to take the stranger's advice, but his own concerned looks told her that he, too, was beginning to worry.

Soon, thirst became a bigger concern than worrying over the Indians. Molly's mouth was getting parched. Her tongue felt sticky. Her lips were already sore from trying to lick them and rubbing them against the back of her hand. A small crack began to bleed, and she felt a small relief as she touched her dry tongue to the blood.

The Indians had given them only a few sips of water early the day before. It had been even longer since they'd had anything to eat. Molly had been thirsty a few times in her life before, but nothing had prepared her for this. She watched the others stumbling along with their heads hanging low. They were thirsty, too, she thought.

Another problem was she had to go. It frustrated her that one part of her body was so dry and the other part wanted to make water. Suddenly, she hated the stranger for pushing them along, the cool prairie wind blowing against their faces. Surely, she thought, he'd stop any second now and give them water and a chance to relieve themselves. Instead, he wordlessly moved on, walking his horse for a spell, then mounting up and riding back a way to look behind them. Molly wanted to stop and pee every time he rode off, but she was afraid he'd come back and see her before she was finished. She knew it would take forever to empty herself. The more she thought about it, the worse it got. Molly felt like her bladder was going to pop and send poison through her whole body.

Almost blind from misery, she tried to speak when he rode past her. Her tongue was so enlarged, she couldn't get the words out. She reached out and slapped at his horse.

The stranger looked down at her and sensed her problem. "I have no water," he said. "Yesterday I crossed a stream. It's a little ways ahead, if you can hold on."

Molly gripped her stomach and bobbed up and down on her feet.

The stranger nodded and halted the group. "I'll ride back a ways," he told them. "If any of you need to relieve yourselves, do it now. We can't waste time."

He'd no more than ridden off than several women began relieving themselves where they stood. Molly tried to walk a few steps, but she couldn't hold it any longer. She squatted down among the other women and did her duty. Any sense of shame or dignity had been lost.

Molly sat there with her eyes closed, the relief rushing through her. Her tongue felt as big as a fist in her mouth, and she was bone-tired, but this was a blessed event. She was still crouched low when the stranger rode back in.

"Let's move," he said. "We can't lollygag very long."

The sun climbed high in the sky. Molly kept looking up, wishing for rain. She had an urge to let her tongue leave her mouth and fly up high in the sky, searching for tiny droplets. Beads of sweat dotted her face. She rubbed her dry lips, unaware that they were now bleeding in several spots. Her tongue was too swollen to probe the cuts.

She had nearly given herself up to thoughts of dying of thirst, when they stumbled onto the little stream. It held water from the recent rains, but the prairie wind was already starting to dry it up. Molly dropped to her sore knees and hands and submerged her face in the inch-deep water. Her nose took up mud, but the water was wonderful. At first, her throat hurt when she swallowed, and it took some time before her tongue was back to its normal size. Molly drank until her belly felt full. She felt a little sick, and her head was dizzy and heavy, but she didn't care.

It scared her to think that she could get in such bad shape so quickly. As Molly drank the life-saving water from the muddy little stream, she tried to remember when she had last had a drink. Had it only been a day ago? It seemed longer than that. But why had she wanted to relieve herself so badly? she wondered. She should have been dry and her bladder empty.

It was getting harder to remember what was real and

what she had dreamed. Molly started to cry, her face just inches above the water. She felt helpless as a baby. Maybe she was going crazy, she thought. The more she tried to think about it, the more she cried. She cried over the fact that she was crying. She cried over losing the most precious thing on earth, her Louisa. She cried over her own selfishness. It should have been her who had died instead of her sister and her family.

She was barely aware that the stranger was taking her by the shoulders. He pulled her to her feet. Muddy water dripped from her face, mingling with her tears. A stream of spittle ran from her lips and was caught in the breeze, stretching thin as a spiderweb before it blew away.

Molly leaned into the stranger's body and pressed her head down against his shoulder. The man grew rigid, yet he patted her back and lightly hugged her. She could tell that he was a man who didn't easily show his emotions.

"We have to move on," he said softly.

"I–I can't," she said.

"Sure you can," the stranger said.

Molly stopped crying and abruptly pulled back. She wiped her nose on her sleeve. She realized how ridiculous she must seem to the stranger and the other women.

"Maybe," she said evenly, "your friends killed the Indians." She looked into his eyes. "There were other men with you, weren't there?" she said.

She thought she noticed a confused look pass over him, but his expression didn't change. "No," he said simply.

34

Jory's insides were turning over at such a rate, he thought he might lose the contents of his stomach. From the location of the smoke that rose into the air, he knew it to be Molly's bunch. Smoke and his warriors had made good on their threats. Jory had no doubts as to what he and Standing Bear would find.

When they were close enough to see the burned-out wagons and the scattered bodies, Jory felt a huge lump rise in his throat. His heart pounded. Why hadn't he stayed with Molly? Guilt consumed him. He swallowed back the lump and tried not to cry openly in front of Standing Bear.

Standing Bear, too, was shaken by the scene below. This was not good, he thought. It would bring on much fighting. He had had many encounters with the white men. For some of them, like Jory Matlock, he had a genuine fondness. Others he detested. All in all, the white men were pretty much like his own people: some he liked, some he didn't.

But war with whites was bad. Not that war among the Indians wasn't bad, too. He himself had little regard for the Sioux, who didn't like the Pawnee and were always driving them south, away from their hunting grounds. White men, though, were different. Once trouble started, white men could kill just for the sake of killing. Standing Bear felt crestfallen at the thought of more people dying.

He wished Smoke had died, back several years ago when he'd been gored by an elk. Smoke had bled and hung on to life for days. All the people had been surprised, after he'd lost so much blood and gotten so sick. But he did live, and now Standing Bear was sad that he'd had a small part in saving his life.

He had been the one who had come along to find Smoke lying in his own blood and struggling for breath. Smoke had thought he'd killed the big bull elk, but it had suddenly come alive and charged him, nearly ripping Smoke's guts out of his body. Standing Bear had wrapped Smoke's belly and hauled him back to their camp.

He had felt regret over that action ever since, but never as strongly as he felt it now. His old eyes searched through the carnage below. The only living beings were his own people, the Pawnee. A deep sadness came over him. He supposed the possibility of lying with milky white thighs was gone like yesterday's wind.

"It is Smoke. He has killed them all, I am afraid," Standing Bear said.

Jory didn't respond to Standing Bear's unnecessary words. His sorrow was deep. This might all have been avoided, he thought. He could have been there to stop the massacre. Even though a part of his mind told him he wasn't responsible, he still blamed himself.

They rode in as close as they dared and stopped. A few of the Indians were lying down, some were seated on the ground, and some were walking around. Jory looked at the bodies, and squinted to see better. He could only make out the figures of men. Where were the women?

"I will go in alone," Standing Bear said.

"The hell you will!" Jory snapped.

Standing Bear moved his pony in front of Jory. His old eyes were tired and laced with pain. "No. You must stay here, Jory Matlock. Smoke will surely not be so generous this time. He will kill you."

Jory's eyes met the Indian's. His face was crimson and the veins on his neck swelled as the two men stared at each other.

"Move aside. I'm riding in with you. I gotta find out what happened to the womenfolk."

Standing Bear understood his friend's pain. He, too, felt angry, but he also knew that Smoke was in a bloody mood. Standing Bear had never known the man to have any regard for anyone, let alone the white man. Smoke was eaten up with hatred, and his appetite for more death would be at a peak.

"You will die. You must stay here."

"The hell I will!" Jory said. "If death awaits me, so be it, but I'll take that son of a bitch Smoke with me!"

Standing Bear could see there was no use trying to talk his friend into staying behind. He could only hope that Smoke would decide to spare Jory's life. He wondered if there was any way to persuade him. Maybe he should mention Smoke's fat mother. Maybe Smoke would think Standing Bear had intentions of sharing the old woman's lodge. That would surely put him in an agreeable mood. Then he could be generous and allow Jory to live.

As he and Jory rode toward the Indians and the death camp, Standing Bear again thought about his dreams of milky white thighs. The dreams had consumed his thinking for days and blocked out any consideration of practical matters for more than a few minutes. Now, though, he knew he must put his friend's needs above his own. He must give careful thought before he broached the subject of Smoke's mother. Surely, he reasoned, there were other ways to gain Smoke's favor. There had to be other things to say that would convince Smoke to spare the life of Jory Matlock. But, try as he might, Standing Bear could think of nothing that would equal the pleasing effect of offering to share the old squaw's bed.

They saw Smoke right away. The big Indian, riding his spotted pony, came out to meet them. As he grew near, Jory could see that he was agitated about something. Jory had never seen this look before on Smoke. All of his remembrances were of a hardened, sour man who seemed ready to kill a man simply for turning his head the wrong way. Smoke's lance stood out like a beacon to a sailor lost at sea. Jory couldn't pull his eyes away from the fresh scalps that glistened in the morning sun. He had a mental image of his own scalp attached to the lance and gave thought to shooting Smoke on the spot. He could take the chance that his horse would outrun the others. Maybe, he thought, if he killed Smoke, no one would even bother to give chase. Maybe the Pawnee, too, would be glad for his demise. He had noticed over the years that most of Smoke's followers held more of a look of fear in his presence than a look of pride in his leadership.

But that was only wishful thinking. There was a pride of honor among the Indians. Even if they all hated and despised Smoke the way Standing Bear did, they still wouldn't let his death go unrevenged. Besides that, Jory had to get into that camp to find out what had happened to Molly.

Still with no plan to carry them over the next few minutes, Jory and Standing Bear watched as Smoke drew near. Jory was somewhat surprised at the arrogant way Smoke rode to meet them, all by himself. His gall alone made Jory want to kill him.

Smoke pulled his big pony up a few feet in front of them and stopped. His jaw twitched and his eyes were bloodshot, but there was little sign of animosity in his demeanor. More than anything, he just seemed to be unconcerned that Jory and Standing Bear were there. Jory got the feeling that Smoke wanted to boast to them about his massacre.

Standing Bear watched Smoke closely. There was no apparent hostility toward Jory, but Smoke was crazy, and first appearances meant nothing. Still, it was good that he didn't have to offer his services to Smoke's fat mother just yet. He could hold on to his suggestion for the time being, and that was a relief.

He knew it might rile Smoke, but just the same, he asked him why he had killed the white people. Standing Bear hoped that Smoke would see that he was now no better than the white man, for this was their way of settling disputes. Standing Bear had not seen this himself, but he had heard stories about the whites riding in their houses on wheels and shooting at passing Indians for sport. He had heard about soldiers killing Indians as they claimed the land to build their forts. This he had not seen either, but he believed the stories to be true. The whites were inferior. He knew that; all of his people knew. Whites were silly,

like children. They did not know how to use the land to
hunt. They wasted food and water and everything else that
they came into contact with. And they beat their children.
Why, his people would never do such a savage thing as to
strike a little one. In tribal custom, they were considered
young and innocent of life's ways. They were supposed to
use their youth to gain knowledge and wisdom, and even
though they could be a nuisance at times, they were nonetheless treated with great love and nurturing. Standing
Bear did not often see this with the white people. They
ruled over their young ones with sticks and strips of hide.

Now, as he sat there, his heart sank and a tear formed
in one of his eyes. It was so: Smoke had lowered himself
to the level of the inferior whites. He should have kept to
his plan of finding the killers and left these settlers alone.
Smoke made him feel ashamed. Sadly, he turned to Jory.

"I do not think Smoke will kill you today," he said.

Jory had seen death many times on the prairie, but he
had never gotten used to human killing. He remembered
the time he'd come across a party of Pawnee hunters. It
had been a few years ago, a hundred miles or so to the
north. The Indians had been slaughtered by the Sioux, every one. Jory remembered the empty feeling that pulled at
his insides as he stood there among the dead. It seemed so
useless to him, that people would murder each other.
Though he was not a virgin to scenes of death, there was
a somberness to witnessing a killing, and each was always
just as startling and new as the first violent death he'd ever
seen.

But this was the worst he'd ever experienced. These
were folks he'd come to know. And Molly. He had developed deep feelings for her and her little niece, Louisa.
Where were they? The fear in not knowing was almost
worse than the surety of their death. Jory walked among
the bodies, almost in a daze. They were grotesque, swelling up, the heads scalped, as they lay scattered about the
burned-out ruins of the wagons. He tried to brace himself
before he found Molly. He didn't really want to see her all
twisted and bloated in death, but it was better to know. He

fought off the urge to turn and ride away. Smoke would most likely protest his leaving, anyway.

He stumbled and almost stepped on Molly's sister, Bertha. Her head had been bashed in by a hatchet. The force of the blow had been so severe that part of her brain had run down the side of her face and dried there. Maggots had already developed and wriggled freely about. Jory could feel himself choking. He remembered Bertha's face the day he had brought Louisa back—the fear that had filled her eyes and how it had been erased at the sight of her cherubic little daughter. Her face had broken into a smile so big and tender, it could only befit a woman's love for her child. Now, that face was bloated with maggots and flies, and his remembrance was tarnished.

Jory grew sick, and he had to draw on his lifetime practice of holding his feelings inward. He gritted his teeth to keep from losing his dignity among the Indians. His legs felt like lead underneath him, but he stiffly moved past Bertha's body. When he reached the skeleton of the wagon he knew to be Molly's, his eyes swept through what was left of her belongings and all around. There was no sign of her. It dawned on him that all but two of the women were missing. Besides Bertha, the only woman he'd seen lay next to the body of a young boy, several wagons away.

There was a faint moan. Jory jerked around to see.

"My God," he muttered.

It was a large man, very large. One arm was nearly severed at the elbow. It lay twisted at an odd angle across his back. He had been partially scalped. His eyes were open and they blinked. The man was alive, but barely. Jory dropped to his knees and took hold of the arm. It nearly came off in his hand. Jory could see that it was barely attached at the elbow. Gently, he moved the arm to a more natural position and turned the man over.

The big man tried to speak. Jory put his ear close to his mouth, but there were no words. The man continued to move his lips soundlessly, staring hopelessly up at Jory with his dying eyes.

Jory wondered who this man was. He definitely didn't belong with these immigrants. Jory would have remembered someone so large. He wished he had his canteen. He looked up in search of some water and saw Smoke, still sitting on his big pony with his jaw twitching. Smoke looked hung over, but he stared at Jory with an insolence.

"You son of a bitch. This man's alive. He needs water," Jory said with his teeth clenched. Such behavior might get a man killed, but dying wasn't concerning Jory at the moment. He had resigned himself to the fact that Smoke would most likely try to kill him. Though he didn't want to die, he was past the point of worrying about it.

Standing Bear walked over and knelt down beside him. "This man is one of the killers we have hunted," he said. "I have talked to some of my people, and they tracked the killers here. Do not look, but someone came during the night and took the women. Smoke has sent Running Dog and others to find them. At first, Jory Matlock, Smoke thought it was you who took the women. But now he knows that it was not you. So we must go, while Smoke is being so generous."

"What about the young'uns?" Jory asked. "I haven't seen but a couple."

"They are two days' ride from here, at the River With Three Forks. My people are camped there. The children were taken there."

"You say someone took Molly ... I–I mean the women?" Jory asked.

"It is not good to talk about that now," Standing Bear said, looking around them. Smoke was not normally a generous and giving sort, but he had drunk so much whiskey that he was greatly hung over and complained of a sore head. He apparently felt too bad to care one way or the other about the two men. Standing Bear knew that when the soreness wore off, Smoke was apt to get in a bloody mood again. Then Jory Matlock would not be allowed to leave without a fight. Smoke might even challenge Standing Bear, for traveling with a white man.

The fact that Smoke had not yet mentioned his mother to him was another sign of his generous nature at this time. Standing Bear was in no mood to press his luck in such matters.

Jory was reluctant to leave, but he knew there was no use in staying. Molly was not here. He wondered who had come and taken her and the others. Whoever it was, he felt a strong gratitude. Standing Bear was right. They had best leave while he still had his scalp attached. They could pick up the trail of Molly and the others. Their rescuer would surely be needing help.

"What about this man?" Jory asked Standing Bear. "Will Smoke let us take him?"

Standing Bear's wrinkled face wrinkled even more as he stared forlornly down at the large man. "Perhaps he will let us," he muttered, "but this man will die soon. It would be best to leave him here. We should not trouble Smoke with such questions."

"Ask him!"

Standing Bear looked at his friend. Surely, Jory didn't expect him to bother Smoke with questions when he was so close to being in a bloody mood again. He shook his head. "It is better to go," he said.

"That may be true. It may be better just to go. Nonetheless, I want you to ask him." Jory stared back at him.

Standing Bear knew there was no use arguing with his friend. Troubled, he turned and moved slowly toward Smoke. He was certain that Smoke would speak to him about his fat mother. The fact that he hadn't so far didn't mean he wouldn't remember now.

Whites were so foolish, he thought. Only a white man would waste his time with someone who lay so close to death. He had figured that Jory Matlock would only be concerned with picking up the trail of the women. He, himself, would like to find them. Maybe Molly or one of the others would lie with him. They would surely be grateful for being taken from Smoke.

Now, though, things grew complicated again. More complicated than they needed to be. The dying man would only be a burden. He should be left to die. In Standing Bear's eyes, the man deserved to be left to the buzzards. He glanced back at Jory Matlock, who was bending close over the killer, examining his arm. Once again, he thought about how foolish the whites were. He thought about just

bidding his farewell to Smoke. He could lie to Jory
Matlock and tell him that Smoke refused to let them take
the man. Then, they could be on their way to find the
women.

In the end, though, he did ask Smoke. And Smoke, who
also thought it was a ridiculous idea, glared at Standing
Bear with his bloodshot eyes and nodded. They could take
the big one, he shrugged. He had fought against the Indians bravely, and deserved to be one of their own people.

They quickly took their leave, devising a rough travois
for the man to lie on, and headed out.

To Standing Bear's surprise, the big man hung on to
life. He had expected him to die before they left the camp.
In fact, he thought the man was already mostly dead, all
but a tiny part of him. Once they were away from Smoke
and the others, Jory finished cutting off the man's arm.
Though both men felt the urge to hurry on their way to
find Molly and the other women, Jory took great care in
cleaning the big man's wounds and bandaging him up the
best he could. Standing Bear sat patiently and waited, his
eyes watchful in case Smoke changed his mind and came
after them.

The morning had pretty much slipped past them by the
time Jory had finished his doctoring efforts. He handed
Standing Bear what was left of his water.

"You stay here with him," he said. "I'll try to catch up
with the womenfolk."

Standing Bear was not happy with the suggestion. "He
is one of the killer men," he pointed out. "Why would you
care about such a man?"

Jory had asked himself that question. He had no answer.
"I reckon it's enough that he's a human being," he said.

"Smoke told me that this man would have been a great
warrior. He said he fought with the courage of ten men,"
Standing Bear said. "Maybe, if he lives, he will kill you,
Jory Matlock."

Standing Bear had never expected the man to live all
this time, but here he was, still alive and being tended to
by Jory Matlock. Maybe this man was like Smoke—too

mean to die. "It is a silly idea. But I will stay, if that is what you want."

Jory picked up the trail easily enough. He circled back around the death camp in the direction Standing Bear's people had indicated to him. Desperation gnawed at him. Standing Bear had said only the tracks of one man had been found. This puzzled Jory. He couldn't imagine who had ridden in and gotten the women out single-handedly. It must have been all the whiskey, he thought. Standing Bear had said one of the wagons had contained enough whiskey to get them all drunk two or three times over. Even the guards must have been drinking. Now they were after one man and several women. From the tracks, he guessed there were a dozen or so Pawnee hunting them.

He knew there was no way he could catch up with the trackers before they reached the women. He hoped against hope that Smoke had ordered that the women be returned unharmed. He pushed his horse hard, while, in his chest, his heart pounded. Feelings of love, real love, had pretty much eluded him in life. It seemed like he always made the wrong decisions, as with Agnes Perring. He could have loved Agnes. He might even have helped save her from the Cayuse. There had been other women that had come and gone, but none of them had given him the thirst to set-tle down and enjoy life like Molly. She was different. He could picture a life with her, up on that farm in Oregon. Oh, he'd get the wanderlust, all right. That was his nature. But his feelings for Molly were of such intensity, he knew he could adjust to settling down. For the first time in his life, he knew it. Jory had always been chasing something, and if he managed to catch up with it, he'd be off chasing something else. He'd never understood or comprehended what made him run in life, what kept him looking to the other side of the mountain, and why once on that other side, he'd just start looking for another mountain. It didn't disappoint him, really, that he held these yearnings. Life was lonely at times, but it had held its satisfactions and ex-citement.

It seemed like the years had slipped past him, so fast it was little more than the blink of an eye. The yearnings ran for something deeper than excitement. He longed for comfort. Nowadays, his body had taken to aching on cold nights. His joints stiffened. His hands were beginning to disfigure. Some mornings, he'd wake up and look down at his red-chafed hands and think of Burley Schultz. He'd met Burley the first time he'd left the States and trekked westward. Burley was a trapper, a tall, thin, big-boned man of about fifty. He'd shown Jory his hands and talked about the ravages of old age. Jory could remember Burley's fingers had become so disfigured, they bent sideways at odd angles. Not long after that, Burley had gotten himself killed by a young Flathead who'd sneaked into his camp to steal some beaver pelts. Rumor had it that Burley had drawn a bead with his rifle on the Flathead, but never got a shot off.

It had been those twisted, swollen hands, Jory thought. They'd been of no use to Burley, and he'd died because of them.

Jory worried about such things. His own joints and fingers often got swollen and sore. He found it harder to wake up in the mornings, and easier to sit longer over his coffee cup. With Molly, he imagined sitting with her on their farm in Oregon and warming his hands by the fireplace. He wouldn't sleep out in the elements any more. Instead, he'd lie with his head cozied up next to hers. And she would be there to take care of him when his hands weren't useful any more.

Now, Jory thought as he rode alone, here he was, chasing another dream. He'd reached for so many others in life. This time, though, he had a bad feeling about what he'd find on the other side of the mountain.

35

Samson could worry over the smallest things in life. Subjects that the normal person wouldn't even think twice about could send Samson into a deep depression. If he were to lose something, he fretted for days, weeks, and, on some occasions, even months. It bothered him to think that he might offend someone by something he said or did. Samson had turned into a private person and enjoyed mostly keeping to himself, but he was extremely loyal to those allowed into his inner circle. He even worried over their lives and concerns, sometimes more than they did.

The fact was, Samson worried over problems that weren't even problems. What might happen, if and when. He wasn't sure what had made him this way. He remembered how his wife had chided him for his frettings over their son. Nancy's and Cordry's deaths had nearly destroyed him, and until Becky had come along, he would just as well have been dead himself. Becky had taken away some of the pain, and now he worried over her.

The one person who had never caused Samson any concern was himself. He rarely thought about his own safety and had never considered illnesses or danger.

Now the thought crossed Samson's mind that his lack of selfishness, although a noble trait, had put him and the women in a perilous position. The Indians were going to catch up with them at any second—of that he had no doubt whatsoever—and he had no idea what he could do to prevent them all from being massacred.

He should have gone back to the wagon train for help.

He should have brought Reuben and about twenty men back with him. Being well armed, they could have easily surprised and overtaken the unsuspecting, drunken Indians. All of these women would now be safe.

Samson thought about his impetuous action. He'd always tended to take the leap before thinking things through clearly. Davy Crockett had warned him about this many times, about how a man should be sure that his actions justified the reactions that followed. It had amused Samson, since Crockett exhibited much of the same spontaneity, himself. Nevertheless, he'd been right.

But Samson was a man who took action in tight situations. He knew nothing could ever change that. He'd seen the women needed help and he'd gone in and brought them out. But now that? Here he was with the fruits of his single-handed rescue. There was no place to hide the women. The prairie, with its wide open spaces, was not the best location for them.

Samson tried to make his plans, thinking over several different scenarios for when the Indians came. It wasn't promising—the conclusions all turned out the same. One man and one gun against a whole group of Indians left little hope. Nervously, he pushed them harder. Some of the women were barefoot, and their feet were cut and bleeding. Most of them kept their eyes fixed straight ahead on unseen objects, having given up on thinking clearly anymore. As if bewildered, they stumbled on forward.

Samson didn't try to talk to them. He knew it was better if they didn't think at all about what had happened to them. Besides, all the thinking in the world wasn't going to change anything.

He was still nursing his guilt and wondering what in the world he was going to do, when he spotted the lone rider approaching from the east. They saw each other at about the same time, and the rider put his horse into a full gallop. It took Samson a few minutes before he recognized Willie. What in the world was that boy doing, Samson thought. He had been left strict orders to stay put with his family. Had something happened?

A sudden panic gripped him. As concerned as he was

over these women and their situation, it was Becky that he most wanted to protect. His love had taken such a grip on his feelings, all other worries paled in comparison.

He spurred his horse and rode out to meet Willie. "What's wrong?" he hollered.

Willie's eyes widened as they danced back and forth from Samson to the women. "Who are they?" he asked excitedly. "Where'd you find 'em?"

Samson grew impatient. "What's happened back there? What are you doing here?" he demanded.

Willie couldn't hide his curiosity. He licked his tongue about his lips and slightly protruding teeth. "What about them women?" he asked again. "Where's their menfolk? Did they have trouble with the Indians?"

"Will you shut up those questions and tell me what in blazes you're doing here?" Samson hollered.

Willie snapped his attention away from the women and looked startled at Samson for his sudden anger. "Why, there's nothing wrong. I got worried about you, is all. I come to check on you."

The jaw muscle began to twitch in Samson's jaw. "You mean to tell me there ain't nothing wrong and you came out here when I warned you not to? Well, you can just turn tail right now. In fact—" Samson stopped speaking and looked back toward the women. His eyes centered on the young girl. She wasn't much older than Cordry. "Follow me," he said to Willie and approached the girl.

"What's your name?" he asked her. She didn't answer, but stared down at her feet and rubbed her knees together.

A woman moved forward and put her hand on the girl's shoulder. "Her name is Christine. I'm her mother, Gloria," she said.

Samson nodded at her. "This here's Willie. Now Christine, I want you to get up behind him and ride double. Willie's gonna take you to a place where you'll be safe. And," he pointed at Gloria, "you get up on my horse. You need to be with your daughter."

He looked around at the other women and pointed. "You. What's your name?"

"Molly Jackson."

"Well, Molly, you get up behind the mother."

"I'm not going," Molly said. "Pick someone else."

Samson shook his head. "No, ma'am. I can see you're having a hard time walking. You're limping. Your knees are all torn up and there's fresh blood all over your dress. I doubt you can make it much farther."

"I'll not leave the others," Molly insisted, "and I'll make it just fine. Look," she said wearily, "I appreciate your help, more than you'll ever know, but I left a sister back there, and I have a little niece—" Her voice caught. "God only knows what happened to her. Take one of the younger ones, please. Take Emma Taggert there. Her life's still ahead of her."

Short, squat Emma Taggert, who was nearly as round as she was tall, stood among the group of women with her head bowed. She had been one of Molly's neighbors back in the States. Just past the age of twenty, she had confided her loneliness to Molly, along with her hopes that in Oregon she would find someone to marry her and give her children. Molly had always felt sorry for the plain little woman. Emma, she decided, deserved to have her dreams come true.

Samson stared at the stubborn woman in silence. This dilemma wasn't going to be solved by deciding which women rode back to the wagon train, and there was no time to be lost in making such a decision. He was just about to give in to Molly's wishes, when he noticed the Indians.

The Pawnee were approaching. Samson guessed them to be no more than a mile and a half to two miles off. He had known it was just a matter of time, but that realization didn't stop the panic that now ran through him.

Willie's face was flushed with excitement. "Boy, there's a bunch of 'em," he said. "What are we gonna do?" His eyes darted back and forth from the Indians to Samson to the women.

"I can tell you what *you're* gonna do, Willie. You're gonna take Christine and ride back for help. Put her on my horse."

"What about her ma and the other woman?" Willie

asked. "Don't you want to us to double up with them?" He looked disappointed that he wasn't going to get to stay.

"It's too late for that now, Willie," Samson said slowly, so the boy would catch his meaning. "If they catch you, son, they'll kill you for sure. Whereas, I don't know what they'll do to the womenfolk. I suspect they'll just gather them up and take them back. Now, you and Christine git and leave me your rifle."

"Don't make me go. If they'd kill me, then they'll for sure kill you. Let me stay and help. Let one of the women take my horse and go," Willie begged.

Samson cut him off. He could understand the boy's lack of respect for the situation. As a youth, he, too, had been prone to taking chances. He'd felt invincible. Now, all he felt was responsible for the young'un and his naive ways.

"Leave me your rifle and git!" Samson said. "I'll hear no more of your arguments." He took Willie's rifle and powder and was surprised when Willie started grinning.

"I brought Pop's rifle too," he said excitedly. He ran to his horse and fetched it, along with the powder horn.

Samson felt grateful, but there wasn't time for thank-yous. Willie and Christine were barely atop the horses when he slapped the animals hard on the rumps and sent them on their way. He watched them for a few seconds, then turned forlornly back to the group of women.

He stared at them, and they stared back. Off in the distance, the Pawnee came.

"I can shoot," Molly Jackson said.

Another woman spoke up. "I'm not much of a shooter, but I can certainly help you reload. I did it for my husband many a time." Then, remembering that her husband was dead, speared by a Pawnee lance, her eyes dropped, then looked back up at Samson full of anger.

Another woman, who had picked up a stick of dry wood to use as a walking stick, waved it angrily in the air. "I'll get me one of 'em," she said.

Samson was impressed by their courage. He had thought them to be broken women. Moments before, they had seemed despondent and broken of spirit, no longer human. Samson had feared that many of them had lost their minds and given up.

But these women had a grit that matched any man's. Battered, hungry, bone-tired, and sore, they had lost husbands and children. They had no weapons and little hope. But here they were, gathered around Samson and ready to take on a band of Indians and fight to the end. Samson had seen that same determined look before, but always in men.

"All right," he said. He handed Willie's new rifle to Molly. "Anybody else got a shooting eye?"

"I do." Emma Taggert stepped out from among the women and grabbed the rifle that Willie had taken from his father.

Samson nodded at them to take position and ordered the women to take cover as best they could. They hurried to collect rocks and sticks, anything they might use to fight off the Indians.

The situation was dismal at best. Samson was nearly overwhelmed. He'd known he couldn't outrun death forever, but now, here it was, lurking right over his shoulder. Back at his home in Tennessee, many a man had died from diseases and the elements, several before they'd reached Samson's age. He'd watched them die, expressed his sympathy, but had never given much thought to his own mortality. Life was a gift—he'd always known that. It was to be taken with appreciation and thankfulness. But Samson had lost that appreciation when Nancy and Cordry had died. He'd given little thought to anything more than facing a new sunrise each day.

Now, as he stood there, it hit him like a bolt of lightning. His time to die had come. He looked at the determination on the women's faces as they grouped around him, and the thought crossed his mind that he couldn't have picked a better group of people with whom to share his last breath.

He gave one last thought to Becky. Softly, to himself, he sent her his silent message. *I love you.*

"All right, ladies. Let's give 'em hell!"

36

⊱———⊰

amson told Molly and Emma to hold their fire until the Indians were close enough for the women to get a good aim. He gave them instructions to shoot at those in front, reload, and shoot again. At his best estimation, they might be able to kill off five or so right away, providing their aim was true. Still, that left close to a dozen Indians who would soon be right on top of them.

He had another theory, however, that he was banking all hope upon. When he and the two women did drop those in front, the rest of the Indians might be surprised by the challenge and hightail it away. He'd seen it happen many times before, with Indians and white men alike. A lot of men liked to fight when they had the upper hand, but quickly ran when the reality of the situation set in. Besides that, these Indians were most likely still hung over from the night before. Maybe they were too soreheaded to give more than a halfhearted effort.

Sweat ran down Samson's forehead and stung his eyes. He rubbed his sleeve over his face. He was holding a bead on an Indian who was riding a pony that looked ridiculously small for its rider. Samson aimed squarely at the center of his chest. He was waiting for the Indian to come a few steps closer, when Emma Taggert fired.

The blast from her rifle made Samson jump. He'd taken it for granted that his shot would be the first. The Indian jerked violently and fell backward, pulling the little pony down with him.

There was no time to waste on whose shot came when.

Instead, Samson felt instantly grateful for Emma's accurate aim. He quickly regained himself and dropped an Indian who had ridden next to the fallen one. He'd barely squeezed the trigger, when Molly's rifle sent a bullet into another Pawnee. The Indian was wounded, but managed to stay on his mount.

The shots startled the Indians. Some of their ponies bolted sideways, others reared and kicked, but still they raced forward. Their war cries shrieked across the prairie sky.

Samson's second shot hit a young Pawnee in the forehead. The Indian grabbed his face and fell over his pony's neck. Emma's rifle misfired on her second try. Molly took careful aim and shot an Indian no more than fifteen feet away.

Samson was trying to get off a third shot, when an arrow dug into his shoulder. On reflex, his hand flew to the wound, as another arrow struck under the right side of his breastbone.

"They've killed me," he muttered to himself. "The sons of bitches have killed me."

Cursing his attackers, he tried to take aim, but another arrow sliced his cheek and went on to strike thirty-five-year-old Katherine Mayweather in the throat. Blood spewed from the severed main artery in her neck, and she fell to the ground. Only the day before, Katherine had lost her husband and two sons. Oregon had been a dream that she and her husband had mostly disagreed upon. She had been happy in her home back in the States, but she'd been unable to sway Abraham from his wandering ways. Finally, he'd convinced her to head westward, and they had started off in Massachusetts when they were first married. They had worked their way farther west, through Pennsylvania and Ohio. Then they had hooked up with the others at Independence. Katherine had been grateful for the company. It had been Abraham's intention to travel alone, but Katherine felt safety in the numbers of others. Now, she was dead, gone to join her family.

Samson took a fourth arrow, but not before he killed another Indian. The arrow was delivered by a brave who had ridden almost directly on top of him. The arrow passed through Samson's upper shoulder. He dropped the rifle and fell forward, striking his head on the earth and taking in a mouthful of dirt. He tried to raise himself up, but he was suddenly too tired. He spit the dirt from his mouth. Funny, but he didn't feel any pain, but hadn't he been hit, more than once? He had to get up and help the others. If he could just get his bearings, he thought. If only the ground would be still underneath him. Then he could help the women.

It dawned on him that the shooting had stopped. The Indians had ceased their war cries. What was happening, he thought. Had the Indians left? Had they turned and run?

He was lying beside a little tree. Somehow it bumped hard against his head. Samson reached out for the trunk to steady himself, but the tree pulled away.

He heard snorting, and the tree turned into a horse's leg that stomped on the ground beside his head. The Indians were still there. Samson blinked his eyes hard, trying to get his mind to think clearly. He knew the futility of getting up, but he couldn't just lie there. The women needed him. Once again, he tried to push himself up, but his body only shook with the effort. He felt so tired, so helpless. As confused as his mind was, his body was even weaker.

Only seconds passed by, but to Samson it felt like he had lain there for days. Slowly, he began to feel the aches and burns from his injuries. His shoulder was hurting badly, and his bloody cheek stung as it lay pressed against the ground. His stomach hurt, too, and there was a cramping in his gut. Suddenly, he felt thirsty.

The ponies were standing over him. Through narrow slits, Samson looked up and into the sun at the figures on horseback. Nothing made sense any more.

The next thing he knew, he was lying on his back, but it was different. The sun was no longer in his eyes, but was blocked by the shape of someone's head. Samson opened his eyes and blinked hard until the face came into focus.

He'd seen that face before. She was saying something to him, but he couldn't understand the words. The hard ground under his head felt soft, and he managed to understand that he must be lying on her lap.

He tried hard to listen closely to what she was whispering, but he couldn't put the pieces together.

Suddenly, Samson felt his body being raised up, then slamming against the ground. The woman's face was gone.

The shadowed riders that surrounded him were Indians, and the soft lap was Molly's. They had pulled her roughly to her feet and dragged her off, and now they were talking over him. Though he didn't understand the words, he knew the angry tone.

The sudden loud shot rang in his ears. Samson expected a new surge of pain, but he felt nothing. It wasn't him they were shooting, he realized. It must be Molly. Were they shooting her?

Then, one of the silhouettes stiffened, and the Pawnee fell from his pony. Horses' hooves pounded the ground all around as another shot rang out. Then, the ponies and their silhouetted figures were gone. Again, Molly was by his side.

She pulled his head to her breast and cradled him as one would a child. His breath felt hot against her chest. Samson thought of his mother, and the fear within him vanished. He felt safe again. Maybe for the first time in years, he felt safe. Molly's ample breast began to shake, and Samson realized that she was crying.

He lost consciousness. When he came to, he was still in Molly's lap. She was holding him tightly against her, so tightly it hurt. His body was burning. He felt like crying out.

There were voices. Someone was tugging at him, then a pain ripped through his shoulder that was so intense, he let out a holler.

"There. I got it out," a man's voice said. "But he's losin' a lot of blood."

The voice was strange to Samson's ears. He tried to sit up, but nearly blacked out from the effort.

"Don't try to move," Molly said to him. "This here's Jory Matlock, and he's our friend." She added, "If he hadn't come along, well . . ."

Samson's eyes searched the man's face. He couldn't remember ever seeing him before. "I'm grateful," he said.

Jory Matlock nodded. "I wouldn't be too grateful so quick. They're still out there. Eleven of 'em. I managed to run 'em off, but it won't be long, I'm afraid. When they realize it was only me that was shootin' at 'em, they'll be back." He looked at Molly and wished he hadn't been so blunt. " 'Course, then, they might not come until dark. I don't know."

"Eleven, you say?" Samson said. His body burned like he'd been dipped in a boiling caldron, but for the first time his mind felt clear enough to do some rational thinking.

"That's what I counted," Jory said. "Four of 'em are dead, and another looked like he was shot up pretty good. We did get a rifle off one of 'em."

"It was my brother-in-law's," Molly said bitterly.

Jory pulled his eyes away from Molly. He hurt deeply for her and wanted to take her in his arms and tell her so. But it wasn't in his nature to be so bold. "Do you know about the children?" he asked her.

"No! Tell me!" she demanded fearfully. "Did you find Louisa?"

"No, but I got a good idee where she's at. They took the children to their camp up north. It's a couple days' ride from here."

The other women drew closer to better catch what Jory was saying. Several began to cry.

Molly looked up at Jory. "We've got to save them."

"How are the women?" Samson asked.

"All things considered, they're just fine," Molly said. Her face turned sad. "Except for poor Katherine Mayweather. She took an arrow and died."

"They were only after you," Jory said to Samson. "As far as I can tell, except for the lady that got hit, none of the other women were even aimed at."

"Where's my rifle?" Samson asked. He felt a new urgency to be up and useful again. He tried to pull free from Molly, but he was too weak.

The fact that he hadn't died had started him thinking about Becky. He wished he was back with her now. He'd give anything to relive that night next to the bush when she'd given her love to him. Samson knew he was hurt badly and might die at any moment, but his only fear was that he might never see her again. He had to talk with her, if only for one last time. It meant everything to him, and he was sure it meant everything to her, too.

"Give me my rifle," he said again.

"You just lie still," Molly said. She pushed his hair back from his eyes. "Harriet Andrews has your rifle. Her daughter, Sadie, is carrying your pistol. Don't you worry none."

She squeezed Samson tight, then reached down and kissed him on the forehead. "I'm forever grateful to ya," she whispered. "I just want you to know that."

The Indians were about five hundred yards to the west. The tension in the air was thick, as Samson, Jory, and the women waited for them to strike again. Each minute seemed like an hour, but they had no other choice but to wait. The women talked about their anger, and they were determined to fight against the savages, but still the fear ran among them that the two men would be killed, and they would be taken back as prisoners to be raped and used as the Indians pleased.

There was considerable concern about Samson, too. Even though he was conscious and seemed to have stabilized, he had lost a considerable amount of blood and was weakened by his wounds.

The afternoon sun was heading west, when the rest of the Pawnee band suddenly appeared on the horizon.

"My God!" Jory announced. "It's Smoke!" There was a resignation in his voice, and the lines in his face deepened with worry.

Molly watched the band intently. The man was hardly distinguishable to the naked eye at this distance, but she could make out the shape of the big Indian on his powerful pony, riding in front. She remembered his cold, mocking eyes, and the shred of hope she'd been holding on to suddenly started to dim. Her faith in the intentions of Jory and this man Samson was strong, but there was no way in God's earth that they could fight off Smoke and his men.

Ever since Jory had mentioned that the children had been taken north to the Pawnee camp, Molly had thought of little else but Louisa. Now, her hopes of finding and saving the little girl were gone like the prairie wind. She knew she might possibly live to see Louisa. She might even end up in the same camp with her. But that would be a fate worse than death itself, for not only would she, herself, be handed from Indian to Indian. She would have to see her Louisa grow up to meet the same fate. Even the idea of being saved for the big Indian alone filled Molly's heart with terror.

She felt tired and drained. She looked at Jory, who was huddled down next to her and Samson, fiddling with his gun. *Poor Jory,* she thought. *They'll kill him for sure.* And Samson, the stranger. She owed her life to him, and he'd be dead before long himself. She looked back across the prairie at the Indians. They were still just specks in the distance.

"Smoke. Is he the big one out front?" she asked.

"That's him," Jory said simply. He looked at Molly. There was an urgency stirring inside him. There wasn't much time, and he needed to talk to her. He needed to let her know how he felt—that it had been she who had tamed his wandering heart. He searched for the courage to look into her eyes and tell her. He wanted to say that he loved her and how he had dreamed about cutting the wood to build their new home in Oregon. About growing crops and spending the rest of their lives together.

This was an inopportune time, but it was the only time he had. On an impulse, he reached his hand out to her. She took it and stared back at him expectantly.

The words wouldn't come. Their eyes held on to each other as their thoughts and feelings passed back and forth, unspoken, but understood just the same.

Molly saw the sadness in Jory's eyes and knew his frustration. She thought about all the pain and the loss. So many lives ruined and wasted. Then she thought about Jory's courage, his kindness, and his gentle ways.

For years, Molly Jackson had wondered if there was a man left alive who could breathe new life into her soul, in a way that only a man could do. She looked a while longer into the eyes of Jory Matlock.

Finally, she stood up and stared at the Indians. Her voice was deep and strong again. There was a new fire burning in her soul.

"I'm gonna kill Smoke, myself," she said.

37

Reuben rode out in front, having taken Samson's place during his absence. He felt lonely and somewhat bored. The wagon train moved at a snail's pace, and he missed Samson's company and conversation.

Sometimes Reuben wished he'd never left the tavern. Why, if he hadn't left, he could be sitting there right now with his feet propped up and a jug nearby, listening to some stranger telling tall tales. Gertie would be taking care of him and tending to the customers. While Reuben liked to handle the money himself, Gertie was much better at the labor end of things. Other men had sometimes made fun of Reuben and his so-called lazy ways, but it didn't bother him any. Actually, he considered himself to be blessed with the trait of intelligence. Most men, he figured, didn't have the slightest clue as to what their own long suits were, whereas Reuben was using his talents to the best advantage.

It prided him to know that he knew how to make money. He could sit down and figure it all out from start to finish while nursing a jug of liquor. He realized that other men viewed this activity as a waste of time, but that didn't matter to Reuben. Many a time, he'd been tempted to tell them. He was like a possum, he'd say. Whereas the possum would play dead, Reuben would play drunk and keep his thinking to himself. Not that he didn't like to get inebriated on occasion. He greatly enjoyed sitting down to a drink with others and listening to their stories while taking in their money.

Well, he thought, that was behind him. He thought about the possibilities of what might lie ahead. He reckoned he'd like Oregon well enough. He'd already laid some plans in his mind to build him a tavern with sleeping quarters in the back. He'd given some thought to putting his sleeping quarters up above and making the place real fancy. He could even take in guests. That would bring in some extra money. Then, he got to thinking about having to climb those stairs, day after day, and pretty soon he came to the conclusion that it would be much easier for him to simply stumble to the back and fall into bed each night. Of course, he reasoned, he could have it both ways. He could keep his sleeping room in the back, and still build a fancy suite of rooms overhead. These were pleasant thoughts, and he enjoyed wrestling back and forth with all sorts of ideas. The only dark spot was the absence of Gertie. Without her, there was no one there to listen to his ideas, silently but agreeably, like she did, or to warm his bed at night.

Reuben was thinking about taverns and guests and Gertie's ample backside, when his gaze fell upon two riders, off in the distance. He could tell they'd been riding hard for a spell. The horses looked tired and ran that way.

One of the riders was Willie, and Reuben recognized Samson's horse running alongside. But it wasn't Samson. It was a girl.

What in the world was Willie up to, riding along with some girl on Samson's horse? Willie's pap was going to be some kind of angry, Reuben thought to himself. He'd been looking for his son ever since Willie had told him he was going off to look for some strays, and hadn't returned. The boy's mother had been near hysterics, carrying on about Indians snatching the boy and killing him.

Willie was waving his arm and hollering something, but he was too far away to make any sense. Reuben gave his horse spur and rode out to meet them, trying to put Willie's words together. The boy obviously needed help of some kind, and what with the girl riding Samson's horse, it didn't take a lot of figuring to realize that Samson was involved in some way.

Willie rode up hard, and their horses nearly collided.

"Now, just calm down," Reuben said, staring at the wild look in Willie's eyes. "Tell me what's happened."

"We got to get help right away!" Willie said. "For Samson and the women!"

"What women are you talkin' about? Willie, slow down some and catch your breath," Reuben said.

"Back there." Willie pointed and nodded over his shoulder. "Samson's got about a dozen women with him, and there's at least that many Indians, to boot. We gotta hurry, Reuben! It may be too late already!"

Reuben was trying to put the pieces together, when Mellner and some of the other men rode up.

"What's going on here? Where's Samson?" Mellner asked. He stared at Samson's horse, then the girl.

Reuben started to try to explain, but Willie talked right over him. "Back yonder. Them Indians are gonna kill Samson and the women if we don't get there to stop 'em. They might have already killed 'em!"

Again, Reuben started to jump into the conversation, when Mellner turned to Tom Sinclair. "Go back and round up some men," he said. He looked at Willie. "How many Indians are there?"

"About a dozen, I 'spect."

Mellner nodded. "Tom, bring about twenty-five or thirty men. Tell them to come well armed."

"Wait!"

The girl's voice startled the men. They turned to her, waiting for her to say more. She wouldn't look at them.

"There's more than that," she said simply.

Willie looked surprised, "Why, I looked good, and I didn't see no more'n maybe a dozen."

"They's the ones that come after us. They's the ones you saw," Christine said. "But there's more. There's lots more—" Her lips quivered, and she started to cry.

"Take her back to the womenfolk," Mellner said quickly to Willie. "Have Missus Mellner get her some clean clothes and food. Hurry, boy."

"Yes sir. But, I didn't see that many Indians. I swear I

didn't. And Samson didn't say nothing about any more," Willie said.

"Shhh," Mellner hissed. "Just take care of the girl, here. Do as I say!"

It wasn't long before Tom Sinclair had rounded up the men. Some of the womenfolk clung to their husbands fearfully, while others cried. A few of the younger boys begged to go along. The children were full of questions. It was almost a circus atmosphere. Impatiently, Mellner ordered the families to return to their wagons and told Reuben to stay back with them to watch over things.

Reuben would hear none of it. "Samson's the best friend I got in this world," he argued. "By damn, I'm goin'!"

Joseph Mellner was faced with a quick decision. He had every intention of going, himself, but then he thought about what the girl had said. There were more Indians, but how many more? Suppose they had already overtaken Samson and were headed this way?

Someone of an authoritative nature had to stay behind and protect the wagon train. Reuben was clearly bent on going. Mellner realized with some disappointment that it was his duty to stay behind.

Tom Sinclair had gathered up a total of twenty-nine men to face the Indians. Now some of the men were questioning whether that was enough. The girl, Christine, had told them there were many more Indians than Willie had seen. With over two hundred men traveling in the wagon train, why should they take a party of only twenty-nine men? If the girl was right, they would surely be slaughtered, they warned.

Mellner weighed all these facts. He still believed his first duty was to the wagon train, yet he felt compelled to send help to Samson and these women. He could take all two hundred of the men. They would be a formidable foe, but what if all the men went out and got themselves killed? Then what became of the women and children on the wagon train?

The girl was delirious. Maybe she was wrong. Maybe Willie, though an excitable boy, knew the truer picture. At a loss, Mellner finally turned to Reuben for advice, figuring that he might know their best course of action. After all, Reuben knew about Indians. He'd been married to one. And, even though Mellner hated Reuben's drinking ways, this was no time to let his prejudices stand in the way of better judgment.

"What are your thoughts, Mister Cook? Do you think the girl is telling the truth?"

Reuben looked surprised. This was the first time that Joseph Mellner had ever spoken to him in a manner that didn't seem condescending. The importance of the occasion wasn't lost on Reuben. He rubbed his chin.

"To tell you the truth, I ain't sure, hoss," he said slowly. "I did pick up from Willie that Samson rescued some women. If I had to venture a guess, I'd say the girl's probably tellin' the truth." He stopped talking long enough to bite off a chew. "Then, on the other hand, I think the boy's tellin' the truth, too."

"How in the world could *both* of them be telling the truth?" Mellner demanded.

"Well, hoss, the way I got it figured, Samson must've run across some women that the Indians stole and snuck in and got 'em out. The Pawnee most likely picked up their tracks and saw it was just one man that did it. My guess is they just sent out a small party to fetch 'em back. 'Course," he shrugged, "I could be wrong."

"Should I send more men?" Mellner said, his voice dropping to where the prairie wind almost covered it up.

"I wish I knew, hoss," Reuben said truthfully. He didn't envy Joseph Mellner for the decisions that he was faced with making. A man could make any number of decisions and they could all turn up right. Or wrong.

"Are we gonna go, or sit here talkin' about it? Time's a-wastin'," Tom Sinclair said.

Reuben couldn't help but give a peculiar eye to Sinclair. He knew the man hated Samson, and he suspected Sinclair would even kill him if given the chance. He'd seen a lot of Tom Sinclairs in his life—men who hated for no apparent reason and looked for trouble. Reuben knew it wasn't any concern over his wife that bothered Tom Sinclair. The fact that she had talked to Samson might have set him off a time or two, but men like Sinclair didn't set their caps on anything as substantial as jealousy or love. It was the taking of other men's hides that they lived for, living at the expense of others.

Samson should have killed Sinclair, Reuben thought. He wished he had. Reuben even thought about killing him, himself. It would surely eliminate a lot of trouble in the future. Some men were just better off dead, and Sinclair was one of those men. Now, the snake was here, offering to lead the charge that would save Samson's life. Why, Tom Sinclair had no inclination to save anybody! He needed the fight, pure and simple.

Reuben decided to keep a close eye on the situation. He had no real idea what thoughts the man was carrying in his head, but he would be on hand, just in case. He'd kill Sinclair, himself, before he let him get near Samson.

He hadn't intended to say anything, but the words popped out before he could stop himself.

"What are you in such an all-fired hurry for, Sinclair? I reckon everybody knows the bad blood between you and Samson."

Sinclair's nostrils flared. His face turned crimson as he glared Reuben's way. "That ain't got nothin' to do with nothin'," he said.

Reuben opened his mouth to answer, but Mellner complained loudly.

"That's enough! I can't believe you'd make such a statement," he said to Reuben.

Reuben couldn't believe he'd said such a thing, either, but he wasn't sorry he'd said it.

They put away their argument and set out together in the direction Samson had taken. The men rode hard for over two hours, overworking their horses into a lather, before they first spotted the Indians about a mile away.

There were many more than they expected. The girl had been right. Some of the men cursed Joseph Mellner for not believing her. But the Indians were just sitting there on their horses. For some strange reason, they hadn't attacked Samson and the women.

"What do you make of this?" Tom Sinclair asked. He had ridden up beside Reuben, and together they looked the situation over. "Given the time it took those young'uns to ride back and fetch us—" He paused, puzzled. "Why do you reckon they haven't attacked?"

"Damned if I know," Reuben said. It surprised him to see that the women were there, sitting together, instead of all dead. He thought he could see two men. One was sitting up, and the other appeared to be lying down. He wondered if Samson was alive among them.

Two opinions started forming among the men. One was to charge in, and the other was to pull back altogether. Tom Sinclair sneered at the idea of withdrawing.

"I say let's go in and kill the bastards!" he said. "We got guns and they don't. Why, it'll be easier than killing settin' ducks on a pond."

Reuben was surprised at Sinclair's brassiness. They might have guns, all right, he pointed out, but the Pawnee looked to be over a hundred strong. It would be a battle for survival on both sides—more than just shooting ducks on a pond.

"Well, hoss," he said, "we didn't ride here to run away, and we didn't come all this way to get ourselves killed, neither. What we need to do is slowly make our way in to where Samson and the women are. We won't make any sudden moves, but just move slow and easy. Why, it could be that them Pawnee ain't gonna do nothin'. They might just let things be and go on home."

"I agree with half of what you say," Sinclair answered. "I surely didn't come this far to turn tail and run, but we're about to miss out on a golden opportunity here. We'll ride in, all right, slow and easy, like you say. But then we'll kill 'em. Kill 'em all before they kill our own women and children."

Reuben was nodding his head. "That's right, hoss. You go ahead and start a war, right here and now. But you just better be prepared to fight all the way to Oregon, if you do. Have you ever fought an Indian, mister?"

"I haven't had the pleasure," Tom Sinclair answered coldly.

"Well, then, let me offer you a word of warning," Reuben said. "First off, we might have better weapons, but you can't match up to them Indians in savagery. Things that you think to be barbaric in nature is commonplace among 'em. No, you'll not equal their brutal ways in times of battle, I'll guarantee ya. A white man'll get knocked down by the elements, but about the only thing that'll kill any Indian out here in the wilderness is other Indians. They spend their whole lives moving along behind the herds. They beat the dryness and the heat in the summer and live through the worst blizzards in the winter. Their hides are tougher than ours." Reuben shook his head. "Nope, I'll tellin' ya, hoss. You don't want to make things any worse'n they are. Something made those Pawnee take to the warpath in the first place. It just ain't their nature to be attackin' innocent folks. They might steal your livestock or food, but they ain't killers. So, until we find out what upset them, we best take a defensive posture."

"That's all pure horse piss!" Tom Sinclair said. "Frankly, I don't give a good damn what caused those savages to do nothin'! I'm goin' in and kill their asses, before they start killin' us!" He looked around at the men. "What about the rest of you? You comin'? Or maybe you'd rather go back to the womenfolk."

"I think we'll just wait a spell," Reuben cut in. He stared a long time at the Indians, then down at the group of women.

Everyone was still. The Indians sat motionless on their horses. He made his decision.

"*You* ain't goin' nowhere, Sinclair. We'll ride in together, real slow. And if them Pawnee make a move, we'll fight 'em." Reuben looked at the men, one by one, waiting for a word of refusal. There was none. Then he stared at Sinclair.

"Now let's go."

38

~~~❦~~~

Samson thought his eyes must be playing tricks on him. He raised his head to get a better look. Yes, it was him, off in the distance. The old man with the silvery, flowing hair sat atop his magnificent white stallion, right next to a large Indian on a big, muscular horse. He was looking this way, as if he could see right into Samson's eyes.

The old man's presence brought a peace to Samson's heart. He wondered if he was dreaming again. He'd been hurting so bad, falling in and out of consciousness, and having terrible dreams. Maybe this was just another trick of the mind.

He looked around him. Molly was still there, and so was the stranger, Jory. He took in a breath and tried to rise up higher, but the pain overwhelmed him. Yep, he thought, he was awake, all right.

But what was the old man doing here, riding with the Pawnee? Surely he wasn't a part of their tribe? No, no, Samson told himself. He couldn't be. The old man had been appearing to him for over a year, in places that were far from Pawnee country. Yet, there he was, sitting with the Pawnee, tall and proud on the stallion, with the prairie breezes catching the silver hair and lifting it gently.

Samson craned his neck to see better. After all this time of seeing the old man and mostly dreading the occurrences, it was now a welcome sight.

Molly was gently pushing him back down. "You must be still," she said softly. "You've stopped bleeding."

"Do you see him?" Samson asked her, pointing toward the old man.

"What's that?" Molly frowned.

"The one with the silver hair."

Molly looked toward the Indians, then back at Samson. He was hallucinating, she thought. Maybe he was about to die. She'd heard about people seeing things when they were near the end. It seemed like all her life, anybody she cared about had ended up dying. Sometimes, it made her feel guilty for living.

Emma Taggert was sitting nearby, watching the Indians. "What are they waiting on?" she said, her voice breaking with emotion. "If they're trying to drive us crazy, they're doing a good job."

"What *are* they waiting for?" Molly asked. "Why haven't they attacked?"

"I don't rightly know," Jory admitted. "Maybe they're having trouble agreeing on what to do with us. With Smoke, though, I doubt there'd be much argument."

Emma Taggert let out a cry. "Look!" she said. "Over yonder! Praise God!"

Off in the distance, riders were approaching. White men. One by one, the women stood up to watch them.

Molly leaned over Samson and smiled. "Christine and your friend, Willie, have sent help," she said.

Samson nodded, but he hadn't really heard what she said. He was looking at the old man with the wisdom in his eyes.

Several of the women were jumping up and down and waving excitedly at the approaching riders.

"I surely don't want to spoil things, but we better hold our celebrating," Jory said. "We're not out of the woods yet."

Molly gave him a hard look. "I reckon the only thing we have left is hope," she said. "Don't begrudge us that."

Jory looked sorry for his remark. He turned to look at Smoke. "Damn him," he muttered. The Pawnee were known to be peaceful for the most part, but they weren't afraid of a fight, either. It was puzzling to him why they hadn't charged right on in and finished things hours ago.

By now, they could already have the women back in the Pawnee camp.

Maybe he was judging Smoke too harshly, Jory thought. Maybe Smoke wanted to stop the killing. But the more he thought about it, the more he realized there was no explanation. Smoke was a strange one, he knew, and he also knew that the man carried a bigger itch for a fight than anyone else he'd ever run across.

Nearby, Samson lay dreamily watching the old man's white horse prancing in its graceful way. There was something about the animal that was soothing. He'd always loved horses, but never had one held him so captivated.

The more he watched the old man and the stallion, the more the pain in his body seemed to go away. *The old man must be intervening,* Samson thought. He had never understood why the old man had begun appearing to him in his dreams shortly after Nancy and Cordry died. It was even more puzzling when he showed up in Samson's waking hours.

"The old man will save us," he said, but his voice was so weak, no one paid him any mind.

Deep down, Samson had always known that there was a purpose for the old man's appearances. At times, he'd tried to explain them, considering that he might be a guardian angel. He'd wondered, too, if Nancy and Cordry had sent the old man along. He'd had a powerful urge to talk to somebody about it, but he couldn't for fear of looking foolish, even crazy.

Samson had always been a deep thinker. As a boy, he'd wondered if he was the only one with such a trait. Once, when he was nine or ten years old, he'd told a schoolmate about a dream he'd had, and the boy had laughed at him. His mother had overheard, and she warned Samson about telling tall tales. People might think badly of him, she'd said. From that day on, Samson had kept his inner thoughts mostly to himself, even with Davy Crockett, who used to talk for hours on end when they'd be camped for the night, telling Samson story after story. Even at Samson's young age, he knew a lot of the tales were stretched far beyond reality.

He remembered how Davy had shared his feelings on just about anything that came to mind. He discussed his views on politics, religion, differences between men and women, whom he liked and whom he disliked.

But for a man who liked to talk so much, Davy had always had a ready ear to listen. He'd encouraged Samson to speak his mind. If ever there was a person Samson could have talked to about things, it was Davy.

Samson sighed to himself and wished his old friend had never made that trip to Texas. If he were here today, Davy wouldn't laugh at Samson and his visions. Most likely he'd nod his understanding, then offer his attempt at explaining what the old man with the silver hair and the white stallion were all about. Not only that, Samson thought. Davy would be easing everyone else's burdens with his stories.

Samson was deep in his musings, his eyes drawn and locked on the old Indian, when a familiar voice cut deep into his thoughts.

"Damn, hoss! They got you good! Here, have a pull on this jug."

Reuben was at his side. He held out the jug of whiskey.

"Reuben, my friend," Samson said weakly. "It's damn good to see you. Where's Willie? Are he and the girl all right?"

"They're both just fine, hoss. Fetched us back here. C'mon, take a drink. It'll do ya right."

Reuben held him up. As Samson took hold of the jug, he felt the old Indian's eyes on him, watching. It was strange, he thought. The old man had never appeared to him in the presence of others. He'd always been alone before. Could anybody else see him? Surely, they all noticed the feeling of comfort that had settled over the situation. Surely, he wasn't the only one privy to such a wondrous thing.

The whiskey burned going down, and Samson started to cough. The movement sent pain through him. He grabbed Reuben's arm and squeezed it hard until the aches eased somewhat. Then he checked to reassure himself that the old man was still there.

Tom Sinclair was looking over the group of women. He walked to where Samson lay and studied the Pawnee, then turned his unfriendly gaze on Reuben.

"What in the hell are those savages doin'?" he asked. He gave Samson a disdainful glance, then added, "Well, there ain't gonna be no better opportunity. We could drop a third of 'em with one volley."

"I doubt that," Reuben said. "They're too far. You're a better shooter than me if you can hit 'em at that distance."

"I know damn well I could drop one of 'em," Sinclair said. "Just aim a little high, and this rifle of mine will bring him down. I guarantee it."

Jory spoke up. "Lookee here, mister. You shoot in among them Indians, and you'll get us all killed."

"Oh, don't pay no attention to him," Reuben said. He stood up to shake hands with Jory. "I'm Reuben Cook," he said. "This here's Tom Sinclair. He's of the opinion that if we kill off these here Injuns, it'll clear the way to Oregon."

Sinclair looked angry. "You mind your tongue, Reuben Cook, or I'll deal with you later."

Reuben spit tobacco juice and just barely missed Sinclair's feet. He wasn't afraid of Sinclair, but he wasn't wanting any trouble, either. Men like Tom Sinclair could cause a lot of worry, because they were crazy. In fact, Reuben figured that the best way to deal with such a fellow was to sneak up on him and hit him with a chunk of wood, or a rock, while he was resting or sleeping. Normally, Reuben would have considered that a coward's way, but in the case of Sinclair and others like him, it was simply the smart way to handle things.

Sinclair was fingering his firearm. "Well, what are we going to do, just sit here and wait?" he asked.

"I say we've got a couple of choices," Jory said. "We could do that—sit here and wait, or we could start pulling Samson and the women out a few at a time. Some of the men could stay here and keep them Pawnee at bay until everyone's out, then hightail it themselves. At any rate, the mere fact that they've been sitting there for several hours puts me to thinkin' that they ain't in no hurry for a fight."

"That's fine, but what about our families?" Emma Taggert spoke up angrily. "They slaughtered our loved ones like animals—like they weren't even human beings!"

"What about the children?" Molly stepped up and said. "They stole our babies. I can't leave here until we get our children back!"

Jory explained to Reuben and the other men about the Indians' attack on Molly's wagon train. He told them about the couple that had been murdered, Jim and Hazel Street, and how he and Standing Bear had been searching for the killers. Those same men had killed some of the Pawnee. The Indians, he explained, had almost been forced into fighting. And the fact that Smoke was their chief only made matters worse.

Jory, who wasn't much of a conversationalist in the first place, talked the best he could so that everyone would understand. He had spent many years with very few problems with the Indians and, though his heart was heavy over Molly's grief for her family, there was a part of him that needed to defend the Indians. He wondered, as he looked at the immigrants' hard faces, if they could understand how the Pawnee felt. One of the reasons he'd become a drifter and a dreamer was because he'd never felt comfortable back in the States. It bothered him how white people would gossip and ruin people's lives with their wicked tongues. He'd heard the word "savage" attached to Indians so often, the mere word itself stood for the red man, just as much as "Indian" did.

To Jory, Indians were like animals. They hunted for what they needed to eat. He'd never seen Indians needlessly slaughter buffalo or deer, or any other food source. Like animals, they only took for their own survival. Even when it came to killing other humans, it was mostly for survival, not just senseless hatred. When the Sioux had massacred the Pawnee, it hadn't been to settle any kind of bad feeling between them. It had been done to drive the Pawnee from their hunting areas. Jory had felt the same way, back then, as he stood there among the dead Pawnee. He had felt sick for them, but not anger. For as cruel and barbaric as it seemed, he realized it was all about survival.

"Look, more killings ain't gonna right any wrongs. The longer Smoke and his people put this off, the better chance we have to get everyone out of here," he said.

"Sh-i-i-i-t. Sounds to me like you ain't much more than a savage yourself. You been livin' around them too long. I say ain't nothin' better than a dead Indian to get a message across," Sinclair said.

"Mister, you got a tongue like a snake. I'm scared of snakes, so when I get around one, I usually cut its head off if it won't go away," Jory said. His eyes bored into Sinclair's with a menace that few people had ever seen, but neither had they forgotten.

"Let's stop the bickering and arguing among ourselves," Molly said. "We gotta get those babies back, and we gotta figure out how."

Tom Sinclair kicked the dirt and cursed, then stomped off by himself.

Molly pointed toward the Pawnee. There was a lone rider heading for the other Indians. "Jory, isn't that your friend, Standing Bear?"

"It sure is," Jory said, surprised. Standing Bear was riding toward Smoke. "I left him with an old boy that was near death. Fellow must have died." He looked at Molly. "We found him back there. He was one of them killers we'd been looking for."

"Was he a big man?" Molly asked. Her voice was soft and concerned.

"Real big."

"That was Calvin," Molly said. "He may have been riding with those men, but he wasn't no killer. Not the way you mean, leastwise. I believe he was a good man, given the right circumstances. He tried to save me and Louisa. Well!" She sniffed, but didn't cry. She had used up most of her tears. "I thought him to be dead already." Her mind lingered on Calvin for a few seconds. She said a quick prayer for his soul.

39

Standing Bear knew he was taking a chance approaching Smoke and the Pawnee. He'd come to try to mediate the situation, but he was fearful that Smoke's fat mother might come up in the conversation.

The Great One, with his silver hair and magnificent pony, had sent him here. Standing Bear had been tending to the big white man, who lay sick, when the old man appeared to him, just as he had appeared to his father and his father's father.

His elders had told him about the old Indian, of how he had come to their fathers, and to their fathers before them with great stories. Once, there had been the tale of a great flood that killed everything on earth, except for a man, his family and animals. A male and a female from each kind. Standing Bear's own father, Skinny Dog, had told him the story of his youth. He had been swimming and got caught in the undergrowth. He knew he was drowning, and just as he was about to go under for the last time, he looked up to the riverbank, and there stood a man with silver hair. The old one opened his arms to Skinny Dog, and the next minute, he found himself out of the water, lying on the ground next to the hooves of the magnificent white horse.

Standing Bear had heard about the old man appearing to his people and telling them stories about floods, and about the small man who slew the giant with a rock. He had come to the Pawnee when they were hungry and led them to food. Once, Standing Bear's father's father had told how he had become lost when the great ice came from the

sky. The old man had appeared to him and presented a
buffalo. His father's father had killed the buffalo, then
crawled inside its skin and survived.

Standing Bear had never seen the Great One, yet he believed the stories to be true, for his father and his father's
father would not tell a lie. He longed to be chosen for this
great honor, but he knew himself to be unworthy for some
reason, perhaps because he had traveled away from his
people so much.

It filled his heart with pride, then, when he looked up
from the sick white man whom he tended and saw the big
white pony pawing the earth, and the man with hair
touched by moonlight. He knew at once that this was the
Great One whom his father and his father's father had
talked about.

The old man had spoken to him in words that soothed
his spirit. His voice was like a melody, telling Standing
Bear to leave the white one and go to Smoke.

Standing Bear wanted to answer, to tell him that his
friend, Jory Matlock, had asked him to stay there. He tried
to speak, but his tongue and throat had grown stiff as a
tree. The Great One understood, for he gave Standing Bear
the promise that the white man would be all right. Standing Bear must quickly go and speak to Smoke, for he understood the tongue of the white men. There would be no
more war. Standing Bear must tell Smoke and the whites
to leave one another in peace.

Standing Bear listened in his silence to the old man's
commands, then obediently mounted his horse. It concerned him that he would have to approach Smoke. Perhaps he would still want Standing Bear to lie with his fat
mother. He wished the great man had appeared to him for
another reason.

With much trepidation, Standing Bear rode until at last
he saw them. When he drew near, he was surprised to see
the great man suddenly appear, sitting on his magnificent
pony next to Smoke. Smoke's own pony was as fine as
any his warriors owned, but, standing there next to the
stallion, it paled in comparison.

Standing Bear looked at his people. Each of them held

his head tilted forward, in reverence to the Great One. Even Smoke's defiant demeanor was humbled. Standing Bear's spirits lifted, for surely Smoke wouldn't be so bold as to talk about his fat mother in front of the Great One.

More confident now, Standing Bear rode up to the two. The Great One's eyes took him in and told him that his burden was lifted. Standing Bear was suddenly filled with a deep happiness. In his mind, he could hear the musical chants and dances of others who had gone before him. The hair on his neck bristled, and he felt proud to be a Pawnee.

He stopped his pony and sat there, again struck speechless, filling his heart with the presence of the Great One in their midst.

Several minutes passed before Smoke was allowed to speak to Standing Bear.

"We will not kill the devils today," he said. "You will go to them and tell them so. Tell them that they must stay here, and I will return the captives to them. Then they will go in peace. You will tell them that they should be grateful for our generosity."

Standing Bear nodded, relieved at Smoke's words. He wanted to think good thoughts of Smoke, but he knew that this was not of Smoke's doing. It was the will of the Great One. Besides, if he spoke of his friendship, it might cause Smoke to remember his mother, and Standing Bear did not wish for that to happen.

Standing Bear and his pony headed toward the whites. His old eyes surveyed the group, off in the distance, and again his heart was filled with pride. The whites looked disheveled and weak.

He wished that they could know how he felt—what it was like to be Pawnee. He felt pity for them, for they would pass through life and never know the freedom and joy that his people shared.

Midway, he stopped and turned his pony to look at the Great One. Many seasons had come and gone before he, too, was privileged as his father and his father's father had been. Once more, he wanted to gaze at the old man, sitting there with his kindness and wisdom. He wanted to feel those loving eyes looking into his own one last time, for he did not expect ever to see him again in his lifetime.

Even at a distance, his old eyes could see the Great One's face as if it were only a few paces away. Again, the hair bristled on Standing Bear's neck. His skin became taut. His spirit soared like an eagle. He took what he knew would be his last look at the Great One, and thousands of words were spoken. In but an instant, he was filled with assurance. It was good. He turned his pony and went forward.

Up ahead, Standing Bear saw Jory and many other white men. They watched him approach with sober faces. He felt superior to these white men, yet his heart cried for them. He wished Jory Matlock had been one of his people. Jory was a good man. Had he been a Pawnee, Jory surely would have taken care of Smoke many seasons ago. He would not have allowed Smoke to lay such heavy burdens on him. Gone would have been the irritation of worrying about Smoke's mother. Standing Bear could have been free to join his people more often.

Jory quickly mounted up and rode out to meet him. He was eager to keep Standing Bear from riding in too close. The one named Sinclair was boiling for a fight and might get trigger-happy. Jory didn't want anything to happen to Standing Bear because of somebody's foolishness.

"It is good to see you, Jory Matlock. I thought you would probably be dead. Have you got tobacco? I have ridden a long ways."

Jory managed a smile and gave Standing Bear the tobacco. He waited as the old man moistened the chew and spit.

"It is a good day, Jory Matlock," Standing Bear said at last. "Smoke is not going to kill you or the others. He wants peace between your people and mine." He looked past Jory and saw Molly watching them, and felt that familiar ache in his loins. "Maybe this time you will let me sleep with one of the white women."

"Maybe, but it won't be Molly, Standing Bear," Jory said. "I told myself back there that, if I was to get out of this alive, I'm going to ask her to be my wife. I'm gonna go on to Oregon with her."

Standing Bear nodded. "I, too, would like to go. I would like to see the big water. I have heard it goes on forever, with no end to it." He paused. "Maybe on the journey, you can talk to one of the white women about my request."

"We'll talk about that later. What are they gonna do about the children?" Jory said. Life for Molly would be meaningless without Louisa. Jory knew the burden would put a heavy strain on the marriage, if she agreed to marry him.

"Smoke has told me that he will send the children. You must wait here."

"Wait, hell! We'll go after 'em ourselves," Jory said with an urgency in his voice.

Standing Bear frowned. "No. It is not good that you disagree. I know you have little regard for Smoke. I, myself, do not like him. But trust me, Jory Matlock. Smoke will keep his word. He would not be able to face my people if he did not."

Jory was reluctant, but he nodded and turned back to tell the others.

Standing Bear leaned over to spit, then turned his pony. He had been right—the Great One was gone. Sadness tugged at him. He knew that here on earth he would never again feel as he just had. For a brief time, he had known true peace and harmony with the earth. There had been a happiness in his spirit that he would remember all his days.

Smoke and the rest of his people had turned away and were heading north to the River With Three Forks. Though he was sad that the Great One was gone, Standing Bear felt as though his burdens had been lifted. For the time being, there would be no talk of Smoke's fat mother.

After so much killing, Standing Bear wondered what kind of reception the whites would give him. He stayed close to his friend, Jory Matlock.

Molly was the first to greet him. She hugged him, and his concerns left him as her touch sent a stirring through

his body. He wished that it was another woman who held
Jory Matlock's heart. Then, maybe he could get his friend
to talk to Molly about lying with him. He was sure that
Molly would fulfill all his desires. Such a handsome
woman he had never seen.

Yes, Standing Bear decided, it would be good for him to
go to this place called Oregon, for he did wish to see the
great waters that went on forever. Standing Bear knew his
age was advanced. Each season, his body lost a little more
of its strength. It made him feel sad, for in his heart he
was still a great warrior.

Now that he had seen the Great One, he could wait in
peace until the day the Great Spirit came for him.

But more than anything else, he could spend his remaining time in hopes that Jory would find him a white woman
to lay with—one who had the same fine qualities as Molly
did.

40

‫‬

Had he not been so sick, Samson probably wouldn't
have accepted Becky's care. He was only half-
conscious when she first came to Reuben's wagon and
dismissed Mrs. Clinger, the immigrant from Baltimore
who had been put in charge of him. He'd been loaded into
Reuben's wagon, since most of the other wagons were full
with taking on the rescued women and children. Reuben
hadn't minded much, except in making room, he'd had to
distribute much of his whiskey supply among some of the
other wagons. This was worrisome, to say the least.

Molly had taken over the care of Calvin. The big man
had somehow lived through the Indians' massacre, and
though he'd lost an arm and would never again be a pleasant sight to look upon, Molly considered his and little
Louisa's survival among life's biggest blessings. Jory understood, and did his part by keeping a watchful eye on
Louisa for her.

Samson improved under Becky's attentions. She knew
nothing about medicine, but she kept him as comfortable
as she could and cleaned his wounds often. His entire
shoulder, extending down to his chest, was purple where
he had taken the two arrows. She worried over whether
he'd ever be able to use his left arm again, if indeed he did
live.

Each time she entered the wagon and bent over him, her
lovely face serious with concern, Samson had to turn his
mind away from his feelings. His pain was so severe during his waking hours, he longed for sleep and was scared

to awaken and not find Becky there beside him. He knew this didn't look right, and he wondered what other folks must be saying. Still, he couldn't bring himself to reproach her for coming to him each day.

Talk did spread among the immigrants. They noticed her frequent trips to Reuben's wagon, and everyone knew that Becky and Samson were spending many long hours alone together. Some folks even felt sorry for her husband, and they said so. It didn't matter that most of them had grown to fear and dislike Tom Sinclair. It still wasn't right for a married woman to carry on with another man in plain sight. Why in the world, they wondered, did Tom Sinclair allow such goings-on?

Reuben, in particular, was wary over the situation. He feared what might happen if Tom Sinclair was to get crazy. Once, when he had Samson's attention, he told him his thoughts on the matter. Why, any minute, he said, Sinclair could show up and kill all three of them. He'd already lost a considerable amount of sleep, wondering if Sinclair might decide to sneak up in the middle of the night and shoot them.

But surprisingly, Sinclair did not come. And he wouldn't come. Unbeknownst to anyone, Becky had promised her husband that if he caused any more fracas as far as Samson Roach was concerned, she would wait until he was asleep and kill him. She meant it, and somehow he knew she meant it. The secret, however, was kept between them.

Standing Bear had made a wise decision to travel with the immigrants. He enjoyed playing with the young children. They constantly trailed after him, having found him a willing playmate, which was rare in an adult. Also, in his play with the children, Standing Bear was able to spend many hours scrutinizing the women. Though he had not found any to match the fine qualities of Molly, he had to admit that there were a lot of good women among the immigrants—more than he had ever imagined seeing at one time.

There was a spiritual bond that drew him to Samson. Standing Bear had felt it the first day he had seen him as he lay wounded on the ground. He did not understand why, but every day he found himself riding by the wagon in which Samson lay, to peek wordlessly inside. The man had shown great courage to come in alone and steal the women away from Smoke. He had bravery and honor and was to be admired among men. He, like Jory Matlock, would have made a fine Pawnee.

A little over a week had gone by, when Standing Bear stopped and peered into the back of the wagon to find Samson up. He was leaning against a whiskey barrel. He smiled as their eyes met for the first time. An odd feeling ran through Standing Bear.

"Would you join me for a drink?" Samson said to welcome him.

Wordlessly, Standing Bear climbed from the pony's back and stepped into the back of the wagon.

"It's Reuben's whiskey. Rotten stuff," Samson said, offering a jug. He was drunk and feeling no pain, save the fire that burned in his belly. The whiskey had his head swirling and his tongue loose.

"Do I know you?" Samson asked, watching Standing Bear take a drink. "You look familiar. At least, I think I do."

"We have not met, but I know of your bravery. You are the one who saved Molly and the other women," Standing Bear said politely.

"I could have sworn I knew ye. I had a friend once and you remind me of him," Samson said.

"Oh? You have known some of my people?" Standing Bear asked.

Samson took a long drink of whiskey and gritted his teeth to keep from coughing. It made his body hurt when he coughed. Besides, he wanted to get so drunk that, when Becky came, he would have the nerve to tell her what he must. He pulled the bottle from his lips and wiped his mouth. The Indian had asked him a question, and he had to answer. He looked back up, and stopped.

The old Indian looked different. The morning sun shone through the rear of the wagon, illuminating the back of the man's head. His gray hair was lit up, and even though the face was black against the brightness of the sun, Samson could see the twinkle in his eyes. He stared, openmouthed.

"I'm talking to you!" he said. "Why haven't I been able to speak to you before this? Did Nancy send you? She and Cordry? Please, tell me, are they all right?"

Standing Bear saw the change in Samson's eyes. He said, very slowly, "I do not know the people you speak of. Do you want me to find them for you?"

"No, please!" Samson begged. "Please! Don't go! You have to tell me!" He hiccuped and groped for the jug. "Where did you come from? Are you an angel?"

Standing Bear looked thoughtful. "I am Standing Bear," he said. "Friend of Jory Matlock. I have heard of the angels in your Bible." His mind drifted back to the great Bible man, Joshua Whittington, and his wife, Kathleen. Again, he recalled the memory of watching her from the creekbank as she bathed, the sunlight glistening on her large breasts, with the tips as pink as prairie flowers.

He watched Samson closely. "Did this angel," he paused, "ride upon a big white pony?"

Samson nodded, and Standing Bear felt the hair bristle on his neck. It wasn't the fact that this man, Samson, was a great warrior, or a brave rescuer of women and children. That was not what had drawn him to Samson. It was something else.

He had seen the Great One.

But, Standing Bear thought, this was a white man. Surely, there must be Pawnee blood flowing through his body.

"Your mother or your father," he said, "were they of my people, the Pawnee?"

Samson didn't know what Standing Bear was talking about. By now he was inebriated to the point where nothing was making any sense. He wished the Indian would just go away and leave him alone. He was too woozy to think any more. He hadn't meant to get this drunk. Now he was too drunk to talk to Becky. And he needed to talk to her worse than anything.

He started to weep openly, hating the miserable situation he was in and hating himself for being the cause of it.

He cried a while, then stopped and wiped his eyes. When he looked up, the Indian was still sitting there, apparently wanting an answer to his question. Samson couldn't remember, though, what the question had been.

"Well, since you ain't no angel, why don't you go on and get out of here?" he asked irritably, slurring his words.

But the old man stayed put, sitting there in front of him. It was just like when the old silver-haired one had sat with him, only this time Samson could talk. He took in a deep breath and laid his head back against a barrel. "Please," he said weakly. "Just go away."

Confused by Samson's attitude, Standing Bear finally got up and climbed out of the wagon. This man had seen the Great One, he kept telling himself, over and over. He must come back later, when Samson was not drunk with whiskey. They must hold council together. Perhaps Samson Roach knew things about the Great One that his father and his father's father had not told him.

Samson lay there with his eyes closed. The floor of the wagon seemed to be moving and swaying under him. He took in deep breaths to fight back the dizziness. At least, he thought, that old Indian with the hunger of conversation was gone. There was only one person he wanted to talk to, once he had his sobriety back.

There was a noise, and he was about to holler to whoever it was to go away, when he looked up and saw Becky. Then he noticed her fragrance. It was the one that would forevermore remind him of her.

She took one look at him and started scolding. "Goodness! What are you doing, trying to kill yourself?" She took the jug from him and corked it. "Just wait 'til I see that Reuben!"

Samson's smile was giddy. "It weren't Reuben. I got it myself, thank you."

"Well, I'm ashamed of you. Do you think I've spent all this time tending to you, so you could go and drink yourself to death?"

"I ain't gonna kill myself," Samson said. "Why don't you just come over here and give me a kiss?"

He'd gotten so drunk, he'd gone beyond his intentions

of gathering up the courage to tell her that, no matter how they felt, they could never be together. Now, all he knew was that he wanted her, more than anything, and the whiskey only made him feel more romantically inclined.

Eagerly, Becky leaned forward. Ever so gently, she kissed him, then took his head in her arms and pulled it to her chest.

"What am I going to do with you?" she sighed, half to herself.

"You could lay down here beside me."

"I could, but I won't." She smiled.

Content, he closed his eyes and nuzzled against her. Soon, he'd fallen into a deep, drunken sleep.

It was nearly suppertime when he awoke. His body was racked by pain, joined by a fresh ache in his head. Becky was still with him. She had waited until he awoke to check him over, to give him his rest.

The wound in his sternum was oozing pus. The area around where the arrow had entered was feverishly hot. Becky dabbed at it with a wet cloth and wiped away the infection as best she could.

Samson's head was throbbing. He knew he could throw up any second, but that would only cause him more pain, so he held back. Why'd he done such a fool thing, drinking like a man with no sense?

Then he remembered why. Samson cursed himself for his weakness of character. Now he and his loose tongue had only made matters worse. Instead of finding his courage in whiskey, he'd have to get it from somewhere inside.

She was wiping his forehead with a wet cloth. He reached up and took hold of her hand. "Becky. I know we've talked about this before, but now you've got to listen to me. You can't come here anymore."

She started to speak, but Samson touched her lips with a finger.

"No. People are talking, and it isn't good, especially not for you. Becky, don't waste your reputation and your life on me. In Oregon, everybody gets a new start. Until we get there, we have to stop seeing or talking to each other. Maybe by then folks will have forgotten all about this."

"I can't let you go," Becky said. "I'd die first." Her eyes welled up with tears. "You don't understand what my life has been like."

Samson fought back the urge to open his arms to her. He stared at her, overtaken by her beauty and by the awful misery that pulled at his heart. Yes, he thought, he did understand. He understood all too well what it was like to live with a deep, empty space inside you. He had loved Cordry more than life itself, and had been happy with Nancy. When they died, his life had died also, until Becky Sinclair came along. But it wasn't just a gratitude for life that she had given him. It was a new kind of love, a passion for life that made each day a reward.

As he studied her perfect features, his heart seemed to quiver inside his chest. He'd rather die than hurt her. He wished he didn't love her so much. Maybe then he could just allow himself to be selfish, to carry her away without a care about what other people said about her.

But he knew that was impossible. Samson knew he couldn't stand for anyone to view Becky Sinclair as anything but respectable.

He reached out and grabbed a piece of burlap bag in his hand, squeezing it in his fist until it hurt. He prayed for the courage to say what had to be said.

"Look," he began, talking slowly so that she would understand, trying to sound impersonal. "I'm sorry I made you cheat on your husband. I guess I was just being a man. I didn't stop to think about the consequences. But, it ain't never going to happen again. You've got to understand that."

"I don't want to hear that nonsense, Samson Roach! I reckon I had as much to do with that night as you did! I love you, and that's all that matters to me." Becky was crying openly now.

Samson cursed the whiskey and himself for getting too drunk. He needed that courage, right now. He forced himself to say the words that he himself hated to hear.

"Well, I wish you didn't, 'cause I don't love you. Oh, I'll admit, I wanted to separate you from your drawers, but that didn't mean it was love. I'm sorry if I made you think it was."

Becky looked like she'd just been slapped. "You ... you can't mean that!" She started to say more, but she couldn't. She bit her lip and swallowed hard, watching him through her tears.

Samson's mind swept backward, over time. He'd give anything for his mama to be here, he thought. He could be a boy again and put his head in her lap and bawl like a baby. She could take care of his burdens. All he'd have to do is stay close to her, and everything would be all right.

But life didn't work that way. Nobody could go back. Not even the man with the flowing silver hair could help him do what he had to do. His knuckles turned white from squeezing the burlap.

"I reckon I do mean it," he said. "Sorry to hurt your feelings, but these things happen. You're a nice person, Becky, and I'm sorry it had to happen to you. Best go on with your life. Oregon's a fine place. You'll get new beginnings there."

Anger swept through Becky. "You just shut up about Oregon!" she said. "You just shut up about everything!" She shook her head. "You don't understand nothing, Samson Roach. I reckon you never will."

She turned from him and was gone.

Then Samson started to cry. It would have been a lot better, he thought, if he was still drunk.

"Yes," he said aloud. "New beginnings."

Epilogue

———⊱≈≈≈⊰———

Jory Matlock assumed duties as temporary wagon master, assuring everyone that when Samson was able, the job was still his.

They eventually came to a fur-trading post that would later become Fort Laramie. There they met Dr. Ephraim Snodgrass of Virginia, who joined them.

The doctor, who was also a professed minister, had obtained his medical degree from the College of Pennsylvania and was looking for a new and promising location to set up his practice. Oregon was just the place, so he had gathered up his belongings, said his good-byes to his family in Virginia, and set out westward. The immigrants were thrilled with the idea of having a physician among them, especially after the fever had claimed so many.

The doctor was an outgoing fellow, and curious. He enjoyed holding audience while he talked about the modern advances in medicine. One of his favorite topics of conversation was the wealth of knowledge one could gain by dissection of the human body itself. Many of the immigrants, though they didn't want to say anything that might ruin the prospect of having a doctor in their new home, were shocked. Dr. Snodgrass tried to explain to them that this was how a physician better prepared himself for the practice of healing. Each time a loved one was lost along the trail, the doctor made his respectful request to have the body for a dissection, and each time he was refused. Only one person agreed to his request.

It was Elizabeth Berringer of Pennsylvania who offered

303

the body of her precious three-year-old, Annabella. The child had succumbed to pneumonia days after falling into a river during a crossing.

Friends voiced their outrage, but the bereaved mother scolded them. Some day, she told them, she would have other children in her home, and she wanted that doctor to know everything there was to know about caring for little ones. If her baby, Annabella, could help him learn, then so be it. Her impassioned oratory calmed the critics, but still no other offers were made to further the cause of science.

Despite the controversy surrounding his ideas, Dr. Snodgrass was given his just due, among them credit for saving Samson's life. Several times, Samson had hovered near death, hanging on to life by a thread. The arrows he had taken in the shoulder would leave their effects for the rest of his life, causing the shoulder to become stiff and painful when damp weather came. It was the wound just below the breastbone, though, that became infected. Samson's fever rose to a dangerous level, and it was feared that he would die any time.

Willie, who had worried over Samson like an old woman, attached himself to the doctor's side and was there to help when Dr. Snodgrass tended to his needs.

The doctor immediately cut into the swollen wound and drained out the pus. Twice a day for three weeks he returned, pushing on Samson's abdomen, squeezing out more pus and bile, then cleansing the wound with a strong solution of sulphate of zinc and water. Later, he used a solution of Castile soap to rinse out the wound. Slowly, the wound began to dry up, and Samson's fever lifted. His recovery was remarkably quick after that.

Willie was fascinated by the doctor's ability to perform such miracles. He decided his calling was to become a physician. Eagerly, he assisted Dr. Snodgrass in everything from removing ingrown toenails to performing some major surgeries. One operation had tragic results for Cornelia Bloodworth. She had gone into a long and torturous labor, and after two days, the doctor decided to do a caesarean section.

The labor had been too much for Cornelia. She died five

hours after the surgery, but Dr. Snodgrass delivered a healthy baby boy into the arms of her grieving young husband.

Another caesarean operation took place near the end of their journey at the Columbia River. Minerva Teske had been in labor for four days. Exhausted and near delirium, Minerva refused to agree to the surgery, but as it looked like her life was ebbing away, her husband took hold of her limp hand and gravely gave the doctor his permission.

Quickly, Dr. Snodgrass cut through the abdomen and placenta. The baby's back was facing him, and the doctor saw with alarm that the cord was wrapped around its neck. Desperately, he turned the boy around, but it was too late. There was nothing he could do to save the infant.

Happily, Dr. Snodgrass's successes far outweighed his failures. He even made headlines in the eastern papers when it became known that he had performed a brilliant ovariotomy on Mary Todd Lowe of Albany, New York. Using a molasses and water enema, he prepared her on the floor of a wagon, with the canvas removed for light. Then, he made an incision from the umbilicus to near the pubis, but had to lengthen it another six inches before he could remove a twenty-four-pound multilocular ovarian cyst. Using silk ligatures, he sewed Mary Todd up. Forever grateful to the young doctor, she lived to fulfill her dream of raising her family in Oregon.

Another noted performance by Dr. Snodgrass was his officiating in the marriage of Jory Matlock and Molly Jackson. The wedding occurred west of Fort Laramie on a grassy creekbank that was overrun with wildflowers. Little Louisa sucked her thumb and held Molly's hand through the ceremony.

As Jory stood next to his new wife and repeated his vows, he felt a transformation come over him. He had a wife and a daughter. They all belonged to each other. The happiness that filled his heart would last throughout the rest of his years.

Jory talked often about his family back in Massachusetts. Molly noticed the sadness that crept into his voice as he wondered what had happened to the little ones, Elizabeth and Sarah Jane, and his older sister, Kara. His eyes would mist as he talked about his mother. Surely, he said, she was dead, but what about his sisters?

Five years after they settled in Oregon, Molly talked him into going back to find his family. Though she dreaded making the journey, she knew Jory needed it more than anything. Together, she, Jory, and Louisa made the long trip.

To their surprise, finding his sisters was an easy task. The three women were all still living in the same area. The oldest, Kara, was happily married. She had four sons, one of whom she had named Jory. Sarah Jane was also married, with a daughter and a son. The baby, Elizabeth, had turned into a beautiful, mature woman. She was raising three young'uns, two boys and a girl by herself. Her husband had been killed just three years before when he'd been struck by a felled tree.

The reunion was filled with many tears of joy. The sisters had thought Jory to be long dead, and they were overjoyed to see him. They welcomed Molly and Louisa with open arms and begged them to stay.

The visit lasted four months. Jory became great friends with his brothers-in-law. Sarah Jane's husband couldn't hear enough stories about Oregon, and one day announced that he and Sarah Jane and their two children were going back to Oregon with them. Elizabeth quickly made her decision. She and Sarah Jane were so close in age, they'd always been inseparable, so there was no question that she would move to Oregon, too.

They all begged Kara and her husband to come along, but Kara said she was too old and set in her ways for such a move. Tearfully, they said their good-byes.

Jory and his new family made it back to Oregon, where he and Molly lived to a ripe old age on their Oregon farm.

Reuben Cook found him another Indian wife and named her Gertie. The young but homely woman bore him three children and served the customers who came to his tavern. Reuben became a wealthy man and enjoyed his family, until he was killed one rainy night by a habitual drunk who accidentally shot him. His oldest son, whom he'd named

Samson, went on to become a lawyer and served two terms in the Oregon Senate.

Willie lost his father to consumption just before they reached Oregon. Broken by her loss, his mother soon took ill. The headaches she had suffered all along the trip became more severe, and a swelling appeared behind her ear. Seven months after they reached Oregon, she died of a tumor.

Willie and Jory helped Samson build his cabin and got him settled, but it wasn't homesteading that held Willie's attention. He sought out Dr. Snodgrass and set about learning everything he could. He worked for several years as the doctor's assistant, until the law dictated that he couldn't practice medicine without a degree from an accredited medical school. With the help of Dr. Snodgrass and money from Reuben, Willie went east to get his medical degree. On his return, he stopped in St. Louis, figuring to spend a year or so there to raise more funds for his return to Oregon. Love intervened, though, when he met and married Lila Fronterhouse. Eight children later, Willie was still residing in the city of St. Louis, happily spending his days regaling his offspring with his experiences and passing on the old stories of Dr. Ephraim Snodgrass.

Joseph Mellner lived to the age of ninety-one, becoming one of the biggest landowners in the valley. Always a man who believed in hard work and little play, Joseph had softened during the passage to Oregon. Though shrewd as ever, he saved many of the immigrants from going bankrupt with his financial counseling and occasional loans. It was said that Mellner had the biggest funeral ever attended in the area.

Calvin Page never forgot the man who saved his life. He went to work for Jory Matlock as a farmhand. With only one arm, he worked as hard in the fields as any two men. Together, they built a fine home for Jory and Molly, then added a smaller house for Calvin on a corner of the property.

Calvin never married, but he was content. He grew fiercely protective of Louisa in her growing-up years. At the age of forty-nine, Calvin died in his sleep of a heart attack. Molly, Jory, and Louisa mourned him deeply.

Louisa went off to school in New York and later married a prosperous newspaper editor. Bored with her pampered lifestyle, Louisa became homesick and soon decided she needed to be near Molly and Jory, to take care of them in their old age. Her husband thought this nonsense, but he loved his beautiful wife. He sold everything, and they moved back to the Willamette Valley, where he started his own newspaper. Louisa was determined to make Molly a great-aunt, but after several miscarriages, she and her husband finally resigned themselves to the fact that they would remain childless. It was at that point that Louisa conceived and, nine months later, gave birth to a healthy son.

Christine Hackman married one of Joseph Mellner's sons and raised nine children. Her mother, Gloria, drowned in the Snake River.

Emma Taggert found a husband, a man from Missouri named George Nixon. He was an abusive, drinking man who held little regard for any woman. Unable to submit to George's cruel ways, Emma shot and killed him just a few days after their third anniversary. The town sheriff, who had never liked George Nixon in the first place, just offered the widow his sympathy.

Emma was to marry twice more. She buried her second husband, who had been a sickly man, and then was wed to a gambling man. He moved her to California that same year, and no one heard from Emma again.

Sadie Andrews, who'd had a brief first taste of love with Sal Musso, never married. Considered by some to be the most beautiful woman in the valley, she became a nurse for Dr. Snodgrass, and rumors persisted that she was his mistress. Thirty years the doctor's junior, Sadie stayed with him until he grew so old and blinded by cataracts that he was forced to close his practice. Still, Sadie remained, claiming she owed him, working as his housekeeper.

When he died, she was forty-three years old. A new younger doctor had taken up practice, but Sadie wasn't interested. Just days later, she left the valley with nothing but her satchel, and paid for passage on a steamer headed south to San Francisco.

Soon after, when the doctor's effects were examined, there was not a red cent to be found anywhere. The doctor had always been considered to be a wealthy man.

For years after, folks talked about Sadie Andrews and the day she'd hurriedly left town, clutching that satchel to her bosom, and speculated on how she'd spent all that money. It was a well-received story that grew a little over the years and provided an entertainment well into the twentieth century.

Sadie's mother, Harriet, buried the reverend and, two summers later, married another preacher man, a Pennsylvanian named Leviticus Baker. They began a church in the valley and lived happily until the day Sadie left town. Harriet never recovered from the heartache caused by all the rumors, and many said she died of a broken heart.

Standing Bear joined the wagon train and started on the trip. He wanted to see the Great Ocean, and besides that, he figured his chances of finding a white woman would be much better among the immigrants. He still dreamed of lying next to milky white thighs, and he mentioned it often to Jory. Finally, Jory mentioned it to Molly, hoping maybe she could help. He guessed he owed it to the Indian, he explained to her. Would she play Cupid for him?

He'd been half-afraid that Molly would be angry, but she seemed to find the whole idea hysterically funny. She laughed heartily, but was touched enough by Standing Bear's urgent desires to speak with Penelope Romig. Penelope was a widow of forty-six who seemed to fit the description of Standing Bear's wishes. A robust woman, she stood five-six and was more than an armful to hold. Her hair was of a light gold and her eyes sparkled when she talked. She was very much a woman, often confiding to Molly how she missed frolicking more than anything else. Sometimes, Molly had tired of hearing about Penelope's secret desires and avoided her. Besides, Molly suspected she had designs on Jory, for she spoke of the handsome men in a desirous way and even discussed just what she'd do with them if she had the opportunity.

When Molly first related Standing Bear's story to Penelope, the widow wrinkled her nose. The more they talked, though, the more interested Penelope became. She started considering the matter, wondering out loud what Indian men were like. Were they built differently from white men? Did Molly suppose Standing Bear's tree was still strong, or had it shriveled any? Molly pretended to ponder the questions seriously, even though she had to keep from laughing outright.

In any event, a meeting was set up between the two, with Jory talking to Standing Bear, and Molly relaying the information to Penelope.

No one knew whether Standing Bear was pleased that night, or whether his fantasy was satisfied. The wagon train was camped near the Willamette Valley, and the sun was hanging low in the sky as Standing Bear and Penelope slipped off by themselves. She was carrying a blanket that her mother had made and sent along on the trip, so that her daughter would have something from back home to dream on.

The next morning, Molly was fixing breakfast when Penelope, her tousled hair covering one eye, stumbled into camp. Her usual effervescent smile had been replaced by a look of sadness and shock.

"He's dead," she said.

Molly stared at her. "Dead?"

"Yes."

"Oh, no. Poor Standing Bear," Molly said. "I wondered about him. I was afraid he was too old."

"Oh no," Penelope sniffed. "He died after, in his sleep." She offered Molly the hint of a smile. "He was not too old at all."

Samson got first pick of farms. He planted a big garden and sold off the produce. He also raised livestock, beef and hogs, which he sold to Joseph Mellner every year. Mellner didn't necessarily need Samson's beef or hogs. He raised enough to feed a third of the valley himself. Still, any time he got word that Samson was ready to turn some stock, he'd promptly send someone over with the fairest price to be had.

Molly took particular care in sending Samson at least two home-cooked meals a week. Other ladies supplemented the other days with their culinary treats. For any other man, this might have created jealousies, but there was more than one woman in the Willamette Valley who felt extremely grateful to this man for saving their lives and those of their children. Molly, in particular, felt a tie to Samson. It wasn't anything romantic, though he was truly the most handsome man she'd ever known. She talked it over with Jory, knowing he wasn't envious, for she gave all of her love to him. Still, she said many times, it was purely confusing how a man with the face of a Greek god could live all alone like that. She'd gladly have tried her hand at playing Cupid, but Jory put a stop to that idea.

Samson lived out the days with a deep, empty void. He still thought of his mama, back in Tennessee. He planned to return for her someday, but somehow he never got around to it.

He lived alone. It wasn't that he wouldn't have enjoyed being held and comforted and having a woman to look after. But he had designs on one woman only, and she was a married woman. Nothing could change that, or the fact that his heart was dead for anyone else.

Becky had become the schoolteacher for the new Willamette Valley School—one dream, at least, had been realized. Occasionally, she sent him letters through one of her students who passed by his place. Each letter was basically the same. Samson had only to give the word, and she would seek a divorce from Tom. She even tried to set up a rendezvous with him on several occasions, but Samson never showed up. He wanted to, but he couldn't. As much as it killed him, he loved her too much to spoil her name.

Nine years to the day after they arrived in the valley, Tom Sinclair was killed when one of his prize racehorses threw him into a stump, breaking his neck. Samson got the news some five days later. He did not go to Becky; instead, he walked to Reuben's tavern and got drunk.

The days and weeks passed. It was late fall, and Samson was sitting by the fireplace, rocking, with one of Reuben's jugs on his lap. Above him, on the mantel, lay a stack of letters, unopened.

It had been eight months since Dr. Snodgrass told him he had the cancer. A year at the most, the doctor had said. Now his breathing had become labored, and the whiskey seemed to be the only thing that helped.

It was better when he was drunk. He could let his mind drift back to another time and place—a better time—when night had fallen over the prairie and two lovers met beside a lonesome bush. Again, the stars glittered in the sky and the soft wind danced through her silky hair.

If he concentrated hard enough, he could still smell the scent of love.